THE SUICIDE SONATA

Books by BV Lawson

Scott Drayco Series

Novels:

Played to Death
Requiem for Innocence
Dies Irae
Elegy in Scarlet
The Suicide Sonata

Short Story Collections

False Shadows
Hear No Evil
Vengeance is Blind

Other Short Story Collections

Best Served Cold
Deadly Decisions
Death on Holiday
Grave Madness

The Suicide Sonata

A Scott Drayco Mystery

BV Lawson

Crimetime Press

The Suicide Sonata is a work of fiction. All of the names, characters, places, organizations and events portrayed in this novel are either products of the author's imagination or are used fictitiously. Any resemblance to actual events, locales, or persons, living or dead, is entirely coincidental.

In Memoriam, Lela J. Vanaman and Sylvia Lawson, two of the best mothers anyone could ever hope for. "May flights of angels sing thee to thy rest."

O Death, Rock Me Asleep

Death, rock me asleep,
Bring me to quiet rest,
Let pass my weary guiltless ghost
Out of my careful breast.
Toll on, thou passing bell;
Ring out my doleful knell;
Let thy sound my death tell.
Death doth draw nigh;
There is no remedy.

My pains who can express?
Alas, they are so strong;
My dolour will not suffer strength
My life for to prolong.
Toll on, thou passing bell;
Ring out my doleful knell;
Let thy sound my death tell.
Death doth draw nigh;
There is no remedy.

Alone in prison strong
I wait my destiny.
Woe worth this cruel hap that I
Should taste this misery!
Toll on, thou passing bell;
Ring out my doleful knell;
Let thy sound my death tell. ·
Death doth draw nigh;
There is no remedy.

Farewell, my pleasures past,
Welcome, my present pain!
I feel my torments so increase
That life cannot remain.
Cease now, thou passing bell;
Rung is my doleful knell;
For the sound my death doth tell.
Death doth draw nigh;
There is no remedy.

poem by Anne Boleyn, music by John Edmunds

Prologue

It was a strange location for a suicide—isolated, far from town in a godforsaken wood. Nelia Tyler stepped away from the body to get one last set of camera shots. But in her haste, she almost tripped on the slimy leaves under the tree canopy.

Turning to fellow deputy Wesley Giles, she asked, "Got everything bagged and tagged?"

"What I could find. That storm did its best to wash evidence away."

Nelia looked past the clearing toward what was usually a sleepy creek, now turned into a raging stream. "They're going to take the body out by boat. Wanna ride?"

Giles snorted. "I hate boats. Even looking at one makes me wanna puke. Think I'll pick door number one and take the car."

"It's over a mile to hike back. And you nearly broke your neck on the way in, falling over that tree root."

"Killer trees I can handle. Boats, not so much."

All joking aside, the trek through the woods to the clearing was a challenge. Without a drone and radios guiding their way, it would be easy to get lost. And they'd never hear the last of it if they had to be "rescued."

Nelia glanced at the young victim's motorcycle parked against a tree. Before the rains, the trail across the creek would have been a little messy, but passable. But it didn't explain why he chose this place to end his life. Nowadays, someone his age would be more likely to livestream it on the internet.

Right as the EMT techs swooped in to put the body in the waiting plastic bag, Nelia spied something. "Wait a minute, guys."

She knelt and used her gloved fingers to flip up a piece of fabric on the deceased's nylon jacket. "Hidden zipper. I almost missed this."

She reached inside the pocket and pulled out a slip of paper. Taking great pains to avoid tearing it, she unfolded the paper and read the writing.

Giles asked, "What is it?"

"If it's a suicide note, it's the strangest one I've ever read."

He peered over her shoulder. "Looks like a poem. Or a song, I guess."

Nelia studied the note. Someone had scrawled the words "soul vibration" in the margins and drawn a triangle next to them. Who would doodle on a suicide note? Didn't make sense.

She said, "Wonder what Scott Drayco would make of this?"

Giles snorted. "He'd take one look at it, tie it in with some obscure ancient Egyptian cult, then tell us exactly what this guy was thinking when he pulled the trigger."

Nelia went to her kit, pulled out a baggie, and sealed the paper inside. "This might mean something, might not."

She placed the bagged note on top of the kit, above the gun found beside the victim. Then she watched as the EMTs zipped up the body bag, studying the scene not just from a forensics angle but also from the human one. She might not have known the young male victim personally—but her mother had.

The few flickering rays of sunlight wafting through the dense canopy illuminated the boy's face like a host of angels kissing that cold, bluish skin. Nelia shook off the fanciful notion and packed up her kit.

As if to emphasize the point, a lone crow settled on a nearby tree and cawed at her. Laughing? Crying? Or was this the same bird that had picked at the corpse's exposed flesh, now annoyed at the loss of dinner?

She said to the black bird, "Crows only live ten years, you know. You'll be here, yourself, soon enough."

Giles, packing up his own kit, looked over at her in bewilderment. "Did you say something?"

"It's nothing. Places like this give me the creeps."

She watched as the techs carried the body to the waiting boat and then gave one last look around. Well, the Medical Examiner would do her thing, and she and Giles would do theirs. And this particular suicide would just be another statistic on the CDC books.

But, as she started the walk back with Giles through the woods, Nelia felt a little shiver of something she couldn't quite identify. It was that damned crow. That must be it. The crow, this setting with its stark loneliness, the tragedy of life cut far too short—this was one of those days she almost wished she'd become an accountant.

She shook it off and continued the trek to the car. It would be followed by a stop at the office with its endless parade of crime scene reports and tedious paperwork. And having to make "that" visit to a worried father telling him his missing son was never coming home.

1

Thursday, June 7

"Drayco, where are you?" Scott Drayco couldn't tell where Nelia Tyler was calling from, but he heard noisy traffic in the background.

He said, "At my townhome in D.C. Where are *you?*"

"In the District, but I won't be here long. Have to return to the Eastern Shore tonight."

"Wish I'd known you were in town earlier. I'd love to catch up."

She let an emergency vehicle with a screeching siren pass by. "I do have something important I want to ask you. But not over the phone."

"A mystery quest. Sounds cloak-and-dagger."

With a nervous laugh, she said, "Hate to disappoint you. No spies. Or CIA or FBI or NSA. Look, if you're too busy—"

"Not too busy for you. Do you want to stop by my place?"

More nervous laughter. "That's not necessary. But that coffee shop nearby—what say we meet there. Around five-ish?"

He consulted his watch. "Sure, I think I can make that."

And he did make it in plenty of time—a little too quickly. No signs of Nelia when he arrived at the café at "five-ish." He went ahead and grabbed some coffee, tasted it, then sprinkled salt into the cup. Much better.

As he settled in to wait on his too-hard metal chair, he indulged his habit of people-watching. One man caught Drayco's eye, and he observed as flies landed on the man's table. The guy snared them one by one in a pool of honey poured on a napkin and squashed them.

Drayco turned his attention from the fly-killer to the other café patrons. Most stayed buried in their phones or laptops, hardly glancing up to enjoy their overpriced lattes and croissants.

Ordinarily, he'd have opted for an outdoor table since it reflected fewer textures, colors, and shapes from sounds bouncing off boxy surfaces. Much more comfortable for a synesthete. The rusty-orange pins of the fly-killer's voice hadn't helped, though Drayco wasn't sure which was worse—that voice or the eggplant-colored scalpels from the coffee bean grinder.

But all of those little dramas paled in comparison to his burning questions from Nelia's phone call. What could she possibly want? A bullet-point list of scenarios scrolled through his head, some good, some neutral, some indefinable. He drummed his fingers on the table, chiding himself. Mustn't let his list-obsession take a flight of fancy to parts unknown.

It was a relief when the familiar blonde entered the shop and headed his way. "Hope I'm not late." Nelia smiled as she walked up to his table and then turned to look at the menu board. "Any recommendations?"

"The Kona brew is pretty good. And the raspberry cheese Danish if you're into cheesy things."

"I like cheesy. Just ask Tim. If I want to annoy him, I'll turn on old Abbott and Costello shows."

The mention of Nelia's husband took Drayco's mood down a few notches. Maybe that was why she'd requested to meet him here—at a café *near* his townhome rather than *at* his townhome? When they'd last discussed Tim, she was considering a divorce. Now, she was acting as if afraid to be alone with Drayco.

His thoughts darted back to the barely platonic evening at the marina they'd shared two months ago. Was she as disappointed as he was it ended that way?

Nelia went to the counter to place her order, which gave him a chance to turn his people-watching skills on her. Hair still plaited into a braid, wearing sensible flats and sporting an equally sensible pale blue dress. Must be cooler than her deputy browns on a sticky June day.

When she returned to the table with an aromatic coffee and red-topped Danish, he asked, "How's Tim doing?" He bit his tongue not to ask, *"And has he hit you lately?"*

"Still employed, though the MS makes it tricky. But we hired a live-in aide to help around the house. Such a load off my mind to have Melanie there."

"You're only in town for the day?"

"Finishing up loose ends from the semester."

"I wondered what your schedule was this summer."

She chewed on her lip and looked away. He hadn't meant his comment as a dig. But she'd not spoken with him since May, answering his phone call attempts with terse text replies. Another clue he'd tried to overlook, perhaps.

"I'm working full time for Sheriff Sailor until fall." She took a sip of the coffee and said, "You're right, the Kona's great."

"What happened to Regina, the woman job-sharing with you?"

"Her baby had medical problems. But the prognosis is good. Hopefully, she'll return to work before law school starts in the fall."

"Benny Baskin will miss your legal research skills this summer."

"Oh, I doubt I'm that irreplaceable."

"Benny would beg to differ. But it must be hard living in three places."

"My tiny apartment here in D.C. is spartan. The Cape Unity apartment is bare bones. And I don't make it to the house in Baltimore much."

Drayco didn't miss the slight gritting of her teeth and the tightened jaw. "Doesn't it get lonely? Living in scattered homes?"

She took a nibble of the Danish and took her time answering. "Two jobs and law school part-time? I don't have a microsecond to be lonely."

Nelia was strong, independent, and direct, traits he found so appealing, but she'd make a terrible actress. He let it slide.

She sighed. "Look, I'm sorry I didn't stay in touch over the past couple of months."

"As you said, you're swamped. I understand."

"I thought about you. Wanted to call."

"Why?"

"I was worried how you were taking the end of your mother's case. Having your Mom charged with murder. And having it end like it did."

It was Drayco's turn to take his time answering, letting the salted coffee trickle down his throat. "I had some cases consulting for law enforcement groups. The normal high-stress dance card. But maybe the frenzy of activity wasn't a bad thing. A distraction."

She chewed on her lip. "I suppose so."

He forestalled any further questioning along that line. "So, what's this big mysterious quest of yours?"

"My mother plays violin in a Virginia Beach orchestra. The son of one of her fellow violinists committed suicide a month ago."

Drayco's heart sank. Of all the things he'd imagined she wanted to discuss, this wasn't on the list. Plus, he'd never liked working suicides, and he knew—dreaded—what was coming. "And the parents can't believe their son would take his own life."

She nodded. "The boy's father, Sebastien Penry. His mother died years ago. But Marty's suicide was totally out of character. The young man never showed signs of being suicidal."

"They often don't."

"I was skeptical myself, at first."

"What changed your mind?"

"Mom was a large part of it. She knew Marty Penry, that's the son, and she swears she believes his father, Sebastien."

"Marty also lived in Virginia Beach?"

"Both father and son used to live in Cape Unity, but only Marty stayed. Since Marty's death happened in Prince of Wales County, Sheriff Sailor looked into it. He made a detailed report, and there are inconsistencies in the case. But that was as far as it went. Officially."

That wasn't encouraging. If Sailor believed it was a homicide, he'd have pursued it. "What inconsistencies?"

"For one, Marty shot himself with a pistol, a Smith & Wesson Model 39, yet he didn't own a gun. But it matches the description of one stolen from his best friend's car."

"You think this friend staged the theft and used the gun against Marty?"

"That's a possibility."

"Did you trace it to make sure?"

"A hand-me-down from the friend's father. Who got it from his father."

"Not in the supply chain, then."

She shook her head.

"Fingerprints?"

"Just Marty's."

"That detail's odd. If it belonged to the friend, why would the suicide victim have wiped off the friend's prints? Was there a note?"

Nelia fished out a paper from her purse. "I found a piece of paper with Marty's body. And you could interpret it as a suicide note. Or I guess I should say a suicide song."

Drayco straightened up at that. "Suicide song?"

She handed the paper over. "Here's a copy of the song with the lyrics. You can keep it."

Drayco read the text:

I'm lost in confusion and melancholy,
Drowning in heartache and rivers of grief,
The hours are slowing, my dreams are all crushed,
Like trees turn to husks and metal to rust.

I live in the shadows, and alone I shall be,
Gone are the days that were bright and carefree,
The flowers are fading, the light becomes dusk,
Ashes turn to ashes and dust turns to dust.

My guilt and betrayal are too much to bear
With nothing to hope for and no one to care,
My time is now fading, like light from the stars,
And peals of the church bells that reach out to Mars

He said, "This isn't very cheery. In fact, it's precisely the type of poetry to attract someone who's depressed. And what does 'soul vibration' in the margin mean? And that triangle?"

"The first two stanzas are from the original song. Marty apparently wrote the third. The margin bit, well, I have no idea."

Drayco concentrated on those last four lines. "I hate to say it, but 'my guilt and betrayal are too much to bear' sounds like a suicide confession."

"Or the victim of that betrayal is at the bottom of this. And staged it as you suggested."

"I don't know, Nelia. The vast majority of suicides are just that. As hard as it is for a family to accept, that's the statistical truth. One reason I hate suicide cases."

Nelia stared at the remaining third of the Danish for a few moments before pushing it away. "I knew a guy while I was in the reserves. He'd been in a war zone, had PTSD and personal setbacks. Yet, when his wife found him in his car with the engine running and rags crammed into the exhaust, she didn't believe he'd killed himself."

She shook her head. "I realize this seems cut-and-dried. I won't think badly of you if you don't want to look into it."

Drayco grabbed the plate with the Danish and pushed it across the table. "Eat, you're wasting away. And you'll need your strength if you're going to help me with this hopeless case of yours."

A smile crept across her lips. "You'll get paid for this one. Sebastien Penry has offered to make your fee. My Mom will kick in the rest."

"With personal ties, evidence will have to be golden to stand up in court."

"If anyone can do it, you can."

Her unwavering faith in his abilities should have made him do a song and dance. But he'd agreed to take the case against his better judgment. And it was possible he'd disappoint a lot of people including Nelia, her mother, and Sebastien Penry. If it were anyone other than Nelia asking him to work a suicide case, he'd say no. They were always the same—the grieving wanting to know the unknowable.

≈ ≈ ≈

Drayco waved at Nelia as they parted company. He walked the short distance to his townhome near Capitol Hill, dodging tourists looking at maps on their cellphones. Once inside, he closed the door and leaned against it with his eyes closed.

After a moment, he headed toward the bookcase and pulled out a biography on Chopin. Turning to the title page, he ran his finger along the dedication, "To my favorite student and future superstar, Scott Drayco. All my best, A. Vucasovich." Touching Vuca's signature made the man feel so real, so alive.

He could still see it clearly. Vuca sitting in the front row as the twenty-year-old Drayco finished playing Beethoven's Emperor concerto with the Boston Symphony, leaping to his feet to lead the standing ovation. Then a week later, the devastation on Vuca's face as he visited Drayco in the hospital after the fateful carjacking, staring at Drayco's shattered wrist and arm. Three months on, it was Drayco's turn to stand and look at Vuca, only this time at a cemetery as Vuca's coffin was lowered into the ground.

Drayco re-read the book's dedication, wondering as he always did when he thought of his former piano teacher—*why did you do it, Vuca?* Maybe there were some things no one could ever know. Or ever should know.

He thought of the copy of the "suicide song" Nelia gave him and grabbed his laptop to do a bit of quick research. Not originally a song at all but based on a piano sonata, one mysteriously linked to suicides. Yet that wasn't what sent a chill up Drayco's spine. The composer of the sonata was Hungarian—a man who also happened to be Vuca's friend before the war.

Drayco slid onto his sofa, staring into space, musing on life's many circles of connection and coincidence. Why this case and why now? The last thing he needed was digging up more emotional graves from his past. But a promise was a promise.

Tired of staring at nothing, he headed for his fridge to grab a bottle of Manhattan Special. Maybe the espresso soda would help? He changed his mind and opened a beer can. He'd need something stronger than a Danish and coffee if this case of Nelia's turned out to be as hopeless as he suspected it was going to be.

2

Thursday, June 14

It took a week for Drayco to tie up his other cases in the District before heading to Cape Unity. The Chesapeake Bay Bridge traffic was thorny, but he made it by mid-afternoon. Driving down Main Street was like driving back in time, with Mom-and-Pop's, no chain stores, and an *Our Town* feel.

Every time he returned to the Eastern Shore, he forgot how much he missed the odor of salt spray and how cleaner the air felt. Nature's aromatherapy for city slickers. Next time, he'd rent a plane, fly over and see it from the air.

He knew what his first stop had to be and was soon parked in the creaky swivel chair in Sheriff Sailor's office. A pile of case folders stacked on the man's desk wasn't a promising sign. The mounted piranha-like fish still glowered at Drayco from the wall, but Sailor's stare was no less intimidating.

Sailor greeted him with, "Once again someone goes over my head to hire you. First Lucy and Maida a year ago. Now, Nelia's mother, of all people."

"I'm not sure this case will take that long."

"You got that right. Suicide note sort of cinches it."

"Not quite a standard note, is it?"

Sailor wadded up a blank piece of paper and tossed it at a galvanized steel trashcan overflowing with paper balls. "I'm sympathetic to the grieving father. But weird note or not, this has the hallmarks of an ordinary suicide. If there is such a thing."

He grabbed a manila folder from the pile and pushed it across his desk for Drayco. "That's a copy of the report. Figured you'd need it."

"I thought you were mad at me."

Sailor smirked. "I am."

Drayco flipped through the folder, stopping first on the photos taken at the scene—the motorcycle, the bullet wound, the blood, the gun. Looked like dozens of others he'd seen before.

He started reading the report next. "Handwriting on the note matched the victim's, as confirmed by the father and Nelia's analysis. Shot with the pistol at close range, one that matches the weapon stolen from his friend's car." Drayco made a note of the name. "Antonio Skye."

"Yeah, that theft was weird, I admit. A week before the suicide, too. But maybe Marty Penry needed a gun, knew his friend had one, and simply stole it."

"If they were friends, surely there were easier ways to get that gun?"

"People not in their right minds and all."

"Any other sources for the weapon?"

"Marty didn't own one. Neither did his father. Or Marty's other friends. Haven't been able to trace it, so can't tell you much."

Drayco studied one entry in the file. "Odd there are no fingerprints on the gun other than Marty's."

"And there's that."

Drayco drummed his fingers on the armrest. "The song found with Marty has a checkered past, apparently. It's based on a piano sonata dating to 1930, written by a Hungarian, Adojan Dobos."

"Marty's father mentioned sheet music. Didn't seem relevant."

"The original piano piece is also known as the 'Suicide Sonata.'"

Sailor's eyes widened. "How's that?"

"A copy was found clutched in a young man's hand after he lay down on railroad tracks as a train barreled through. A few years later, it also turned up beside a woman who'd slit her wrists."

"Two incidents? Hardly enough to make a piece of music infamous."

"The sonata's melody was the basis for a popular song translated into several languages under the title 'Melancholy Morning.' There are reports of a dozen people committing suicide after becoming obsessed with the song. The composer himself took his own life decades later."

Sailor got up to drain the coffee pot into two cups, handing one over. "Adds more weight to Marty's death being exactly what it appears to be."

"On the surface."

"I don't get it. Why are you bothering with this one?"

"A guy's gotta make a living."

"You get plenty of cases. Important ones."

"A favor. Friends and all."

"Uh huh." Sailor gave him a skeptical eye.

Drayco took a taste of Sailor's coffee. Same old sludge, burnt smell and all. So thick, you'd expect a teensy Creature from the Black Lagoon to rise from the murk. He choked some down.

"There are lots of performances of the 'suicide song' on the internet. The sheet music is hard to come by—only one or two sites where you can download it. Don't suppose you looked into that, Sheriff?"

Sailor shrugged. "Doesn't matter ultimately, does it? Marty found it, obsessed over it, died for it."

"Legal downloaders have to pay, so there may be records. I'll need law enforcement muscle to get the site owner to cough up the name." Drayco handed over a list of websites. "Here you go."

Sailor snatched it from him. "Nice to know I'm good for something."

"What about Marty's father saying the suicide was out of character?"

"That's the father's rose-colored glasses."

"Well, have you at least got the tox screen results yet?"

"You kidding? Backlogs, my friend."

"Too bad. It would help if we knew whether he was on drugs."

"No reason to pull strings and request a rush job. Suicides aren't going anywhere." Sailor grimaced. "Drug crimes are on the rise around here, but Marty Penry wasn't on my radar for that."

Drayco tapped the folder. "You said Marty's friends, plural. Who were these friends other than Antonio Skye?"

"We spoke with them. It's all in the report."

Drayco put down the coffee-sludge to search the folder documents. He found the appropriate page and read the names of Marty's girlfriend and other close friends. Not a long list.

Sailor half-smiled. "You're memorizing those, aren't you, Mr. Eidetic Memory? One word of warning—don't talk to the third name on that list, Deirdre Pinnick, without calling her father first. Or better yet, let me be there when you do. He's an attorney and itching for a fight."

"Why?"

"Had a restraining order taken out against Marty Penry. Alleged stalking of his daughter who dated him, then dumped him. Pinnick and his wife are social climbers around here if there's any social to climb. He's Randolph Squier's attorney. If that tells you anything."

"That tells me everything. Thanks for the warning." So that's who took on Squier's case after the man's arrest. Drayco didn't want to dwell on the fact he'd helped put Squier behind bars. And that Drayco was occasionally seeing Squier's ex-wife, Darcie.

Another sip of the coffee made Drayco wish he carried around a salt shaker. He coughed out, "Wouldn't this attorney-father, Emmerson Pinnick, be happy to see Marty Penry dead? That would stop Marty from hanging around his daughter. Permanently."

"The restraining order seemed to do its job. Why take it further?"

Drayco flipped through the folder and stopped on one piece of paper. "This says Marty was reported missing by the marine biology station when he didn't show up for work. And your team found the body in a remote spot several days later. Did you use his cellphone GPS to find him? Or just look for a circle of buzzards?"

Sailor glared at him. "Smart ass. He didn't have his cell with him. Which we still haven't found, by the way. It was Police Work 101. We asked his most recent girlfriend—"

Drayco interrupted, "Lena Bing."

"Lena Bing, yes, and she said they'd gone there a few times on their motorcycles to 'make out.'"

"Have you subpoenaed the—"

"Cellphone records? We put an order in. But we're low priority since it's deemed a suicide. Hell, even when it's an active criminal investigation, I'm lucky if I get a warrant through the court in six weeks."

Flip, flip, flip. Drayco scanned the report's pages as fast as he could. "The M.E. had to determine time of death from insects. And it's approximate. How are the alibis?"

"Without an exact TOD, all his family and friends have alibis galore. But if it's a suicide, that won't matter."

"How remote is this area?"

"We used our new drone to fly in and spot a body before moving in. There was a heavy rain between the time Marty rode there on his motorcycle and when we found him. The one road into the area was flooded."

"How did you get the body out?" Drayco scanned the evidence summary.

"Used a dinghy. Unusual, but it worked."

"Anyone else in his circle own a motorcycle?"

"Yep. Lena Bing."

"Any stolen motorcycles reported?"

"What? Oh, no reports I'm aware of. I can have Giles double-check. In his *spare* time. Again, we have real crimes to solve around here."

Sailor's report had sketches and photos from the site where Marty was found. Drayco focused on the one with the body—a young man in his prime, attractive in an actor-ly way, lying on a bed of bloody leaves as if staged for a crime drama. "Gunshot was on the right side of his head. Was Marty right-handed?"

"I asked his father, and yes. None of that bullshit about the wrong hand being used."

Drayco pulled out his copy of the suicide song Nelia had left with him. "What of the song verse Marty wrote himself? Guilt, betrayal, could be a motive hidden in there."

"For suicide, yeah."

Drayco read the last sentence of the verse. "'And peals of the church bells that reach out to Mars.' Was Marty religious?"

"Sensing his demise, he turned to a deity? His father didn't say. At his final moments, maybe he was trying to make peace with his Creator. Who knows?"

"Yes, but, the 'peals are fading,' his 'faith is fading'?"

"Deathbed conversions. It happens."

"And what of this 'soul vibration' thing in the margin?"

"Again, who knows? Madness and all." Sailor pointed at the song in Drayco's hand. "Tyler gave you the copy?"

"When she asked me to take on the case as a favor to her mother."

Sailor shifted in his seat. "About that. I told Tyler she can't act on behalf of the department, per se, due to her mother connection. But she can assist you in *her* spare time. As long as she makes it clear she's working for the victim's father."

Drayco scanned the rest of the pages in the folder and returned it to Sailor's desk. "Doesn't mean you and I can't schedule lunch at the Seafood Hut for old times' sake, does it?"

"Can't."

Drayco blinked at him. "You're that busy?"

"The Hut had a fire a month ago."

"I had no idea. How bad?"

"Bad enough. They'll be closed for the foreseeable future. The upside is they were insured and can rebuild."

Drayco groaned. He'd really been looking forward to the world's best crab cakes. "Well, I've got to check in with the Jepsons at their B&B, anyway."

"You came here first?" Sailor put his hand over his heart. "I'm touched."

"Some of your employees might say you're touched, all right." Sailor allowed a smile. "Good to have you back, Drayco."

3

Drayco pulled in front of the English Tudor-styled Lazy Crab, the B&B bathed in a golden glow from the late afternoon sun. He probably should have stopped by the Opera House first. When it came to *that* place, procrastination was his middle name. He had a good contractor he trusted, but the building was turning out to be a major headache. More of a nightmare than he hoped when he decided to restore it after a client bequeathed it to him—with a body inside. Still, it kept him involved in his former music life, in a way. And the community was excited about it, so there was that.

He was also putting off seeing Nelia and her mother until tomorrow since they were having a hard time coordinating schedules. Looked like he'd have to make the drive to Virginia Beach if he wanted to meet Sebastien Penry, his new client.

Before Drayco climbed out of the car, he made sure his Glock 27 lay hidden in its safe place. He'd take it with him, but the B&B's co-proprietor, Maida Jepson, hated having firearms in the house. She greeted him with a bear hug and a glass of "iced-tea-syrup," as she called it, and told him dinner would be ready in an hour or so.

He excused himself to take his suitcase to his room, pleased to see it hadn't changed one bit since the last time. Same cool aqua walls, one of the inn's many fireplaces, and a vast four-poster bed with toffee-colored down comforter. As always, the dark paneling on the walls smelled of pine and bayberry, an agreeable mix. The Lazy Crab was an immortal monument locked in a time bubble.

He started to unpack but decided to deal with that later—except for one item he pulled out of his bag. After placing the Chopin biography with Vuca's dedication on the nightstand, he headed downstairs.

Drayco waved out the kitchen window at Major Jepson, who was in the backyard. The man was potting something that looked like a mini version of the carnivorous Audrey II from *Little Shop of Horrors*. Moments later, the patio door banged, followed by the gurgle of running water in the mudroom sink.

When "the Major," as everyone called him, popped into view, Drayco said, "You didn't have to stop what you were doing on my account."

"Tell that to my back. My old, tired, and very aching vertebrae. Guess I should try some of that yoga or pale-ay-tayze."

Maida handed her husband a glass of the tea syrup. "It's pronounced pill-ah-teez, dear."

"Should be called pretzel-teez, if you ask me."

"That reminds me," Maida pulled out a tray and placed it on the table. "Appetizers, anyone? Have some pretzel-ring beer cheese dip."

Drayco nibbled on a soft pretzel section, burning his tongue, and slid into a chair carved like a sailboat. "It's only been a month since I was last here, and your garden has exploded. Major, your thumb isn't green, it's a magic wand for plants."

"Learned it from my father and his father before him. They found the gardening gene in that human genome project, didn't they? One of those CATG combo thingies?"

Maida pulled out a chair to join Drayco. "Since we're on the topic of genetics," she peered at him over a set of chartreuse glasses. "We didn't discuss it much last time, and I don't want to open raw wounds. But I can't stop dwelling on your mother and that horrible murder case. How's your father taking it?"

"As far as he's concerned, it's closure."

"And as far as you're concerned?"

He hesitated. He'd thought of that very question every day over the past couple of months, but easy answers always eluded him. "Sometimes I wonder if we were better off before she came back. I know how that sounds—"

"It's okay, dear. Can't imagine too many shocks greater. Think she's still alive?"

"When I was a boy, and she vanished, my father told me she was dead. I believed the lie. Now she's disappeared once more, I should trust my own instincts."

Maida put a hand on his arm. "What are they telling you?"

"That she's alive. But I'm not sure it means I'll see her again."

"Do you want to?"

"Under different circumstances, yes."

"Then, I hope you do. In the meantime, consider this your adopted home for whenever you need us."

Drayco shook his head. "You might regret that. I seem to attract trouble."

The Major blurted out, "Thank god. Things can get dull around here."

Maida got up to check her Cajun venison casserole in the oven. The pungent aroma of onions, garlic, and cayenne was already filling the room. "I'm glad you're looking into Marty Penry's death, Scott."

"You are?"

"Marty Penry came to talk to me once." She stuck an oven thermometer into the dish and pulled it out to read.

"Here?"

"At the church. Told him I was a lay pastor, and if he needed a good therapist, I could arrange it."

"Can you tell me more? As much as you're comfortable revealing."

"I'm not a psychiatrist or a Catholic priest. That whole confidentiality business doesn't apply, especially if this turns out to be a criminal case. After chatting with Marty, I could tell he was a nice young man. Troubled, but a good soul."

"When you say troubled, what do you mean?" Drayco poured himself more of the tea.

"You know how young people are in their twenties. That first taste of adulthood can be a doozy. Mostly girl problems and work stress. Certainly didn't seem suicidal. But he did want to chat about one odd thing."

"Odd in what way?"

"The Akashic Records."

Drayco choked on his tea. "How in the world did he get interested in the Akashic Records? That whole multi-dimensional, astral plane philosophy?"

"That's the one. It's a little out there, pardon the pun. But I've heard stranger beliefs in my day."

Drayco grabbed his cellphone to look it up on the internet. "According to this, there's a Hall of Records with all knowledge and experiences, past, present and future. Your soul can gain access through psychic readings."

"It's all woo-woo, if you ask me." Major finished munching on a pretzel and half-bowed to Maida. "That's one point my wife and I disagree on. But we have an understanding. I don't go to church, and she doesn't try to convert me. We've been married forty years, so I guess it works."

Maida shoved the casserole into the oven. "Woo-woo or not, Marty was worried over 'karmic debts.' Unfinished business or pending lessons the soul has yet to learn. I think that's how he worded it."

"Like he was seeking forgiveness?"

"I got that impression."

"You're probably right." Drayco trusted Maida's instincts more than those of most psychologists. "Did he mention 'peals of church bells that reach out to Mars?'"

"No, but that would tie in with the whole astral plane thing, wouldn't it?"

"I'll ask Marty's father tomorrow when I see him."

Maida stood with her hands on her hips. "Don't know whether to hope it's suicide or murder. Either way, the poor boy is dead."

"If it's murder, then he deserves justice."

"And if it's suicide, his father will have to live with the guilt." She frowned. "I swear young people are taking their own lives more often."

"The CDC says suicide is the second leading cause of death in Marty's age group."

"It was different when we were kids. Or not reported as much. Or youngsters were less stressed and happier. No one talks to anyone these days. It's all done on tiny screens."

Drayco thought back to his observations at the D.C. café. Maybe they weren't on the same astral plane, but he and Maida were thinking along the same lines. "Does this mean you don't play games on your cellphone, Maida?"

"I only got a cellphone last year. One of those 'dumb' phones. It's one time dumb is better if you ask me. Talk about not stopping and smelling the roses. People don't even *notice* the roses anymore."

Drayco agreed with her on that. Modern young people practically had their phones wired into their hands. So why did Marty Penry not have his with him when he died? Or if he did, where the hell was it now?

The cellphone gods must have been listening in, because Drayco's own phone rang and made him jump. The gruff baritone on the other end said, "Hey, son. My client, who's a pilot, flew us into Salisbury for the day. Said he needed to stop by Accomack Airport on our way back to D.C. I know this is short notice, but we've got thirty minutes." He paused and then added, "If you're available."

"It'll take me ten to get there, but I can make it."

"Great. See you in ten."

After Drayco rang off, he said "Speak of the devil" and then told Maida and Major the plan.

Maida replied, "Tell him he's missing out on a great dinner. Sure you can't get him and his friend to stay?"

"Sounded like Brock's client is on a tight schedule."

Maida grabbed some of her homemade peanut-butter fudge, bundled it into a container, and handed it over. "Consolation prize."

After thanking her and apologizing again for having to leave after he'd just got there, Drayco headed up US 13 and onto Airport Drive. He passed by some invasive Tree-of-heavens trying to out-evolve the native boxelder and pignut hickory. At least, no turkey vultures strutted around the runway like last time.

A slender, distinguished man with short, graying hair stood outside the small terminal. He strode over to Drayco's car and opened the door. "We've got ten minutes for a whirlwind tour of the town. You up for it?"

"Whirlwind Tours at your service."

Drayco's father hopped in, and they headed toward the heart of Cape Unity. Brock asked, "Is the Opera House nearby?"

"Not too far. The interior's torn up, and things are a bit of a mess."

"Driving by the building itself will be enough."

Drayco parked at the Opera House to let his father take in the patterned shingles and weathered copper rosettes flanking the gables. Drayco said, "You should have seen it a year ago. The windows could best be described as dingy. We've patched up the cracks in the front steps and gussied up the paint."

"Looks better than I feared."

"What were you expecting, then?"

"A disaster."

Drayco gritted his teeth. "You were never on board with this whole project, were you?"

Brock grunted. "Still think you should sell it."

"A little late now. Besides, you were always the one who told me to miter the corners. Do it right, make it tight. Follow through."

Brock softened his tone. "Tell you what. If you can make this thing a success, I'll buy a front-row ticket for opening night."

"I'll hold you to that. And make it two. We could always use the money."

Craning his neck to get a better look at the top of the building, Brock asked, "This is a suicide case you're on, right?"

"The client, the boy's father, doesn't think it's suicide."

"That's what they all believe. I thought you didn't like suicide cases."

"I detest them."

Brock turned to face him, studying Drayco for longer than he was comfortable. "This isn't just about that boy, is it?"

"It's a favor. For a friend."

"Hmm. And for Vuca, perhaps?"

"Music *is* connected to this case." Drayco pinched the bridge of his nose. This was not a discussion he wanted to have. "And the composer was a friend of Vuca's. It's complicated."

"I think I see."

"You do?"

"Vuca was there for you when I wasn't. You owe him."

Drayco fixated on the dashboard as they sat in silence, save for the whirring of the AC and rumbling of the engine. Finally, Drayco cleared his throat. "It's ancient history, isn't it? Forward, upward, onward."

Brock gave a half-smile. "That's what your mother used to say." He looked at the time on the Starfire's dash. "And unfortunately, onward means I need to get to the airport where we'll be going upward soon. Sam gets cranky when he misses dinner with his wife."

Drayco turned the car around, and they made it with a few minutes to spare. Before his father got out, Drayco handed over the box of fudge.

"What's that?"

"A gift from Maida Jepson. Trust me—anything she makes is gourmet fare."

"Please give her my thanks. I'll meet her on the next trip. Maybe when I buy that front-row seat."

He slid out of the car. "And give Darcie my regards, too. Hope she's doing well."

Drayco winced. "I haven't seen her in a couple of weeks. But soon."

Brock gave Drayco one of his bayonet stares. "Couple of weeks. Breathing room's always good, right?" He gave a quick wave as he added, "Keep me posted on the case," and headed inside the terminal.

Breathing room. Another coded phrase from Brock, who hadn't warmed up to Darcie. But he wasn't enthusiastic about any of his son's girlfriends, not even Drayco's ex-fiancée, Tatiana.

Drayco should go inside the building to see his father off properly, but he was on a schedule, too. Maida's schedule. He pointed the

Starfire along Airport Drive and realized he'd forgotten to ask how his father's case was going. For two former FBI agents, they were woefully lacking in investigating each other's lives.

℞ ℞ ℞

When Drayco returned to the Lazy Crab, Maida's dinner wasn't quite ready. So, he headed to the den and sat at the Jepsons' mahogany Chickering piano. He'd brought his downloaded copy of the original Suicide Sonata with him from D.C. and propped the sheet music on the stand.

It wasn't the first time he'd played it, having tackled the piece at his townhome. But on the vintage Chickering, it took on a different tone. Maybe it was the expressiveness of the sound. Or the coppery bass, beveled-jade midrange, and crinkled bamboo treble it created in his brain. Or maybe it was knowing a Chickering was the house piano at Ford's Theater the night of Lincoln's assassination.

He couldn't deny it was a gloomy tune. Set in the key of D minor, like the Mozart, Fauré, Bruckner, and Reger Requiems. Study after study attempted to show why minor keys sounded "sad" to Western ears. But none had linked minor keys to suicide.

He dug into the notes, transported back a century when the composition was new. The first half of the piece set up the dark mood—murky chords in the bass, tremolos, and a haunting melody making heavy use of tritones.

If the first part was dark, the second was positively despondent. Drayco's fingers glided through the arpeggios, as the bleakness of the broken minor chords drew him in. Beauty in sadness, darkness in joy.

Through the haze of concentration and feeling oddly dizzy, he became aware of a presence in the room. He turned to see Maida standing in the doorway, listening. "I hate to disturb you, but dinner is ready."

"Of course. Hope I didn't keep you waiting."

"Other way around, I'd say. But whatever was that piece? It's lovely but rather sad."

"It has a bizarre backstory. I'll tell you later."

As he followed her out of the den, he took one look back at the piano. The sheet music was still on the stand, a paper link between a tragic past and a tragic present. Something about that disturbed him. But no, it must be the dizzy spell—probably low blood sugar.

As he watched, a page fluttered, seemingly on its own. Ghosts of his imagination? He looked around and saw an air-conditioning vent pointed at the piano. It should be funny, so why didn't he feel like laughing?

4

Friday, June 15

Maida packed Drayco a portable breakfast for his trip down U.S. 13 through the Chesapeake Bay Bridge-Tunnel into Virginia Beach. Since it was a ninety-minute drive, he'd gotten an early start, arriving five minutes ahead of schedule.

Sebastien Penry's bungalow wasn't on Virginia Beach proper. It lay on Sandbridge Island, perched along the Currituck Banks Peninsula coast at the Outer Banks' northern tip. The winds blew over the water, bringing the tangy aroma of seaweed and briny air, much stronger than in Cape Unity.

When Nelia greeted Drayco and ushered him to the cedar deck in back, he saw the location's charm. Picturesque views spread out toward the inlet with clumped marsh grass ringing the greenish-blue water. The relative quiet appealed to Drayco's synesthesia. He'd happily take the violet fog of the water and golden grooved bird calls over the khaki sabers of the raucous city.

A man and a woman, seated on blue metal chairs around a matching table, stood up when he entered. The man stuck out his hand. "I'm Sebastien Penry. And I am so relieved you're taking my son's case, Mr. Drayco."

Nelia turned to the tall, slender woman with an equal amount of gray hair threaded through the blond. "And this is Olive Tyler, Drayco. My mother."

There was a strong family resemblance between mother and daughter, making Drayco think of the Major's comment on "those CATG combo thingies." Definitely good genes, there.

Mrs. Tyler also shook Drayco's hand, with a smile. "I've heard so much about you. Former piano star. Now a brilliant consulting detective. Meeting you in person doesn't disappoint."

Drayco raised his eyebrows at Nelia, who grinned. "Your infamy follows you around like a puppy."

"Good to meet you both." Drayco looked at Sebastien and Olive in turn, adding, "I wish it were under happier circumstances."

Sebastien perched on the deck railing, his face the color of the distant storm clouds over the ocean, dark and ashen gray. "Sheriff Sailor and everyone else wrote off Marty's death as a suicide. The grieving father grasping at straws. But my son deserves better than that. And I deserve the truth."

Drayco asked, "Wherever that truth may lead?"

"I'm prepared for all possibilities."

"I'm curious why you waited weeks to hire me. More so if you suspect it was murder?"

"I was too numb. The more time went on, the more I couldn't believe it was suicide. It makes no sense. And all those bizarre inconsistencies. It's all joed up."

"Joed up?"

"Sorry. Construction lingo. When something's been fabricated wrong."

"In this case, you mean the gun?"

"The gun, the location, the timing, the motive. Make that lack of motive." Sebastien waved his hands in the air. "Take your pick."

Drayco studied the other man. "Are you okay discussing this? I know it must be hard."

"I'm ready. I *need* to do this."

"All right, let's start with Marty. Tell me more about him. His childhood, his interests." Unlike the sheriff and Drayco's former FBI partner Sarg, Drayco didn't take notes on site. He memorized everything and wrote it down later—eye contact was too important.

"His mother died when he was ten. Ovarian cancer. Hard on me, but harder on him. I did my best."

Olive spoke up. "Of course, you did."

"We have family up in New York but nobody close. It was mostly all on me."

Drayco asked, "He was a pianist?"

Sebastien smiled briefly. "I taught him piano when he was a boy, Bach, Chopin, Mozart. I know you must think it's odd for a construction worker to be a classical musician—"

"Not at all."

"Marty did the usual teen rebellion thing and went all-rock. Until college. Took a music history class because he needed a humanities credit. Got hooked on classical again."

"You're familiar with the 'Suicide Sonata' song found with him?"

Sebastien slid off the railing and onto a chair. "Don't know where he got that. I knew he had the piano sonata sheet music, but that was all."

"Where did he get his copy of that sheet music?"

"I have no earthly idea."

Olive Tyler sat next to him and patted his hand. "Must appear damning for that song to be found with him. But Marty was by and large an upbeat young man. Loved that job of his."

"His twin passions were music and marine biology. I was so damned proud when he got his master's degree. He had such great plans for his career." Sebastien flinched as he fixated on a red stain on the table.

"Were the two of you on good terms? Any arguments, estrangements?"

To Drayco's surprise, Sebastien answered in the affirmative. "We got along fine most of the time. Except for the day he went missing. We'd argued over the phone." He choked up and covered it with a cough. Olive rushed into the house to get him a glass of water.

Drayco gave him a moment to regain his composure. "What was the source of this disagreement?"

"A girl. Isn't it always a girl? Or money. Marty belonged to a group at Cape Unity High School, five kids who hung together. Antonio Skye was one, and then the three girls. Lena Bing, Deirdre Pinnick, and Tess Gartin."

All recognizable names from the sheriff's folder. "And the argument concerned one of the girls?"

"Deirdre Pinnick. He'd dated both her and Lena—Lena most recently, I think—but it was Deirdre he was obsessed with. Even after that asshole father of hers took out that restraining order."

"Yet, it was Lena Bing who told the sheriff where he might find the body."

"They were engaged once. Broke it off when he started dating Deirdre. When Deirdre dumped him, he hooked up with Lena again."

"Why the broken engagement?"

"Too young. And it was brief. When they got back together, they weren't talking marriage anymore."

"Could any of those relationships lead to violence? If Marty didn't take his own life, that's the alternative. Murder."

Sebastien's lips compressed into a white line. "I'd hate to think that. But if one of them is a killer, that means Marty didn't do it."

"Is there anyone else who hated Marty? Any threats?"

"I've sat up night after night going through Marty's life. To answer that very question. He was a typical kid. Never had so much as a detention."

Drayco paused for a moment, keeping an eye on Sebastien, who kept rubbing his trembling hands together. "If we're ruling out suicide, it would help to know if Marty talked about death lately. Or about making a will. Or had started giving away possessions."

Sebastien replied in a flat tone of voice, "He didn't say any such thing to me. And going through his apartment, I didn't see much missing."

Drayco sat down a bench against the wall, but the moment he did, a yellow ball of fur scrambled out through a doggy door and hopped beside him. The golden retriever lay his head on Drayco's knee and looked up at him with soulful eyes.

Sebastien said, "Drago rarely warms up to strangers."

Olive added, "My Aunt Jess always said dogs could see people's auras. Guess you must put out friendly body language."

Drayco scratched the dog's ears. "Drago?"

Sebastien chuckled at that. "Didn't think of the connection. You're a Drayco, and he's a Drago. Both terms for 'dragon.' Guess it makes sense he'd like you."

"Mr. Penry—"

"Please, just Sebastien."

"Sebastien, did Marty have any vices, alcohol, drugs?"

"Never saw him take anything harder than beer. I suspected he dabbled in marijuana. But he'd been on a huge health kick."

"Was he religious? The verse he wrote for the song leaned in that direction."

"We stopped going to church when my wife died."

Olive grabbed Sebastien's hand. That was the second or third time. Was she unsure of the suicide angle, herself, but didn't want to upset her friend? Or was it something else entirely?

Drayco said, "Does the Akashic Records ring any bells?"

Sebastien stared at him. "The what?"

"Something that was mentioned to me."

Since the other man's confusion seemed genuine, Drayco changed the subject. "I hate to bring up the gun. But the sheriff said you didn't own any weapons. Have any idea where he got it?"

"I heard it was Antonio's. The one that was stolen. Or so they said."

"You don't believe in the theft scenario?"

"Such an odd thing to happen right before. . ." He took a deep breath. "Right before Marty's death."

"Was there any bad blood between Antonio Skye and Marty?"

"The opposite. Despite Marty going off to college and Antonio staying behind to work in the chicken plant, they remained close."

Sebastien pulled a photo from his wallet and handed it over to Drayco. "That's the two of them. Found it among his things. Printed out from a cellphone."

"Marty's cellphone? Did you find it with his other possessions?"

"No, no phones of any kind."

"Did he not use it much?"

"On the contrary. He was on it constantly."

Drayco studied the photo which had a date stamp, an odd detail. The smiling pair of young men stood side by side, each with a fishing pole. Marty was taller, with his sandy-colored hair and a smattering of freckles. Antonio was half a foot shorter, his dark eyes dancing with laughter.

"This was six months ago." Drayco passed the photo back. "Do you have any other of his personal effects? There may be clues there."

"Haven't cleared out Marty's apartment. The landlord is cutting us a break. Grudgingly, but I'll take it."

He had a blank expression as he gazed out over the marsh. Drayco wondered if he'd get additional info from the other man, but Sebastien surprised him a second time. He said, "I'll be back in a moment," and bolted into the house.

Drayco continued scratching Drago's ears, a blissful smile on the doggy face. Drayco said to Nelia's mother, "Your daughter's told me a lot about you, too, Mrs. Tyler." As she opened her mouth to object, he hastened to add, "That is, Olive. I'd hoped to meet J.B., as well."

The skin around Olive's mouth tightened so slightly, he almost missed it. "My husband travels on business quite a bit. After he left the military, he took consulting jobs that send him around the world."

"Next time, then. J.B. stands for Jean-Baptiste, doesn't it?"

Olive replied, "Yes, and your French accent is quite good. You must speak the language."

"*Je parle un peu mal français.*"

"Not that badly." She laughed.

Sebastien rejoined them and held out his hand to Drayco, a key dangling from a seahorse-shaped keychain. "This is the key to his place. If it'll help to go through his belongings, you have my blessing."

The man glanced at his watch, and Drayco asked, "You have an appointment?"

"Just started a new contracting job, first one in a while. I could manage taking off a few hours today. But only a few."

"Is that where you got the injury?" Drayco pointed at a bandage on Sebastien's arm.

"Had a fight with a bunny gun, and I lost."

"A bunny gun?"

"Cable cutters. Don't ordinarily handle those, but I picked up a pair from the ground."

"Glad to see it wasn't worse." Drayco stood up. "Well, Sebastien, thanks for your time. If I think of anything else, I'll give you a call."

After a parting hug from Olive, Nelia walked Drayco to his car with Drago following along. Nelia patted Drayco's car. "Good old Leonora, your lovely Starfire."

"I manage to keep her running."

Nelia chewed on her lip. "Did Sebastien help with building a case for a possible homicide?"

"Not much. But it's early, and I have a few motives worth tracking down."

"And that sonata?"

"And that mystery sonata, yes, in its various forms."

He looked around for something to throw Drago to chase. Nothing. "How long has your mother known Sebastien Penry?"

"Seven years, since he moved here."

"Enough to vouch for his character?"

"Of course."

Drayco leaned over to rub the dog's ears. "From what you've told me of Olive, she doesn't suffer fools gladly. I'll keep that in mind."

"You don't trust him?"

"I've seen too many people with a hidden dark side. Since he's my client, I'll give him the benefit of the doubt. For now."

Drayco opened the Starfire and slid into the driver's seat. After starting it, he cranked up the AC. Despite being mid-morning, it was already hot, one reason he'd opted for a white shirt. He wiped beads of sweat from his forehead and hoped he wasn't getting underarm lakes. The guy who'd invented air conditioning deserved a posthumous medal.

As he drove off, he saw Nelia waving in the rearview mirror with Drago barking his own goodbye.

5

Nelia watched her mother bend over to smell the orange Floribunda roses. Following the meeting at Sebastien's, both women soon had to return to work—Nelia to Cape Unity and her mother to practice for a concert with her orchestra in the evening. But Olive seemed as reluctant to go as Nelia. They decided to take a quick stroll through the botanical garden in town, a place neither had visited in years.

Olive straightened up, looked toward a small building with a plaque on the side, and pulled Nelia toward it. "I thought of you when I heard of this new exhibit they've installed. Right up your alley."

Nelia read the plaque. "The Poison Patch?"

Olive grinned. "Let's go in."

A curator greeted them inside with a few cautionary instructions, while an armed guard kept a close eye on them. Nelia could see why. The shed contained beds of *ricinus communis*, the castor oil plant, the seeds of which contained the toxin ricin. There was a laburnum tree with its various poisonous parts that can cause frothing at the mouth and coma. And last but not least, monkshood, so deadly a drinking well contaminated with its roots could poison an entire town.

Olive shuddered as they passed a display of hemlock. "I'm not sure I'd come here on my own. And since you rarely make it down here, anymore, there's that."

Nelia silently counted to three. "Mom, I try. But with two jobs, law school, and Tim, there's no time left to breathe, let alone travel. You're welcome to visit me any time."

Olive stopped next to a planter with opium-producing poppies. "These are lovely, aren't they? Death from beauty."

Since the curator warned them not to touch or smell any plants, Nelia's mother opted for a cellphone photo. "Nelia, dear, you haven't mentioned Tim this entire day. How's he doing, really?"

"Nothing new. The MS is stable, so say the docs. He's his same cranky, demanding self." Nelia's voice sounded bitter to her own ears. But Tim was always going to be a sore point between them, wasn't he?

Olive stepped in front of her daughter to keep her walking further. "And how are *you* doing, really?"

"I'm fine. Overworked. The usual stress."

"Work stress or marital stress? Reading between the lines, I'd say your marriage is in rocky territory. Are you thinking about divorce?"

"I don't want to discuss it. Not now." Nelia always knew her mother could read her like a Nelia encyclopedia. Nelia hadn't mentioned the "D" word to anyone but attorney Benny Baskin. And Drayco. God, why had she mentioned it to him? Of all people?

Once more, her mother showed her maternal telepathy. "I like that Scott Drayco. You made a good choice."

"A what?" Nelia gaped at her. Oh, she meant investigator. "Yes, yes, he's good. I mean, he's very good at what he does. Sheriff Sailor respects him, which is a ringing endorsement if there ever was one." Nelia reached out to touch the nightshade plants but stopped herself. "But I don't want to waste his valuable time on a wild goose chase. And waste Sebastien's money."

"Waste his time? Do you honestly believe that?"

"It's a possibility. You have to admit it."

Olive shook her head. "I do not have to admit it, not at all. I firmly believe Sebastien's instincts about his son. Just like my instincts about you. And if he thinks his son didn't commit suicide, then he didn't. But if *you* don't agree, why did you ask Scott Drayco to help?"

Nelia sighed. "Because I love you, and you want this. And because the whole thing does feel off." She rushed to add, "But whatever truth we find, I hope you'll be ready to accept it."

"I promise, dear." Her mother made her way toward a large flat-topped rock and perched on top.

Nelia approached a white flowering plant and read the label. "I always wanted to see hemlock in person."

Olive laughed. "That's my daughter."

Nelia caught a whiff of something fragrant and tracked the aroma to a plant with pink tubular flowers. The tag read *Daphne odora - all parts of the plant are poisonous to humans.* The scent was a combination of citrus blossoms, lilies, and roses. Heavenly.

"When is Dad coming home, Mom? He's been gone longer this time."

"Jaunting all over the world is unpredictable. But he loves his work."

"Drayco's been eager to meet you both. I guess fifty percent is better than none."

Olive hopped up to join her in admiring the *Daphne.* "Why do you call him 'Drayco' instead of Scott?"

"We're colleagues and professionals. I don't call Sheriff Sailor 'Ernest.'"

"But the sheriff is your boss. And you and Scott don't work in the same department." She paused, then added, "And that's why Scott Drayco calls you 'Tyler'?"

"Naturally."

Olive took a deep whiff of the plant. "When you're an attorney and no longer a deputy, you can drop all that formality."

Nelia hadn't considered that. She had three years of law school left, so no rush to change the status quo. Was there?

An image of their near-kiss in D.C. hit her full force, and she felt her cheeks flush. What would it be like if she'd given in? Maybe that's why she kept Drayco at arms-length. She was afraid she couldn't resist next time.

"What were your impressions of Marty, Mom?"

"A nice, polite young man. I could see his father in him, in looks and temperament."

"He didn't appear depressed to you?"

"Hardly. He was cheerful, joking."

"Could he have been faking it?"

"Faking? Why would he do that?"

"Young people often don't show signs of suicidal thoughts. Until it's too late."

Her mother's face had a steely look that Nelia knew all too well. "We're back to that? That he did commit suicide? Are you sure you're not prejudiced against other possibilities?"

Nelia tried not to take offense at that. She was taking offense far too easily as of late. "Did I not mention I was a professional? When I said we'll follow the truth wherever it leads us, I meant it."

Olive looked up at the building's skylight. "That's what worries me."

Nelia wanted to push her on what she meant by that, but Olive started walking toward the exit. "You have to make the return trip to Cape Unity, and we've had enough poison for today."

Her abrupt change in demeanor alarmed Nelia. Was her mother hiding something from her? Nelia tried to push that notion aside, but her mother's words and the aroma of the deadly *Daphne* followed her out the door.

6

Drayco altered his course to the marine biology station where Marty had worked to see a place Drayco hadn't visited in a while. Where a mini-forest once stood on the properties of Earl Yaegle and Oakley Keys, a three-story skeleton—make that monstrosity—of a building now shot up from the sandy soil.

The new condo development was around forty feet tall. Through the steel-and-concrete framework, Drayco caught a glimpse of the Bluedog Creek marsh beyond. For now, anyway, until the building was completed and blocked the view altogether. What had become of Oakley's heart-shaped garden and the rock shrine that used to be there? A depressing thought.

Forcing himself to focus on the present and not the past, he accelerated the Starfire toward his goal and finally pulled into a gravel lot. The sign read, "Eastern Shore Laboratory of the Virginia Institute of Marine Science." The front of the blue wooden-panel building didn't look all that large. That is until he poked his head around the side. A much longer section jutted out into the water with a small marina attached.

If the pungent smell of fish was strong outside, it permeated every inch of the interior as he made his way toward a front desk. Not seeing anyone, he tapped the bell and looked around while he waited. The exhibits scattered along the walls—sharks' teeth, whale bones, mounted fish that would put Sheriff Sailor's to shame—seemed tailored for school groups. Regular visitors, no doubt.

After five minutes and no sign of anyone, he walked through the hallway noting one side room sporting tanks with bay scallops, small crabs, and eels. Another room held a small screen and chairs. The murmur of voices lured him toward an ample space in the rear with more tanks and pumps.

When an older man and his younger female companion, who were deep in conversation, didn't notice him, he cleared his throat. "Dr. Judson Kolman?"

The man whirled around. "We don't allow tourists outside of special hours. There's a sign-up sheet in front—"

"I'm not a tourist. I'm Dr. Scott Drayco." He rarely pulled out the Ph.D. "card" but sensed this was one of those times it would help.

"Ah, a colleague. We weren't expecting anyone today."

Drayco replied, "Criminal science, not marine, I'm afraid. I'm looking into the death of Marty Penry on behalf of his father."

Kolman turned to the young woman, and they exchanged confused glances. "I don't understand. The sheriff concluded it was suicide."

"Tying up loose ends, looking for motivations, closure."

Kolman replied, "Not sure how we can help." He turned toward a small office on the other side of the hallway. "But I don't want to be an ungracious host. I think I have coffee left. Cream? Sugar?"

"Thanks. I take it black. With salt."

"Salt?" Kolman laughed and swept his hand toward the water in the tanks. "We have plenty of the marine kind. Don't know of any condiment kind in this building." He stroked his mustache. "On the other hand. Hang on a moment."

He ducked into the office and returned with a paper cup, a wooden stirrer, and some salt packets. "Left over from a picnic last month."

Drayco doctored the coffee as Kolman watched in amazement. "As much as I'm around salt water, it never once occurred to me to try that."

"Makes coffee less bitter."

"Well, then. It goes on my list. Now about those questions. . ." A cellphone interrupted him. After looking at the number, he tapped the screen and made a face. "It's the state bureau. I'll take this in my office and be with you shortly."

Kolman turned to the young woman. "Tess, feel free to answer any questions Dr. Drayco has. We need to do whatever we can to help Sebastien Penry." He disappeared into his office and closed the door.

Drayco studied the young woman he assumed was Tess Gartin from the list of Marty's Group of Five. Her outdoorsy tan matched her dark, close-cropped hair—easier to put on a scuba mask? "You're Tess Gartin, a childhood friend of Marty's?"

She motioned toward the marina. "Can we chat while I'm working? I'm behind on my *Crassostrea ariakensis* project."

"Oysters?"

"Are you sure you aren't a marine scientist?"

"I know a little Latin. *Ostrea*, oysters."

"People think we're all about dolphins and whales and seals, the cute animals. But it's so much more."

He followed her outside to the pier where she pulled up a rope from the railing and read the attached meter. "Marty and I weren't childhood friends. Didn't know him until high school. We had our group that hung together."

"Misfits?"

"No more than anyone else in high school."

"And you stayed friends?"

After making a note on a chart, she replied, "A fun little club. Until Marty messed everything up. Dated two of the girls more seriously. Obsessed over one in particular. A right frickin' mess."

"Girls as in Lena Bing and Deirdre Pinnick?"

"You've done your homework. It was fun and carefree. Weed, booze, free love. Hang out, have a good time, de-stress."

"Why didn't you and Marty date? Part of the club bylaws, it seems."

She snorted. "Marty wasn't my type. We were rivals. Went to the same college, but I was the better student."

"You both got a master's degree in marine science, and both came to work here. Seems friendly enough."

"You take gigs where you can get 'em. But I believed I had the upper hand to be Senior Marine Scientist."

Drayco took note of the flash in her eyes and her jutting jaw. "Marty was promoted instead?"

She folded her arms across her chest. "I'd say it's because Dr. Kolman was a second father figure to Marty. But it's probably more of that frickin' sexism thing. We women scientists face it every day. Makes me sound like I'm happy Marty's dead, but I'm not. He could be fun to have around. Until he got all mopey."

Finally, someone was saying Marty wasn't all smiles and yucks. "How long ago did this change occur?"

"Months. Might have started when Deirdre dumped him."

"Breakups can make people suicidal."

"He was in the dumps, like anyone after a breakup. On the other hand, Marty was a health nut."

She made a face. "His favorite drink was this homemade smoothie with bitter greens. Kale and dandelion. Along with green apple, avocado, and hemp protein. Those big tubs of powder you add to liquid. Had it with him all the time."

Drayco grinned, "I doubt he got the recipe from the Akashic Records."

Tess gaped at him. "What? Oh, you mean that project of Deirdre's. Kinda weird hokum. But no, I don't remember any recipes." That managed to get a small smile out of her.

Kolman rejoined them. "Sorry for the interruption. Gotta keep the state bureaucrats happy. So, Tess, were you telling Dr. Drayco what a good employee Marty was?"

Noting Tess's wide eyes, Drayco rescued her from embarrassment. "You appointed him Senior Marine Scientist?"

"Higher than that one day. Assistant Director." The older man rubbed his forehead. "He had dreams of being the next Jacques Cousteau. Guess I was a bit of a hard-ass. But you have to build slowly, work your way up. I didn't want him to become bitter and disappointed."

Kolman stopped to watch an amberjack as big as a mini-sub as it jumped out of the water. "Those other friends of his weren't a great influence. Was hoping he'd mature, so I practiced tough love."

Drayco said, "Did Marty understand this 'tough love' of yours?"

"He never complained. But it's kept me up at night, wondering."

The noise from a chugging boat engine drew closer, and a small cabin boat pulled up and docked expertly at the pier. Tess went to help the pilot carry what looked like lobster traps into the building. Lobsters? Not around here, surely. Probably crayfish.

Drayco said, "Must take a host of resources to run this facility. Personnel, money."

Kolman picked at a knothole in one of the pier's wooden planks. "Sure, but we work hard to pull in grants for our projects. And we've done a bang-up job with the place. If I do say so, myself."

Tess returned in time to hear what Kolman had said. "Dr. Kolman has to fight for every penny."

Her boss added, "Sucking up to rich people who don't care about the environment but want a tax write-off. Or something to brag about at cocktail parties."

Drayco had an uncomfortable image of his rundown Opera House and its expensive renovations. "You have my sympathies. I suppose Marty had to deal with that, too?"

"He was working more with budgets. Bought new gear. Made a few questionable purchases, but he was learning. I was pleased with his progress."

"Tess said she noticed Marty had grown moodier lately."

"Moody? I don't know. Distracted. Quieter, I guess. Afraid I'm not an expert on human psychology."

Drayco pulled out his copy of the suicide song and held it up for them to see. "Did the sheriff ask you about the note found with Marty? The so-called 'suicide song'?"

Tess spoke up, "It was like an obsession. And the sheriff did ask that question, but my answer is the same. I mean, what the hell?"

Kolman added. "I dismissed it as a fad, if not a macabre one. But I don't keep up with pop music."

Drayco put the copy away. "It's more classical than pop. And so obscure, hardly anyone would know it. That's the problem."

Tess dropped a meter she was holding on the pier where it fell with a clatter. "Marty showed me the real sonata once, the one for piano. Said it was nicknamed the 'Suicide Sonata,' which he thought was funny. The song was based on that, wasn't it?"

"It was. What did you mean by 'obsessed' with the song, Tess?"

She took her time bending down to pick up the meter. "Listened to it over and over. Thank god he used earbuds most of the time."

Drayco nodded toward the building where the new arrival had vanished. "Did your boat operator know Marty well?"

It was Kolman who answered. "Besides three full-time positions—myself, Tess here, and Marty—the station has temporary and contract people who come and go. None long enough to get to know Marty much. We added George there three weeks ago."

That bit of news gave Drayco mixed feelings. It meant fewer people to interview but fewer people with potential answers. Or motives. He thanked Kolman and Tess for their time and headed toward his Starfire.

A goose stood in his way, flapping its wings and squawking with the most ungodly sound any bird could make. A cross between a siren and a donkey's braying that hit his brain with orange needles and beige glass shards. It was times like this he wished he weren't a synesthete.

Drayco planted his feet in the gravel and stared down the goose. "Out of my way, or you might end up as somebody's dinner."

After a few more seconds of the bird's protests, it waddled away. Was it warning him? Not mating season yet so that couldn't be it.

According to Tess, Marty's Gang of Five were proficient with that whole mating thing. And if Marty was obsessed with Deirdre Pinnick, then the breakup could have hit him hard—and possibly lead to suicide. Even if Tess didn't support that hypothesis.

Marty had a great job, a loving father, supportive friends, another girlfriend, and was on a health kick. That made his suicide an attitude one-eighty, unless there was another motive, a hidden financial crisis, perhaps. Another subpoena for Sheriff Sailor—who wasn't going to be

Drayco's best buddy if he had to go after bank records in addition to websites.

The notion that a "tough love" boss would cause Marty to take his own life seemed far-fetched. But if he were depressed and felt his Cousteau dream was in jeopardy, perhaps. On the other hand, Tess's rivalry with Marty was intriguing, but murder? She could have simply bided her time and taken another job elsewhere.

At this point, motive-wise, Drayco was ready to blame the goose. Drayco looked around for the bird, thinking he should apologize for that dinner crack. But it had vanished.

As investigational starts went, this was limping right out of the block. Was that why he was uneasy? He'd felt unsettled since his mother's case three months ago. This was just more of the same, more of the sense he'd lost some of his emotional footing.

With a sigh, he headed toward his car. He'd made a promise to Nelia, and that's all his "emotional footing" needed to know.

7

On a whim, or more of a calculated guess, Drayco drove by one of the giant chicken processing plants that dotted the Delmarva Peninsula. It wasn't hard to miss, going by the occasional whiffs of bird-scat "fertilizer." Chicken was big business in the area, accounting for fifteen percent of all poultry produced in the U.S. But it wasn't that or his new poultry friend, the goose, Drayco had on his mind.

It was near three o'clock, the usual time for shift changes—and he was in luck. As he sat in the parking lot watching the stream of workers filing out of the building, one particular person caught his attention. The dark-haired young man was the spitting image of the shorter boy from Sebastien Penry's photo.

His angular face contrasted with his five-eight stature as if someone had swapped head and body from different people. The polypropylene hairnet mashed his thick, dark hair into a blob making his head resemble a jellyfish.

Drayco rolled down the window and called out, "Are you Antonio Skye?"

The worker narrowed his eyes. "Who wants to know?"

"Scott Drayco. I work with Sheriff Sailor. Sebastien Penry hired me to look into his son's death, to get some closure." He motioned to his Starfire. "Have a moment to chat?"

The boy looked like he'd rather climb into a de-boner machine with the chickens. But he seemed drawn to the Starfire, running his hand along the hood. "I got fifteen minutes."

"You have to be somewhere else?"

"I wish. I'm on break."

"And these other workers?" Drayco opened the passenger door, and Antonio slid into the seat.

"They're going home. I take my breaks outside where I can get fresh air."

"I imagine the smell could be irritating."

"You get used to it."

Drayco caught a whiff of that smell on Antonio's blue uniform. Yikes. Like someone had blended ammonia, sulfur, and sewage into a joke cologne. Make that a "gag" cologne. Drayco rolled down the other windows.

Antonio peered at the dashboard. "Classic car. Maybe I can afford one of these someday. My car's held together with duct tape and superglue. Somebody busted out my window."

"I heard of the theft. The gun that was stolen."

The young man slumped in the seat. "He killed himself with my gun. My. Gun."

"You believe Marty stole it from your car?"

"He must have. But why bother? He knew where I kept it."

"Did you teach him how to shoot?"

Antonio's jaw hung open. "I hadn't. . .I mean, no. Marty didn't like guns, so I never tried."

Drayco used a more soothing tone. "Mr. Penry showed me a photo of you and Marty. You must have been good friends."

"He was great. Smart and funny. Never gave me grief over my old man."

"Your father?"

"He's in state prison. Murdered some guy. Twelve years ago." Slouching further, Antonio picked at his cracked nails.

"I'm sorry to hear that, Antonio. Sorry about Marty, too. Were there any signs he'd been having problems?"

"Seemed okay to me. The day he went missing, we were going fishing. I tried calling him. No answer. Figured he was busy with work. When I found out what happened. . ."

The young man rubbed his eyes. "Wish I'd called somebody to go find him. Anybody. They could have stopped him."

"You're convinced he took his own life?"

"But I thought. . .that's what they said. The forest, the gun, the note?"

"We're checking all angles to be sure."

The younger man straightened up with a quick check of the clock on the car's dashboard. "Look, if you're going to ask more questions, it'll have to be in there," he pointed toward the plant. "If I want to keep my job. Could get you in with a guest pass. Gail owes me a favor."

Drayco almost said he'd catch Antonio another time. But it could be enlightening to see the place—and Antonio's part in it all.

Gail, who was the receptionist, agreed to the guest pass especially after Antonio told her Drayco was a friend of the sheriff's. Antonio got a bump cap and a lab coat for Drayco and guided his "guest" into the bowels of the plant.

As they passed by a room bathed in black light with the label "Live Hanging," Drayco regretted agreeing to the tour. Workers were lifting the birds from their crates on a conveyor belt and hanging them by their feet on a moving line of hooks.

Antonio said, "Those guys have the highest-paying job in the plant. The night shift's more."

Drayco had heard the plant's jobs were decent pay for unskilled laborers, but he wasn't sure it was worth it. Acutely aware of the limited time he had with Antonio, Drayco hurried to ask, "I spoke with Tess Gartin, one of your high school gang."

"Tess is fun. We hooked up briefly, but I don't know. It wasn't right."

"You were all good friends, your group?"

"Well, we weren't jocks. Around here, sports is king. If you aren't into it, you're weird."

"Where did you hang out?"

"Where *didn't* we?"

"What sort of things did you talk about?"

"It could get kinda deep. I mean, that whole Akashic bit of Deirdre's."

Drayco's ears perked up. "The Akashic Records?"

"Supposed to be all positive and rah-rah. It was kinda spooky to me."

"Like that suicide song?"

Antonio's face blanched at the mention. "You can't get it out of your head. I mean, you just can't." He grabbed his cellphone from his pocket and thumbed through the menu. He pressed play, and the suicide song started up.

Drayco asked, "Did Marty give that copy to you?"

Antonio stopped the music and replied, "He sent it to my phone."

"Did you ask him to do that?"

Antonio shrugged and then headed down the hall with a hand wave for Drayco to follow. They next passed the "Kill Room" that resembled a scene from a horror movie. Not that the "Evisceration Room" was much better, with more hanging hooks and claws and a fast-moving wastewater canal. As the old saying went, if you like laws and sausages—or in this case, chicken—you should never watch either one being made.

"Why was Marty obsessed with the song?"

Antonio closed his eyes for a moment. "Wish he hadn't been. Wish I'd never heard it. It's cursed."

"Did Marty feel it was cursed, too?"

Antonio shrugged again.

"Where did the two of you first hear of it?"

"Marty didn't say. But we looked it up on the internet. The history and all. Found a recording and listened to it."

"Is it possible Marty visited internet chat rooms that focused on suicide? He might have come across it there."

"He didn't tell me anything like that. I mean, why would he?"

It was evident before they passed the next section why it was called "Chlorination." Add in the smell of wet feathers and the occasional whiff of Eau de Barnyard, and Drayco could understand why Antonio had needed that fresh air.

"Were you aware Marty wrote a third verse to that song?"

"Not until the sheriff told me."

"Does it have any particular meaning to you? Religion or the Akashic Records?"

Antonio thrust his hands in his pockets. "Nothing has any particular meaning to me. No offense, but I don't want to talk about this anymore. And I've got to get back to the line. Can you find your way out?"

It wasn't hard, thanks to the trail of the various smells. Drayco turned in his guest pass, coat, and hat, and returned to the full parking lot. Always full, perhaps? Shift worker bees in, shift worker bees out.

Drayco didn't believe a piece of music could be cursed, but it was curious Antonio thought so. Both he and Marty researched the sonata and likely discovered its shady past. If Marty learned of its ties to suicides in Hungary, did it influence him to copy the 1930s victims?

Drayco paused when he reached his car, thinking back over his "chat" with Antonio. The young man was helpful in one area—he'd filled some holes in a motive for Marty taking his own life. Other than a few minor personal relationship problems, there didn't seem to be a reason for anyone *but* Marty to kill Marty.

It was only Drayco's second day in town. But he was ready to tell Sebastien Penry to keep his money and spend it on a good therapist.

8

Drayco used the key from Sebastien Penry to enter Marty's apartment, the bottom half of a '60s-era duplex. The building's shutter-less windows took on the air of eyes dazed by the early evening visitors disturbing its nap.

Sheriff Sailor, following closely behind, took one look around the interior and said, "What a dump."

"First time here? No search after Marty's death?" Drayco handed Sailor a pair of nitrile gloves he'd extracted from a box in the Starfire's trunk.

Sailor glared at him. "The M.E. said it was a suicide. We had a gun with the victim's fingerprints. And we had a suicide note. Of sorts."

"It wasn't an accusation. Just curious." Drayco stooped to pick up mail pushed through the slot in the door. Electric bill, water bill, credit card offers, store circulars, and one flyer from an upcoming marine biology conference. He opened that one and scanned it. Judson Kolman was a scheduled speaker.

Marty wasn't the world's neatest tenant, and it was clear what the sheriff meant by "dump." Peeling gray paint decked the walls, mold speckled the baseboards, and rust streaked around the air vents.

Drayco peered into a closet. "Despite the mildew perfume, this place smells better than the chicken plant."

"Like living next to a paper mill. Or so says my cousin. Wore a clothespin on my nose when I visited. He never understood why."

Marty was an avid reader, judging by the books on the shelves. Mostly marine science, a few books on music, one astronomy textbook, and a biography of Jacques Cousteau. No religion, no Akashic Records.

Drayco held up the biography for Sailor to see. "Judson Kolman said Marty dreamed of being the next Cousteau."

"You're saying he had too much to live for? Don't forget all the rich people and celebrities who've gone before. Newspapers are full of 'em."

Drayco flipped through the book and then returned it to the dusty shelf. "Not saying anything of the kind. It's just incredibly depressing."

Sailor opened a cabinet door. "This whole damned place, hell, this whole damned case is depressing. I hate suicide cases."

Drayco and the sheriff weren't always on the same page, but they agreed on that point. "Sarg and I consulted on a couple. The last, involving a wealthy stock trader, was suspicious. Until we discovered his son had gambled away his fortune and embezzled from a charity."

"And you want to know if Marty had financial problems, too. Thanks for piling another subpoena on my plate. I'm getting full, thank you very much. I can do without dessert."

To punctuate Sailor's complaint, Drayco handed the bills he'd picked up from the floor over to Sailor. The sheriff glared at him before placing them in a pile on a chair.

Sailor went through the rest of the cabinets in the small kitchenette. "Now that you mentioned Sarg, how's your former FBI partner doing?"

"Cantankerous. Sarcastic. Stubborn. In short, normal."

"I'd like to meet him. Get dirt on you."

"Then I'll avoid arranging a meeting at all costs."

Sailor opened a desk drawer and filed through the contents, holding up items for Drayco to see. "Sticky notes, paper clips, orange highlighters, a packet of wintergreen gum. A real desk, yee haw."

"You don't seem happy. Have something against office supplies?"

"I'd hoped to find his missing cellphone."

Drayco bent to look under a couch and then said as he straightened up, "Why not search his apartment for the cellphone before?"

"His father said he'd searched here. And the Medical Examiner—"

"Said it was suicide. I know. You're a broken record."

Sailor turned to glare at him. This had turned into a three-glare project so far. Sailor growled, "Did you not say *you're* leaning toward the suicide theory?"

"The song, the missing phone, the strange gun theft. I may be leaning, but I've got my feet planted firmly in the center."

The sheriff examined the laptop on the desk and turned it on. "We searched through his social media accounts. The ones we know of."

"And you didn't find squat. Neither did I." Drayco's search for Marty's online posts found the conventional selfies, memes, movies he'd watched. Marty hated superhero flicks. He enjoyed nature documentaries and old spaghetti westerns. But nothing indicated he was suicidal.

After a minute or two of booting, the screen came alive. "Damn," Sailor grumbled.

Drayco joined him. "Password protected. I can take it with me and give it a look."

Sailor switched it off. "Be my guest. Better you than us. We've had a spate of synthetic opioid arrests. Plus the usual tossed salad of domestic arrests."

"Dessert? Salad? You must be hungry, Sheriff."

"You haven't heard my stomach rumbling? My wife's making her famous scalloped oysters for dinner. This better not take too long. Why'd you want me along, anyway? My department mostly closed the case."

"Chain of custody. In case we find anything incriminating."

Sailor snorted. "When has that stopped you? Good luck with that. I've seen more incriminating evidence at a church bingo game."

An unlabeled white plastic container on the tiny kitchen table lured Drayco to peek inside. The green powder inside reeked like a freshly mowed lawn with tobacco added in for good measure. This must the powdered protein mixture Tess mentioned.

Leaving Sailor to check the sofa cushions, Drayco headed to the one small bedroom. A pair of khaki shorts and a T-shirt saying "Reel men know how to fish" rested on the bed—as if waiting for their owner to reappear any minute and put them on. Next to them lay a graphite fishing rod, and a small tackle box with a see-through lid rested on the floor. Drayco checked inside the box. Empty, save for a few rainbow-colored fishing lures.

After searching under the bed and in the closets, he found jeans, shorts, and shirts, plus a pile of messy papers in the closet. Thumbtacks and string held three framed photos of Cousteau's ship, the *Calypso*, on the wall. Marty was seriously obsessed with his hero.

The *Calypso* trio were the only photos in the room. None of his father, his late mother, or Deirdre or Lena or any other friend. Did young people no longer bother because the entire universe was on their cellphones and the internet nowadays? Everything was "virtual," even relationships.

As always, when Drayco entered the personal space of someone who'd met a violent end, he felt a sense of profound loss. But also one of connection. He inhaled the hodgepodge of aromas in the room—the powdery scent from an open dried-out deodorant stick, the lingering sweat from socks worn but not washed, a rag soaked with fishing-reel grease.

He noticed the way the fading light made jagged shadows on the wall. He listened to the squeaking of the struggling AC compressor outside and the buzzing from an old-style clock radio. He rubbed his fingers along the soft jersey fabric of the plaid bedspread.

In this way, Marty became alive, as if Drayco had met him in person. As he found out more about the idealistic young man, he was sorry he didn't have the chance.

Drayco snagged the one curious item in the room, a silver chain necklace with a clay ball hanging on the end—etched with a crimson triangle and downward arrow. He carried it into the living room where Sailor stood surveying the space as he said, "Not much here."

"Except for the computer."

"And you'd better keep your promise to take care of that angle."

"There's also this," Drayco let the necklace dangle from his hand.

"What's that?"

"The symbol on it may be important. Looks like the triangle found on the suicide song, in a way. Don't think his father would mind if I borrowed it."

"Doesn't look useful, but knock yourself out."

Drayco grabbed the plastic container from the table. "You might want to have this analyzed."

Sailor raised an eyebrow. "What's in it?"

"Marty's protein powder. No aroma of marijuana, although you never know."

The sheriff hesitated and then snatched the can from Drayco. "What did I say about adding to my plate?"

"You said you're hungry."

Sailor opened the tin and took a whiff. "Not for that." He closed the lid with a cough.

Drayco walked around the perimeter of the room, looking for lumps or openings under the carpet. "By the way, I found clothes suitable for fishing and a rod on Marty's bed."

"So?"

"His friend Antonio Skye said they were going fishing the day Marty died."

"Suicides can be spur of the moment. Besides, maybe Antonio planted those on Marty's bed to back up his story."

"Which would mean Antonio had something to hide."

Sailor growled. "Yeah. If."

"What's most interesting are the items we didn't find."

"Such as?"

"His missing cellphone. Plus, Tess Gartin said Marty showed her a copy of the sheet music for the Suicide Sonata—the actual piano piece. I didn't see it anywhere."

"He could have tossed it."

"For what reason? And there's an absence of anything showing Marty was on the edge. No morbid paintings, drawings, sketches. Only that one verse tacked onto the suicide song."

Drayco noted a small filing cabinet in the corner of the room and went to take a closer look. "Did you move this?"

"No, why?" Sailor came to join him.

"See those dust lines in the carpet? Someone moved this recently."

"So? Marty's father said he'd been here."

"But it's been a month, and this line has no dust in it. I found a similar situation in the bedroom with the nightstand. And papers in his closet were dumped there recently, judging from the lack of dust on them. Like someone was in a hurry."

"Doesn't prove somebody rifled through the place. What would an intruder want to find?"

"The missing cellphone. Or the copy of the Suicide Sonata sheet music. Or something else incriminating."

Drayco pulled out the necklace he'd found and studied the symbol on the clay charm. "Wonder if this has to do with the Akashic theme?"

"Bless you. That *was* a sneeze, wasn't it?"

"Akashic Records. A spiritual belief rooted in cosmology and Sanskrit. Higher realms of consciousness and astral planes. Marty asked Maida about it once, and Antonio told me their little group dabbled in it."

"Don't see how it relates to this case. Unless we're talking a weird cult. Or Marty heard voices in his head."

Drayco had considered the voices angle. When reading up on suicides, Drayco ran across cases where the victim complained of hearing voices. Some were on meds, some weren't.

Sailor watched as Drayco packed up the laptop in a small case he'd nabbed from under the desk. The sheriff said, "Too bad Marty didn't use mental health resources."

"Many patients don't want treatment. Committing a person into a facility against their will gets messy."

"Had this discussion with my wife after a former schoolmate of hers turned up dead by his own hand. The guy was homeless. Suffered problems for years."

"Marty wouldn't have lasted long working for Dr. Kolman with those kinds of problems."

Drayco picked up the laptop and gave a long, last look at the apartment before following Sailor out the door. For a moment, he imagined he heard strains of the John Denver tribute song to Cousteau's ship, "*Calypso*," ringing through the air.

9

Saturday, June 16

Drayco walked up the stairs onto the porch of the immaculate Victorian with recently added newel posts and teal door with stained glass insets. The "historical" part of Historical Society was in name only, if you went by pristine architectural status.

He tried the lever, and the door opened with a bell announcing his arrival. Once inside, cries of "Drayco sorry, Drayco sorry," greeted him, followed by a loud squawk.

A man dressed in golfer's plaid knickers and a matching vest popped out of a side room. "You should be honored Andrew here remembers you. It's been months."

"It's not been that long." Drayco gestured toward the African Grey parrot on its fuzzy blue perch. "Still watching the NASCAR channel?"

The Society's director, Reece Wable, grimaced. "Lord, no. He was saying 'vroom vroom' too much. Then I tried the Golf Channel. But then he said 'in the hole' all the time. He gets to watch tennis now."

Andrew Jackson started making popping noises, and when Drayco figured out what they were, he laughed. "Uh oh. I think he's imitating the tennis ball going back and forth on the court. You should try television without audio."

"Duly noted. Not that I'm sorry to see you, Scott, but you owe me big time. It's my day off, and Lucy and I are having a picnic later. Yet, here I am giving up my Saturday morning."

"Did you get my text regarding suicides—both the older Hungarian ones and any recent ones on the Eastern Shore?"

"Yep. Hardly seems urgent."

"I'm looking into Marty Penry's death for his father."

"According to the *Eastern Shore Post*, standard suicidey stuff. But if you're here, I'm guessing not so much."

Drayco peered around the corner toward the reading room. "I assume you have documents?"

Reece crooked his finger at Drayco and headed down the hall. When they entered the reading room, folders lay stacked on the table, waiting. Drayco grinned. "You knew exactly what I was after."

"Research R Us."

Drayco surveyed the piles of folders. "I really appreciate this, Reece. I wanted to see if you could dig up something I haven't. Any order to these files?"

"Chronological. The Hungarian bits are in the first file. Though I have no idea why Marty's case has anything to do with suicides from the 1930s. That's followed by the Eastern Shore articles. Starting with the oldest right here and ending up with the local newspaper article on Marty Penry way over there."

Drayco sat at the table and grabbed the first folder. After making a quick scan through the contents, he said, "No hints of murder. The local police in the various Hungarian jurisdictions put the suicides down to mass hysteria. After ninety years, murder would be hard to prove now."

"You seem disappointed."

"Death is death, no matter how you get there. But I'd wondered if there weren't a serial killer hiding behind that hysteria."

He placed that folder on the table and reached for the next one. When he flipped it open, the top headline read, "Coffee Heir Found in the Drink." Drayco scanned the details. The son of the JFR Coffee Company, who couldn't swim, waded past the shallow dunes into open water until it was over his head. Authorities found his drowned body a day later.

Drayco glanced up at Reece who was pointing at the headline. "Tabloids of today have nothing on those of yesteryear."

"Titillation sells, then and now." Drayco read some more. "Pretty sad tale. He fell in love with the daughter of a rival to the family business. Her father said no, so the son took the easy way out."

Reece rubbed his chin. "Easy way out?"

Drayco didn't know why he'd phrased it that way. "Sorry. Seems so pointless."

"Most suicides do. To the survivors."

Drayco scanned the other folders and clippings Reece had laid out for him. Some star-crossed-lover scenarios. A few bankruptcies and financial ruin. Alcoholism, drugs. No obvious pattern, not that he'd expected it.

"Can't find what you're seeking, Scott?"

"Not sure what I was seeking. A link, a clue, anything." Drayco tapped the article about Marty. "This doesn't describe the so-called 'note' found with him."

"Did the reporter get it wrong?"

"Guess Sheriff Sailor held onto that tidbit. It was a copy of a song."

"Please don't tell me it was 'March of the Damned.'"

Drayco glared at him, and Reece hastened to add. "Gallows humor."

"A song created from a piano piece nicknamed the Suicide Sonata."

"There was a brief mention in a report from Hungary. Thought it was a myth."

"People were obsessed with the sonata and took their own lives after hearing it. Some songwriter got the brilliant idea this would make a good pop song and added lyrics to the melody. More suicides ensued. Hence the name."

"And they found that pop song with Marty Penry?"

"Along with an additional verse Marty apparently wrote himself."

Reece scratched his head. "Makes it hard to find that closure. Can't ask a poet to explain his work after he's gone."

Drayco fingered the slim folder containing the articles about the coffee heir, snapshots of a brief life long gone from the cosmic timeline. Unless those articles were digitized somewhere on the planet, preserving a record of the young man's existence in bits and bytes.

Drayco gently laid the folder aside. "Anything in your files mention cults?"

Reece grabbed a single folder from a filing cabinet. "Cults must be a big-city affliction."

"That's all you have?"

Reece tossed it to him. "In 1935, a Miss Livia Peebles of Pungoteague was accused of being a Satanist. Mostly because she liked to wear black. And dance naked around a certain juniper tree during the full moon."

Drayco scanned the article which took all of a minute to read. "I see mention of huckleberry schnapps."

"The Greeks had their Eleusinians, the Romans had their Mithras, and we had a drunk exhibitionist spinster."

"I'd love to ask a friend of mine, a former religion professor, his take on that. But Dr. Jaffray is in the middle of the Himalayas."

Drayco closed the folder. "Nothing with the Akashic Records?"

"That's the astral projection thing, isn't it? Sanskrit or something?"

"Parts of it date to the nineteenth century. Other parts are more of a contemporary take, kind of a universal encyclopedia you can access."

Reece snorted. "That would put me out of business. Don't find it, 'kay?"

"Not sure there's anything to find. I gather it was more of a case of youthful Dungeons and Dragons."

Drayco offered to help file the materials, but Reece waved him off. "I'll have Mrs. Hammontree do it tomorrow. She loves filing, Bless her."

As they headed out of the reading room and up the hallway toward the front, an object in a side room caught Drayco's attention. He stopped dead in his tracks. After ducking inside, he studied a wheelbarrow-sized stone marker with a heart etched into one side and G-clef into the other.

He said, "You didn't tell me this was here."

"When I heard they were putting up those dreadful condos on the former Keys's property, I got the okay to bring the rock here. Historical significance and all. Wasn't easy."

Drayco knelt and traced the clef with his finger. "I'd wondered what happened to Oakley's shrine. It never occurred to me to rescue it."

"That's why you're the crime guy, and I'm the history guy."

Drayco stood up but continued to admire the marker. That stone had outlasted Oakley and would long survive Drayco or Reece or pretty much anyone currently alive. Even those digitized files.

He should take comfort in that and perhaps a part of him did. There were so few psychological rocks, so few anchors in life. People came and went. Lived and died. Appeared and disappeared.

He bid Reece farewell and told himself he wasn't at all envious the other man was going on a picnic with his girlfriend. He stepped outside and squinted. Sunday was living up to its name, and after he'd climbed into his Starfire, he cranked up the AC. But it wasn't getting any cooler, only blowing out ambient air.

Great, just great. A shot compressor could mean another grand or two he'd have to shell out. And what lovely timing, right as the highs were forecast to soar into the 90s.

"Drayco sorry, all right," he muttered to himself and nosed his car-sauna out of the parking lot. He'd have to turn vampire and do his sleuthing at night.

He turned on his satellite radio to a classical channel. Opera. Gounod's *Roméo et Juliette*, no less. If that wasn't a bad omen, he didn't know what was. After turning it off, he started humming but stopped when he realized it was the Suicide Sonata. Irritated, he switched to a rock station and cranked up the volume.

10

Drayco tripped over the boxes of red oak acoustical panels parked next to stacks of tongue-and-groove planks and rolls of maroon carpeting. He'd planned on stopping by the Opera House last night after searching Marty's apartment but was too tired. Besides, it would be quieter on a Saturday morning with the workers off. Or so he'd thought.

His contractor trotted onto the stage, making Drayco jump. "Howdy, Scott. Didn't know you were coming."

"Sorry, Troy. Should have called ahead. I've wanted to see how things are coming along."

Troy Mehaffey rubbed the bridge of his nose, crooked from his former boxing days. "Slowly. Can't finish rewiring the electrical system since I maxed out the budget."

"I'm working on that. We've got a new grant, and that money will be in the account soon."

"I'll see what I can do in the meantime. If I don't run into the unexpected. These old buildings, they hold surprises. And mysteries of the architectural kind. Guess that's more your thing, right? Me, I love bringing history to life."

"That's why I hired you. That Opera House you restored up in Wilmington is a marvel."

Troy's eyes lighted up. "She's a beauty, isn't she? Sounds sexist, but I imagine buildings as having personalities. Some male, some female. That one was a princess. You know, from a fairy tale. Like Sleeping Beauty."

"And this Opera House?"

Troy grinned. "The fading movie star who stumbles on the fountain of youth."

That made Drayco chuckle. Troy had nailed it. With ties to two murders and untold drama through the years, "fading movie star" was a good fit—especially one who specialized in noir.

Troy asked, "I came to pick up my briefcase I left yesterday. But you got any questions for me? Orders? Marching, or otherwise?"

"No questions, but don't you dare quit. Otherwise, I'll have to kidnap you and force you into Opera House labor."

"I can think of worse." The contractor took a look around and then said with a wave, "See you around, Scott. Sooner next time?"

Drayco winced at that but assured Troy he would as he let him out the rear door. When he was alone, Drayco stood on stage and clapped his hands. The audience seats were at the warehouse being restored, and their absence, plus the lack of carpeting, made for a very live space.

Happily, the Steinway Hamburg-D was still there. He ducked into a small side room used for storage, pushed the piano to the center of the stage, and removed the blanket. He'd almost forgotten how sexy the instrument was, its curved lines luring him like a mythological Siren.

Opening the lid gently, he slid the stick into the lid prop groove and massaged the rim. "Sorry you were all cold and lonely in there."

After an arm-soaking in the green room sink, he grabbed the piano bench and sat down to roll off a few scales. That was more like it. And only a fraction out of tune. He flexed his fingers in preparation for Chopin's Nocturne in B flat minor but a text alert on his phone stopped him.

He would have ignored it, wanted to ignore it, but since he was on a case, he had to check. It was Nelia. *Maida said you were at Opera House. Love to see the progress. OK if I stop by?*

He texted, *Sure. Let me know when you get here.*

After the reply chime, he read, *At the back door now.*

He hopped up and opened the door for her. She looked around and pointed to the floor. "No bodies on stage today. That's a relief."

As she joined him in the crook of the piano, their closeness took him back to the almost-kiss in February at the Columbia Island

Marina—when she said she wished they'd met years ago. Not for the first time, he wondered what would have happened if he'd given in and gone for that kiss.

As the light reflected off the silkiness on her lips, and he caught hints of a minty fragrance from her hair, it was intoxicating. Their eyes locked for a moment, and he saw his own confusion reflected back at him.

They'd never addressed it. Should they now? Get it out in the open and let it have some air? "About that night in the District. At the marina—"

"I know. I remember. Maybe it was a touch of moonlight madness." She rubbed her arm, looking at him, looking away, looking back again. "But Tim. And Darcie. It wouldn't work out."

"Wouldn't it?"

"This is safer." Her eyes pleaded with him to drop the subject.

Reluctantly he gave in, swallowing the objections stuck in his throat. He could do "safer" with the best of them. "Your mother's orchestra should play here once the work is finished. *If* it's finished."

She maneuvered around him to sit on the piano bench. "What do you mean, 'if'? Isn't the sale from the Chopin manuscript financing renovations?"

"Can't decide if Konstantina Klucze hiding it in the Opera House all those decades ago was a blessing or a curse."

"I don't understand."

"Haven't told you the latest. Once news of the auction got out, a couple of very distant relatives of Konstantina came forward to claim ownership. It'll be tied up in the courts for God knows how long."

"Isn't there other funding? You mentioned grants."

"Corporations aren't flocking to fund the arts anymore, wealthy donors are shying away. I'm worried—or I should my CPA is worried—we'll come up short. This place has a daunting list of violations to fix to bring it up to code."

Nelia inspected the empty room where the seats should be, frowning. But then a small grin crept across her face. "I could organize a bake sale."

"Maida's pies might do the trick. Sweet potato, rhubarb, cherry. She's got a wide-ranging repertoire."

When Nelia laughed, it sent dancing lines of squiggly blue pipe cleaners straight to his brain. Some laughter could be painful to his ears but not hers.

After she caught her breath, she spied the book Drayco had placed on top of the piano and grabbed it. "This looks well read."

"My former piano teacher gave that to me."

Nelia opened the book and stopped at the inscription. "A. Vucasovich?" Then she looked at the rest of the title page. "The author?"

"He was like a second father during my touring days. When I was semi-estranged from Brock."

"You're still calling your father 'Brock'?"

"Old habits. I'm working on it."

That made her shake her head. "It's great you and your Dad are on a better footing. But you should thank Alexander Vucasovich by inviting him here for a concert. *When* the place is finished."

Drayco ran his hand along the piano's gleaming ebony lid. "He died not long after my carjacking incident sixteen years ago."

"Oh, that's awful. What happened?"

"Suicide."

She grimaced. "That's an odd coincidence. Any hints beforehand?"

"Not much. Vuca did say one odd thing, a quote from Marcus Aurelius. That 'death isn't the greatest loss to fear, it's never beginning to live.'"

Drayco would never forget the look on the face of Vuca's wife at the funeral. And how it felt like someone sucked all the air out of his Drayco's lungs.

"Was he married? I mean, surely his wife saw signs?"

"She was as shocked as everyone else, and he didn't leave a note. The timing still haunts me. Happening so soon after my injury, me telling him I was quitting piano to work for the FBI."

"What a nightmarish rough patch for you. The carjacking, loss of your music career, his death. Scott, I'm so sorry."

That was the first instance she'd called him by his first name. And it sounded pretty good.

She flinched. "I shouldn't have come to you with Marty's case. It's roiling up bad memories. And the parallels are there—no signs beforehand, no explanatory note, just mysteries and a trail of heartache."

"I have to admit, I almost didn't take the case. But now I'm glad I did."

"You are?"

"Being in Marty's room yesterday, he felt so alive, and there was this energy. Even if it's suicide, I want to know why he did it."

She gave a small nod. "How's it going in the motives department?"

"Girl trouble, job stress, religious fervor, mental illness, the usual possibilities." Drayco paused for a moment. "I know I asked you this before, but how well does your mother really know Sebastien Penry? A number of suicides by young people stem from sexual abuse as children."

Her lips tightened into a white line. "No, not Sebastien. Absolutely not."

"You're sure?"

"Positive. Another family member or teacher, maybe. But you don't think—"

"Marty didn't have the symptoms. Dissociation, low self-esteem, social withdrawal, panic attacks. But I had to ask."

She stared at her feet. "Sheriff Sailor told me he hates suicide cases. This is my first, and I'm starting to understand why."

"There was your Army Reserve colleague."

"But not a case. It's different somehow."

"Yet hard, either way."

"Yeah." She kicked at a loose nail on the stage, making it roll toward the wings as the clinking echoed around them.

Drayco pointed to the maroon carpet rolls next to her feet. "We tried to match the old flooring to keep it as much like the original decor as possible. You approve?"

"It's a lovely color. Can't wait to see it laid out with the seats."

"Glad you like it." For some reason, her approval made him ridiculously happy. "I know it seems like I'm harping on Sebastien Penry. But he said he argued with his son before his death. Could parental guilt be driving him to find a scapegoat?"

"My mother wouldn't agree."

"She's put a lot of faith in him."

"Music colleagues. Birds of a feather. You've experienced that, right?"

He recalled the character back-stabbings he'd seen through the years. Not always a musical love nest. "I'd hate to see her confidence in him misplaced."

"Keep digging. The truth is there." Then she added wistfully, "I'll help as much as I can. As long as I don't violate those conflicts of interest Sailor's so worried about."

"Still don't see how your assistance on this would cause problems."

"The sheriff got burned on a case helping a family member. He vowed not to make that mistake again."

"But you're not in uniform today. This look suits you." Drayco took in her straight-leg jeans and the pale yellow blouse that matched her hair. Then he hastened to add, "And civvies means you're just a friend helping out a friend."

She jumped up, strode over to him, and tousled his hair. "There. Since you're hardly ever in jeans or shorts, that's as close to civvies as you get."

He caught his reflection in the piano. "It's an improvement."

Her smirk lifted his spirits for a moment. But a glance at the Chopin book brought them right back down. "Did Sailor mention the Akashic Records angle?"

"It's that whole Universal Consciousness idea? From the Sanskrit, right?"

"You are correctly informed, ma'am. Marty's Gang of Five were interested in it in high school."

"He says it's bunk. But do you think that explains the suicide note?"

"It's a possibility."

Nelia frowned. "A teenage cult gone wrong?"

"Sailor mentioned the cult angle. I don't think he was on board that theory, either."

"Are you?"

"When they were teens, but now? I haven't found a strong link. Yet."

She slid back onto the piano bench. "How was the search at Marty's place last night? Sheriff Sailor hasn't filled me in."

"I gave him more homework. He wasn't pleased, but I gave myself homework, too. Fair is fair. Marty's laptop, and it's password protected."

"You should figure that out quickly. If not—"

"I know where to go. The Bureau would have loved you."

"No offense, but it wouldn't be mutual." She wrinkled her nose.

"You can still apply as an attorney once you get your JD."

"And ruin my chance at being Benny Baskin's partner? Fat chance."

Was she serious? "Benny" and "partner" were a combination that had never entered his mind. But Benny had seemed quite taken by Nelia during her internship. They'd be one big happy family. Benny, Nelia, and Drayco. And Darcie Squier.

That was one visit he'd put off since hitting the shore. But why? Darcie was fun to be with and a very satisfying partner. Or was Brock onto something with that whole "breathing room" thing?

He couldn't postpone it much longer. Darcie was definitely going on his "to do" list today. When his rational brain noted the double entendre, he started coughing. That prompted Nelia to jump up and rub him on the back. Her soft, warm touch only made things worse.

"Sawdust?" she asked.

"You have no idea," he replied, grateful she wasn't an actual mind reader.

She bid him farewell and left him alone with the piano. He had time for a Bach prelude and fugue, didn't he? But as his fingers eased into the notes, the gleaming black finish on the piano kept reminding him of Darcie's gleaming dark hair.

He gave up and returned the instrument to its cave, giving it a pat before closing the door. "Later, my friend."

He was actually looking forward to seeing Darcie if not her Cypress Manor home. Two long weeks without her and not a word. Was she under the weather? Feeling guilty for not having attempted to contact her in earnest, he suddenly needed to find out if she was okay.

11

Drayco balanced the bouquet of sweet-scented Stargazer lilies and purple iris in his hand as he tried the doorbell for the second time. No answer. Maida said she'd seen Darcie around town, so she couldn't really be ill, right?

The door finally opened and revealed Darcie in one of her more form-fitting dresses. Her shock soon turned to a pasted-on smile as she grabbed the flowers and handed them to a man standing behind her in the doorway. "Put these in water, won't you? This'll just take a minute." She pulled the door shut.

Drayco asked, "Who's your guest?"

"A friend. He owns a big media corporation. It's headquartered up your way."

"I see. Wealthy, then." He hadn't got a good look at the fellow, but Drayco guessed him to be thirty years older than Darcie. Distinguished, graying hair, wearing a gray wool suit despite the warm spell they were having.

"Harry's such a dear. He owns this incredible house in McLean with a giant pool and this huge garden with a grape arbor. Like out of *Architectural Digest*. And he's taken me out on his yacht. It's moored at the Occoquan Marina. He's promised to take me hot-air ballooning next week."

Drayco looked toward the door. "All that in two weeks since I saw you last, Darcie?"

She had the good sense to be embarrassed, her cheeks turning a pale pink. "Maybe a little longer."

"How much longer?"

"Oh, you know." She smoothed a wrinkle on the tiny sleeve on her tiny dress. "A couple of months."

Drayco stood very still for a moment. "You hid that incredibly well. If I didn't know about him, did he know about me?"

"There's no reason for anyone to know about anything, is there? I mean, we're all having fun, right?"

"Look, Darcie. I never had any delusions regarding our relationship. I knew you were accustomed to a certain lifestyle. And I knew I couldn't give it to you."

"But you and I have so much fun." She moved in closer and lowered her voice. "The last night we were together was amazing, wasn't it? In bed, in the kitchen, on the—"

"I remember, thanks."

"And you're so adorable when you get out of the shower. That dark wet hair and that sexy chest and, of course, your—"

"Darcie. Stop. We shouldn't discuss this here. Or anywhere. Besides, it sounds like I won't be seeing much of you. And I think that's for the best."

She gave a quick look over her shoulder toward the house and then lowered her voice to a whisper. "I need to see you. I crave you. Two weeks is too long."

Drayco ran a hand through his hair. "And should probably be longer. As in, this is a good time to cool it off."

Her lips formed into a pout. "That's not what I want."

"Darcie, I'm not sure you'll ever know what you want. But I do know money makes you happy. And from what you say, this Harry guy has it in spades. Ergo, he should make you very happy. Blessings on you both."

As he turned to leave, she grabbed onto his shirt. "I don't want to leave it this way."

He put his hand over hers and gently pried it off. "Enjoy the flowers. And give my best to Harry."

He strode to his car and hopped in before she tempted him any further. Pealing out of the long driveway, he headed the Starfire toward downtown and the courthouse where he'd first met Darcie over a year ago. He drove on past, not knowing or caring where he was headed and ended up in the parking area of Powhatan Park.

After climbing out of the car, he strode to the gazebo. It wasn't much of a haven, with a nausea-inducing odor of acrid solvents from fresh paint. Looking north along the small beach leading to the marsh's edge, he saw something else that was new. Rising in the distance above the channels, inlets, and tree maze was the top of the three-story condo development. So much for the view.

Everything changed, not always for the best, not always for the worst. Sometimes change was just change. Still, Darcie's double-timing was more of a sucker-punch than he cared to admit.

She'd dated the new guy while she'd been sleeping with him? Was he jealous? No, that wasn't it. Not being a one-night-stand kind of guy, relationships weren't only about sex. There were layers of companionship, emotions, attachments. Even if it wasn't love, it was something.

As he let off steam by pacing along the boardwalk trail for the better part of an hour, his thoughts turned to Marty Penry's "gang." Their relationships were more complicated than the mere "free love" assertion by Tess Gartin. Complicated enough for suicide? Or murder? Untangling the connections between them was like untangling a fishing net filled with traps, trash, and discarded tackle. Like him and Darcie in a twisted way. And perhaps Nelia, but he didn't want to go *there*.

This being a sunny June weekend, other park patrons soon joined Drayco, taking advantage of picnic tables under tupelo and poplar trees—one family of five and one young couple. Most other people were likely at the Assateague or Chincoteague beaches on the northern end of the Eastern Shore. Or Kiptopeke State Park and Cape Charles on the southern tip.

This small park was a less-popular jewel he and Maida enjoyed visiting. Before the condo development, you could feel as if you were on your own private island cut off from the rest of civilization and the techno-trap that went with it. No Wi-Fi or cell service around here.

A squealing laugh caught his attention. The two younger kids romped along the small beach, running after birds, as the parents watched. The oldest child, a boy wearing a backward ball cap, stayed seated at the picnic table glued to a noisy video game app on his cellphone.

Drayco's other companions, the young couple, seemed to be enjoying each other's company. They were around the same age as Marty and Antonio and Lena and Deirdre and Tess. The infamous "Gang of Five."

He forced all reminders of Darcie out of his head. Plenty of opportunities later to mourn whatever it was they'd had together. He was in town for a much different purpose, and it's time he met a few more of the players in Marty's fateful little group.

12

Drayco stood outside the Lazy Crab baking in the hot sun. Marty's most recent girlfriend, Lena Bing, had agreed to meet him after her shift at the chicken plant ended, but it was twenty minutes past her scheduled ETA.

He scrutinized every vehicle as it passed by the inn, but they sailed on, a land-flotilla of pickup trucks, SUVs, and the occasional Mercedes. One loud backfire startled him as a rustbucket truck chugged by in a cloud of smoke. Its bald cigar-chomping driver clearly wasn't Lena.

Finally, a faint motor grew louder and louder, signaling the arrival of an aqua motorcycle some might kindly call "vintage." The driver wore jeans with horizontal slits above the knees and a tank top with a squirrel dressed in camouflage. The caption read, "Protect your nuts."

She pulled into the Crab's small parking lot and motioned to him. He had to lean in to hear her over the helmet covering her face and the roar of the motor as she asked, "Scott Drayco?"

He nodded, and she dipped her hand inside a storage box at the rear of the cycle, pulled out a helmet, and thrust it at him. "Put this on. State law." It was complete with face guard, no goggles required.

She impatiently patted the seat behind her, and he hopped on board. As he looked around for straps or handles, she grabbed his right hand and put it around her waist. Human straps, then.

They roared off, bypassing the downtown and heading off U.S. 13 for a narrow road Drayco didn't know existed. When the paved road ended, they continued on a dirt path that quickly led to no path—only a carpet of leaves, twigs, and grass beneath the loblolly pines and hackberry trees.

After crossing a shallow creek, they parked in a small clearing. Lena waited for him to slide off the bike first and then she followed, ripping off her helmet. Strands of straight flax-colored hair wedged inside the helmet tumbled out, framing a pale, elfin face that didn't have a trace of makeup.

She said, "Marty and I used to come here to make out."

Drayco stowed his helmet back in the storage box. "Does 'make out' mean what it used to?"

"Sex. Is there anything else?" She wiped her hand across her nose, leaving a small smudge, then pointed to a specific spot on the ground. "That's where they found him. Under that sweetgum. From what the sheriff told me."

He studied the space for a moment. "Appreciate you bringing me here. I'm a little surprised you agreed to it."

She paced along the pine straw. "Here's the deal. I don't think Marty committed suicide. Heard you were going to prove he didn't. So I want to help."

Drayco took a closer look at the location she'd pointed out and studied the markings on the ground. Over four weeks had passed since Marty was found there, but that wasn't the main problem. From faint footprints and dragging marks, Drayco could tell where the sheriff's team and the EMTs had conducted their business. It made any virgin evidence impossible to spot. If it existed in the first place.

Drayco did spy faint traces of a set of deep motorcycle tracks leading into the center of the police activity. Marty's bike? He circled around the tracks, looking at the tires on Lena's motorcycle for comparison.

He asked, "If Marty didn't take his own life, then who did?"

She scrunched up her forehead. "Everybody loved Marty. You know, always the life of the party."

"You didn't notice any suicidal signs? Depression? Withdrawing from his friends?" He was so programmed to ask that question by now, he felt like Reece Wable's parrot. So far, he had different answers from everyone.

Lena hesitated before giving her own non-answer. "Doesn't mean he'd kill himself. Not Marty. We all get the blues."

"By 'the blues,' what do you mean? Had his behavior changed?"

"That creepy music."

"The suicide song?"

She winced. "He fixated on that thing."

"You feel the song was connected with his death?" Drayco looked up as a crow cawed at them from a low tree branch.

"It was stupid. You know, a game."

"What kind of game?"

"Okay, more a joke than a game. But it's just music, you know? I don't get what he saw in it."

Drayco bent down to look at treads in the ground and ran his finger along the pattern. "When did you first learn of the song?"

"Last year, I guess." She rubbed her hand as if to flick off an invisible insect.

"And that's when you noticed the attitude change?"

"He didn't want to go out, didn't talk as much. I worried he'd gone schizo and told him he should see somebody. He refused. That was one reason I broke up with him."

"What was the other?"

Her hands balled into fists. "It was personal."

"Did that 'personal' have to do with Deirdre Pinnick?"

Her frown deepened. "As I said, personal." She walked over to him as he straightened up. "Find something?"

"Have you been here since his death?"

"This is the first time. Wanted to tell you 'no' when you asked to see it."

He gave her a brief smile. "I appreciate you not wanting to meet me at the chicken plant, Lena. Antonio took me on a tour. Once is enough."

"It's not glamorous. Not much else around. You got tourism, the Wallops space gigs, fishing, or chickens, you know?"

She grabbed a stick and poked it at into a small hole in the ground. "And the chicken plant gigs may disappear soon. Robots taking jobs. Mine would be one of the first to go."

He pulled out his cellphone to take a photo of her tires. Then he took another of the various tracks on the ground, mostly partials. "Marty's father said he never saw his son take drugs harder than alcohol and marijuana. And that he was on a health kick."

"We all smoked weed and drank. Who doesn't, you know? And yeah, he'd become Mr. Universe. Always lecturing me about eating crap. And drinking those god-awful protein shakes. Had at least three a day."

"He carried the powder wherever he went, or so says Tess Gartin." Drayco fought the urge to add a "you know" to keep up with Lena.

She wrinkled her nose. Drayco wasn't sure whether it was due to the mention of Tess or the powder. "Guess Marty did go overboard. Those shakes, that sonata thing, the whole dream of being the next Cousteau."

"You're good friends with Antonio Skye? I understand he's a member of your group and also works at the chicken plant."

"Our group isn't much of a group anymore. And the plant's gone to weird shifts. Don't see Antonio much."

"He never spoke to you of any problems with Marty?"

"You mean that gun of his, right? There are a lot of guns around here. And a lot of thefts."

"Do you own a gun?"

"I'd have to steal one, too. Can't afford it."

She gently picked up a leaf. As she held it in the air, he saw a black-and-blue swallowtail butterfly perched on top. For a moment, her eyes sparkled with wonder. "Marty loved fish. I love these. Both have short lives, but butterflies get to soar."

As the insect flitted off toward the creek, Drayco gauged the distance from the clearing to the main road. Around a fourth of a mile away as Sheriff Sailor had said.

Drayco motioned to a faint set of tracks under the shelter of a tree. "These don't match your bike. Do you recognize them as Marty's?"

"Don't know. This spot is popular with other kids. A great make-out spot, not just for me and Marty."

He took another photo. The tracks weren't recent and didn't match Lena's or those he'd speculated were Marty's. But they looked to be made around the same time.

He'd have to check them against Marty's bike at the sheriff's impound lot to see if the treads matched. If not, where had the other treads come from? If the creek were flooded for a while, then no young lovers would have headed here. Unless they liked "mud wrestling" of the intimate kind.

"Did Marty come here alone?"

"Too busy with work. Cherie kept telling him to slow down, take it easy. You know, enjoy being young."

"Cherie?"

"Cherie Kolman. Judson Kolman's wife. Mr. Kolman is Marty's boss. I started working for Cherie to make extra money after my aunt was disabled."

"You live with your aunt?"

"I'm an orphan. Don't you love that term? Little Orphan Annie was all songs and dancing, you know? That's not like it at all. My aunt's been great, but she had to go on social security after a car accident hurt her back. Funny, that's what's wrong with Cherie, too. Her back."

Drayco took a photo of the area beneath the sweetgum tree. "Another accident, I take it?"

"Scoliosis. She needs a housekeeping aide—me. Plus I help out with her hobby, coin collecting."

Lena shivered and wrapped her arms around her body. "I'm getting cold chills here. Guess that's why I didn't want to come." Her laugh was hollow. "And yet I visit Marty's gravesite every day. He's buried next to his Mom."

Thankfully, she hadn't asked him to meet her there, either. He'd been to too many graveyards lately. "Both you and Marty's father admitted he did some drinking. Did it get out of control? People can act out of character when they're drunk."

"You think him shooting himself was an accident? He was plastered when he did it?"

"Or it led to his recent behavioral changes. As can happen with closet alcoholics."

Lena thought a moment. "I would have smelled it on him. Seen it when I went to his place. And I never did. Sure, we got drunk more than once. And there was this one time."

She got a faraway look on her face, so he asked a little more loudly, "One time?"

"Not long before he died. We stopped by the Boardwalk Bar near Chincoteague, had some beers. A shitload of beers. He made this weird comment. That something big that was going to happen soon. But when I asked him what, he got all tight-lipped."

Drayco filed that away for future reference. "The two of you were engaged at one point, isn't that right?"

"We were nineteen. My aunt said we were too young. Guess she was right. Marty was the one who broke it off to date someone else." She didn't mention Deirdre's name, but she didn't have to.

"You got back together?"

"Because I loved him. But that was a mistake."

He didn't have a chance to ask her if loving him was a mistake or getting back together was a mistake when she marched to her bike and grabbed her helmet. "Look, I gotta go. My aunt needs me to help with supper."

Drayco took one last look around the clearing before donning his too-tight helmet. The one aspect that impressed him most about the site was how quiet and still it felt. With only birds and squirrels as witnesses, it was the perfect spot for death.

13

The crimson rays from the setting sun painted brush strokes on the dusky canvas of purple clouds, creating an abstract landscape painting over the Chesapeake. The chirping of the crickets and katydids followed Drayco as he joined Sheriff Sailor on the postcard-perfect lawn.

Sailor quipped, "This is two evenings in a row I've spent with you. My wife is getting jealous."

"So this is the Pinnick residence?"

"Yep."

"Looks like a brick colonial trying way too hard to be a mansion."

Sailor snorted at that.

They were expected, but the frown on the man at the door was so deep, it looked like he'd be happier shoving them off the pier in back. Seeing as how he was the attorney for Darcie's ex-husband, Drayco wasn't stunned at the man's attitude toward Drayco. But the guy was only slightly more polite to the sheriff.

The gloves came off right away. "Don't know why you had to get involved in this, Mr. Drayco. I've said all I have to say on the matter. I want to make it abundantly clear I'm only agreeing to this out of courtesy to Sheriff Sailor."

Emmerson Pinnick motioned for them to follow him to a den where the floor-to-ceiling glass windows afforded a vista of Willow Cove's indigo water. He disappeared for a moment and returned with his arm around the shoulders of an unsmiling young woman. She sported cherry-red hair and a small neck tattoo of a crescent moon and three stars. He guided her to a chair opposite his guests as if to keep her as far away as possible.

"This is my daughter Deirdre. I've told her not to answer questions I determine are unreasonable."

Meaning, they wouldn't get much out of her. Drayco understood why the sheriff strongly suggested he tag along on this outing.

Drayco smiled at the young woman. "Deirdre, I want to thank you for helping us out. Marty's father wants to put closure to this case. Find out more about what happened. And why."

She looked at her father, and he nodded, so she nodded.

"You met Marty in high school, is that correct?" More nodding. "And at some point, you started dating. But you later broke up with him?"

"Marty was too uptight. I wanted an open relationship. He didn't."

Her father butted in. "And after she broke up with him, after he started dating that other girl, he kept on pressuring Deirdre. Following her in his car, calling her at all hours, pleading for her to give him another chance."

"And that's why you took out that restraining order a year ago?"

"Damn straight. She's had zero to do with him since."

Drayco aimed his question at the daughter. "How upset were you with Marty's stalking behavior? And how did you feel about the restraining order?"

She jumped in before her father could open his mouth. "It was my idea, but I don't want to dwell on the past. It's ancient history. I'm engaged to Dale Messineo now. He works at Wallops Flight Facility as a Systems Analyst. That's where we met, I'm a receptionist. And we have a house near Wallops Island."

His father beamed with satisfaction at the way she'd evaded the question. Drayco glanced at Sailor who was shooting him sympathetic looks. "Deirdre, you and Marty were part of a small group of friends that included Antonio Skye, Tess Gartin, and Lena Bing?"

"That's ancient history, too. High school nonsense. I'm much more mature now and would never hang around with those types anymore." She kept fiddling with her engagement ring.

Before he could ask another question, she continued. "If you're wondering if I feel any guilt over Marty's death, I don't. It's not my fault. He was unstable."

This was going nowhere, faster than a Wallops Island rocket. "Do the Akashic Records mean anything to you?"

She blinked at Drayco. Her father seemed confused, but Deirdre didn't bother to look at lawyer-daddy this time. "Did a class report on it. My friends and I had some fun with it, that's all. No bigs."

She folded her arms across her chest, "You should ask Lena what *her* project was about."

"I will, thanks. Marty didn't seem enamored of the Akashic Records or any other religion?"

She twisted strands of her hair with her fingers. "No."

"And yet he was obsessed with the so-called Suicide Sonata, or suicide song."

"I told you. He was unstable."

"Do you remember how he got interested in that music?"

More hair-twisting. Then more ring fiddling. "No."

Emmerson Pinnick sneered. "She was right to dump that young man. People are talking behind our backs. My wife's utterly embarrassed. We're fourth generation Eastern Shore, and we have a standing to protect."

A middle-aged woman with two-toned—or was it three toned?—blond and blond and blond shoulder-length hair entered the room. Her navy blue dress matched the water behind the house, and her grooming was as postcard-perfect as the lawn.

She strode up to Deirdre's chair and perched on the armrest. "I overheard your conversation. Hope you gentlemen don't mind. But I want to set the record straight. My daughter had nothing to do with Marty Penry's death. She didn't cause his suicide, and she certainly didn't kill him."

Funny. Drayco hadn't said anything about murder. "You didn't approve of Marty dating your daughter, either?"

She waved a hand in the air, making the dangling bracelets on her wrist jingle. "Gracious, no. He's not her type. His father is a contractor."

Emmerson Pinnick's eyes had darkened further when his wife started talking. "Now, Barbara. Marty seemed normal until the whole stalking business. But I feared it might escalate."

Barbara's Pinnick's voice rose half an octave, "*Might* escalate? It was already escalating. Out-of-the-stratosphere escalating. To think what he could have done to our daughter in his state. Horrible, truly horrible. Why, he might have tried to take her with him. And then, there'd be two graves."

She grabbed a nearby magazine and started fanning herself. Her husband coughed and looked away while Deirdre kept her eyes glued to the floor. Barbara Pinnick had taken lessons in Overacting 101, and her husband and daughter were accustomed to having season tickets.

Drayco wasn't in the mood for theatrics. "Deirdre, did Marty mention to you recently about 'something big' he was working on? A special project? A new venture?"

For the first time, he'd caught Deirdre completely off-guard. She stared at him, her mouth half-open. "Not to me. Who did he tell? Tess? Lena?"

Emmerson Pinnick sprang up from his seat. "That's enough questions for now. We've been more than accommodating. Too accommodating."

Sheriff Sailor jumped out of his chair, and Drayco eased himself up to follow. "Thank you for your assistance, Mr. Pinnick." He smiled at the two women, "Mrs. Pinnick. Deirdre."

Once back on the postcard lawn, Sailor paused outside his car. "I warned you. Pinnick's prickly. And he kept his daughter on a tight leash."

"Maybe not that tight."

"What do you mean?"

Drayco waited for a flock of chattering black starlings as they fluttered among the trees. "When I asked Deirdre about Marty and the 'something big,' I specifically said it was a *recent* reference. She allegedly broke up with him a year ago and hasn't seen him since. Yet, she didn't correct me."

"Fathers don't always know what their daughters are up to. Perhaps Emmerson Pinnick's restraining order wasn't as restraining as he thought." Sailor threw his hat into the car before climbing in.

Drayco poked his head inside the open driver side window. "If she and Marty were still seeing each other and her parents found out—"

"Motive for murder, got it. You don't like making my life any easier, you know that?"

Drayco studied the starlings as Sailor drove off. Aggressive, noisy creatures, like Pinnick. As much as Pinnick's heavy-handed efforts to protect his daughter annoyed Drayco, he understood. That didn't mean he wouldn't try to find another way to question Deirdre sans lawyer-daddy. He just had to figure out how.

14

Sunday, June 17

Drayco awoke to the beeping of a cellphone text alert and peered at the bedside clock. Six-thirty. Who would be sending him a text so early? He didn't recognize the number, but the message said, "This is for you," and it had an attachment.

At any other time, he'd dismiss it as a spammer, but a hunch told him this was different. After a split-second hesitation, he clicked on the link. It was a music file, and soon the unmistakable music of the suicide song filled the room.

He listened to the whole thing, half-expecting a stinger. But when the song ended, there was nothing else. He dialed the phone number back but got a message saying the number wasn't in service.

After grabbing his laptop, he checked a few quick phone databases. Not listed. Had Antonio sent this? What was with the "not in service" message? That had to mean the phone was switched off. Or the caller had removed the battery after sending the text. That was an awful lot of trouble to go to just to send Drayco music he already had.

But *were* the songs identical? He listened to the copy he'd downloaded himself for comparison, and the two were indeed the same. As jokes went, it wasn't very funny. And if it were a warning, it wasn't very specific.

It rattled him more than he would have expected. Maybe it was due to waking him from a deep sleep and a pleasant dream starring Darcie. Then he remembered his recent visit to see her and how that had ended. Well, this was a lovely start to the day.

He sat on the edge of the bed listening for signs of life in the inn. Deciding to chance it, he ran through a quick series of Krav Maga calisthenics and exercises. But even pushups, burpees, and shadow-punching weren't enough to let off all the steam.

Always the perceptive face reader, Maida frowned when she saw him at breakfast. "What's the matter?"

"The cellphone woke me. Not to worry."

She said, "Hmm," and pointed to the table. "Mr. and Mrs. Litton left early this morning, so it's you and Major and me."

After he grabbed a chair, she brought out pastries with a purple filling and a plate of an eggy creation. "Berry crossovers and Eggs Benedict will cheer you up."

A door slam at the back of the house heralded the arrival of the Major, who slid into a chair beside Drayco. "You made Eggs Benedict? You never make me Eggs Benedict."

Maida scooped one onto her husband's plate. "You never ask."

Like all Maida's cooking, it was five-star and had a special "Maida touch," in this case, the addition of scallops. Much better than Drayco's usual breakfast of instant coffee and leftover takeout. He didn't tell them he'd given the B&B a five-star rating on various travel websites, but it wasn't a lie.

Maida poured them all mimosas and perched on the window ledge. One of her occasional cigars lay unsmoked on a nearby ashtray. "You must tell me how your chat with the Pinnicks went last night."

Drayco grimaced. "Emmerson pulled the lawyer card. Deirdre was the obedient daughter. And Mrs. Pinnick wouldn't win any Oscars, though she sure tried."

"Barbara Pinnick didn't want Marty for a son-in-law, that was obvious. Even to Marty, who mentioned it when he came to talk to me.

"Ouch. Poor Marty."

"That wasn't the sole problem. Marty was the son of Sebastien Penry—and Penry and Emmerson Pinnick weren't on the best of terms. Plenty of bad blood."

"The restraining order?"

She shook her head. "Started long before that. Emmerson filed a lawsuit against Sebastien over a contractor job at his law firm. I think it was a misrepresentation of how the building was going to turn out. But Sebastien counter-sued and won."

"Sheriff Sailor never mentioned it."

"I only know because Marty told me. As I recall, the suit was filed under the firm's name, but it was all Pinnick's doing."

"And Marty got caught in the middle."

"In more ways than one. Barbara Pinnick is a true snob. Since Marty was the son of a 'blue collar' worker," Maida made air quotes with her fingers, "that wouldn't do for her precious Deirdre."

Drayco wrapped his hands around the cool glass with the mimosa. "Deirdre didn't seem to mind."

"Romeo and Juliet."

"Look how that turned out. Adds more weight to the idea Marty's death was suicide, like Romeo."

The Major piped up, "With her upbringing, you wouldn't think Barbara would cop such an attitude, now would you?"

"Upbringing?"

"Parents died young. Overdoses. Meth, as I recall."

Maida added, "She ended up in a series of foster homes. Could be that inspired her to make something of herself, which I applaud. But trying to become an 'important person' isn't the right type of aspiration to me. Guess when you're an outcast as a child, you end up with a burning desire to fit in."

Drayco replied, "To the extreme." Well, now. The fact her parents died of drug overdoses might not be ancient history if there were a drug connection in all of this.

Maida asked, "Are you still considering murder?"

"I promised Nelia and her mother I'd pursue this to the bitter end."

"What are your instincts telling you? I don't know anyone with better."

He didn't have a chance to answer before a knock at the front door made Maida get up to check who it was. Moments later, laughing young voices and a wheelchair signaled the arrival of two people Drayco was delighted to see. He'd been keeping tabs on them ever since the case a year ago that brought them into his life.

Barry Farland, wearing his customary Goth blacks and silver lip ring, wheeled Virginia Harston into the kitchen. When the girl saw the drink glasses, she said, "Oooh, mimosas. Can I have one?"

"You can have one with ginger ale instead of alcohol," Maida replied, as she hurried to the fridge to whip one up.

Virginia groaned. "I'm thirteen. In France, they let kids drink wine when they're babies."

Maida peered over her glasses at the girl. "Your mother would French-fry me if I tried."

Barry held out his hand. "I'm legal."

She handed Virginia her drink and then made another for Barry. "And you get a half-mimosa because you're driving."

"That's fair. Mr. Haffey would fire me in a second if I got a DUI."

Drayco leaned back in his chair. "To what do we owe the honor of a visit from Cape Unity's premiere artistic duo?"

Virginia giggled. "To see you, silly. And to thank you again for my birthday present."

"You're quite welcome. I heard you had a big party. Sorry I couldn't be there."

"Two parties. One with each of my Moms. Having two mothers is turning out to be great."

Drayco pulled out his cellphone, flipped through the photos, and showed one to her. "The painting you made of my sister is framed and hanging on the wall behind my piano."

Her smile could have outshone a Christmas tree. "You better keep it safe. It'll be worth a fortune when I'm famous."

He laughed. "I'll hold you to that." Not that he'd part with it. Nope, it was staying right where it was.

Barry poked Virginia in the arm. "Tell them about the prosthetics."

The look on Maida's face told Drayco she was as startled as he was. He asked, "You're getting prosthetics?"

Virginia bit her lip. "It's not a done deal. But I've been thinking about it." She pointed at the stubs of her legs that ended below the knee. "So I can go wherever I want to paint scenery. And there's too many places a wheelchair won't work."

"Your Moms approve?"

"They both say it's a great idea. The new house Mom is building is close to the one Vesta Mae bought. I want to walk back and forth between them instead of getting a motorized wheelchair. Besides, I'm going to need to be able to walk on stage when I get my Hugo Boss prize."

The fact Virginia and Lucy Harston were no longer poor might have something to do with the change in attitude about the prosthetics. But Drayco didn't care about the motive, he was happy as long as Virginia was happy.

Barry grabbed a pastry and sat in a chair backward, dribbling crumbs on the floor. "You solve the Marty Penry case yet?"

"How did you hear about that?"

"Word gets around. Guess Mr. Penry doesn't want anyone to think bad of his son, right?"

The young man's insight echoed what Drayco was thinking all along. "Barry, did you have any interactions with Marty and his group of friends?"

"You mean Antonio, Lena, Deirdre, and Tess? Didn't know 'em personally. I knew who they were. Another type of clique or whatever. High school is a battle zone. This clique here, that clique there."

"They're a little older than you, so it's understandable you didn't hang out together."

"I was a sophomore when they were seniors. But I see 'em around town now and then."

When the young man eyed the plate of pastries, Drayco handed it over. "Did you hear them mention the Akashic Records?"

Barry wolfed down another pastry, then licked his fingers, prompting Maida to hand him a napkin. "Rings a bell. Maybe once, at lunch. It's all bunk. A teenage version of fairy tales and make-believe or whatever."

"You don't think they took it seriously?"

"Teenagers don't believe in much of anything except sex, do they?" He reached out to put his hands over Virginia's ears. "Sorry, Ginnie. You didn't hear that."

Drayco said, "Odd that Deirdre would belong to that group. Surely her mother would have pushed her to be a cheerleader. Or student body president."

Barry grinned. "Kids do the opposite of what their parents want."

"Another odd fit is Tess Gartin. She and Marty ended up rivals."

The younger man got up to refill his mimosa, but Maida headed him off with a cup of coffee, which made Virginia giggle. Barry replied, "Yeah, Tess and Marty went to the same college. For the same thing. Lot of folks around here don't graduate from high school, let alone go to college. And they chose the same school and degree? Weird."

"And then they wind up working at the same place, only Marty gets the job Tess wanted."

"But I guess she gets the gig now, huh? Now that Marty's dead."

Drayco couldn't argue that fact. Nor could he deny Tess was a conundrum. Her social media presence was unusually sketchy as if she took pains to stay invisible.

As Drayco watched Barry and Virginia laughing and joking with the Jepsons, he had a more profound sympathy for Sebastien Penry. These two young people were the closest thing to kids Drayco had, and a fierce, protective instinct hit him full force. He wouldn't have accepted a suicide ruling for them, either.

Had he gone about this all wrong? Was he was too prejudiced by Vuca's death to believe in the murder scenario? Or maybe music was too much in his blood, making him think it also infected Marty by way of that sonata and song.

What was that Latin proverb? *Music induces more madness in many than wine.* The question was, who had introduced that song—that madness—to Marty and why?

15

Tess scowled at her boss. "You said to adjust the power filter and pump, so I adjusted the frickin' power filter and pump." She crouched on the floor and flipped open the side panel to the tank. "I've done this umpteen times before, and it's worked fine."

Judson Kolman stood with his feet planted as wide as his scowl. "This is a very delicate project. At such a crucial stage. We can't afford to have all that work go down the drain. Literally."

"I've got this. Had to maintain this same type of gear at UNC. I learned tons of workarounds."

Kolman heaved an audible sigh that only made Tess tenser. She was regretting coming in to work even if it meant making sure the *Crassostrea ariakensis* were doing okay.

She said under her breath, "You wouldn't have questioned Marty's decisions."

Kolman had moved to peer outside to the marina where a pleasure boat was puttering not far from the station. But he'd still heard her jibe. "You think I'm harder on you than Marty? I'm hard on all my staff."

She didn't answer and reseated an O-ring on the pump.

He added, "You don't learn anything if you're told everything you do is perfect. Even when it isn't."

He kept looking from her to the marina, and she couldn't tell if he was more annoyed with her or the pleasure boat. With a loud grunt as the boat's motors grew louder, he marched outside the room, leaving her alone with her oysters.

She wasn't all that different from him. He was happier being with porpoises than people. She was happier being alone with the oysters, every funky, slimy, musky-smelling last inch of them.

It wasn't long before Kolman rejoined her. "The signs plainly say this isn't a public dock. And these boaters spoke English well enough to read."

When she looked around for a screwdriver, he anticipated her and grabbed one from the workbench. She nodded her thanks. A bit of *détente*.

Kolman rescued his neglected coffee cup from the same bench and took a sip with a grimace. "This coffee is bad when it's warm. Cold, it tastes like krill juice. Or what I imagine krill juice would taste like. I should try some of Dr. Drayco's salt."

That made her smile. A little. More so, when Kolman pointed at the tank as the bubbles began to circulate. "Good work."

She buttoned up the panel and was grateful to stand, shaking out her cramping quads. "Fancier labs have better gear. Here, you gotta learn how to punt. Marty was great at it." There, she could be magnanimous now that Marty wasn't around.

Still grimacing, Kolman swigged more of the cold coffee. "I've had sleepless nights worrying if I pushed him too far. He never complained."

"Guess it's normal to wonder what any of us could have done differently." Tess had suffered a few sleepless nights herself lately, reliving their conversations before Marty's death. She'd felt they were getting along better. Joking around.

She rummaged through the feeding station, picked up a bottle of a gooey, green algae "milkshake," and measured a small amount into a long syringe to feed the oysters. "What if Sebastien Penry's right, and it was murder?"

The chugging of another approaching boat made Kolman growl. "Wait here," he said, tossing the remainder of the coffee into a sink.

He was gone longer this time, and when he returned, he was in full-blown anger mode. "The weekend boaters are the worst. Drunk from partying the night before. Or, on their way to getting drunk, from the size of the beer-filled cooler I saw."

He opened a small refrigerator and pulled out two root beers, handing one over. "I can't think of anyone who had a bad word against

Marty. Unless it was the Pinnicks. They had it in for Marty's Dad. Could be they took it out on his son."

Tess felt her cheeks grow warm when he uttered the Pinnick name. "Couldn't be Emmerson Pinnick. He's an attorney, he knows better."

Kolman lifted an eyebrow. "Attorneys aren't saints. More than a few weasels and snakes among their numbers. I'm surprised you'd defend him."

"Deirdre is a better suspect. Or Lena, the woman scorned."

"I admit I don't know Lena well, but she's very good to my wife, Cherie. But Deirdre, now that's interesting. What about Pinnick's restraining order?"

"If a guy were stalking your daughter, you'd do the same as Emmerson did."

"Stalking?" Kolman dug into the supply cabinet to pull out a few test tubes. "Marty was no stalker. He loved her, that's all. Merely trying to change her mind about breaking it off."

At the noise of yet another boat outside, Tess held up her hand. "I'll take care of it. Don't want your blood pressure to explode."

She headed out toward the dock but found he was following her. Fine. They'd double-team the new arrivals. As they passed the equipment room, she paused. "A new magnetometer?"

"Marty purchased that."

"Did he tell you he was getting it?"

"I gave him a budget, but he didn't mention his interest in this. I found out after the fact. Frankly, I don't know whether we'll be able to keep it. Sure would be nice to have for seafloor magnetic shifts and whale migrations."

"Wouldn't a manned submersible be better? Our ROV is long in the tooth."

"Last time I priced those human-operated jobs, they started at a couple million."

"Marty was a dreamer, all right. He watched every episode of the old Jacques Cousteau show. More than once." Tess grabbed her drawstring sunhat off the rack by the door.

Kolman chuckled. "I didn't do that, and they were brand-new shows when I was a lad."

"He felt he could make a difference. Had an idea for clearing up the plastic messes in the ocean, like that Great Pacific Garbage Patch. Wish he'd written it down."

Kolman rubbed his mustache. "I'll ask his father if he found the plans among Marty's effects."

They headed out to the marina where a red-and-white boat with the name *SexSea* painted on the side pulled up to the pier. The half dozen or so twenty-somethings were laughing and pushing one of the bikini-clad girls out onto the dock.

She stumbled out, bumping into Tess. "Gotta use the head," she slurred.

Tess peered at Kolman, whose scowl was the width of the Chesapeake Bay. He growled, "This isn't a public facility. It's a research station."

The girl belched, then said, "I've done it before. That cute young guy said I could." She looked around. "Said his name was Marty."

A young man from the boat called out, "Hurry up, will you, Bobbi? We ain't got all day."

The young woman yelled at them. "This jerk here says I can't use the bathroom."

Her companion growled, "Oh, yeah? Who says?"

Tess sized up the guy, noting he was a good seventy pounds heavier than her and six inches taller than her boss. She thought she saw Kolman's eye twitch, something he did when he was nervous.

But he rested his arm casually on top of a post and said, "Who says? The Virginia Marine Police who patrol this area and hand out heavy fines and jail time for trespassing. But, since I'm a nice guy, I'll let this young lady—Bobbi, is it?—inside today. From now on, however, you should opt for the public marinas at Chincoteague or Wachapreague."

After a few tense moments, the younger man shrugged and said, "Whatever, dude."

Tess followed Bobbi to the bathroom and waited outside, keeping a careful watch. But Bobbi had enough booze to make her unsteady and hardly in thieving mode. Tess kept her eye on the girl until she'd rejoined her boat, and it motored off into the distance

Tess felt the knot of muscles at the back of her neck relax some. "I can see Marty letting her in. He was too kind-hearted at times."

Kolman replied, "I suppose," and headed inside.

Tess watched the boat until it was a tiny dot against the sea channel. It wasn't only that Marty was too kind. He was too trusting for his own good. She'd witnessed that herself, hadn't she?

She rubbed a hand across her eyes. *Oh, Marty. If only you'd left a clue.* With one last look at the disappearing dot, she made her way to the lab where the oysters would be a welcome distraction. And *they* never talked back.

16

Drayco's circulatory caffeine reservoir was empty, and that would never do. Time to stop by the Novel Café for their killer coffee. Cup in hand, he headed over to the bookstore side, where he took note of a woman with curly gray hair who was using metal crutches.

When she inquired at the counter whether a book she'd ordered had come, the clerk asked her name. She replied, "Cherie Kolman."

The book had indeed arrived, and Mrs. Kolman paid for her new treasure and went outside. She sat at a table in front of the store, and he headed toward her. "I don't want to bother you, but you said your name was Cherie Kolman?"

The woman squinted at him. "Do I know you?"

"The name's Scott Drayco. Sebastien Penry hired me to look into his son's death. I spoke with your husband at the marine biology station. Do you mind if I join you? I could get you a coffee. Or iced tea."

She smiled at him. "No coffee or tea, thanks. But do have a seat. If you've spoken with Judson, it must be fine."

The sloping of her left shoulder and the curve in her spine were evidence of the scoliosis Lena had mentioned. She maneuvered reasonably well and didn't wince as if in pain. He was grateful for that when she reached to move her crutches to the side before he could do it for her.

He pointed to her book, *Fielden's Guide to Rare Coins*. "Lena Bing told me you had a coin collecting hobby."

"I make a little money from it. Better than being on disability. Lena's a big help with that. And housework."

"Did Marty ever join Lena when she assisted you?"

"A few times. And we had him and Tess over for dinner, too. He was a bright boy, that Marty. A bit troubled. Nothing unusual. All young people today carry their share of burdens."

"Troubled in what way?"

"Not suicidal. I'd swear to that. I'm hoping it was just a tragic accident."

She picked up the book and rubbed her hand along the spine. "We watched Tom and Jerry cartoons together. Marty had a sharp sense of humor. And he especially loved satire. He was such a sweet boy."

"So I've heard."

"Judson had high hopes for him. He was devastated when news came of the suicide."

Drayco moved his feet to avoid bumping into her crutches. "Your husband admitted he was hard on Marty at times."

"Oh, that's Judson's way. He got that from *his* father. Very strict."

"He did mention tough love."

She hesitated. "Judson has hinted his father hit him and his mother. And belittled my husband's decision to be a marine biologist instead of a doctor making 'good' money. My poor Judson."

She paused, and a brief flash of pain crossed her face. Was he wrong about scoliosis causing her discomfort? But when she continued, he understood. "Marty was like a son to him. Our own boy, Jack, died of a drug overdose when he was fourteen. That's another reason Judson was so hard on Marty. So lightning wouldn't strike twice."

"I'm terribly sorry. I had no idea. Your husband didn't mention it."

"He wouldn't. He never talks about Jack. It devastated him. Devastated us both."

"Then you may understand why Sebastien Penry is seeking a reason for his son's death."

"I'd want the same thing." She grabbed a napkin from a dispenser on the table and dabbed at her eyes. "I think Judson's more affected by this than he admits."

"Suicides can take a heavy toll on the survivors."

"Judson seems despondent when he doesn't know I'm looking. He's got so many other burdens. Responsibility for the station, his staff, funding, grants."

Drayco was getting a taste of that with his Opera House. He replied, "I understand."

She clutched the napkin in her hand. "Judson thinks he's failed because he can't give me the life I should have. But I assure him I'm content as long as I have him."

"By all accounts, Marty was reasonably content until recently. Did he mention a Suicide Sonata or song by that name?"

"Not to me. But Judson told me about it. He said Marty was obsessed, and no one understood why. Judson looked up that song out of curiosity. He's never expressed an interest in the supernatural before, but it spooked him."

A male voice from behind Drayco's shoulder spoke up. "Dr. Drayco, you aren't harassing my wife, are you?"

Drayco turned to see a scowling Judson Kolman, whose narrowed eyes and tense posture made it clear he wasn't joking. Before Drayco had a chance to reply, Cherie said, "Did you say *Dr.* Drayco? I didn't know you were a scientist, too. Anyway, Judson, it's fine. Dr. Drayco and I have been having a nice conversation about Marty."

Kolman put his hands on his wife's shoulders and kissed her on the head. "My mistake, dear. I always overreact when it comes to your well-being. So sue me."

She covered his hands with hers and squeezed them gently. "I'm a lucky woman."

Kolman looked over at Drayco, "The reverse is closer to the truth. Cherie is an extraordinary person, and I'm not saying that because she's my wife. Stronger and smarter than most folks. And as lovely as the day we got married."

Drayco should have winced at that. It was often a false declaration—as if a man was expected to say it, so he played the role. But in this case, the look of adoration on Kolman's face spoke volumes.

"Now, my dear, your chariot awaits. Sorry if I left you hanging. My errands took longer than planned."

She grabbed the edges of the table to hoist herself up, and Drayco secured the crutches and handed them to her. She gave him a little wave as the couple headed toward their car.

After they'd left, Drayco sat alone with his cooling coffee and lukewarm thoughts. Seeing a few other book lovers at tables around the corner, he wished he'd brought his Chopin biography. The book was out of print now, but it had won an award shortly after Vuca wrote it. Depending upon which expert you believed, Chopin himself may have suffered from bipolar disorder, depression, or schizophrenia—complete with hallucinations he called "a cohort of phantoms."

Drayco tried to relax into his metal chair with the barely there cushion, studying the people, the traffic, and catching snatches of conversations as they came and went. The main change from his people-watching days of yore was that a high percentage of those passing conversations were now on cellphones. Those who weren't chatting on phones were texting on them. Couples, friends, side-by-side glued to their phones. If the art of real conversation wasn't yet dead, it was on life support.

He'd been at it for half an hour when his phone blurted out a text alert, and he dutifully checked it. When in Rome and all. It was identical to the mysterious text he'd received before, *This is for you.* Clicking on the attachment led to another audio file of the suicide song.

He compared the phone number to the previous one. They were different. Why would someone send him the song twice via different phones? Or was it more than one person, or someone covering their tracks by using burner phones? Either way, bizarre. And suspicious.

As with the last time, he listened to the song all the way through to the final verse, "The flowers are fading, the light becomes dusk, Ashes turn to ashes and dust turns to dust."

He half-expected to hear someone singing Marty's extra verse, but it was the commercially available version from the internet again. He wasn't in a great frame of mind before. But if the sender of the song wanted to bring him down, it worked.

A call earlier in the day from Sheriff Sailor with a disturbing accusation against Sebastien Penry added to his black mood. He'd wait and deal with that tomorrow at a meeting Sailor was arranging.

After staring at his phone for a minute, he did a web search and found the phone number for Vuca's widow, Lydia. He punched in the number, but after the first ring, he hung up. What would that accomplish? No need to unleash his own cohort of phantoms.

On a whim, Drayco popped back inside the Novel Café to check out the philosophy section. When he didn't see what he was after, he headed to the register hoping to see Zelda, the regular clerk. She wasn't in, so he asked the seller on duty, "Do you have any books on the Akashic Records?"

"Don't think I've heard of that. But let me check." She tapped the computer keyboard and scanned the screen. "We did have one book, *The Akashic Records: Unlock Infinite Universal Purpose.* But we sold it. Sorry—can we order you another one?"

"How long ago did you sell it?"

She checked the display. "In January."

January. Four months before Marty's alleged suicide. Drayco smiled at the clerk. "I'll check to see if that's the one I'm looking for and get back with you."

Possibly a long shot. But every one of Marty's gang had mentioned the topic, describing it variously as 'spooky,' 'kinda interesting,' 'kinda funky,' or merely a class project. In Drayco's day, it was the humble Ouija Board kids toyed with.

As he made his way to the street, one look at a passing car made him hurry to his Starfire and take off after it. Tailing in this small town wasn't easy, but he doubted this particular driver would notice since his expression was like something you'd see in a zombie movie. Where was he headed in that state of mind and why? Only one way to find out.

17

Antonio wasn't lying when he said his car was held together with duct tape and superglue. Drayco spotted right away which window was smashed during the gun theft, judging by the black plastic trash bags taped across the right rear glass.

He kept a safe distance, knowing Antonio could identify the Starfire. But his hunch Antonio wouldn't notice a tail was correct. The younger man drove first to a hardware store where he stayed five minutes, walking out with a tiny brown bag. Then he traveled to a store that sold tobacco and guns. That was more interesting, but he came out empty-handed.

After a few more miles, Drayco was ready to give up and peel away. Then Antonio suddenly jerked his Ford Escort across two lanes of traffic so fast, he barely avoided hitting an oncoming delivery truck. Had Antonio seen him? But no, when Drayco caught up to the young man's car, it crept along a now-familiar street, its driver still oblivious to much of anything.

Drayco parked down the road from Antonio, who pulled in front of Marty's duplex and stared straight ahead with the engine idling. Then Antonio hopped out and pressed his hands and nose against the front window, staying frozen in that position for one minute, two, then five minutes.

Drayco watched, waiting, as the moments ticked by. Would Antonio break the glass? Or maybe he had a key? But the young man finally roused himself from his paralysis as he bolted into the car and roared off. Drayco continued to tail him as they proceeded to another familiar spot, the chicken plant, where a flurry of people and vehicles coming and going signaled a shift change. Antonio plodded his way into the building with as much enthusiasm as a schoolboy heading to class after summer break.

The odd work schedules the young man mentioned didn't get him off on a Sunday, it seemed. Feeling more than a little sorry for Antonio despite the fact he was a chief suspect in Marty's death, Drayco headed toward the center of town. Time for something he hoped would be more positive.

Yesterday's visit to the Opera House was way too brief, cut short by Nelia and then his encounter with Darcie. He'd barely had a few minutes with the glorious Steinway, and now he heard the piano calling his name. Maybe the Akashic Records had it all wrong, and the inanimate objects were psychic. The instrument somehow knew Drayco needed it, needed its comforting presence.

Following the standard arm-soaking in the Opera House green room to loosen up his muscles, Drayco made his way to the piano and eased himself onto the bench. But he didn't start playing right away. It was too hard for him to shake the image of Antonio staring into Marty's apartment as if its former occupant would stroll out any minute.

What was Antonio hoping to see inside? Memories? Ghosts? Or evidence he'd left behind? Drayco stared at the pink, branching scars stretching from his palm to his elbow. Antonio had scars, too, just not as obvious. Having a father in prison for murder was the kind of thing that sent more affluent people into years of pricey therapy.

Drayco had a sudden burning desire to play the original "Suicide Sonata" by Adojan Dobos. As he played, he pictured himself living in the era of its composition. What was there about the piece that would cause a young man to lie across railroad tracks or a young woman to slit her wrists?

The sonata didn't make Drayco suicidal, but it didn't make him want to get up and dance, either. He stopped and switched to Debussy's *Reflets dans l'Eau*. Much better. And a water theme, no less. The rippling arpeggios of the piece matched the play of light and shadow reflecting off the marshy waters at Powhatan Park.

After finishing the Debussy, he couldn't help himself and started playing the Suicide Sonata again. Marty had the sheet music and was a good enough pianist to tackle it, so he must have played it, too. But could it really have contributed to his downward psychological spiral? The Hungarian "curse" striking again?

Yet, the song *based* on the sonata was what was found with Marty's body, not the sonata itself. So why was the sheet music missing from Marty's apartment? And was "soul vibration" merely an Akashic Records reference? None of it made any sense.

Drayco switched to playing a transcription of the suicide song he made on the fly, singing the words as he played. At the end, the last strains of the word "Mars" echoed around the stage, bouncing back to him from the exposed metal pipes and the bare walls.

He swung his feet around and faced the empty hall, now still and quiet. He'd never needed an audience to connect with music or to channel a composer's spirit with each note. And yet, this empty hall depressed him. Everything seemed to be depressing him. Was this how it started for Marty? For Vuca?

Shaking it off, he headed toward the stage exit. What would help was one of Maida's potable potions—magic in a glass. Before he left, he spied a shiny copper penny on stage and plucked it from the floor. He wasn't prone to superstition, but this case was turning out to be so frustrating, he might need all the luck he could get.

18

Another morning, another trip to Café Sailor where the sheriff handed over the usual cup of mud. Drayco smelled something fried and followed the olfactory trail to a greasy paper bag with a half-eaten sandwich on top. He saw bits of flour-battered chicken inside—the result of Antonio's handiwork? Or another worker at some other chicken plant.

As they waited for their "guest" to arrive, Drayco told Sailor about the two texts sent to his phone, making Sailor frown. "We can try a trace. Not sure a judge or the phone company will go along with it. Likely a prank. But look, if they get threatening—"

"I'll let you know."

Sailor drummed his fingers on his desk, which made Drayco say, "My habits are catching."

"What?" Sailor glared at his hands and stopped the drumming. "Thanks a lot. For that and for turning this into an official department investigation."

When Sailor's desk phone rang, and he answered, Drayco heard Nelia's voice on the other end. "He's here. Should I show him in?"

Sailor gave her the go-ahead, and she ushered in Sebastien Penry. Sailor pointed to the remaining seat in the office for the man to sit. Drayco looked at Nelia and half-rose from his chair, but she shook her head and stayed standing.

Sebastien's face had a glimmer of hope as he asked, "I appreciate the updates you've phoned me, Scott. Nelia didn't tell me what this was about. Hope you've had a big break."

Sailor was stone-faced. "We're hoping you can help us out with that."

Sebastien's smile faded fast. "I don't understand."

Sailor tapped a piece of paper on his desk. "You've had financial difficulties lately."

"Contracting work comes and goes. There's the pittance I get from playing in the symphony part-time. Plus, I have modest savings in the bank. I'll be okay."

"You were passed over for that new condo development, right?"

The muscles in Sebastien's face tightened. "It happens."

"Must have been a big blow." Sailor pushed the piece of paper to him. "We found out you had a life insurance policy on your son. For a quarter of a million dollars."

As the realization of Sailor's implication hit him full force, Sebastien's voice took on a darker edge. "I purchased that years ago on the advice of a financial planner. He told me it locked in Marty's ability to qualify for more life insurance. Especially if he were to develop a medical problem. My brother died in his twenties from a genetic heart defect."

When Sailor didn't respond, Sebastien added, "Look, Marty cashed some in to use for college expenses. And I've made arrangements to donate the rest to the Ocean Foundation and Chesapeake Bay Trust. In Marty's name."

"The life insurance policy isn't the only thing, Mr. Penry. You were arrested for assault ten years ago."

"Self-defense. The guy was an asshole. He came at me first. Got what was coming to him."

Sailor continued. "Must have been pretty angry with him. And you were pretty angry with Emmerson Pinnick. That lawsuit he brought against you. And then the restraining order against your son."

"Hell, yes, I was angry. You would be, too. What of it?"

"What if you found out, say, that your son was still seeing Pinnick's daughter? It could make you so angry, you killed Marty in anger even if accidental. You told Drayco you'd argued the day he died. Over a girl."

"Are you seriously implying I'd follow my son to that isolated spot to argue with him? And then shoot him in the head? You're fucking insane."

"Barbara Pinnick made nasty comments to you. That Marty wasn't good enough for Deirdre. In fact, she was desperate to keep him away from her. That had to rankle after the lawsuit Emmerson Pinnick filed."

Sebastien crossed his arm across his chest and said, "I can't believe this," and then he glowered at Drayco. "I ask you to look into my son's death, and you try to frame me for it."

Drayco replied, "No one wants to frame anyone, Sebastien. But you have to understand how this looks on the surface. And if *we* don't ask you, someone else will."

Nelia added, "We can check out the charitable donations. That should help clear this up."

Sailor gave Nelia a sharp look but stayed silent.

Drayco asked Sebastien, "Did Marty recently mention 'something big' that was coming to him?"

"I don't recall. Unless he was going to get a raise. Or a promotion. Or had another job offer. But he didn't say squat to me."

Sebastien jumped up from his chair. "Look, this is one giant FUBAR. I'll be lucky if I make it to my job site by noon. I got a new gaffer and boomhand starting today, too."

Sailor started to interject, but Sebastien kept up his rant. "I'll get canned if I do this often. And I can't afford that, as you so forcefully reminded me. If this line of questioning is going any further, I'll want my own attorney before I say more."

Drayco stood to join him. "I'll walk you to the front if that's okay?" He peered at Sailor, who waved them off.

Sebastien was still steaming as they made their way down the corridor. Drayco said, "If it helps, you aren't high on my suspect list."

His companion stopped dead in his tracks. "Then why the hell am I here?"

"The sheriff has to check all angles. Standard procedure."

"Didn't sound all that standard to me. What a shitshow. I mean, he's convinced I killed my own son."

Drayco stopped for a moment when they entered the beige-and-gray front lobby. "I promised you and Olive Tyler I'd pursue this wherever it leads. Haven't changed my mind."

Sebastien's shoulders dropped an inch or two. "I hope not, Scott, I truly do. The sheriff was right on one point. I'm not a wealthy man. Hiring you isn't easy on my bank account."

"We can work something out." Sebastien hadn't mentioned contributions from Nelia's mother. Did he know? Or did Olive Tyler not want him to know?

Sebastien asked, "You're saying you'll keep an open mind?"

"I don't know any other way."

"Then I'll hold you to that. And Olive still trusts you, which counts for something."

With the other man slightly placated and safely on his way, Drayco rejoined Sailor and Nelia in Sailor's office. He said to the pair, "I'll grant you Marty's death could have been an accident in the heat of the moment. But there's the gun stolen from Antonio's car—that smacks of premeditation. If Sebastien wanted to kill his son, he had easier ways to do it."

Sailor grumbled, "Could have hired a hit man and framed Antonio."

Nelia asked, "If he's being honest about giving away the insurance money, where's the motive? Seems more likely he'd hire someone to kill the Pinnicks."

"Yeah, yeah, hitting me with your logic. It's a small chance, okay? But I've had small chances pay off big."

Drayco said, "I'd love to stay and spar, but I promised Virginia I'd pop by to look at her latest artistic creations."

He looked at Nelia with a quick nod, hoping she'd join him. But Sailor said, "Tyler, can you stay a minute? I want a brief word."

She avoided looking at Drayco as she shut the door behind him for the conference with her boss. He had a good idea of what had upset the sheriff, but he wasn't going to get involved. Sailor and Tyler would have to work it out.

He paused in the lobby pretending to look at the mug shots on the wall, a decision that paid off a few minutes later when Nelia stalked through the lobby. She stopped when she saw him. "I thought you'd left."

"On my way out. Admiring these handsome gentlemen here."

She tried to smile, but it was a spectacular failure. "I shouldn't have told Sebastien checking into the charity would clear him. The sheriff warned me about letting this get personal."

"We all do it." Drayco held out two fingers pressed together. "And it was only a Lilliputian slip-up. Sailor trusts you."

"I've let my personal feelings get in the way too much." Her cheeks turned pink, and she hurried to add, "I should go catch up on paperwork." She vanished so fast, she left a breeze in her wake.

In the days since he arrived in town, he'd only seen her briefly a few times. Not one word of her relationship with her husband. Not that it would matter to Drayco's love life. Darcie was history, and Nelia was probably an enigma that would forever stay an enigma.

Despite how dispirited that made him feel, he had to put on a bright face for Virginia. The anticipation of seeing her new paintings cheered him. Hopefully, they included pleasant subjects or colorful abstracts because he could sure use a lot less dark realism in his life right now.

19

After spending a lively afternoon with Virginia and marveling at how her talent was blooming at such a young age, Drayco returned to the Lazy Crab. He waved at Maida and went straight to his room where he did more research on his laptop for clues to the mystery phone caller. No luck.

He delved more deeply into the social media accounts for Marty's little Gang of Five. Tess, as usual, was largely absent. The postings from Lena and Antonio trended toward the melancholy side with several centered on Marty.

Drayco was surprised to see Lena had even written a poem after Marty's death. Maybe she had a hand in writing the last stanza of Marty's "note"? He compared her work with Marty's but didn't see any clear similarities.

Deirdre, on the other hand, had scores of photos with her smiling new fiancé and snaps of clothing, shoes, and other banal observations. Lots of selfies from her recent trips to Miami and the Keys. Few of her beside landmarks, but several of her leaving Dolce & Gabbana and Gucci stores loaded with shopping bags. Did anyone really care she got an "adorbs" calfskin fanny pack for ten percent off?

His main task was hacking the password on Marty's computer since the first attempts a few days ago were unsuccessful. After a few more tries, he gave up on getting lucky. Next up was bringing out the big guns via a Linux Live CD. Bingo.

A quick survey of files found various work-related documents. Budgets, purchase orders, and drawings and schematics for an ocean cleanup project. Drayco studied the schematics. Looked interesting and very creative. Had Kolman seen this?

Drayco scanned the other work fodder, but not seeing anything remarkable, he moved on to the rest of the files. Nothing much there, not surprising since younger people used their cellphones for everything.

Maybe email? He found a link to one account, also password protected. He tried using Marty's name with various passwords but struck out until he had an idea and typed in "Calypso." That worked.

Paging through Marty's email folders, Drayco found the young man used the account primarily for business. No rambling essays filled with depressive thoughts. No links to suicide forums or websites although a few linked to info on headache cures.

If Drayco had hoped to find a browser history of visits to suicide-related chat rooms, he struck out there, too. He did find one link to a recipe for a protein powder. He wrote down the ingredients, which were pretty much as Tess described. Kale and dandelion greens, dried green apple, dried avocado, and hemp protein. No marijuana, drugs, or intentional poisons.

The one other item of interest Drayco found on the hard drive was a copy of the suicide song where Marty composed his final verse. Seeing it there on the screen was harder than seeing it on the paper found with his body. This was where Marty contemplated mortality, played a game with it, and lost.

Drayco rubbed his eyes and then stared at Marty's words again. *And peals of the church bells that reach out to Mars.* Where had that come from? Even the Akashic Records didn't mention anything like it.

He pushed ahead, checking the hard drive where he found a folder with photos Marty downloaded from his phone, including the one of him and Antonio fishing. Drayco sat up straighter when he found one—and only one—photo of a forested area that looked identical to the clearing where Marty's body was found.

The date of the file was a month before his death. That verified what Lena said, that Marty had visited the clearing before. But why take only a single snapshot of the place and without Lena? Or so much as a selfie?

After an hour of fruitless searching, Drayco slammed the lid shut and considered taking a nap on the oh-so-inviting bed with the down comforter. Instead, he picked up Marty's clay necklace and studied the etched markings. What did the triangle and downward arrow mean? And when had he made this?

A knock on the bedroom door interrupted his musing, and he opened it to find an apologetic Maida. "Hate to disturb you. Judson Kolman is downstairs."

Drayco stuffed the necklace in his pocket and made his way to the study where Kolman rose from his chair to shake his hand. "I'm glad you agreed to meet with me, Dr. Drayco."

"If this is about my conversation with your wife—"

"I must apologize for that. I was out of line. My wife's not in the best of health, but I shouldn't treat her like a fragile doll. She's stronger emotionally than most men I know. And she said the two of you had a nice chat."

Drayco eased into the wingback chair as Kolman sat across from him and asked, "What can I do for you?"

"I've thought more about Marty and the sonata. And the deaths of those other people who listened to the song. You don't think there's anything to this, do you?"

"You mean, is there a curse on that song?"

"Sounds silly coming from a scientist." Kolman chuckled. "When I was a lad, it was Beatles backward records that were all the rage."

Drayco leaned forward. "Doesn't matter what you and I believe about that music. It's what Marty believed."

"Seemed like hogwash when he first mentioned the thing."

"What made you change your mind?"

"He listens to music called the 'suicide song' and then commits suicide. That can't be a coincidence, can it?" Kolman stared at the aqua-and-teal braided rug. "If only I'd been more forceful, maybe talk him out of listening to that music. Paid more attention to his frame of mind."

"At the marine biology station, you said Marty was more distracted, quieter recently. Could there be another factor? He told a friend 'something big' was coming."

"Whatever did he mean?"

"When pressed for details, he clammed up. Were you getting ready to promote him, give him a big raise?"

"That Assistant Director title was a few years off. But, as I say, if I'd paid attention, he might have been more open."

Kolman grabbed a dog-eared hardcover book from the table next to his chair and stood up to hand it over. "This is the main reason I dropped by."

Drayco checked the title, embossed in gold. "*Moby Dick?*"

He thumbed through the book as Kolman pointed to the front. "A volunteer at the station found it in a drawer. Hidden, forgotten, who knows? It's inscribed."

Drayco turned to the beginning and read the handwritten inscription aloud. "To my beloved Marty. May you enter the Universal Consciousness in Akasha and tap into the seventh vibration. Love, Deirdre."

"Speaking of the Beatles, that inscription could be straight from the '60s."

"It's from a class project of Deirdre Pinnick's. A spiritual mysticism known as the Akashic Records."

"Well, then. Sorry if I've wasted your time. At the very least, Marty's father might want the book. For sentimental reasons."

"I'll pass it along when I see him next. He's got a new construction job in Virginia Beach."

Kolman rubbed his mustache. "Good to hear. Marty was worried when his father missed out on that condo project."

An image of that monstrosity—that wasn't being fair, more like abomination—popped into Drayco's mind. "New building projects are springing up everywhere around here."

"Plenty of eyesores left. There's the crumbling train depot in Savage Town. And that abandoned amusement park in Paintersville. Don't think we're in jeopardy of turning into Ocean City."

"Lord, no. I prefer the old-world charm and slower pace of life."

"Then you should come out on the boat with me. No civilization in sight. You sit in one spot for hours gathering data and specimens."

Drayco smiled. "You must love your job."

"I care about our oceans. Their health is our health. If they die, so do we. How can you not be passionate over that?"

Drayco handed him the clay necklace he'd brought downstairs with him. "You have any idea what those symbols mean?"

Kolman studied it, then passed the necklace back. "Resembles a Native American artifact. Local archaeology?"

"It was Marty's. And from the looks of it, handmade."

"I had no idea he was interested in crafts. But he was a multi-talented young man."

Kolman excused himself to head home to Cherie, and Drayco started to drop the book and necklace off in his room before deciding to seek out Maida instead. She was working on dinner in anticipation of two new B&B guests that evening.

"Hate to interrupt you, Maida." He handed her the book so she could read the inscription. "But when you and Marty discussed the Akashic Records and 'karmic debts,' was there talk of anything like this?"

She studied the words Deirdre had written. "Not that I recall. What in the world is the seventh vibration?"

"The Akashic philosophy is complicated. Basically, there are seven planes of existence. The first is our physical realm, and the others are forms of energy. The seventh, or highest, level is pure energy where you transcend time and space. Vibration refers to the movement of the atomic structure, a manifestation of the Creator."

Maida re-read the inscription. "Everyone has to find their own way to God. One way or another, we all get there in the end."

"Even suicides?"

"I'm aware various religions frown on suicide. Deny them mourning rites or bury them in unsanctified ground. To me, that's a bigger sin than the act of taking one's life. I don't see them denying other mentally ill people a proper burial."

"No argument here." Drayco walked to the fridge and peered inside, hoping for iced tea. With a happy sigh, he grabbed the pitcher. He'd just poured himself some and raised the glass to his lips when his phone rang.

It was Reece. "I know this has nothing whatsoever to do with your case. But I happen to have info you'll find interesting. Well, *I* find it interesting. As a mere mortal, I don't think I'd be allowed in."

"Allowed in where, Reece?"

"That construction site where the new condos are going up. I got a call from an informant—" he headed off the retort Drayco was going to say. "We historians have those, too. *My* informant tells me when the crew was digging up a trench for utilities, they found something strange."

"Please tell me it's a pirate treasure. That would be fun."

There was a pause on the other end. "How did you know?"

"Reece, I was joking."

"You must be psychic. Not sure I'd call it a treasure per se since a single gold coin was found with the skeleton."

"Skeleton?"

"Ah-ha! I know something you don't. Yep, they dug up a skeleton. The sheriff and his team are there now."

"And you can't wait to find out if it's fodder for the Historical Society."

Drayco could practically see Reece beaming on the other end. "I knew you'd understand. You'll go and report back?"

"Wild horses, Reece." Drayco hung up and said to Maida. "I may be gone a while. Don't set a plate for me tonight in case."

She picked up a roasting pan complete with chicken. "Did I hear you mention a skeleton?"

"You heard right. It's ironic—it was found on Oakley Keys' old property."

Maida dropped the pan but caught it before it hit the floor. "I don't know whether to laugh or cry."

Drayco held the oven door open for her. "Let's hope this is one skeleton who found his seventh vibration."

20

It was dusk, but there was enough light for Drayco to see the tableau before him. On the right, a couple of the sheriff's deputies in their short-sleeve browns were talking to hard-hatted construction workers. Another group, composed of Nelia, Deputy Wesley Giles, and an EMT squad, stood over on the left.

As Drayco got out of his car and headed toward the left group, a man in a security guard's uniform held out a hand to stop him. A booming voice called out, "S'okay, Monroe. You can let him in."

Drayco took note of the string grid lines laid out, the shovels, spades, and brushes heaped in a pile, and the specimen baggies tagged. Nearby, Giles's camera and tripod lay on top of their case. The sheriff's crew had already been at the scene a few hours, likely arriving not long after Drayco left Sailor's office.

He joined Sheriff Sailor who was staring at a body bag being zipped up. Sailor gave Drayco a sideways look, saying, "Not terribly shocked to see you. But it means I have a mole in my department."

Worried Sailor would think it was Nelia, Drayco hurried to reply, "None of your staff. Another source may have mentioned a skeleton."

"What's left of one. The construction excavator demolished the entire crime scene. With any luck, we got most of the bones and fragments."

"Are you sure it's a crime, Sheriff?"

"Hard to say. Not until the M.E. in Norfolk gives it a thorough inspection. I'll order a rush on it for a quickie prelim. What's your opinion, Mr. Crime Consultant?"

"Perhaps it's the Eastern Shore Mafia burying bodies under construction sites."

"Closest thing we have is the always-slippery Caleb Quintier, who somehow manages to stay out of prison."

"How is ole Caleb doing? Haven't heard you mention him lately."

"Been lying low since that incident with you a year ago when you almost nailed him. Wouldn't put it past him to do this."

"He practically told me he prefers burying his bodies at sea."

Sailor scratched his head. "You serious?"

"Wouldn't call it a true confession. But he wasn't terribly worried what I thought."

Sailor tipped his hat brim. "With any luck, this will turn out to be a private grave from days of yore. I'll get my deputies to track down everyone who owned this damned property. From the Keys and Yaegles back to the Stone Age."

"Any signs it was recent? Maybe someone took advantage of the construction and hoped the body would be entombed under a million tons of concrete and steel."

"As I said, the workers obliterated any signs. We did find this," Sailor dangled a baggie with a gold coin inside.

Drayco took it from him and held it up for a closer look. "Looks old."

"Could be somebody buried a pile of gold here. That gold could come in handy—Sebastien Penry, for instance. He was determined to get this contracting job. Perhaps he wanted the chance to excavate the property first."

"Or someone planted the body to make the construction company look bad. I read of a similar incident in California."

"Only guy I know who hated the company enough to do that is Sebastien Penry."

Nelia said something to Giles that Drayco couldn't hear, then she trotted over to join Sailor's group. Drayco handed the baggie to her. "What do you make of this?"

She grabbed the bag by the corner with her dirt-caked gloved fingers and studied the coin through the plastic. "Handwriting and chemical analysis are more my area. But this could be nineteenth century or earlier."

Drayco replied, "Cherie Kolman may be able to help. She has a coin collecting hobby."

"You don't say," Sailor rubbed an ungloved hand across his chin. "By the way, Tyler, spread the word we need to keep this gold coin news quiet. Don't want every treasure hunter in creation tromping all over the place."

Drayco winced. "That little bird I mentioned may already know."

Sailor groaned. "I do have a mole."

"Not necessarily. One of the construction crew could be the culprit."

The sheriff barked out, "Tyler, add that crew to your list, too."

Right before the EMTs loaded up the body bag onto a gurney, Drayco stopped them. "Mind if I take a look?"

The head EMT eyed the sheriff who nodded, and the technician unzipped the bag filled to bursting with dirt that surrounded the remains. Sailor wasn't kidding with his "what was left of it" comment. More a pile of disconnected bones than a fully realized skeleton.

Nelia had followed Drayco and pointed inside the bag. "Parts of the jawbone are intact with some teeth."

"And part of the pelvic bone. We might get a gender." Drayco peered further inside. "Fragments of clothing, too."

A hard-hat-wearing crew member charged toward them, his face dark and pinched as he confronted the sheriff. "Your deputy tells me we can't work tomorrow. We're running way behind. My boss'll have my head."

Sailor gazed at the crewman calmly. "I'll speak with him. And let him know how important it is we have time to cull through the area. Every inch of it. Your excavator scattered evidence far and wide. It's going to take time to assess it all."

The man smacked his hard hat against his thigh. "That damned fool Johnson. Told him not to dig too deep. Not to stray from the painted outline my engineer laid down. And he did both. The idiot."

He turned on his heel and hurried to a small group of construction workers where he proceeded to read one of them the riot act. Poor Johnson. Drayco took one final look at the skeletal remains. Then he waved at the EMTs, and they promptly re-zipped and stowed the bag and were soon on their way.

Nelia knocked the dirt off her gloves. "Going to be a long night. Have to secure the area, for one. If you're right about that coin detail getting out, Drayco, we could have all kinds of treasure hunters trying to sneak in. It's times like this, I hate my job."

"Hate your job?"

She shook her head so hard her ponytail wagged like an actual horse's tail swatting flies. "Hate this kind of job."

"I'll do my part and tell my little bird not to tweet the details."

"Reece?"

"How did you guess?"

"Seems like something he'd know."

Drayco said, "Do you need coffee since you'll be here into the wee hours?"

"If I drink too much coffee, the hours won't be the only 'wee' I'll have to worry about." Nelia peered at the portable toilets and shuddered. "Should have you get me something salty instead."

"Your wish is my command, m'lady."

She smiled. It was a while since he saw her smile like that and the dimple that went along with it. "If you snag rations for me, you'll have to get some for the entire crew."

He took a head count. "Consider it done."

After they watched Sailor bark out commands to Giles, Nelia said, "Sorry if I snapped at you today. Guess it's all the stress."

"More than usual?"

"The same, but it wears you down. Not sure I can handle law school and part-time work. And there's Tim."

"You're going through with the divorce, then?" Drayco was tired of tip-toeing around that issue.

She cleared her throat and stooped to run a gloved hand through the dirt as if looking for bone fragments. "We've not had that talk. He's on the new meds, he has the new live-in assistant. Things are going better than they have in, well, I don't remember when."

"Does he still give you grief over the law school decision?" He didn't add, *And me?*

"He's been more upbeat. Hasn't brought up law school in months."

She changed the subject abruptly. "Assuming Sebastien Penry didn't kill his son, how's your suspect list doing?"

"The entire Pinnick clan have better motives."

"High-strung people, for sure."

"To be truthful, it could be any of Marty's friends or colleagues."

Nelia picked up an object from the soil and studied it before tossing it aside. "A rock. Yep, it's going to be a long night."

She straightened up, and he put his hand on her bare arm to steady her. It hit him that he shouldn't have done that. It's not something he'd do for Sailor, but she didn't appear to mind. For a moment, the look in her eyes was that of someone who hadn't minded at all.

What were they—teenagers? Talk about things wearing you down, this strange dance of theirs was worse than trying to play Bach fugues on a honky-tonk piano.

When Sailor tramped over to them, being careful to walk around the trench area, Drayco asked, "Soda, tea, or stronger? I'm buying."

"Don't tempt me with the stronger part. I could kill for a vodka and tonic."

"Sodas, it is. Have a feeling you'll need the caffeine."

Drayco headed off to Limping Mike's Bait Shop, figuring he may as well pick up a few bottles of Manhattan Special espresso soda for himself. If they still carried it. They were the lone store selling the drinks in the area, but with the changes happening on the shore, you could never predict which institutions would hang in there.

The approach of dusk brought with it the calls of katydids, crickets, and chorus frogs. An odd mix to his synesthesia brain. A combo of purple sparklers and turquoise darts.

It was on a June night like this when Alexander Vucasovich took his life. Drayco had just gotten word from his orthopedic surgeon they wouldn't have to implant screws or plates in his hand. But the doc also said Drayco might never regain the full feeling and range of motion, as good as death to a pianist. Drayco went to Vuca's house to tell him and. . .

No, no more of that. Not now.

The evening critter chorus conjured up an impression of an interwoven community that still talked to one another. If only they'd witnessed the demise of the person whose skeletal remains were wending their way to Norfolk. But perhaps they did? Maybe their ancestors were there and had handed down the story to successive generations.

Drayco slid into the driver's seat of the Starfire and turned on the cheap plastic battery-operated fan he'd mounted to the dashboard next to his toy piano ornament. He should check out Sailor's vodka and tonic because Drayco's zoological musings could be a sign *he* needed something stronger than soda.

The skeleton find disturbed him, but why? If it turned out to be old, then it didn't matter, did it? This was one coincidence that was probably a coincidence. Too bad he couldn't get that message through to his instinct-o-meter, which was pegging off the chart.

He had the sudden urge to seek out the comfort of Darcie, but that ship had sailed and sunk off the coast, for better or worse. Yep, Sheriff Sailor's vodka and tonic sounded pretty damn good.

21

Tess stifled a series of yawns. What did that adage say? "Early to rise makes a man healthy, wealthy, and wise?" A frickin' man, yeah. Wasn't doing much for her today if it ever did.

She wasn't a huge fan of piloting a boat, but there were a few upsides to going out early in the morning—calmer, quieter, just her and a few fishing boats. But after taking water temperature and nitrogen measurements and collecting specimens, she was eager to get back and start work in the labs. She powered down the engine to maneuver into shore and spied a figure on the pier as if waiting for her.

When she pulled into the slip and secured the boat, she saw her visitor was Antonio. Why wasn't he at work this morning? Then she remembered they'd started that weird schedule thing at the plant. A Tuesday morning might be different from a Wednesday morning. God, what a bitch that would be.

She hadn't seen him since Marty's funeral, and he didn't look himself. He sported a few days' worth of stubble, it looked like his hair hadn't been washed in a week, and his shirt was stained. Even his basketball shorts were on inside-out, the tag flapping in the breeze.

Tess tied up the boat and called out to him. "What's up, Antonio? Why are you here? Couldn't this wait until after work?"

He hopped into the boat with her and sank down on the bench seat. "I know what you're up to. You think you can keep it up without anybody knowing? It's gonna come out."

She grabbed the specimen box filled with sponges, sea slugs, and polychaete worms from the floor of the boat and hauled it onto the dock. "I know what I'm doing. And it's none of your business."

"If Marty was here," Antonio slumped against the side of the boat, "he wouldn't like it. He'd tell you to stop."

Antonio's eyes were bloodshot, but Tess didn't smell any booze. She sat next to him. "Look, Antonio. I hate seeing you so unhappy. It makes me unhappy."

He fixed his gaze on her specimen box and didn't respond. He was so skinny, she wondered if he'd skipped breakfast. And a lot of other meals.

She said, "Marty's death hit you hard. I understand how you felt. How you really felt. You had a crush on him, and I'm okay with that."

Antonio lifted his head. "A crush?" He laughed bitterly. "I loved him. But he only had eyes for that skank, Deirdre."

"If it makes you feel any better, you'd have been much better for him."

His bleary eyes opened wider. "Can't believe you'd say that. I mean, I thought nobody would understand."

She had to fight the urge to push his hair off his face and stroke it. He had such lovely soft, thick dark hair. Even now, looking at him made her heart flutter and her stomach do flip flops. "I understand you more than you think."

He watched as a fish jumped out of the water, high enough to vault right into the boat, before it descended into the depths. "Wish I could do that."

"What?"

"Disappear. Get away from the world. Down there where it's dark and quiet. Swim along wherever you want, and nobody notices."

She lightly touched his arm. "Have you talked to anybody since Marty died? Maybe at a church—"

"They can't help. They can't undo what I did. No one can."

Tess must have missed something important because she wasn't following him at all. "What did you do?"

"It was my gun that killed Marty."

"But someone stole it. That wasn't your fault."

Antonio buried his head in his hands and stayed silent.

Tess felt increasingly desperate. She'd do anything to cheer him up but didn't have the slightest idea how. "I could get you get you a job here at the station. You wouldn't have to work in the chicken plant anymore."

She barely heard his muffled voice, but she made out the words. "Trading the smell of chicken shit for rotting fish guts. No, thanks."

"But I know how much you and your mother need the money. This gig would pay better than the hourly wage the plant pays you. Salary and bennies."

He lifted his head. "I'm such a disappointment to Mom. She deserves better."

Tess wracked her brain, trying to come up with something, anything, to nudge him out of the dumps. "She loves you, Antonio. That's all that matters."

"It's that song. That song did it. It's all my fault."

She knew what he meant, and she was damned sick of hearing it. "That frickin' song didn't kill Marty. And you're being a drama queen. Besides, I suspect Marty's father and that detective think it was murder. Unless you're the one who murdered him, you don't have anything to feel guilty about."

Antonio clutched his knees with his hands so tightly, his knuckles turned white. For a moment, his eyes flashed, but he didn't say a word.

Oh my god. Had she hit on the truth? That someone did kill Marty, and that someone was Antonio? Could he? Would he?

No, he'd never do that intentionally. Not gentle, soulful Antonio. "Look, Antonio, if there was an accident—it wouldn't be your fault, right? Talk to me. I can help."

He jumped up so fast, the boat rocked violently, and Tess grabbed on to the edge to keep from slipping onto the bottom. He yelled out, "No one can help. Marty's gone, and that's that. It's too late."

"Antonio—" But her cries fell on deaf ears as he scrambled onto the dock and ran around the side of the building.

She toyed with running after him, grabbing him in her arms and holding him tight until he calmed down. Should she? *For once, Tess, stop thinking, and just do it.* She sprinted along the dock in the same direction he'd taken. By the time she got to the front, he was in his car and peeling out of the parking lot.

Judson Kolman popped outside, a quizzical look on his face. "Everything okay?"

Tess replied, "That was Marty's friend, Antonio. He's not taking Marty's death too well."

Kolman rubbed his mustache. "Marty mentioned him on more than one occasion. They went fishing together. Knew each other since childhood."

"They were very close. And Antonio feels guilty it's his gun that killed Marty."

"I knew Marty didn't own one. But I didn't know the gun he used belonged to a friend."

"It was stolen. I told him none of this was his fault. He didn't want to listen."

"If he trusts you, you can chat with him after work. I'll bet he could use a good friend."

Yeah, she'd try to catch him at home later. Give him the name of a therapist to see. Who was that minister Marty said he'd talked to once? Maida Jepson, wasn't it?

Despite the warm air that was eighty degrees at ten in the morning, goose bumps popped up on her arms. Antonio was so many things—sensitive, funny, gentle. Or he was once. He was also the last person on Earth she'd dream could be a killer.

If only everything were different, weren't so frickin' mixed up. She could have made him happy, could have helped him reach his potential. Could have saved his soul.

22

Drayco pulled up in front of a house with warped white siding, one of three nearly identical homes in a row. He tried not to yawn, but he'd stayed up late talking to the sheriff's crew at the construction site last night.

The person who answered the door wasn't who he'd expected. "I might have the wrong house. I wanted to speak to Antonio Skye."

The woman looked him up and down as if assessing potential threats. "I do not need a new roof. Or windows. Nor does my son."

This must be Rosita Skye. He saw a family resemblance, the same wavy black hair and upturned nose, though she was much shorter than Antonio. "I spoke with your son the other day at the plant. He helped with questions I had concerning Marty Penry."

She thrust out her chin. "We talked to the sheriff."

"I don't work for the sheriff. My name is Scott Drayco. Marty's father hired me to make some sense of his son's death."

"*Qué pena.* I feel very sorry for that man, his father. Must be painful for him to live with such a horrible thing."

Her eyes landed on his blue Starfire out front, appraising it, still appraising him. "You missed Antonio. He came home an hour ago. To grab something from his apartment, then off to work."

Drayco asked, "His apartment? I have this as his home address."

"*Sí,*" she said, pointing to a smaller garage-sized building behind the house. "Studio, one bath."

The garage didn't look that big, but since few Eastern Shore homes had basements, it made sense. "Maybe you can help me. Marty and Antonio were such good friends, you must have known Marty pretty well."

She chewed on her cheek, her chin jutting forward. But instead of the dismissal he expected, she waved him inside. Rosita might not have much money, but you couldn't tell it from the interior of her home. He'd always heard of floors so clean you could eat off of them, but this was the first time he believed it. The space was decorated much better than his townhome.

During his quick scan of the room, he began to understand the depths of Rosita's creativity—an end table crafted from an old decoupaged suitcase, a coffee table made from a recycled door with glass panes. He caught a sweet, citrus-honey aroma and traced it to a vase of magnolia cuttings.

"You have a lovely home here, Mrs. Skye."

She smoothed a ridge in the pastel-blue sofa cover. "*Gracias.* My Antonio never notices such things."

"I understand Antonio and Marty were friends since childhood. When did you last see Marty yourself?"

"A week or two before he passed."

"Did he act normally at that time?"

"I not talk to him. He go straight to Antonio's apartment."

Drayco took a stab in the dark. "You didn't like having Marty in your home?"

"I did not want them to be friends. Not after. . ." Her cheeks flushed a deep red.

"They had an argument?"

"Oh, no, I do not think so. Antonio and I did."

"You argued over Marty?"

Rosita rubbed her finger along the Bible on the end table next to her. "My son, he was under his spell. Antonio had unnatural feelings for Marty."

"You were afraid Antonio was gay?"

She hissed through her teeth. "That word, gay. What does it mean? Sounds so happy. But it does not make Antonio happy, does it? I give him books to read. To make him see he is wrong. That I am praying for him."

She grabbed a patchwork-quilted pillow on the sofa and squeezed the edges so hard, Drayco was afraid the stuffing would explode. "So many rumors. So much ugliness. I know what they think, what they say."

Before Drayco could ask her to explain further, she continued, "They think my Antonio did it. Killed Marty. The gun was his, they say. This, after he reports it stolen. And the police, they saw the broken window, they saw the damage."

"Antonio said the gun used on Marty was his, a Smith & Wesson. I understand it originally belonged to his father?"

"*Sí.*" She squeezed the pillow harder. "My husband is in prison, Señor Drayco. For murder. But not using that gun. Choked a man with his bare hands."

"It must have been hard on you and Antonio."

"I work with people who whisper about my husband. And now they whisper about my son. Like father, like son, they say. I would leave, but it is the one job I can get."

"Does Antonio hear the gossip?"

She shook her head. "I do not know if he hears like I do. Off in his world. A world where I cannot go. But I hoped he would do better. Like Marty. Go to college, make something of himself."

"Why didn't he?"

"My husband was lazy. Now, Antonio."

"Was Antonio jealous of Marty and his success?"

"Jealous?" She frowned. "He did not say so. He is a bright boy, my son. But he never felt he belonged. I blame myself."

"Why?"

"His father in jail, his *mamacíta* working at the plant. I was afraid to be too strict. That I would push him away."

"He can still go to college if he chooses. He might be a late bloomer."

She half-smiled, exposing a few missing teeth. Thrift store salvage worked for design but not for dental care. "I spoke with him the other day. About community college. His eyes, they lit up. Maybe as you say, a late bloomer."

"If Marty and Tess and Deirdre can do it, then Antonio can, too. The other member of their high school group, Lena Bing—she works with you at the plant?"

"Lena is a such a nice girl. I wish she and Antonio. . .but no, she had eyes for Marty. Then look how he treated her. *Asqueroso.*"

Drayco asked, "She broke it off with him the second time, as I understand it. Said he was aloof, acting oddly."

"She came to her senses. Good for her."

He doubted Lena would entirely agree. "Has Antonio mentioned the 'suicide song'?"

"He would not have anything to do with such a song. So evil. Suicide is such a selfish thing to do, why would anyone make a song about it?"

"And he never brought up the Akashic Records?"

She sounded it aloud slowly. "Ah kah shik? Is that where you play this suicide song? On that record?"

He tried not to smile. "It's more of a spiritual philosophy."

She shook her head. "I raise my boy in the Catholic church. No cults. Such wickedness. I always knew Marty would corrupt Antonio."

"From what I can tell, it's harmless, Mrs. Skye. If Antonio believes any of it, he'll be in no danger."

Drayco shifted in his seat. Way too low for his six-four frame. "Getting back to the gun, were you aware Antonio kept it with him in the car?"

"I did not want it in the house, so he took it away." She clutched the pillow to her chest, wrapping her arms around it, holding it, holding in a lot more.

Seeing her distress and not wanting to push her any further, Drayco thanked her and let himself out. As he sat in his car with the engine running, he replayed their conversation in his mind. She hadn't faked her distress. But the source of it was the question.

Was she only thinking of Antonio's well-being? Or was she so upset with her son's crush on Marty, so fearful of a perceived evil, she took matters into her own hands? She wouldn't be the first religious avenger to do so. And a Mama Bear whose cub was threatened would do anything to protect him. But why break into her son's car to get the gun? That break-in made no sense from any angle.

He checked the time. Three-thirty. He had a slight chance to catch a normally tethered bird during one of the few times she was untethered. The Wallops Visiting Center closed at four, and with any luck, he just might make it.

23

"I shouldn't talk to you without my father," Deirdre said, sliding next to Drayco on top the Wallops Visitor Center observation deck. He'd caught her right before closing, but she still offered to take him upstairs to the viewing area. The stiff breeze at that level threatened to whip her pleated plaid skirt over her head, Marilyn Monroe-style.

He replied, "You're not charged with a crime. And I'm not stalking you."

"The stalking part, now that's a shame." She smiled up at him and twisted a strand of red hair around her fingers. "Romantic up here, isn't it?"

"Perfect for watching a rocket launch." He studied the metal audience risers on the ground, with some of the Eastern Shore's untamed tidal marshes spreading out beyond.

"One of the best around. There's also Assateague Island, the Chincoteague Museum. Mason and George Island landings. But this is much better."

She edged closer. "Don't keep me in suspense. What did you want to ask me?" By now, she was a mere foot away. He had to wonder how committed that engagement to her fiancé was.

"I'm confused about your restraining order against Marty. Seems like innocent lovesick behavior, despite what your parents say. Why take such a drastic measure?"

"I didn't. I know, I know. I told you and the sheriff it was my idea, that I made my father do it. No bigs."

"Then your father orchestrated the whole thing?"

"Actually, it was all my mother's doing. She never approved of Marty. Too low class. Beneath me." Deirdre stopped smiling, her fists clenched by her side.

"You didn't agree?"

"My mother has to do things her way or no way. Everything must be perfect. She went ballistic when I got this." Deirdre pointed to the tattoo on her neck. "And god forbid if I gained two pounds. Or wore the wrong jeans. Or cut my hair short. Or went to college for anything other than an MRS degree."

"What did you major in?"

"Home Ec." She shuddered. "Mom picked it."

"What degree did you have in mind?"

"Something in the sciences. Not marine biology like Marty. Another kind of biology. Or engineering. My uncle gave me a construction set when I was a kid. I loved it, but Mom took it away. She said that's for boys."

Drayco opted for a little more personal space and took a step back to lean against the railing. "Your fiancé is an engineer. Marty was a marine biologist. I don't see where your mother's 'low class' idea fits in."

"Dale's father is a doctor. Marty's father is in construction. It's all about pedigree."

"And you didn't agree with this pedigree issue?"

"My mother and I can't agree on anything. And Dad, he goes along with what she wants. Yes, dear, whatever you say, dear."

Drayco moved again to avoid a wasp. "Did she actively hate Marty?"

"You should ask her. If you can get a straight answer. She's an old pro at turning everything back at you."

"Did she hate him enough to kill him?"

Deirdre's eyes widened as if the notion had never occurred to her. "I can see why Dad didn't want me to talk to you."

"And yet, you are."

"You have such fabulous blue-violet eyes. You've got me hypnotized. Or that's what I'll tell Dad."

Drayco tilted his head. "And he'll believe you, just like that?"

"I've got him wrapped around my finger. Daddy's baby girl. He'll believe anything I say."

"Okay, then. Stare into my eyes and tell me about Antonio Skye."

Her hands unclenched, and she fiddled with the hem of her sleeve instead. "I thought Antonio would turn out to be a sculptor or whatever. The broody type. We all played musical partners for a while. Experimental sex. It was fun. No strings. Antonio's heart wasn't in it. Or he had a thing for Lena."

"You said experimental sex. Did Marty hook up with any men?"

Deirdre stopped fiddling with her sleeve as a smile flared across her face. "Marty was definitely hetero. Oh my, did he know how to make a girl sing. If you get my drift."

"Was he in love with you?"

She laughed. "You don't pull any punches, do you?"

"Boxing is fun."

"I wouldn't know. But I do know love isn't all it's cracked up to be. I mean, couples together for decades end up hating each other."

"I take that as a 'no,' Marty wasn't in love with you?"

She shrugged. "Does it matter now?"

"Would he have killed himself when you didn't return his affections?"

"No."

"You're that certain."

"Yes. I'd know." Her answer came a little too quickly.

He studied her face as her gaze darted back and forth between him and the door. "When I was at your house, you said you didn't feel guilt over Marty's death. That it had 'nothing to do with you,' he was unstable. You really believe that?"

She didn't say anything for a moment and then replied slowly, "Except for the unstable part. I mean, so he was a bit down lately. No bigs. Who isn't?"

"What I find depressing is that a healthy, bright young man died for no good reason."

"You said died."

He stared at her, unsure what she meant, and she added, "You didn't say he killed himself. You think it was murder?"

"I honestly think you're not being straight with me."

"Oh, I'm straight, all right. Very." She winked at him.

"Let's discuss the other two members of your high school group, Lena and Tess."

"What's there to say? We hung out for a while, grew apart."

"Lena was a rival for Marty's attention."

Deirdre laughed. "Not so much. She wanted him for herself, I wanted to have fun. He preferred my kind of fun."

"Why break up with him?"

"Mom made me. Threatened to take away my allowance. I was barely twenty and living at home. Besides, since Marty was in college in North Carolina by then. I didn't get to see him."

"And then he hooked up with Lena a second time."

"Is there any doubt he got depressed? She's a real downer."

"And Tess?"

"Tess is a free spirit, like me. We get along fine. But we're not besties. We text each other now and then."

Drayco ran his hand along the weathered railing and was rewarded with a splinter. "The whole Akashic Records bit is an odd philosophy to attract a free spirit. Like Tess, like you."

Deirdre nibbled on her fingernail. "Look, I should get back down below. I'm closing today. Got to make sure the center is secure when the guard arrives."

She turned around so fast, a key ring fell out of her pocket. The dozen keys it held jangled to the floor as it skidded to the edge of the deck. "No!" she cried out and slipped as she lunged to snag the keys before they fell off the building.

Drayco beat her to it, grabbed the key ring, and handed it over.

"Thanks. It's not *my* keys I'm worried about. Got some of Dad's on here, too." She seemed more in a hurry to leave, and he followed her as she flew down the stairs into the reception area.

Right before he left, he asked, "The other day, you said you had no idea how Marty became interested in the suicide song. Remember better now?"

Deirdre hesitated and then said, "Oh, look, there's Pete Jarden, the guard. Guard Jarden. Never noticed it rhymed before."

She hurried to the front door and held it open for Drayco. "Enjoyed our chat. We'll have to do it again. As long as we don't talk shop."

She stopped babbling and put a hand on his backside and pushed him toward the door. "Nice ass, by the way."

He barely made it outside before she closed the door tightly. The security guard eyed him with suspicion as Drayco walked toward his car. The guard continued to keep a watchful eye until Drayco was driving away onto the access road toward the main road.

Since his new battery-operated fan wasn't much help, he opened his car windows. The tang of the salty breeze and muskiness from the live eelgrass followed him for miles. The only other time he'd visited the Wallops launch facility was a trip with attorney Benny Baskin. But it was hard to forget what a contrast the place was—the wildness and simplicity of nature hosting the most technical pursuit of humankind.

What to make of Deirdre? She'd developed the fine art of manipulation honed from years of pitting her father against her mother to get what she wanted. That didn't make her a killer per se. But why did she shut him down whenever he brought up either the Akashic Records or the suicide song?

Drayco got a sudden whiff of fishy air as the wind direction changed. Not all that unpleasant, unlike the occasional rotten-egg smell from the tidal flats. Surprising how quickly you got used to it. Like Sailor's cousin and his paper-mill neighbor.

An osprey flew from its perch in a nearby Spanish oak tree and soared into the air as if trying to do its best impression of one of the Wallops rockets. Drayco envied it. Flight without engines.

He braked hard when a sika deer ran across the road right in his path. The Eastern Shore's natural version of a texting pedestrian not paying attention? He watched with awe as the animal expertly skipped among the mini-islands in the marsh until it disappeared in a thicket of scrub. In the District, the chief wildlife specimens were rats the size of house cats.

They fought for survival, these deer and those rats. What did they feel? Pure instinct or more? They didn't have Marty's Cousteau dreams or Vuca's music, and every day was a fight for existence.

Maybe it was better not to feel, to dream, to imagine you can strap yourself into a tin can on top of a rocket and be shot toward the moon. Maybe the human brain hadn't yet adapted to reconcile the subsistence-versus-stargazer factions fighting for dominance.

He saw the curious face of the deer peeking at him through a gap in the scrub as if to say, *Is this human going nuts?* Drayco released the brake to continue on his way. Sheriff Sailor's favorite vodka and tonic sounded better and better all the time.

24

Lena said she and Marty were at the Boardwalk Bar on the night he mentioned "something big," and Drayco tracked the place down. It wasn't in Chincoteague proper but outside town and whimsically named. As in, the "Boardwalk" Bar was nowhere near the water and didn't have so much as a sidewalk, let alone the board variety.

If the building *had* possessed the good fortune of being on the waterfront, the cobalt-blue sky would be meeting the cerulean-blue water about now. It was something Drayco called the twilight two-step, when the ocean began its dance with the night. The lack of sea breezes wasn't helping the heat wave much, making the Starfire's on-the-fritz AC situation particularly painful.

Before he went inside the bar, Drayco pulled off his sweat-soaked shirt and put on a black tee from the Starfire. His black shirt and black pants blended in nicely with the black paint in the darkened bar. The place must have had to pay for windows by the inch as there were few of them.

He passed a table of three men as he walked inside and stopped dead in his tracks when he heard the word "skeleton." He gave a quick survey of the trio and recognized a construction crew member from the condo the other night. Fortunately, the guy didn't remember Drayco— but the sheriff's orders to keep the find quiet obviously weren't being taken seriously. Was this "the mole?"

Drayco headed to the bar and the lone bartender, a tall Nordic type who sported the name tag, "Greg." Drayco pointed at the tag, "Don't often see bartenders wearing those."

Greg snorted. "Got tired of 'hey you,' so I thought I'd try this. Works ten percent of the time."

Drayco scanned the room and the patrons. "You don't get a bunch of regulars?"

"Trade comes and goes with the seasons. And the workers."

"I was hoping there might be one or two regulars I can talk to. I'm seeking information on a young couple who were here. Little over a month ago."

Greg picked up a glass and wiped it with a towel. "A month is an eternity in here. But if it's information you want, you should chat up Dennis Frischman. If that's his real name." Greg nodded at a man seated in the back corner, alone. "He's in here every day, same time."

"Not his real name?"

"Shady background. Doesn't look that smart, but he sees more than people know. A former Wall Street type, or so they say. Quit after he got tired of the rat race and is living off his savings. Or got canned when he got caught doing something illegal. Take your pick."

"An interesting character. Is he always alone?"

"Always. Has a reputation for being tough. Gotta wonder if it's more mystique. But the roughest guys in here avoid him, so there's that."

Drayco stuffed a twenty into the tip jar. "I'll keep that in mind." He headed toward the table Greg had indicated, pulled out a chair, and sat down.

Frischman looked at the chair and then at Drayco. "Not many people have the guts to do that without asking. Must be a cop."

"Private."

"You don't look it."

"And you don't look like ex-Wall Street." Frischman wore a mustard-yellow floral shirt, a navy beanie cap, and a golden fishhook earring in one ear that matched his golden beard—although ashes from his cigarette threatened to turn that beard gray.

"Do marine salvage now." Frischman observed Drayco through his teashade glasses, hardly blinking. "Let me guess. You want information."

"That's what I do for a living. Dig for dirt. Just not the same kind as our construction friends over there."

"What makes you think I want to help?"

"Absolutely nothing. And I used my last twenty on Greg." Which was true, since Drayco hadn't made it to the bank yet to replenish his wallet.

"Not a very successful private cop, then, are you?"

"Depends upon who you ask."

Frischman studied him for a full minute in silence and then said, "Go ahead with your questions. And I'll decide whether I like what you're asking."

"Fair enough. There was a young couple in here a month ago, in their twenties, a man and a woman. Both would have been on the thin side, with sandy-blondish hair. And he had a soul patch with a mustache."

"That type would have stood out like Girl Scouts in here."

"You did see them?"

"Once. I heard the kid call his friend Lena." Frischman tapped his cigarette into an ashtray. "Kept an eye on them in case. Babes in the woods."

Thank god the air from the ceiling fans was blowing the cigarette smoke away from Drayco. The last thing he needed was burning eyes. He said, "On one of their visits, the young man told Lena 'something big' was coming his way."

Frischman took another drag on the cigarette and blew smoke in Drayco's direction. So much for the burning eyes. "Might have caught bits of their conversation. Overheard what you said, but I figured the kid was getting an inheritance. Or he had an insider stock trading trip." Frischman chuckled at that.

"You didn't hear any details, then?"

"The kid had drunk too much. Clearly wasn't used to handling it. They left shortly after."

"Did either of them come in—together or separately—later?"

"Haven't seen them since. Have to admit the kid made me jealous. Mentioned new tech gear. I took it from what he said, he worked at the marine biology station. Sure could use gear like that for wreck salvage and finding boat parts. It's wasted on fish."

"Does the name Marty Penry mean anything to you?"

"Should it?"

"That's the young man you overheard. Allegedly killed himself a month ago."

Frischman blew out a perfect smoke ring. "In my day, it was guys throwing themselves off tall buildings. But we don't have tall buildings around here. That new three-story condo development is as tall as it gets. Why would a bright kid like that kill himself?"

"It's possible he didn't."

"Murder by suicide? And this 'something big' is in the middle of it?"

When Drayco didn't reply, Frischman said, "You don't know." Then, he added, "You said his name was Penry? The guys in the front," he waved at the construction group, "mentioned that name once. It was a Sebastien Penry."

"That's his father."

"Don't know they had either good or bad to say about the guy. Keeps to himself, they said. Doesn't hang out with the guys much. But he's a contractor, right? The boss, not the bossed."

A tall man to Frischman's left lurched up from his table, swaying, and stumbled against Frischman. The man swung around and put up his fists as if it were Frischman's fault. But when he saw who he'd stumbled into, he dropped his fists and backed away. "Sorry, man. My mistake."

Drayco was itching to learn Frischman's story since he hadn't met any ex-Wall Street types who could get that reaction from the spitting image of Hulk Hogan. Drayco glanced at Frischman's full beer mug and noted the lack of alcohol odor on him. "You're a recovering alcoholic?"

Frischman raised his mug in salute. "Guess you're not such a bad private cop, after all."

"Why come here? Most former alcoholics would run far and fast."

"To prove I can do it. I get one of these every night. And I pour it out in the bathroom every night."

"You've never been tempted, not once?"

"Every single damn night. That's why I come."

"Face your fears head-on?"

"Exactly."

Drayco excused himself to order a soda and an extra mug from Greg. When he returned to the table, he poured half of his soda into the empty mug and pushed it over. "I don't like to drink alone."

Frischman grinned and took a gulp. "Would be better with rum."

Drayco smiled briefly and chugged some to keep up with his companion.

Frischman asked, "How'd the kid die?"

"A gunshot to the head in a lonely clearing in the middle of nowhere."

"Doesn't make sense. Three-quarters of suicides occur at home."

"Are you an expert on the subject?"

"Knew someone who did it, so I read up. Hell, we all know someone, right?" He studied Drayco's face. "You do, I can tell. I know the look."

Drayco didn't like being on the receiving end of psychoanalysis, so he surveyed their fellow barflies. Other than the construction trio and the staggering drunk, their only other companions included two rejects from Edward Hopper's *Nighthawks*.

He asked, "You must know your share of locals. Say, Emmerson Pinnick and his wife?"

Frischman grunted. "Pinnick had a spot on the local radio station. One of those very loud, very obnoxious ads. He's an ambulance chaser."

"He and his wife, Barbara, fancy themselves as more high society."

"Known of plenty of attorneys in my day. All ambulance chasers at heart." Frischman slurped the last of his soda. "Not too bad. Don't have to go to AA for sugar addictions, either."

He thumped his chest and belched. "Did you say his wife was Barbara Pinnick? My ex-girlfriend knew a Barbara Pinnick. Gotta be the same one. My ex hated her guts."

"Why?"

"A master manipulator, that one. They were both up for president of some charity board or other. Someone started a rumor my ex was a druggie. And the day she was scheduled to go to a pre-election meeting to give her stump speech, come to find out someone had slashed her tires with a knife."

"Your ex thinks it was Barbara who was behind it?"

"She did a little investigative reporting and traced the rumors to Barbara. And who else would have cared that badly she not make it to the speech?"

"I'll lay wagers your ex didn't win the election."

Frischman patted the side of his nose. "That's the way of the Backyard Bitch since time immemorial, right? Me, I'd handle it in a back alley."

He grinned, revealing a set of perfectly matched teeth. His "salvage business" must be doing gangbusters if he could afford expensive dental care, unlike Rosita Skye.

"Make sure it's not Caleb Quintier in that back alley with you."

The half-smile on Frischman's face morphed into a steely glare. "You friends with Quintier?"

"We bumped into each other on a case a year ago. He took me out on his nice boat."

"And you came out alive?" Frischman's face relaxed. "Then you truly are a good private cop."

He leaned forward to add, "You wanted information, so I'll give you a tip. Mr. Ambulance Chaser is in debt up to his eyeballs, my ex found out. If he makes partner in his firm, it's an extra hundred grand a year to start. After five years, another hundred."

"And law firms prefer partners-to-be with solid reputations."

"This young Marty fellow. Did he have something incriminating on Pinnick?"

Now there was an interesting idea. Perhaps the restraining order on Marty wasn't only about Deirdre. But what could Marty have discovered that was so dangerous it would lead an attorney to murder?

Drayco drained the rest of his soda. When he pulled out his last ten-dollar bill and slapped it on the table, Frischman pointed at it. "What's that for?"

"A down payment. I'll give you the remainder some other time."

25

Was it being closer to the seashore or the relaxing comfort of Maida Jepson's TLC? Whatever the reason, Drayco slept orders of magnitude better in Cape Unity than the District. Most of the time. Before going to bed last night, he'd made the mistake of playing the original Suicide Sonata on the Jepsons' Chickering piano again. And then listening to the suicide song on his phone over and over.

He had not slept well.

He'd tried his best not to be cranky at breakfast with the Jepsons, but when he entered Sheriff Sailor's office, the man immediately said, "Someone got up on the wrong side of the bunk."

Drayco didn't sit in his usual chair, preferring to perch on the edge of an olive-green wooden storage locker. When Nelia popped in, Drayco motioned for her to take the chair. She looked at him as she sat. "Bad night?"

"Too much caffeine," he lied. "So, Sheriff, you managed to sweet-talk the M.E. in Norfolk?"

"I keep sending Dr. Fireside business. She likes me." Sailor corrected himself. "Strike that. You're the one who keeps sending her the corpses."

"This skeleton isn't my doing."

"You're right. But if you were hoping for a tie-in to the Marty Penry case, forget it. Unless Marty's father found the skeleton somewhere else. And then planted it to get revenge on the construction company. Oh, and the report rules out everyone's favorite local villain, Caleb Quintier."

Nelia spoke up. "The skeleton must be old, then."

Sailor picked up a legal pad where he'd jotted down notes. "Dr. Fireside found fragments of clothing, including buttons that date to around 1710, give or take a few years."

Nelia replied, "Few residents on the Eastern Shore at that time. There were Native Americans, but I doubt they wore buttons."

Sailor added, "And a few English settlers, right? History wasn't my best subject."

Drayco said, "Blackbeard, Calico Jack Rackham, and other pirates sailed these waters in the early 1700s. On both sides of the shore, the Atlantic and the Chesapeake."

"That again?" Sailor grimaced. "Last thing I need is a horde of treasure hunters descending on the town digging up property. Even Giles got all misty over it. Said it could pay for gear for those new twins of his."

Nelia shook her head. "If it's not buried in some safe hidey-hole, it's probably long gone. Anyway, we don't have pirates now. Unless you count oyster poachers."

"And *they're* out of my jurisdiction." Sailor tapped the legal pad. "One weird fact about that skeleton. The M.E. thinks the poor schmuck had six fingers on his left hand. Oh, and he was likely murdered."

"Murdered?" Drayco got up to peer over Sailor's shoulder at his notes and read them aloud. "The skull had a hole in one of the skull fragments. And Dr. Fireside found a musket ball among the debris in the body bag."

Nelia pursed her lips. "An ancient murder mystery is interesting, but it doesn't help with the Penry case. Or any other of our current cases."

Drayco asked, "What happens to the skeletal remains now? And any luck on tracking former owners of that property?"

Sailor grimaced. "The M.E. says she has no further claim or interest. But I got her to hold on to the remains a little longer. It was on

Earl Yaegle's property line, not Oakley Keys's by the way. We called Earl at his new home in Palm Beach. Said he'd never developed that area where we found the skeleton. Let it stay forested for privacy purposes and hunting."

"As I recall, Earl and his wife bought the property forty years ago."

"Could be a prior owner going way back. Giles is digging through the records and going down the list. So far, the other homeowners are all deceased. A dead end in more ways that one."

"The ancient murder may not be relevant to the Marty Penry case. But there may be more gold stashes buried around here. Or somebody found a treasure map."

When Sailor glared at him, Drayco replied, "Hey, it could happen. It's not only in the movies."

Nelia said, "If Marty was the one who found such a map and was digging up gold, someone might have killed him for it."

"Or, he discovered another person digging it up, and they killed him to hide their tracks." Drayco pictured the clearing where Marty was found. No signs of digging, but he hadn't checked the environs farther out. Something to add to his list.

Sailor groaned. "That's reaching, you two. Odds are, there's no connection between our skeleton and Marty Penry. Mere coincidence." He held up his hand when Drayco opened his mouth to speak. "Yeah, yeah, I know you hate coincidences. But they do happen, or there wouldn't be a word for it in the dictionary."

Drayco replied, "Marty did tell Lena 'something big' was going to happen soon."

Nelia nodded, but after looking at Sailor's scowl, she added, "Could have been a new job offer. Or a prestigious award or a big grant."

Drayco interjected. "But I haven't found any evidence of that."

Sailor pushed the legal pad away. "That may be, but I've got burglary cases, I've got drug cases. DUIs, sexual battery, and buckets of misdemeanors. A three-hundred-year-old murder case is at the bottom of my list."

Drayco took one last look at Sailor's notes, memorizing them. "But you don't mind if I poke around."

"Knock yourself out. You'll be on your own. Tyler here is needed with all those real cases I mentioned. Giles, too. When he's through contacting those homeowners, that'll be it for him."

Drayco headed toward the door with a parting comment, "Guess I'm not the only one in a bad mood."

"County board said 'no' to a budget increase. For the umpteenth time. Hell yes, you could say I'm a bad mood." Sailor pointed at the door. "Have fun with your pretend cases."

Nelia followed him out of the office. "You sure you're feeling okay? You've got dark circles. Make that craters."

"Maybe I've just been playing the Suicide Sonata too much."

She narrowed her eyes. "If that's supposed to be a joke, Drayco, it's not funny." And with that parting shot, she darted away from him toward the back part of the building.

Pissing off the entire sheriff's department. *Way to go, Drayco.* He headed to the lobby, waving at Giles, who grimaced with his ear glued to a phone when Drayco passed by the deputy's office. Must be in the air. The stench of crime that never took a day off?

Drayco had a sudden craving for something aromatic, a mocha or a double espresso. Too bad the Fiddler's Green Tavern wasn't open yet—a mocha beer would be more the ticket. Dark drinks for dark moods. He'd have to trademark that and put it on T-shirts and mugs. Could bring in spare change for the Opera House.

He hopped into his Starfire and peeled off too fast, flinging pieces of gravel onto the body of the car. Was he going to need to add paint repair to his mounting list of car expenses? Slowing down, he forced himself to go the speed limit, not one mile per hour over or under. He was rewarded with a series of irritated drivers honking their car horns as they passed around him. Sometimes, you couldn't win.

26

Making do with an aromatic peppermint mocha coffee from the Novel Café, Drayco climbed up the steps to the Historical Society and opened the door lever with his elbow. He located Reece and handed him a chai latte. "Don't know what you see in these, but here."

"I get high on chai," Reece took a big slurp of the drink.

Drayco groaned, prompting Reece to retort, "This from a guy who puts salt in his coffee. Which begs the question—is that peppermint I smell?"

With a shrug, Drayco said, "They were on sale."

Reece grabbed a teaspoon sitting on a table and spooned a tiny amount of the latte into the soil of a potted African violet.

Drayco crinkled his nose. "I know you love your plants, but, really?"

"Tea has flavonoids and tannic acid. Great for plants."

"The violet does look spectacularly healthy. Do you give any to Andrew Jackson?"

"Caffeine is toxic to birds. Might try decaf one day. A teensy bit." Reece replaced the lid and took another loud slurp. "You said you had interesting news. Spill. As in news, not coffee."

"The Medical Examiner determined Mr. Bones dates from the early eighteenth century."

Reece whistled. "Who do I have to pay off to get my hands on that skeleton? Think of all those tourist dollars."

"More so, once they find out Mr. Bones was murdered."

"Murder you say? Oh, this is delicious."

"Don't look so happy. The poor guy was shot in the back of the head with a musket ball."

"Tell me they kept that musket ball." Reece had the air of a tiger fixated on prey.

"I assume so. But someone has to trace the remains. And if it turns out to be Native American, then the tribe involved will want to bury Mr. Bones."

"Thanks very much, spoilsport."

"If it helps, I know how you feel. Did I tell you Konstantina Klucze's distant heirs found out about the Chopin manuscript and filed a lawsuit?"

Reece's non-glass-eye widened. "Holy *merde*. Do they have a chance?"

"My attorney's not sure. They're from a branch of the family in Poland estranged prior to the war. Bottom line is, the Opera House's bottom line is hurting. The pace of these court cases can be glacial. Meanwhile, I've got contractors and workmen waiting to get paid."

"We'll have to arrange a raffle. A date with the world-famous detective Scott Drayco as a prize?"

"That wouldn't raise enough to pay for one new seat. I like Tyler's idea of a bake sale better." Drayco did a mental count of how many pies they'd have to sell. At eight dollars each, something like a million. He really didn't want to think about it. "Reece, do you have any documents or books on pirates in the area?"

Reece chewed on that for a moment. "We do. Oh, Mr. Bones. Think he was friends with Jolly Roger?"

"It's a possibility, considering the gold coin found with him. Did you get my text not to mention it further? Sailor was apoplectic about a leak."

"I did, and my lips are sealed. And thumbs—no texts."

He motioned for Drayco to follow him to the file room and headed for one particular book on a shelf. He leafed through it while Drayco grabbed a seat at the table.

After a few minutes, Reece exclaimed, "I knew I remembered this section on pirates around the Eastern Shore."

"Don't suppose it mentions a pirate with six fingers on his left hand?"

"Six?" Reece scanned the book, running a finger down each page and flipping through them in rapid succession.

Drayco asked, "Do you have a robotic lens in that glass eye of yours?"

"Now that's an interesting idea. Definitely going on my Christmas list. Nope, just an old-fashioned speed reading course. With the thousands of books and documents in our archives, what else to do?"

"Digitize it all."

"Not again with the digitizing. And here I was going to hold out my hand for some of that Chopin manuscript windfall of yours. Our micro-budget barely keeps Andrew Jackson in birdseed."

"Sorry. Couldn't Mrs. Hammontree help?" Drayco hadn't seen any sign of Reece's volunteer assistant.

"Mrs. Hammontree's skills with filing are legendary. With technology, not so much."

Reece kept flipping through the book. "Those pirates were bloodthirsty monsters. Your Mr. Bones was lucky he got shot. Better than evisceration. Or being roasted alive. Or getting his lips, ears, and nose cut off. And here's one who pulled out his victim's heart and—"

"Reece, six fingers, remember?" Reece's own ancestors must have had some pirate in them from the way Reece seem fascinated with the gruesome details. Was Reece's ownership of a parrot a genetic link trying to reassert itself?

"I'm afraid I don't see anything. Oh, wait a minute." Reece stopped on a page and read aloud, "Grabbing Irons Greaver."

"Grabbing Irons?"

"In eighteenth-century naval speak, fingers. Or so it says here. There's a good reason he had that name."

"Six grabbing irons on one hand?"

"The left. According to this account, he was born with six fingers on both hands. A finger on the right hand got cut off in a fight."

"Does it say anything else about Greaver?"

"Had a running feud with another pirate, Rawley Burrowes. When Greaver vanished, it was assumed Burrowes won that grudge match."

"A feud over what?"

"You're going to love this. Sheriff Sailor won't. But they had a falling out over treasure they stole. Greaver said it was lost overboard, Burrowes accused him of stealing it—and hiding it on the shore."

"You're right. Sailor will hate it. But think of the exhibit you can mount if you manage to get Mr. Bones, er, Mr. Greaver, for the Society."

"Might find a patron who'll pony up dough for a new wing for him. Maybe a certain pirate-themed fish restaurant chain?"

Drayco drummed his fingers on the table. "Have any resources on gold coins of that era?"

"'Fraid not. You should check with Cherie Kolman. She's an amateur numismatist. Came by a few years ago looking for books on the subject."

"I'll do that." He already had that one his list. "Has anyone popped in wanting to research pirate treasure by any chance?"

"That would be convenient for you, but no." Reece slammed the book shut. "You'll have to dig harder." Reece beamed at Drayco over the pun.

After Drayco left the Historical Society, he made a note to check with a friend at the Smithsonian later. If the plan he was hatching up worked, he'd be able to help Reece and maybe rewrite a few history books, to boot.

∾ ∾ ∾

Once outside the building, Drayco pulled out his cellphone to look up a number. When the target of his call answered, Drayco asked, "Stewart Cooperman?"

"Speaking."

"This is Scott Drayco—"

"Alexander Vucasovich's star pupil. I appreciate your help with the biography."

"My pleasure. I hope you'll pardon the out-of-the-blue call. But during research for the book, did you find that Vuca played a piece called the 'Suicide Sonata'?"

"I know the piece you're referring to. That Hungarian insanity, right? No way he'd do that. It's nonsense."

"Is it so far-fetched? The composer of the original piano sonata, Adojan Dobos, was a friend of Vuca's. Both men took their own lives."

The voice on the other end sighed. "Yes, but Vuca didn't stay close to Dobos as the years went on. I can't believe there was a connection."

"Did Dobos leave a note of any kind?"

"Not per se. His daughter did say he was despondent over the deaths attributed to his sonata." Cooperman hastily added, "And no, I didn't find any references whatsoever to Vucasovich playing such a piece. Even if it was written by a friend. Besides, Dobos pulled it out of publication for years. Tried his best to bury it."

"I can understand why."

"Whatever made you think of it?"

"It's a case I'm working on. And you're right. Doesn't seem like Vuca's style."

When Drayco's phone vibrated with a text alert, he thanked Cooperman and rang off. It was Darcie, asking to meet with him. That was one minefield he wasn't sure he wanted to cross, so he took his time answering. He typed out the reply, *Don't think that's a good idea.* But right before he sent it, he deleted that and instead replied that he would meet her.

Call him crazy, but thanks to all the talk of skeletons and suicides, he was ready for an actual flesh-and-blood encounter. Even if it was with an ex-girlfriend. Ex-whatever. Although he certainly wasn't going to admit to himself how much he missed her.

No, this "reunion" probably wasn't a good idea at all. So why the hell was he going? He was beginning to believe what he really needed was a top-notch shrink.

A flash of reddish-pink caught his eye from the corner of the Historical Society's porch. A rosebush. It lay nestled in a ring of caladium with heart-shaped green and crimson leaves. Perhaps Maida was right when she'd said people not only didn't stop to smell the roses, they didn't even notice the roses anymore. After all, he'd never noticed that bush before, had he?

Spying one fallen rose that seemed undamaged, he picked it up to take to her, giving it a quick sniff. It didn't have much of a scent, but at least he could tell Maida he tried.

27

Darcie's choice of a setting for their meeting should have given him pause. He pulled up in front of a small graveyard next to a cracked foundation slab—the church had burned a decade ago. Like the last time he met her here, the headstones still leaned, and there were still no flowers. It would look like this a hundred years from now. Forsaken and mostly forgotten.

Moments later, a red Corvette roared into the spot next to his, and Darcie climbed out. Her dress, what little there was of it, matched the car. If her hair were as red as Deirdre's, it would be hard to tell where the driver began and the car left off.

She smiled at him. "Glad you came. I was afraid you wouldn't."

"I almost didn't."

She grabbed his arm and pulled him around the headstones through a grove of witch hazel shrubs to a small drop-off leading to the water. "You did say it was the nicest view of the bay around."

The same oak tree was there with Oakley Keys's carvings on it, untouched. Maybe Reece should chop it down and add it to the rock in the Historical Society. Drayco didn't have time to consider that notion further when Darcie pulled his head away from studying the tree to capture his lips in a passionate kiss. The woman was a top-notch kisser, he had to hand it to her.

After they came up for air, he said, "Does Harry Dickerman know you're here with me?"

"No, but wouldn't it be awesome if the three of us got together?"

"By 'get together,' you mean dinner?"

She wrapped her hands around his hips and pulled him closer to her. "Dessert. With lots of whipped cream in special places."

His jaw dropped. "Don't tell me you're thinking of a three-way."

"Why not, darling?"

"No. No no no no no. Just no."

Darcie pouted. "I was hoping it would keep him from needing Viagra."

"Darcie, stop right there. That's way too much information."

"I doubt he expects me to be *entirely* faithful since he's not 'potent.' A lot of people have side dishes to go along with their entrée. It's the modern way."

During their first meeting at this very spot, she'd seduced him until he'd pushed her away because she was married. Here she was trying the same thing while dating another man. Incredible.

"If you want to make me ecstatic, Darcie, tell me about Emmerson Pinnick."

She moaned with exasperation. "What is it about this place? It's always business with you. Here I am offering you great sex, but you want to talk shop."

She frowned but didn't remove her hands from his ass. "I despise the man. He represented Randolph at his embezzlement hearing, which is okay, I suppose. Somebody had to do it. But he also represented Randolph in the divorce."

"Then you're hardly unbiased."

"He painted me as a witch who'd cast a spell over my husband and led him astray. And that I shouldn't expect to get anything out of Randolph. Yet, I got the house, didn't I? Guess Emmerson Pinnick isn't that great an attorney. Or mine was better."

Drayco tried to ignore Darcie's hands as they roved around his body in very sensitive places. "Surely you've met Barbara Pinnick? She's quite the social climber."

"Oh, I met her. Before that whole Oakley Keys case when you came into our lives, darling. We invited the two of them to the house for a dinner party. I usually adore parties. I didn't enjoy that one at all."

"Why was that?"

"Barbara Pinnick has antifreeze in her veins—to keep her cold heart from turning to ice. Didn't have a good word to say about anybody. Everything was all about her and her standing. And how they were going to build a house bigger than Cypress Manor when her husband made partner. Like she had this 'how to become the center of the universe' checklist."

He couldn't avoid smiling at that. He would have loved to see the two women circling each other at a WBA boxing match.

Darcie saw the look on his face and scolded him. "Even I'm not that bad. I'm just a girl who wants to have fun."

"We're not going to have *that* kind of fun here." He headed off her protest to ask, "You don't have any other dirt on Emmerson or Barbara Pinnick?"

She pushed away from him, and he told himself he didn't miss the contact. "During the divorce case, I might have overheard him talking on the phone."

"Might?"

"He was in the middle of an argument, so I hung around the corner. No need to intrude."

"But it was okay to eavesdrop?"

"It wasn't like everything was hush-hush. He said, 'don't you think that's too extreme'? The voice on the other end was so loud, he held the phone away from his ear. I'm sure Barbara was behind all that shrieking."

"What was she saying?"

"'I want him away from her, and I want him gone, and I don't care how it's done.'"

"How did Emmerson respond to that?"

"Don't know. My attorney needed me, so I had to leave."

"Thanks, Darcie. As always, you're a big help."

She grinned at him. "When you said I gave you an idea before, you thanked me good and proper in my bedroom at Cypress Manor."

He remembered. How could he forget? Although just then, he really wanted to. "I need to get back to town. Besides, your bedroom has another occupant."

Darcie reached for his hand and clasped it in hers. "Harry is a nice man. I don't love him. But I've never been anything other than a rich man's wife."

"There's always a first time. Try something different."

The corners of her mouth trembled, and her eyes grew bright with unshed tears. "I've never loved anyone before you. But I'm not sure I know how to do that, either."

He pulled her into a hug, kissed her on the top of her head, and said softly, "Love isn't always enough."

28

Drayco chugged his triple espresso in the parking lot of the marine biology station. He needed the extra caffeine after getting a text at five in the morning—from yet another phone number with yet another copy of the suicide song. Not the way he wanted to start his day. At the rate he was consuming coffee, not only would his blood turn brown, he'd be having A-fib before long.

This time, when he entered the building, a volunteer was on reception duty. She told him Judson Kolman was away doing fieldwork, but Tess Gartin was outside. After telling the volunteer he knew the way, he headed toward the back.

He paused for a moment outside the equipment room. All that scuba gear—buoyancy compensators, regulators, dive scooters—was making him itch for another dive. The last one was, what, two years? Three? The other equipment was more unfamiliar but looked impressive. Outside Drayco's budget, for sure, and even for salvage operator and recovering barfly-with-perfect-teeth Dennis Frischman.

Drayco eventually found his way toward the dock area he saw on his first trip. Tess wore a sunhat, bent over long rectangular boxes with screened bottoms floating in the water alongside the pier. She looked up with a scowl as he approached. "Dr. Kolman—"

"Is out doing fieldwork. The receptionist told me. But I came to see you." He peered into one of the boxes. "Looks very green. And slimy."

"Eco-engineered macroalgae. You may know them as seaweeds. Could help oyster aquaculture."

"Oyster aquaculture?"

"We cultivate oysters to replenish critically low stocks. We hope these seaweeds can filter out excess carbon dioxide and other pollutants—they're bad for oyster growth. Plus, industries use the seaweed for food and other products."

"Sounds like a win-win."

"Should be, if it works." She rinsed her hands under a dockside faucet. "Looking at this green goo, I always wondered if that's where Marty got his inspiration for those green protein smoothies."

Drayco hadn't expected her to bring up the topic on her own. "You said you'd never tried it. Did he share it with anyone else?"

"Not me, that's all I know."

He inspected a long golden cylinder lying on a table that had CTD on the side. She saw him looking at it and said, "Measures conductivity, temperature, and pressure. And the concentration of salt and other inorganic compounds in seawater."

"I passed by the equipment room inside. Lots of interesting-looking gear."

"Some of it was the gear Marty ordered. The synthetic aperture sonar, a magnetometer, a fish finder. He wanted to explore the newly discovered deep-sea canyons and corals. I would never have bought all that. Too impractical, and we need other gear more."

While drying her hands on a towel, she squinted up at him. "Why do you want to see me?"

"You and Marty picked the same college and degree. Marty was interested in marine biology since he was a boy, but how did you get involved?"

"If you live around the shore, you can't help being inspired. Guess hearing Marty go on and on piqued my interest. As far as the school choice, it's a highly regarded program."

"Yesterday afternoon, I chatted with an assistant prof in the UNC marine sciences department. He remembered both of you. Said you were accused of cheating off Marty on a final exam."

Tess looked daggers at him. "I was innocent, but they made me retake the test. It was frickin' humiliating. Even back then, I was in Marty's shadow."

"And he gets the job here that you had your sights on."

"Yeah." She flung the towel onto a table with such force, it knocked over a glass soda bottle.

"Guess that means you had no romantic interest in him?"

Tess righted the bottle and glared at it as she took her time replying. "Look, I know this will make me sound guilty. But I hated him a little bit."

"A wise man once said the opposite of love isn't hatred but indifference."

"I wasn't indifferent. Exasperated. Marty was too much the Boy Scout type. Always dreaming of big things he couldn't possibly achieve."

Drayco walked closer to get a better look at the algae boxes. "Why not?"

"This is reality. We don't get what we want. We all settle. Haven't you?"

He had a fleeting thought of his piano career. "I'd settle for figuring out how Marty got obsessed with that Suicide Sonata and why."

"I can't answer you there."

"You have absolutely no idea why it was so important to him?"

She shook her head. "Why does anybody develop an obsession? Or believe in a conspiracy theory?"

"Let's chat about Antonio, then. It was his gun allegedly used to kill Marty."

Another long pause before she asked, "What, you think Antonio helped him do it?"

"Or killed Marty himself."

Tess dug into a vinyl bag, grabbed some gloves, and yanked them on. She fumbled with a test tube and scraped some of the green goo inside. "Two people could answer that, and one of them is dead. Don't know what you expect me to say."

"For starters, you can tell me if you think Antonio is capable of murder."

"Every day, I deal with predators, Dr. Drayco. Fish eat plankton, bigger fish eat smaller fish, the largest fish eat everything. We humans evolved from aquatic creatures. I'd say we've all got the predator lurking inside ready to jump out."

"I take that as a yes."

"Antonio is an innocent, sensitive soul who cares about things way too deeply."

"Wouldn't take much for someone who cares that deeply to be pushed to his limit. Watching his unrequited love for Marty thrown back at him by Lena and Deirdre."

She gaped at him. "How did you know Antonio was in love with Marty?"

"His mother hinted at it. She didn't approve. The question is, was she upset enough to do something permanent about it?"

"That's way too Hollywood."

"Perhaps. Have you spoken with Antonio lately?"

She hesitated again and didn't reply, slowly capping the test tube and putting it into a small holder.

Reading between the lines, Drayco asked, "When?"

"A couple days ago. He scared me if you really want to know. Talked about 'that song' and how 'that song' did it, and it's all his fault."

"What did he mean?"

"I don't know. I tried to reassure him. Tell him he didn't cause Marty to commit suicide. Goddamnit, now you're standing here telling me it's true."

"Not necessarily. I'm trying to understand what could have happened."

"I was going to stop by and check on him. But I got cold feet."

A sudden wind gust knocked her sunhat off, and she repositioned it and tightened the drawstring. "Antonio can be a drama queen. And I mean that in the true sense. He got the Best Actor award at the school play. When he said what he did, he had me guessing what was real and what wasn't."

"Marty's death was real enough."

Tess shifted her gaze toward the waterfront as the noise from a passing motorboat reached their ears. "Look, if you want to chat more, we should do it another day. Judson will have my ass if he sees me here wasting time."

"Works you that hard, does he?"

She sighed. "I have a worklist the size of a mountain to get through. So, if you don't mind?"

Drayco took the hint and left her to her test tubes and macroalgae as he made his way back to his car. His chat with Tess wasn't terribly productive. Or he was still sleepwalking after that early morning "wake-up call." More and more, he longed for the good old days when people didn't carry a phone around. You could count on peace and quiet and time to think.

That reminded him of a more troubling aspect of the whole suicide scenario. Where the hell was Marty's cellphone? The treasure hunters could have their coins and maps—to Drayco, that cellphone was a prize worth more than gold.

He stood beside his car, peering around for his goose friend but didn't see it. Just in case, he grabbed the packet of wild bird seed he got from the Major and sprinkled it on the ground.

As he straightened up, he saw sunlight glinting on something in the zoysia grass lawn and snagged it. It was a shell with swirled bands of pink, tan, and blue with a striking maple-colored eye in the center.

Who'd dropped it? Tess? Marty? Didn't look valuable, so he stuffed it in his pocket. His mini-contribution to marine biology conservation.

Tess's encounter with Antonio was troubling but intriguing. It was long past time for another chat with him, far from the chicken plant—and preferably upwind of it. But would Antonio agree to it? He didn't jump for joy to speak with Drayco the first time.

For a people who should bend over backward to help a grieving father, few among Marty's associates seemed willing to talk in detail about his death. Grief could do that. Guilt, too.

Funny how humans always say they want the truth and then run in the other direction from it as far and fast as they can. He whipped out his cellphone and called up one of the new numbers he'd programmed into his address book. Maybe Rosita Skye could help the pursuit of his particular truth inch forward a little bit more.

29

Drayco combined GPS readings and Maida knowledge to find the out-of-the-way beach hidden by hawthorn trees and salt scrub. With the late-morning sun beating on him, Drayco took off his shoes and socks before heading out through the small dunes to the shoreline. It was far too long since he walked barefoot on a beach. During those summers as a boy spent at his great-aunt's beach house, it was all he did. Maybe on his next vacation—that is, if he ever had time for another one.

He zeroed in on his target and plowed through the sand. "Good morning."

Antonio stared at Drayco in shock. "How'd you know where to find me?"

"I checked with your mother. She mentioned a 'crooked beach.'"

"A what?"

"I wasn't sure what she meant, either. Until I studied a map and found a 'Hook Head' spot on the map."

"Oh. Why'd you have to bother her?"

"Just wanted a chance to talk with you. You're hard to pin down due to your odd work schedule."

Antonio replied, "The chicken plant's shaking it up. Instead of folks doing the same shift, they switch it around. Sometimes in the same week. It's murder on sleep."

He had a tan burlap bag with the strap slung across his left shoulder. As he bent over and picked up a shell and put it in the bag, Drayco asked, "Beachcombing a hobby of yours?"

"This is one of the better spots. Me and Marty used to come here to look for shells. Or to fish. Came here once at night, too. Saw a shooting star." For a brief moment, Antonio's expression held a hint of awe.

"The sheriff and I went through Marty's apartment. I didn't see any seashells."

"Shelling's my thing. Marty looked for more unusual stuff."

Antonio put another shell in his bag, but Drayco couldn't tell why he'd picked that particular one. "Did Marty find any interesting items?"

"A silver belt buckle. Old bullets."

"Did either of you use a metal detector?"

"Marty wanted one. Something else to carry, I told him. Lena's aunt owned a metal detector, but I never saw her using—"

Antonio stopped and pushed Drayco so hard, he nearly fell to the ground. Before Drayco could react, Antonio pointed at the sand where Drayco's bare feet had come within a few inches of crossing. "Portuguese man-of-war. Marty told me he knew a guy who stepped on one. Ended up having his foot amputated."

Drayco grabbed a nearby piece of driftwood and lifted up the blobby corpse. "I've heard of these. Dangerous after they're dead?"

"Yep."

Grateful for Antonio's reflexes, Drayco kept a lookout for other venomous creatures. "Thanks for saving my foot. I can pay you back by helping you with your hunt. What type of shells are you looking for?"

"Today, shark's eyes." The young man dug into the sack and pulled out a bluish-gray-tan shell with a dark eye pattern at the tip of the spire. Identical to the one Drayco found in the grass at the marine biology station.

They continued their walk, scanning the beach in silence for a while. Drayco spied one and dug it out of the sand. He passed it to Antonio, who added it to the sack.

"Sebastien Penry showed me a photo of you and Marty with fishing poles. From six months ago."

Antonio skidded to a halt. "Where did he get that?"

"From Marty's place."

"Marty took a selfie of us with his phone. Guess he printed it." A small smile spread across Antonio's face.

"What was their relationship like, Marty and his Dad?"

"Got along okay. I mean, they argued over girls and money."

"Had they argued recently?"

Antonio grabbed another shell and put in his bag. "Don't know. Some, I guess."

"Did Marty mention his father taking out a life insurance policy on him?"

"What?" Antonio's brows knitted together in confusion. "Nope."

Drayco kept looking for shark's eye shells, but mostly he saw broken shards, the surrealist puzzle pieces of forgotten life. "Marty's other friends say he'd grown moody recently."

"I guess. Kinda like he was worried."

"He didn't say why?"

"Had this headache. Couldn't get rid of it. Guess he was starting to take it out on other people. He bitched about his boss, bitched about Tess, bitched about Lena, bitched about the Pinnicks."

"Deirdre, too?"

"Never Deirdre. He called her his Venus." Antonio muttered under his breath. "Even after she borrowed all that money from him for an abortion."

Had Drayco heard him right? "What was that last part you said?"

The younger man didn't reply and kept on walking. They walked in silence for several minutes until Antonio said, "I know you're trying to help and all. But you're asking the wrong person. Hadn't seen Marty in a couple weeks before he died. Not that I didn't want to."

"Too busy?"

"Too something." Antonio snagged a few more shells. "Guess my energy field and vibrations were off."

"Sounds like something from the Akashic Records."

"Most of it doesn't make sense. Hell, nothing makes sense to me, anymore." He stabbed at an empty clamshell with his toe, flipped it over, and kicked it into the water.

"Did you send copies of the suicide song to my cellphone?" Drayco hadn't forgotten Antonio playing it for him at the chicken plant.

"What? Why would I do that?"

"You said you can't get the song out of your head."

"Gives me nightmares." He picked up a broken sand dollar, rolling it in his hand before he crushed it and let the powdery remains fall in the water.

"Did Marty introduce you to it or vice versa?"

"Marty did."

"When did he first mention the song?"

"Guess it was a year ago. I forgot all about it until he started listening to it again."

"Listening when?"

"I dunno. Couple months."

Drayco kept staring down to avoid stepping on another critter, which is why a forceful wave took him by surprise and drenched him up to his knees. Antonio didn't break a smile as if he hadn't noticed.

The young man tightened the drawstring to his shell bag. "Gotta get back. To clean up before I have to be at work. And I need to make Mom's supper and put it in the fridge. When she gets off her shift, she's too tired to cook."

"You're handy to have around. She must be grateful."

Antonio just sighed and trudged toward the path that led to the small clearing where their cars were parked. Without a word, he climbed into his car, cranked up the engine, and drove up the short turnoff between two banks of swamp red bay shrubs.

It was an odd encounter. Drayco couldn't put his finger on it, but there was an air around Antonio that was off. Not so much he was hiding something as he was hiding *from* something.

The Prokofiev ringtone on Drayco's cellphone startled him—he'd gotten used to the spotty cellphone reception on the shore. The sheriff's voice on the other end did nothing to dispel Drayco's general uneasiness. "Got news you'll find interesting. Where are you?"

"Returning from the beach."

"Perfecting our tan, are we?"

"I had a disquieting chat with Antonio Skye."

"You can fill me in when we meet."

"Before or after lunch?"

Sailor didn't reply right away, and Drayco heard his muffled voice as he put his hand over the phone to talk to someone in the background. Finally, he said to Drayco, "Tell you what. The Seafood Hut may be unavailable, but you gotta eat. What say we meet for lunch at the Island View Restaurant. They get fresh flounder from Wachapreague. You can dine al fresco. You city boys need more fresh air."

His attempt at humor didn't help lift Drayco's spirits. But Sailor was right, he had to eat. And with the promise of freshly caught flounder, what could he say? Better to eat sea creatures than step on them.

30

Drayco hated to admit blasphemy, but Island View Restaurant was more aesthetically appealing than the Seafood Hut. Bigger, brighter, with a small lighthouse-painted tower at the top where you could look out over the barrier islands. It also had the outdoor deck seating Sailor promised, which is where Drayco found the sheriff sipping an iced coffee.

The water vista was different from Sebastien Penry's house with its mere hints of the open water beyond. Here, you could see more of the salty banks of the deep inlet that spread out into the Atlantic Ocean. The nearby dock had a few moored fishing boats, including one unloading its seafood bounty packed into round wooden bushels and blue plastic bins.

Drayco dropped the book he'd brought with him onto an empty chair before sliding into his seat and pointing at the drink. "You've gotten citified."

"This would have Bailey's in it if this were later in the day."

"Vodka, now Bailey's? Does Mrs. Sheriff know you're turning into a heavy drinker?" Drayco scanned the menu, then tossed it aside to study their surroundings.

Sailor reached for Drayco's book. When he bdid the title and author, he did a double-take. "A book on suicide. By Dr. Andrew Gilbow. Wasn't he the one who—"

"Yeah. It's a highly regarded book. And I didn't know how long I'd be waiting for you."

Sailor thumbed to the table of contents for a quick look. "Did you learn anything from this?"

"That the whole suicide song business could be the Werther effect."

"Werther? As in Goethe?"

"I'm impressed, Sheriff. You're living up to your middle name of Hemingway again. In Goethe's novel, *The Sorrows of Young Werther*, the title character shoots himself after he's rejected by the woman he loves. Shortly after the book came out, there were reports of young men using the same method to kill themselves."

"Copycat suicides?"

"It's not unusual. After Marilyn Monroe's suicide, there was a twelve percent increase in suicides."

Sailor replaced Drayco's book on the chair. "Not sure you're going to need this."

They waited while the waitress dropped off sweet potato biscuits and water for Drayco and waltzed away with their orders. Drayco asked, "Is that the news you hinted at on the phone?"

"The M.E. did a re-test of Marty Penry's stored tissue samples. This, after I got the lab results from that green powder."

Drayco couldn't contain his excitement. "Not kelp and kale?"

"Oh, plenty of that. But it was heavily spiked with the SSRI sertraline hydrochloride. And there was a high concentration in Marty's tissue."

"The antidepressant? That reinforces the whole suicide theory."

"In normal doses. These were off the charts. Much more than you'd get with a normal prescription. The pills were crushed and mixed into the powder."

"Did you check with Marty's father?"

"He was genuinely shocked. I rushed through a warrant, we checked with pharmacies around here. No prescriptions for Marty."

"Internet, perhaps?"

"Not impossible. But did you find any evidence on his computer?"

"Nothing. Not about pills, not about depression in general." Drayco grabbed his cellphone to look up sertraline.

Sailor held out his hand to stop him. "I know what you're thinking. And I looked it up."

"The side effects? I recall a news report on that class of antidepressants. Caused suicidal thoughts in some patients."

Sailor replied, "The FDA issued a black box warning for links to suicidal behaviors. Greatest risk is young adults. Eighteen to twenty-fourish."

"Marty was twenty-five, around that range. I'm told he'd suffered from a case of the blues. And Antonio also said Marty had a headache he couldn't get rid of."

"Common side effects of sertraline in high doses."

"Someone could have spiked the powder hoping he'd commit suicide. Coupled with the sonata and his melancholy state of mind, it worked."

Sailor mopped his sweating bald head with a napkin. "A hell of a risky plan. I mean, murder by sertraline and a song? Besides, if the kid was depressed, he may have ordered the powder himself. Just went overboard."

"As you say, no record of him ordering it on his computer. We still haven't found his cellphone."

"Yeah, there's that."

Drayco drummed his fingers on the table. "That troubling you as much as it has me?"

"No self-respecting kid goes anywhere without his cellphone. I doubt a possum or raccoon decided they needed a phone to text on."

The waitress reappeared with their orders, placing a fried flounder fillet sandwich in front of Drayco and something rather frightening in front of Sailor. After she scurried off, Drayco said, "What in the world is that?"

"Soft-shell crab."

"I've heard of that. A separate species?"

"Chesapeake Bay blue crabs that get too big for their shells and molt. You catch them at the right time then fry 'em up. All the glory of crab without having to dig around in the shell for itsy-bitsy pieces."

"But it's whole."

"They take out the gills and parts of the abdomen first. And the face and eyes, natch."

Drayco studied the legs poking out of the bread. "At least it won't stare at you as you eat it."

"Now who's the one that's citified?"

Drayco watched with fascination as Sailor crunched on the legs. Drayco said, "Everyone in Marty's circle knew he carried that green powder with him. And how obsessed he was with this recent health kick. Ample opportunity for any of them to doctor the powder."

"But come on. Old-fashioned murder would be a hell of a lot easier."

"Easier, but messier. What better way than to frame the victim for his own death? With Marty's obsession over the Suicide Sonata, makes for the perfect recipe."

Sailor bit off another crab leg, and from the way he gulped it down, he wasn't chewing by the numbers anymore—no more counting up to thirty. "I've put Tyler on the meds angle. See if she can come up with any other sources. And trace them to Marty."

"It must be nice having Tyler back."

"Regina Reymann's good, mind you. Just not in Tyler's class. But don't tell either of them I said so."

"If Regina's baby's medical problems keep her from working, what will Nelia do with the job? Give up law school? Or will you have to hire someone else?"

Sailor didn't bat an eyelash at Drayco's use of his deputy's first name. "Don't know. All depends on the county. And how willing they'll be to go along with this arrangement. I need a full-time position, not part-time. Even if it's job-sharing."

Sailor had eaten the legs first and began concentrating on the middle, meatier part. "Seen Darcie lately?" So the man *had* noticed. The sheriff's subtle poke was a reminder he still disapproved of any attraction between Drayco and Sailor's deputy. Such as it was.

"I have. She's in danger of losing Cypress Manor to bankruptcy."

Sailor paused with his sandwich halfway to his mouth. "What, and hitting you up for money from the Opera House funds?"

"Not exactly. She's dating a rich businessman three decades older. He's the president of a 'big media' corporation."

Sailor squinted at him. "Kinda sudden."

Eager to change the subject, Drayco asked, "Any news on your skeleton's gold coin?"

"Just what you and Reece found. Possible historical pirate, complete with gold. And threats from the condo developer about turning over 'his' gold."

"But one single gold coin? Pretty unsuccessful pirate, Sheriff."

"You thinking treasure hunters?"

"Marty and Antonio were beachcombers. They might have found a treasure map or a link to that skeleton."

"Not seeing how they could have dug up the skeleton's booty. No one had touched that area in decades. If not centuries."

"As you aptly noted, the construction crew decimated the site. Hard to tell much of anything." Drayco took a bite of his sandwich. The flounder was so fresh, it was almost wriggling.

"Your scenario would make Antonio the treasure-hunting partner. Decided to keep it all for himself—and killed the only threat to his plan?"

"One or more of Marty's friends and colleagues could be in on that plan."

"A big stretch. Plus, gold like that is hard to sell without a trace-back."

"I've done some initial checking on that front. No gold coins from that era have come on the market. But there *are* the not-so-public channels."

Sailor threw breadcrumbs to a pair of of seagulls on the deck. "Digging into the black market would take more resources than I have. Besides, we don't have proof this gold exists. Maybe our skeletal pirate's coin was his lucky talisman. Or stolen by his murderer long ago."

Drayco had to hand it to him there. But pirates were known for burying their loot in more than one place. "You have the green powder and the sertraline. That's evidence."

"Still think it's an iffy way to get rid of somebody." Sailor grabbed the small dessert menu from the table and started looking at the pies. "But I've heard of stranger."

So had Drayco. But like his odd reaction to the crab sandwich, Drayco was finding it repulsive to imagine a killer who preyed on a young man's depression.

As he watched a yellow-headed brown pelican take flight above the water, one thing was clear. If someone spiked Marty's powder, then Drayco's fear of disappointing Nelia's mother and Marty's father had flown away and disappeared just like that pelican.

31

Lena was late again as Drayco waited for another parade of cars to pass by the Lazy Crab. At the fifteen-minute-late mark, her motorcycle roared into the B&B's driveway and skidded to a stop in front of him. She fished into the storage console and grabbed a helmet, but this time he knew the drill.

When he'd called her earlier to say he wanted another chat with her, she wasn't thrilled to hear from him. He seemed to be getting a lot of that lately. He offered to stop by her house, but she nixed that idea outright. No reason, just a flat "no."

As a compromise, he suggested she show him a place where she and Marty and the other "gang" used to meet. She'd agreed to that, but as the motorcycle traveled miles out of town, he couldn't help but wonder where she was taking him. Much more remote than the clearing where Marty died.

After leaving US 13 and traveling miles of winding side roads, Lena slowed to navigate a bumpy off-road patch of grass and rocks. Drayco had to duck as they plunged through an opening in a thicket of trees and shrubs. Even so, the hawthorn and yaupon holly branches reached out to grab him and left bleeding scratches on his arms.

They pulled into a clearing where an abandoned Victorian house loomed in the center. A few of the original gingerbread roof tiles remained, along with streaks of robin-egg blue paint on the plank siding. The rest of the place was the stereotype of a haunted mansion. He took in the torn screens, curtains flinching behind broken windows, steps that didn't look step-worthy, and a porch on stilts ready to fall off.

"How did you and the other kids get to this place? Off the beaten path doesn't begin to describe it."

"Motorbikes. We all had them. I'm the only one who kept mine. Well, me and Marty."

Drayco studied the house. It's what the Historical Society would look like if given a makeover for a horror movie. How many more skeletons were buried in such places, and no one knew they were there?

She climbed off the bike and yanked off her helmet. "This place has been empty since forever. Don't really know its history. Don't really care."

"Houses have stories to tell. Like people."

"Our story is simple. This is where me and Deirdre and Tess and Marty and Antonio met to hang out. And talk about this or that. Like that Akashic thing."

Drayco slid off the bike. "What does that Akashic 'thing' mean to you?"

"It was Deirdre's idea." She twisted the helmet around by its strap like a toy top. "It's all about higher levels of consciousness above the astral plane or something. Guarded by these beings of light."

Funny how they all described it in similar terms like cult zombies. "Beings of light?"

"Guess some religions call them angels. Or aliens." She grinned. "And there's the bit I never understood—tapping into this seventh vibration thing. Where you see past lifetimes."

"I'm not quite clear on how you'd do that."

"With trances, sacred prayers, breathing. Weird shit, you know?"

"What was your method?"

Her grin turned mischievous. "Ours was mostly weed."

"Anything harder?"

"We wanted to. Get a little coke or smack. Maybe acid. But we never did. It's not like we had a drug dealer."

"Then where did you get the weed?"

"In the forest. There's a big patch of it there. Dry it, roll your own. Free and easy."

Since the cannabis that grew wild didn't contain high levels of THC, Drayco had a feeling the kids had unknowingly raided somebody's private "farm." They were lucky they weren't caught, especially since the "farmer" probably had guns.

"Did Marty order any drugs or meds off the internet? Or from a dealer?"

"That would be Deirdre or Tess. I mean, they had more money to do it, didn't they? Marty and Antonio and me, we didn't have any."

She paced in front of the house, just like she had in the clearing where Marty died. "I told him before we broke up, he should see somebody. Get meds. But he refused. Said he didn't like taking drugs. That whole health kick he got on, you know? But it didn't help with his blues. The more he did it, the worse he got."

That would fit with the side effects from the spiked green powder. "When did this health kick start? The protein powder, in particular."

She stopped pacing. "A year ago. I tried it once. Ugh. Give me donuts and potato chips any day."

"I have to agree with you there. It smells terrible."

"I told him I didn't want to kiss him after he'd had some."

Drayco smiled at that. "His mood must have been pretty bad for you to suggest he take something to help."

"Look, we're all on edge, right? I mean, everybody's taking antidepressants." She strode over to peer inside one of the windows in the house.

"Including you?"

"Why not? There's a doc who comes to the chicken plant's health clinic. Doesn't take much to get him to hand over pills."

"Why antidepressants, Lena?"

"You kidding? When you spend your days in the Evisceration Room, pretty much everybody's holding their hand out for pills."

"What type are you taking? Is it sertraline, by any chance?"

"Never heard of that."

Drayco walked over to join her at the window. The interior of the house was even worse than the exterior. Warped floorboards, chunks of plaster missing, and a carpet of leaves, animal droppings, and rusted nails. A child-sized wooden chair with faded pink paint sat alone in one corner.

He asked, "Does this plant doctor give you any counseling, too? Or just pills?"

"Asks a few questions, writes a prescription. Look, I'm not suicidal."

"There are hotlines you can call."

"I've seen the TV commercials. Blah blah blah, one eight hundred something."

"Did Marty call any suicide hotlines that you know of?"

"How many times do I have to say it? He wasn't suicidal. So he wouldn't need it. End of story. Next question?"

"All right, then. Going back to the Akashic Records, I understand you wrote an interesting paper in that same class, according to Deirdre Pinnick."

Lena snorted. "She *would* bring that up, wouldn't she? Trying to make me look guilty or something."

"Want to tell me about it?"

"No, I don't." But after a moment of him staring at her, she added, "It was on unsolved murders, okay?

"That's an odd topic for a high school student."

"If you must know, my mother was murdered. My father had a heart attack a couple months after. People thought he did it because he beat her and me. You happy now?"

She seemed so young and vulnerable right then, he was almost sorry he'd brought it up. "Not happy about that, no. But I have to ask hard questions to get at the truth. For instance, were you jealous of Marty's job? Better pay, better benefits, and no Evisceration Room."

She sat on the edge of the porch which groaned and creaked under her despite the fact she hardly weighed more than one-fifteen. "He worked hard for what he got. And he was damn good at it. Besides, he was going to get me a job there as a clerk."

She glared at Drayco. "Don't know why you're trying to pin this on me. I'm the one who wanted to help you, remember? If you think I killed Marty, you're wrong. I loved him. And he was my ticket away from this place."

A howl suspiciously like a coyote's reached their ears, sounding less than a mile away. She folded her arms across her chest. "This house always did give me the creeps. The weed made it look nicer. Like it jumped out of a fairy tale."

"The one where the witch lures children to her gingerbread house so she can bake them into a pie?"

"Does being a detective make you suck the fun out of everything?"

He moved closer to inspect the rickety porch. . .it was as unsafe as it looked. He stood at the ready to catch her in case she fell in. "Tell me more about how you help Cherie Kolman with her coin collecting."

"Never knew it could be so fascinating. Talk about stories. Those coins have them like you wouldn't believe."

"What sort of stories?"

"Did you know a 1913 Liberty Head nickel fetched a million at auction? Then there was this kid who found Viking coins. Those are now worth a bunch."

"Does Cherie have any old coins herself? Around two hundred to three hundred years old?"

"She bought a few from a beachcomber. Pirate booty or whatever. I'm not as interested in those stories. Too much like blood money."

"But she sells coins, too, right?"

"That's how these collectors do. Buy some, trade some, sell some. People specialize in different types. Cherie's into the Revolutionary War. British coins and the like."

"Hobbyists make good money dealing coins, don't they?"

"I guess. But it's not like the Kolmans are living in a palace with a giant swimming pool and driving a Beamer."

The coyote howl grew closer, and that was close enough for Lena. "We should leave." She took one last, long look at the decrepit house. "Don't think I'll be back. And I'm not at all sorry. Too many painful memories, now that Marty's gone."

She stood still for a moment, her bottom lip trembling. "I kinda wish he'd had cancer or something. That would have been easier."

She grabbed her helmet, and he took that as his cue. After securing his own helmet, he climbed behind her on the motorcycle, and they thundered off.

What would the coyote make of that sound? Another predator invading his territory, perhaps. Like Drayco and Lena invading the Victorian house that once served as someone's happy home, now crumbling into dust.

That thought and Lena's plaintive words washed over him with a tidal flood of gloom, something this case was doing more and more. But once again, he shrugged it off. Besides, Maida said she was planning on making her famous—and hopefully undrugged—Chocolate Blackout Cake, a near-perfect prescription for the blues.

32

Drayco had hoped to catch Judson Kolman early in the morning, but the man was getting ready to head out on a cuddy cabin boat. Kolman said, "Making a quick run out to a barrier island for a project check. Want to come along? Won't be gone more than an hour."

Drayco took a look at Kolman's rubber waders and then at his own khaki chinos and leather loafers. "Am I appropriately dressed for the occasion?"

"You're not going swimming. I've got a spare hat you can use. What do you say?"

"Sure, why not? Would give me a chance to see the type of work Marty was doing."

With Kolman's borrowed Panama hat in place, Drayco hopped in the boat, and they headed out along the channel into open water. His last boat ride was with the notorious Caleb Quintier, and he'd forgotten how pleasant it could be—if you weren't worried about becoming fish bait.

Great weather for boating, with hardly a cloud in the sky. When the blazing sun glinted off Kolman's silver necklace with its small key and silver dolphin, Drayco was glad he'd brought sunglasses. Blinded by a dolphin—how many people could say that?

"Nice to be away from technology." Drayco raised his voice to be heard above the engine and added, "Other than motors and GPS."

"No cell service unless you've got a satellite phone, which I do. For emergencies."

"Too expensive for web surfing, I'm guessing."

"At ten dollars a minute, you decide."

With a check of the GPS, Kolman altered course a few degrees. "Sometimes I come out for deep-water fishing, but don't tell Tess. She refuses to eat seafood."

It took only fifteen minutes until they pulled up near a long stretch of sand rising above the water. Several of the barrier islands were more sandbars than islands, but this one had sparse grass and leathery scrub Maida called Wax Myrtle.

After anchoring the boat, Kolman hopped out and waded to a pole sticking up in the middle of the island. He then attached a long line to it and walked to the edge of the water before taking a measurement and heading back.

As Kolman recorded notes in a logbook and took photos of the island, Drayco said, "The isolation and barren landscape are appealing. Who owns this one?"

"The Nature Conservancy owns all or part of most Eastern Shore islands. They've partnered with groups like us to help monitor them. We do the low-tech grunt work on the ground, they use LIDAR from a plane."

"What are you looking for?"

"Large-scale loss of shore salt marshes. They're feeding grounds for waterfowl, nurseries for marine species. And help absorb wave energy and pollutants."

"Is that loss accelerating?"

"Unfortunately." Kolman started up the boat's motor. "Now we go check the marsh."

Drayco stood beside Kolman be to be heard above the motor noise. "Did Marty take the boat out often?"

"As much as possible. It was his favorite aspect of work. Tess loves dipping her hand into the tanks and peering under a microscope. Marty was more of the old-fashioned kind. Getting out, going right to the source. Boats, diving, whatever it took."

"Like Cousteau."

"Marty's wildly improbable dreams aside, he was a huge help to the station. And to me."

A few minutes later, they were at the shore where Drayco saw another pole planted at the water's edge. Kolman pulled out two bottles from a small chest and handed one to Drayco. "Bug spray. Mosquitoes, ticks, and biting flies." Then he navigated the boat carefully through the seagrass and followed the same procedure of anchoring, wading onshore, and using the measuring line.

Drayco called out to him. "I was on the beach with Antonio Skye the other day. Came a few inches of stepping on a Portuguese man-of-war."

"Good thing you didn't. The pain is nasty, the venom's effects worse. *Physalia physalis* aren't jellyfish. It's not an 'it' but a 'they,' an animal made up of a colony of organisms working together. The tentacles can grow more than a hundred fifty feet. In the old days, you'd never see them this far north."

"I doubt it's good for the ecosystem. Or for tourism."

Kolman laughed at that. "I don't care about the tourism part." He folded up the line. "People ask me why marine biology? What's it good for?"

"And what do you tell them?"

"Take the jellyfish, the actual species. Jellyfish blooms are exploding because overfishing has taken out predators. Since jellies eat fish eggs, the fish population declines. In the Black and Caspian Seas, that population crash wiped out a commercial fishing industry worth four hundred million."

"If you can't appeal to people's environmental sense, then the financial aspect gets their attention, right?"

"Exactly." After noting his measurements and trying to restart the boat's motor, it sputtered. Kolman said, "Damn. Got grass wrapped around the propeller."

Hopping out a second time, he splashed around toward the boat's stern. He reached under the boat and tugged hard, prompting more cursing and then a shout to Drayco, "Try cranking her up. But don't rev it. That'll stir up the bottom making all that sand go into the engine."

Drayco gave it a crank, but it sputtered—until sparks flew off the engine and ignited a pile of oily rags below, instantly flaring into a small fire. He spied a fire extinguisher, grabbed it, and sprayed the rags until the fire was out.

Kolman growled. "Grasses must have blocked the raw-water intake. Motor overheated. Good thing I brought you along." He ducked behind the boat, hauling up more grass that he tossed aside. "One more time."

After Drayco cranked the engine a second time, the boat came to life, and Kolman clambered in with a pat on the side. "This tub is an old sailor like me. But she still works."

Despite Kolman's optimism, Drayco kept a close watch on the motor as they made their return trip to the marine biology station. "How did Marty and Tess get along? Bit of a rivalry?"

"A friendly one, I'd like to think."

"You promoted Marty over Tess. That had to rankle."

"Tess is a professional. She knows as we all do such things happen. She probably brought up the whole gender issue. That wasn't why I promoted Marty over her. Marty had higher grades, better recommendations, and his thesis was on a topic that fits in perfectly with our mission here."

"You never heard them argue?"

"Typical disagreements—how to do tasks the best way, schedules, and such." Kolman bit the inside of his cheek. "There was this one incident. I walked in on them looking like they were ready to brawl. Red-faced, shouting. They broke apart as soon as I entered."

"Why were they arguing?"

He hesitated. "I hate to relay it, due to the way it'll come across."

"Try me."

"It was the tail end, but she said, 'And if you tell anyone, I'll kill you,' or words to that effect. Typical locker-room talk."

Drayco mulled that tidbit. Young people, hell, even older people, threw language like that around figuratively. Few turned it into literal murder. But he couldn't deny it suggested Tess had something to hide.

"All these questions you're asking, Dr. Drayco. Seems more than simple closure for Marty's father about a suicide. He thinks it's murder, doesn't he?"

"He wants to make sure nothing is overlooked."

"A diplomatic way to phrase it. Can't say I blame him. I'd want the same thing for my son." Kolman rubbed a hand over his eyes.

"Your wife told me about your son Jack. I'm sorry."

Kolman nodded but then turned his focus back to piloting. When they pulled into the marina, Drayco noted Kolman was right—it had only taken an hour, even with the mishap. Drayco helped tie up the boat, and the other man said, "If you get an itch to change careers, we could use the help. Or you could volunteer. Need those, too."

Tess was out on the deck, this time tending to an outdoor tank with juvenile stingrays. She waved at the two men briefly then returned to her work. Kolman said, "Told you she enjoys working around tanks."

A few moments later, Tess cried out in pain, and they hurried over. She held up her hand. "Frickin' stupid mistake. A piece of a barb got my finger."

Kolman dashed inside to get a first-aid kit, then returned carrying that and a bowl of what looked like plain water. He inspected her hand. "A small wound. No stinger bone."

She dipped her hand in the bowl, and Kolman explained, "Best way to ease the pain of a stingray barb. Soak the wound in very hot water. Heat neutralizes the toxin."

Drayco asked, "Is there anything I can do to help?"

"She'll have to soak for an hour or so. Then some of this," he held up a tube. "Analgesic and antibiotic cream."

Tess groaned. "I don't have time for this."

Kolman smiled at her. "Your first sting, right? I've had four stingray jabs. Goes with the territory."

As her boss bent over the wound, Drayco would have expected a look of appreciation from Tess. But her narrowed eyes and gritted teeth said otherwise. She obviously didn't idolize Kolman as much as Marty had. Or was there an unidentified "monster" lurking under the deep waters at the marine biology station?

Drayco gave them a parting wave and let the two of them get on with the treatment. On the way to his car, he stopped by the bathroom to wash off the bug spray. The chemical felt like a hot poker on his scratched skin from yesterday's forest ride with Lena.

Drayco then massaged his temples. He'd also developed a headache, and he hardly ever got headaches this bad. Why now? Too much sun? Hopefully, Maida had some pain pills.

It was disappointing his goose was still AWOL, not that the bird's screeching would help his headache. The wild bird seed was gone—a good sign. He thought he heard his cellphone beep out a text alert but was thwarted there, too. Every time it chimed, he half-expected to see another copy of the suicide song.

Last night, he'd dug further into the suicide song-related deaths from the 1930s and '40s. One obscure, long out-of-print newspaper article was uploaded online only in the last week. It detailed how most of the suicide-song victims suffered from the stock market crash and then the war. Their livelihoods, their families, lovers, friends, all gone in the blink of an eye. That made the song cursed, all right—cursed with the blood of millions, distilled into a few, dangerous words.

It was entirely possible, even likely, Vuca played one final song before he shot himself, but only the universe and those Akashic Records knew for sure. Drayco wracked his brain, thinking of what he'd choose to play for his last moments here on Earth. Bach, Beethoven, the usual? No, maybe Brahms, the Intermezzo in E-flat minor, op. 118—with its dark, despairing mood, snippets of the Dies Irae chant, and an ending that quietly fades away. Like life itself.

33

Drayco's headache was growing worse, like a throbbing timpani beat in his skull. He didn't think it was his boat trip with Kolman or the pesky financial paperwork for the Opera House he'd worked on for hours afterward. Having to apologize—again—to Troy Mehaffey for being late on payments to the restoration crew hadn't helped.

Time for medicine in the form of something from his favorite food group, the caffeine family. He felt guilty skipping the Novel Café but wanted to try a new place he passed yesterday while driving to his meeting with Sheriff Sailor.

The interior of Grounds for Glory was an old-new fusion. Decorative tin panels on the counter and weathered wood planks on the walls competed with a curious blend of mismatched chairs and an upholstered sofa. The dizzying array of colors, from orange to black to tan to paisley made the place resemble something out of a clown's yard sale.

The aroma of burnt coffee grinds wasn't terribly encouraging. Nor was the smell of over-steamed milk. A tray of freshly baked chocolate chip cookies was trying its best to referee the competing odors by sweetening the deal.

Like the Island View Restaurant, fewer people sat outside on the deck than inside. He'd attribute the lack of al fresco drinkers to the early afternoon heat, but the mid-eighty temps were pleasant with the winds blowing in from the water. Lack of outlets to charge phones, perhaps?

The scene wasn't as picturesque as the restaurant's view, but shore-ish all the same. Adding an exclamation mark, a blue heron made a rather ungainly two-point landing and perched on a rock nearby.

Eventually, more people both inside and out showed up for Drayco to continue his hobby of people-watching.

Taking a sip from his salted and only slightly burnt-tasting black coffee, he jotted notes on a piece of paper he'd tucked inside Gilbow's suicide book. For decades, health care workers had tried hotlines, personal therapy, shock therapy, thrown pills at patients, staged forced hospitalizations, and had people sign contracts saying they wouldn't kill themselves. Yet the suicide rates kept climbing. Anyone else would say Marty was just another statistic in that list, but Drayco wasn't "anyone else." And Marty deserved better than that.

When Drayco's stomach rumbled, he reconsidered his decision earlier not to get any food and ducked inside for a decadent pastry. It was a surprisingly difficult decision. He opted for a chocolate croissant, in honor of his former FBI partner, Sarg Sargosian, who had a soft spot for them.

He reclaimed his seat to nibble on the not-too-sweet pastry, but when he took a swallow of coffee to wash it down, he gagged. Suddenly, the coffee didn't taste right. He'd known food to alter the flavor of drinks before yet this was different.

He studied the people nearby, who were in the same positions as when he'd left. One man was reading a newspaper, and the other two patrons stayed engrossed in their cellphones. None was having similar problems with their drinks.

Drayco took a whiff of the coffee. It smelled off, too, like menthol. He grabbed the plastic spoon he'd used to stir in the salt and scraped the bottom of the cup. Nope, no bird poop or kamikaze bug corpses.

He held it out to dump the liquid and get a clean refill, but something made him stop. What else could make the coffee taste so different so fast? Should he write it off as headache-induced or not? Decision made, he grabbed his book, notepad, and the cup and made his way to his car.

When he walked into Sheriff Sailor's office, the lawman looked at him with exasperation. Seeing the coffee cup in Drayco's hand, said, "Our swill not good enough for you anymore?"

Drayco put the cup on Sailor's desk. "Does this smell off to you?"

Sailor dutifully grabbed it and sniffed. "You want me to close Grounds for Glory on the basis of stale coffee?"

"Might have been tampered with."

He detailed the situation to the sheriff, whose expression grew more serious. "Shouldn't be hard to analyze. Maybe take a day or so to get lab results. Let us know if you start feeling funny."

Sailor dipped his pinkie into the liquid, put it on his tongue, and grimaced. "Does tastes 'off,' but it would be easier to tell if you didn't put so much damn salt in your coffee."

Nelia poked her head inside the doorway. "What tastes off?"

Sailor held up the coffee cup. "There's a chance Drayco had a Mickey slipped in his drink."

She studied the cup. "That's from Grounds for Glory. Were you sitting inside or outside?"

"On the deck."

Nelia thought for a moment. "I was there the other day. The seating area has a path from the parking lot that winds around the building. Easy to slip in and out. Someone could pretend to be another customer wandering around."

Sailor added, "See anyone acting suspiciously, Drayco?"

"No. But you'd think one of the patrons would have noticed a guy dropping drugs in a cup."

The sheriff handed the cup to Nelia to examine. "So you ticked someone off, and it's a retaliatory prank. Like those texts you've been getting. Who've you spoken with?"

"The marine biology staff this morning. And Lena, yesterday afternoon. She's on antidepressants, by the way. Were you aware of that?"

Sailor and Nelia shook their heads in unison like tennis spectators, which made Drayco think of Reece's parrot. "She says the clinic doctor at the chicken plant hands out pills like candy."

Nelia asked Sailor. "You want me to call him in for a chat?"

With a brief nod, Sailor added, "Check and see if there are any complaints regarding this doc. And any reports of overdoses or drug abuse by other plant employees."

Nelia turned a worried face toward Drayco. "Are you feeling okay? Drink much of the coffee?"

"I'm fine. Really."

Sailor gave him a stern look. "Just keep track of your coffee, 'kay?" He grumbled, "Feel like I'm giving advice to a daughter to cover her drink to avoid date-rape drugs."

That brought a rare full-face grin to Nelia's face. "Now there's an image for you. Are you going to give him a curfew, too?"

Sailor grunted. "I wish. Sure would keep him out of trouble."

Drayco tapped his chest. "He's right here."

The sheriff replied, "*He* should go home and rest or have Maida fix you some pie. Better yet, tell her to set a place for me, and I'll come by later to join you."

Drayco hopped off the chair. "She made blackberry cobbler last night," he teased, playing to Sailor's notorious pie obsession.

Drayco waved himself out the door, with Nelia following part of the way down the hall. She said, "You should take his advice."

"About the pie?"

"About being careful. First those texts to your phone with the suicide song. Now this."

"How could I be in any danger with the Tyler-Sailor cavalry ready to gallop to the rescue?"

She squeezed his arm gently and added, "I can't tell you how grateful Mom is you took this case. I realize you're doing it because she asked, not Sebastien Penry."

Still feeling her touch, his mind must not have fully re-engaged as he blurted out, "I also did it for you."

She smiled, the small dimple forming in her cheek. "I know." Her normal demeanor returned as her eyes twinkled. "I'll have to think of a proper way to thank you later."

He gaped after her and then hurried outside to his car. One minute, she was acting like he was poisonous, the next, she seemed to want. . .hell, he wasn't sure what she wanted. Or what *he* wanted.

The afternoon sun angle reflecting off the Starfire's headlights made it appear the car's "eyes" were mocking him. He glared at it, "Not you, too."

Drayco leaned against the Starfire as he watched a couple of deputies hauling in a prisoner in handcuffs and carting him into the jail admitting area. Nelia was lucky since she was one of only two CIs in the department, meaning she got called out to the more interesting cases. She didn't have to deal as much with drunk drivers, domestic assaults, and robberies—a waste of her skills. He admired Sheriff Sailor for supporting her in her quest for a law degree despite being clearly unhappy to lose her.

Drayco took a moment to picture the coffee shop layout as Nelia had described it, trying to see it with fresh eyes. It was time he acted more like a CI himself since he'd totally missed someone spiking his drink. *If* it were spiked.

His carelessness wasn't normal. Were his emotions getting in the way? No, that couldn't be it. He'd managed to work through a case where his own mother was suspected of being a murderer. Why would this be any worse?

So much for the filaments of gloom clinging stubbornly to his psyche. Instead of wallowing in doubt, he needed to be proactive. It was better therapy for him than any antidepressant ever could be.

34

Drayco traced a path from the Grounds for Glory parking lot to the outdoor seating area behind. Was Nelia right? Could it be possible for someone to stroll in from the lot, doctor his coffee while he was inside getting the pastry, and leave without anyone noticing? Granted, the "anyones" at the time had consisted of one newspaper reader and a couple of absorbed phone-zombie patrons.

Galvanized metal planters filled with towering bamboo blocked sight of the front parking lot, another point in favor of Nelia's hypothesis. But that meant someone was following him, and he hadn't spotted a tail—unless his focus was as "off" as the coffee.

As he pictured possible scenarios, he remembered his research notes—sertraline came in liquid form. Much easier to drop into coffee that way by someone casually passing by, as Nelia suggested. He grabbed his phone to do quick research. One site described liquid sertraline as having a menthol aroma. Bingo.

In an act of defiance, he ordered another cup of java, same as last time. The male barista, who sported two mismatched earrings and a perpetually blank expression, said to him, "You must love our coffee. Weren't you just here?"

Drayco replied, "The coffee's. . .interesting," and added a bill into the tip jar. He took a tentative taste after adding his usual salt. Normal-ish, like when he'd ordered it before.

Deciding not to stay this time, he drove along Main Street with a quick pass by the Opera House. "Later, old girl," he said, as he sailed on by. But then, he saw something that made him slow down and pull into a slot near Virginia Harston's favorite place, the Art of Arts Gallery.

He watched as Emmerson Pinnick and Tess Gartin sat in a car together talking. Make that arguing since the talking part was more heated than amiable. After ten minutes, she got out and stormed into a shoe store while Pinnick drove off alone. Drayco stayed with Pinnick and followed him until the man arrived at his law office, slammed his car door, and strode inside.

What could Tess and Pinnick have to discuss, let alone argue over, in the middle of a workday? The possibilities filled his head with a running slideshow of scenarios to find one that fit with Marty Penry. What was it Judson Kolman said? That Marty and Tess had argued, ending with her ominous threat, "If you tell anyone, I'll kill you."

Maybe he needed to speak with another member of the feminine Pinnick flock without legal-eagle Emmerson hovering around. Drayco made his way to the Pinnick's wannabe-mansion address and knocked on the door, unsure of the reception he'd receive. But nothing ventured and all.

Barbara Pinnick froze when she saw him. "You're Mr. Drayco, that detective, right?" The word "detective" had never sounded so sleazy.

He corrected her, thinking it could help ease into her good graces. "It's Dr. Drayco."

She hesitated, swaying in the doorway. He smiled encouragingly, glad he'd worn the designer linen shirt Darcie gave him. After a few tense moments, Barbara waved him in.

She led him to the fenced backyard garden and pool area which was immaculate with not a weed anywhere. This was a Stepford Garden, too perfect. He didn't want to step off the patio's tan-and-silver slate tiles for fear of tromping on a single blade of grass.

After seating him at a teak table, Barbara ducked into the kitchen and brought out lemonade with a sprig of mint on the rim. Perfectly placed, of course.

"What a lovely garden you have, Mrs. Pinnick. It must take an incredible amount of work to maintain."

"It's so hard to get the gardener and pool boy to do everything right."

"I can just imagine."

"It's taken me years to find people I can trust. Most workers want to do as little as possible. Grab your money and run."

She drained her drink in record fashion and excused herself to snag a refill. When she returned, he got a whiff of alcohol. That explained her flushed cheeks and shrill laugh. But why would the Stepford Wife with the Stepford Garden need to anesthetize herself with spiked lemonade?

He turned the conversation back to Deirdre and the Gang of Five. "I ran into Lena Bing the other day. She's been deeply affected by Marty's death."

"I wish Marty Penry stayed with her instead of pursuing my Deirdre. Things would have worked out a lot differently, wouldn't they?"

"Why do you say that?"

"Do you actually believe that I—that we—liked taking out that restraining order? All our friends were whispering behind our backs. I could barely hold my head up in public."

"What did you think of Lena?"

"Deirdre never invited her friends to the house. Not that I minded with that group of hers. I didn't want them around."

"Including Tess Gartin?"

Barbara played with the sprig of mint on her glass, arranging and re-arranging it. "Of all her friends, I was most hoping Deirdre would stick with Tess. That girl is trying to make something of herself, plus she dresses nicely. And her parents were good people. He was a pulmonologist. So tragic."

"Tragic?"

"That accident, when Tess and Marty were in college. Marty was supposed to pick Tess's parents up from the train station. Anyway, Marty couldn't make it, and they took the bus from the station—Wilson, I think?—to Wilmington. Hit by a tractor-trailer. Crushed the side they were in. Killed instantly."

So, Tess's antipathy toward Marty wasn't all grades and missed promotions. What other psychic skeletons was Tess hiding?

He sniffed his lemonade. Smelled like lemons and sugar, no alcohol or hopefully anything else. "Antonio Skye belonged to your daughter's group of friends. What were your impressions of him?"

She frowned. "A non-entity. A ghost friend of hers. Deirdre met him at school along with the others."

"Was Marty at your house often while he and Deirdre dated?"

More sips of the lemonade cocktail. "Once. It's not like I wanted to have him over for dinner. Besides, it can get hectic. Emmerson's work, my social calendar. Overseeing the gardener and such." She was beginning to slur her words.

"You must have truly hated Marty to put out that restraining order."

"I didn't hate the boy so much as I hated what he represented. I saw too much of it growing up."

Her eyes blinked lazily as she looked out at the pool. "You think I'm a horrible person. But I know what it's like, being an outcast. When my parents died, I had to go into foster care. Kids in foster homes can be cruel."

Her voice took on a bitter tone. "You have no idea how hard it is to overcome that. Everyone looking at you, judging you. I'm not going to let my only child suffer like I did."

"Having your daughter interested in Marty must have been a low blow. A problem worth getting rid of by any means possible."

Her half-lidded eyes flashed for a moment. "Are you suggesting I'd kill him?" Her laughter resembled a hyena's if the hyena had swigged some bourbon. "I can't kill a bug. I have Emmerson do it for me."

And if it came down to it, she'd have Emmerson do the killing of a human pest for her? Hard to visualize Emmerson knowing how to use a gun—or his wife for that matter. Too lowbrow.

Judging from Barbara's watery eyes, flushed face, and the slurring, Drayco was pretty sure the addiction gene was alive and well in her. Before she slipped out of reality, he hurried to ask, "Did you see the words of Marty's suicide song?"

"I have no desire to. It has nothing to do with me." She clutched the glass in her fists. "It's just so déclassé."

By then, it was clear her "checkout" time was imminent, but he got in one final question. "Does this mean anything to you?" He recited the stanzas from memory, "My guilt and betrayal are too much to bear; With nothing to hope for and no one to care; My time is now fading, like light from the stars; And peals of the church bells that reach out to Mars."

She sniffed. "Terrible poetry, isn't it? It's obvious the poor boy wasn't in his right mind. Another reason to keep him away from my baby." She slumped in her seat, staring at her drink.

As he excused himself to leave, she didn't look up or say goodbye. He turned for one last glance as he let himself out the side gate. Barbara put her head on her arms now sprawled across the table. He couldn't be sure, but he thought he heard her sobbing.

35

Saturday, June 23

Tess walked into the Island Trader Store and headed straight for the Chincoteague Seafood Sauce. Once an addiction, always an addiction. Might as well grab some Mango Peach Tango while she was at it. She snagged a wooden shopping basket and dropped the sauces in.

When she saw her reflection in a mirror, the light caught the sapphire stone on her necklace. She smiled as she fingered the stone. She shouldn't wear it, but who would know? With a sudden twinge of guilt, she popped the necklace under her dress so only the chain showed. What she was doing was risky, but it was too much fun to stop.

With her attention on a pile of kitschy tourist T-shirts, a voice calling out her name startled her. She whipped around, surprised to see Deirdre Pinnick of all people approaching her. They hadn't had much to do with each other since the funeral.

Then Tess had a panicky thought—does she know? No, she couldn't. "Wouldn't expect to find you here, Deirdre. Isn't Saks more your thing?"

Deirdre rolled her eyes. "Dale has a birthday coming up, and he's obsessed with salt water taffy. I can't stand it, but Island Trader has the best. Why are you here?"

"Every Saturday morning, the Trader's got Skipjack nuts on sale."

Tess grabbed a can to add to her food stash. But then her eye caught a marine specimen encased in a crystal ball. "This is an endangered juvenile Atlantic Sturgeon. I should report this."

Deirdre clenched her jaw. "Can't take your mind off work for one minute, can you?"

"At least I love my job. And it's worthwhile, too. I help make the planet better by protecting our oceans."

"Are you saying my job isn't worthwhile?"

Tess sighed. She hadn't meant to start a fight. "Didn't peg you for the receptionist type. You were such a party girl, and that job seems so, well—"

"Ordinary? Maybe I want ordinary. Being a party girl takes time and energy. I mean, you have to settle down sometime."

"With Dale?"

"With somebody. And Dale is handy. Good job, good salary, respected."

"You're starting to sound like your mother."

Deirdre didn't stamp her foot, but her body language was every bit as angry as if she had. "I am not. This isn't about her. It's about what I want."

"Really? Is that why you and Marty were still screwing around despite the restraining order? And despite your engagement?"

Deirdre gasped. She moved in closer and spoke in a whisper as her gaze darted around the store. "How did you find out? Did you talk with that detective?"

"I couldn't refuse to talk, could I? Not that I told him everything. I'm still not sure I trust his motives."

Tess put down her basket, which was getting heavy and making her hand cramp. "That detective comes across as laid-back. But he's got these intense violet-blue eyes. They're intimidating."

Deirdre gave a small smile. "Detectives are supposed to be fat old alcoholics." But her smile soon vanished. "Tell me you didn't narc on me and Marty."

"I figured it wasn't any of his business who you were having sex with."

"Then what did you two talk about?"

"What you'd expect. Marty. Our group. That ridiculous suicide song."

Deirdre picked at the fringe on an aqua cotton beach wrap. "Did he accuse you? Or any of us? I mean that his death wasn't suicide?"

"He wouldn't be here if he believed it was suicide, would he? Guess he's doing it mainly as a favor for Mr. Penry. Can't say I blame Marty's Dad. When a person dies like that, you want to blame someone. And settle the score."

"You never settled the score with Antonio."

"What do you mean?" Tess felt her blood pressure go up, which always made her face red and spotty. She saw signs of it in her reflection from a mirror above a display table.

"It was so obvious you had it bad. And equally obvious Antonio couldn't care less."

"Doesn't matter anymore. Besides, he wouldn't have noticed unless my name was Trace or Ted."

"You mean he's gay?" Deirdre laughed. "All that time we were together, and I had no idea. You think he and Marty. . .?"

"I think he wanted to with Marty. But those feelings weren't mutual."

"Is that why they had a falling out?"

Tess started to pick up her basket, but that made her stop in her tracks. "Falling out? When?"

"Not long before Marty died."

"Is that one of the things you told that detective?"

"Like you said. None of my business. Figured I should keep my mouth shut. Especially with my father breathing down my neck."

Tess softened her tone. "Is that why you continued to have sex with Marty during the restraining order? To get back at your Dad?"

"Yes. No. I don't know. My parents have stage-managed my whole life. Like I'm an actor in their little play using their script. Marty was a break from all that. He was fun."

"And your fiancé? Isn't he fun?"

"My parents like him. So, I like him." Deirdre picked up the wrap and placed it around her waist as if trying it on for size. But she soon wadded it up and tossed it on the table.

Tess was starting to wonder about Deirdre's strange relationship with her parents. Deirdre's folks were being unreasonably furious with her over Marty.

That sudden insight startled Tess—how furious were they? And how far would they go to keep Deirdre from being with Marty? Maybe that restraining order was only the first step.

She felt a cold shiver along her spine, the same feeling as when she suspected Antonio killed Marty. Dear god, she was a mess. This whole thing was a mess. Why couldn't Marty's father have accepted it was suicide? Nothing would bring Marty back.

Deirdre went to the wrap she'd wadded up to unfold it and smooth out the creases. For a woman who was engaged and getting ready to celebrate her fiancé's birthday, she looked pretty miserable.

Tess blurted out, "You were in love with Marty, weren't you?"

Deirdre didn't answer, grabbing a pair of sunglasses from a display rack and trying them on. Tess was sure the other woman was trying to hide the glint of tears in her eyes. More messes, more pain, more lies.

Tess asked, "Did you tell your parents you loved him?"

Still no answer. "Did he love you?"

This time, she didn't wait for Deirdre to answer as Tess voiced a sudden thought out loud. "If he did, it must have killed him when you got engaged to Dale." When she realized what she'd said, Tess froze.

Deirdre whipped off the sunglasses and jammed them into their slot. "I've got to bug off. Stuff to do, places to go, and all. I've got my target practice at noon. And Dale and I have plans tomorrow to drive to Norfolk to catch a concert by Thirteen Machine. I'll need to find a new outfit to wear." She grabbed a box of taffy and headed for the checkout.

Tess found she'd lost interest in her items and put them all back. Instead, she snagged the crystal ball with the baby sturgeon inside. She paid for her purchase and took it outside where she collapsed onto a bench. Goddamn that Marty. He left a trail of sorrow and grief in his wake, alive or dead. It was like that Akashic nonsense. Karmic debts, patterns, and blockages in your channels or some other gibberish.

Antonio, Deirdre, Lena, all loved Marty. So what was the matter with her? His competitiveness, his drive, always being in his shadow. And her parents.

Her face was hot again, and she knew what that meant. This was frickin' ridiculous. She needed a vacation. Or the bottled equivalent. Spying the Shanty Bar across the street, she picked herself up and headed over.

A little Sex on the Beach would do fine. With extra vodka. Anything to get those song lyrics out of her head, *I live in the shadows, and alone I shall be, gone are the days that were bright and carefree. . .*

36

For most people, Saturday mornings meant sleeping late or a more leisurely schedule. In Drayco's line of work, Saturday was like any other day, depending on the caseload. He'd made a dozen phone calls after breakfast, with one guiding him shortly after noon to a specific target—an appropriate term seeing where his quest led him.

The range was a new addition since his last trip to Cape Unity. So small, you might miss it, tucked away on what was once farmland.

He walked across the half-grass, half-gravel lot, past the sign that read "BJ's Skeet and Shoot," and around a fence of wooden slats. Behind lay two cinder block towers on either side of a semicircular dirt ring with spoke patterns.

A few people milled around, but the ring and towers for skeet weren't the main activity at the moment. At the rear of the field, he spied a target launcher with a table of clay pigeons beside it.

He walked up to the small group as a young woman balanced a shotgun on her shoulder and yelled out, "Pull!"

A clay target soared into the air before arcing toward the ground. The woman fired and missed. "Damn. Three misses in a row."

Drayco moved closer to Deirdre Pinnick until she saw him out of the corner of her eye and whirled around. She ripped off her ear protectors. "Somehow I'll bet you're not here for target practice."

He squinted at the spot where her target had flown. "I don't know. Pays to keep one's skills sharp."

She studied him and then thrust the gun at him. "Have at it."

He took the pump-action shotgun, flipped it over, and pointed it at the ground to check the chamber for shells, but she cut him off. "It's got three shells left and ready to fire." Then she put her ear protectors on his head, followed by her safety glasses.

With a nod at the man operating the pigeon launcher, Drayco pumped the shotgun and hoisted it to his shoulder. He took a few moments to slow his breathing and then gave the cue, "Pull."

The pigeon soared fifteen feet into the air, and Drayco nailed it on the first try, shards of the clay exploding in mini-fireworks. When Deirdre said, "That was a lucky first try," he nodded his approval for the staffer behind the launcher to send up another one.

She interrupted the man, "Uh-uh. To prove he's not just lucky, John, fire up two targets."

Drayco pumped the gun again and waited for John to signal ready. He called out, "Pull," then listened to the whirring of the machine's launching arm as it engaged. Two clays rocketed skyward, and Drayco aimed for the lower one first. Strike, eject, pump, strike. Two for two.

When he handed the gun and gear to Deirdre, she asked, "Where did you learn how to shoot like that?"

"FBI."

"I thought it was the CIA who did all that sniper stuff."

"Not a sniper. A good student."

"Could have fooled me."

He glanced around at the uncomfortably close group of people. "Mind if we chat out there for a minute?" He motioned toward the parking lot.

Deirdre handed her shotgun to John and followed him to the lot where they were alone. She smiled up at him. "If I didn't know better, I'd say you were flirting with me."

Drayco smirked. "It's just nice to get you away from your father. He can be rather—"

"Strict. Overprotective. Authoritarian. Smothering. Take your pick."

"With your best interests at heart."

She snorted. "*His* best interests, you mean. Image, reputation, career. I'm another extension of that."

"Isn't your mother the image-conscious, controlling one of the pair?"

"She's the more desperate of the two. Dad's a typical attorney."

"My sympathies."

"Well, it could be worse."

"How would you define 'worse'?"

She sat on the hood of the Starfire, making Drayco wince. "A drunk. That would be worse."

He recalled his visit to see Barbara Pinnick yesterday and how he'd left her slumped over her self-spiked lemonade. "I'm surprised your mother approves of your sport shooting."

"When she learned skeet shooting's in the Olympics, she decided it was a grand idea. Something rich people do. Besides, Dad was into competitive bullseye shooting. Before he and Mom got married."

So much for Drayco's bet that Emmerson Pinnick wouldn't be interested in guns. "Did Marty join you here?"

"Marty?" She shook her head. "He told me he hated guns."

"And he never practiced here or at any other shooting range?"

"Not that I know of. Besides, he had this eye-hand coordination thing. I think they call it cross dominance."

"Meaning he was right-handed but had a dominant left eye."

"He found out when he took golf lessons. The instructor told him it was throwing his depth perception off. Or something like that."

Deirdre's voice grew so soft, he barely heard her as she added, "But I guess that doesn't matter when you're putting a gun to your head."

An image from the crime scene of Marty's body and the bullet wound came to Drayco's mind. She was right—it wouldn't have mattered. But this was the first hint of anything other than defiance from Deirdre when mentioning her dead friend.

He asked, "Then where did Marty learn how to use a weapon?"

"I hadn't thought of that. Antonio? I mean, he had a gun that was stolen."

"Allegedly stolen."

"There you go again. You law types are all 'allegedly' this and 'allegedly' that."

Drayco had to scoot closer to the Starfire to avoid being hit by an arriving car. "Marty was allegedly on a health kick and was fond of a green protein powder. Did you try it?"

She frowned. "He didn't use that while we were dating. Before we broke up and that whole restraining order thing."

Carefully worded in a way her legal-eagle father would approve. He pressed her further, "And you didn't see him at all after the breakup?"

She paused for a microsecond again before giving him a long once-over and a coquettish smile. "I want to hear more about you. How did such a hunk get to be a private eye?"

He ignored her diversion tactic. "Did you borrow money from Marty for an abortion, Deirdre?"

Her eyes widened to the size of clay skeet discs. "Who said that?"

"Antonio."

"The nerve of that prick. Look, okay, I borrowed money from Marty. But it wasn't for an abortion, it was for body piercings. I didn't have the cash. Couldn't ask my parents 'cause I knew my mother wouldn't agree, considering where they are. You want me to prove it to you?" She started to pull up her top and bra, but he stopped her.

"I'll take you at your word for now."

Her frown morphed into a smile in a nanosecond. "You didn't answer *my* question. About how someone like you got to be a private eye."

"I'm pretty boring. I just help people."

"And ask a bunch of questions."

"That's how I help people." Her father would not approve of the look she was giving him. In some ways, she reminded him of a younger version of Darcie, if Darcie had dyed her hair red.

"Well, you can help *me*," she said.

"In what way?"

"Drop this Marty investigation. I mean, it's so obvious it was suicide. Don't you think it's making his father miserable by stringing this out? Giving him false hope?"

"Mr. Penry doesn't see it that way."

She crinkled her nose. "It's all Lena Bing's fault. Marty didn't love her, and she couldn't handle it."

"Do you mean that in the figurative sense—as in, it made her upset? Or in the literal sense, as in she was jealous enough to kill him?"

Deirdre fiddled with the engagement ring on her left hand and didn't say anything for a moment. Then she replied, "It's always the quiet ones, right?"

"I wouldn't say always."

"All I know is, she was as obsessed with Marty as Marty was with that suicide song."

"Did Marty tell you of this 'obsession' on Lena's part? Or did you observe it firsthand?"

"Lena saw him as her ticket out of poverty. Marty could sense her desperation. But you want me to come right out and say she's capable of murder, right?"

"Is she?"

Deirdre stared at his shirt. "You've got something on that, right over there."

"What?" He looked down to where she was pointing.

"Come here," she motioned for him to come closer to where she was sitting.

He obliged, and she grabbed his shirt and pulled him in so quickly, he fell on top of her. She laughed, wrapped one arm around his waist and the other around his neck, and captured his lips in a deep kiss.

When she let him up for air, she winked at him and hopped off the car. As she walked toward the shooting range, she called out over her shoulder, "Something to remember me by, Mr. FBI."

Drayco watched her go with the passing fancy that he saw why Marty was attracted to her. At the very least, her kissing skills would be a big draw.

Marty was cross-dominant? Interesting. That wouldn't have made much of a difference when using the gun sideways, close to his head, as Deirdre noted. But why would a young man who disliked guns choose that as his suicide method?

On the other hand, Deirdre could handle a gun, even if she weren't an expert. So could her father, the former competitive bullseye shooter. But it wouldn't take an expert to kill their victim at close range.

Drayco walked around to the driver's side of his car, the gravel crunching under his feet. The same type of sandstone dotted the shores of the creek near the clearing where Marty died. Lena had traversed that creek with her motorcycle like an old pro. And as Deirdre said, Lena had as much of ax to grind with Marty as any.

Deirdre wasn't being a hundred percent truthful with Drayco, he knew that. She certainly wasn't being straight with her fiancé if her flirting was any sign.

Every time he came to the Eastern Shore, relationship lies were an epidemic. No, that wasn't fair—the plague was truly universal. Relationship lies were a human affliction no vaccine would ever cure.

Flipping through his mental "scorecard" of all those lies was making his headache throb harder. The thunder of gunfire sending grayish-umber comet fragments into his brain added to the throbbing. He slid into the Starfire and kept the windows rolled up despite the heat until he'd left the range far behind.

37

Drayco hovered over Reece as the other man snapped photographs of the construction site. The skeleton might be gone, but Reece seemed determined to document the site for the Historical Society. He was even antsier after Drayco told him his big news.

Reece adjusted the aperture of his digital camera. "You made my day with your phone call. Hell, my whole month."

"It's not a done deal, but it's looking good."

"When you said a Smithsonian forensic anthropologist was going to get custody of Grabbing Irons, I had a heart attack. I've come to consider him as 'our' skeleton. You think I'm obsessed, but he belongs to Cape Unity now. I mean, he's been here longer than anyone else."

Drayco nodded. "That's what I told Berkeley Naylor. Fortunately, he's a good guy and agreed. I don't know when the Historical Society will get the bone fragments since Berk wants to scrutinize everything. After he's finished, Grabbing Irons is all yours."

Reece pumped a fist in the air. "Haha! I knew this would all work out. I owe you a lobster dinner. Even better, I'll give the Opera House a cut of the new tourist dollars the exhibit will pull in."

"I'm a little disappointed your new pirate obsession is due to the money. A bit shallow, for you, isn't it?"

Reece snapped a few more photos. "If you must know, Mr. Judgmental, my Grandpapa had six fingers on one hand. I was embarrassed as a tot and didn't want to be seen with the 'monster.' He died when I was seven. I've always hated myself for not spending more time with him. Gramps had a wicked sense of humor."

"He probably understood."

"Who knows now? But having Grabbing Irons here, well. Kinda like I'm bringing my grandfather home."

Drayco stepped around to avoid Reece as the historian knelt for a different camera angle. "You said you had news for me?"

"Funny how our news dovetailed. I have a few friends in high places, too. Ancestry gurus. They traced the lineage of Grabbing Irons. No heirs."

"No claims, then. Lucky you."

"Precisely. For grins, I had them trace Rawley Burrowes, the pirate feuding with Grabbing Irons—and the number one suspect in his murder."

"Let me guess. He returned to England rich from his ill-gotten gains and had dozens of children?"

Reece stood up and dusted grass and dirt off his pants. "*Au contraire mon frère.*"

"These pirates were British, not French, Reece."

"Whatever. Burrowes returned to the mother country before Grabbing Irons's disappearing act. He couldn't have killed him."

Reece stopped taking pictures to look through the digital gallery. Drayco peered over Reece's shoulder at the photos. "That one's pretty good."

"Wish I'd got snaps with the actual skeleton."

"I'll see if Sheriff Sailor can help out there. Deputy Giles took several."

Drayco surveyed the scowling construction crew who were watching them. The men didn't want to be here on a Saturday, but the skeleton discovery had set their schedule back.

He said, "How will you place the pirate's death in context without the whole story?"

Reece sighed. "It will have to stay a mystery."

"You have any info on Grabbing Irons's last known whereabouts?"

"That book I showed you said his last ship was the *Sea Strumpet*. Vanished when he did."

"Was there a crew roster or manifest?"

Reece tapped his chin. "I'll have to get back to you on that."

When one of the construction crew pointed in their direction, Drayco said, "You've got all you need, right? Giles can fill in the rest."

"I suppose." Then Reece brightened. "I'm all curious now. My new mission is to find out about that crew, come hell or high water."

"On a flat peninsula like this, hell *is* high water." Drayco made a big production of returning to his car to encourage Reece to do the same. Hopefully, that would discourage the foreman from charging over to chew them out. "If you get any crew names, zap me a copy."

Reece squinted at Drayco out of his good eye. "We can race each other. To see who uncovers something first."

"You're on, History Man."

❧ ❧ ❧

Drayco sat at the kitchen table sipping Maida's newest concoction, rum punch "with a twist." It was an alcohol-gourmand-guessing-game to suss out her secret ingredients. This time, he'd put his money on the Angostura bitters family, a pinch of bourbon, and possibly apricot brandy.

He didn't care what was in it as long as it dulled the pain from his headache. How many days had it been now? Too long. Maybe that was why he took a wrong turn on his way back to the Lazy Crab, a path he'd driven countless times before.

He'd returned from the construction site with Reece in time to catch the B&B's latest guests departing to North Carolina. Drayco asked Maida, "They weren't leaving early on my account, I hope."

She handed him a coaster. "They're bird-watchers. Came here hoping to see a black-bellied whistling duck, a pink-footed goose, and a Barrow's goldeneye. They're traveling along the coast for more sightings. Up next, Cape May. They mentioned a black-capped petrel."

"You have a good memory for bird species. I'm impressed."

She picked up a pad of paper. "Wrote them all down. Major and I should pay more attention to our fowl friends."

The man in question sidled into the kitchen, grabbed a glass, and poured himself some punch. After taking a sip, he said, "Tastes apricoty."

Drayco grinned. "When do your next guests arrive?"

"Next Saturday." Maida added, "But our favorite guest is already here."

"That's the first time I've been called anyone's favorite anything in a long while."

"I find that hard to believe." She refilled his glass with more punch.

The Major said, "Guess how long you get to stay depends upon this suicide thingy. And that skeleton they found?"

Out of deference to the sheriff, Drayco hadn't told the Jepsons about the skeleton and the coin, though he trusted them. But it seemed Reece's loose-lipped friend had been busy. "The skeleton appears to be a pirate from the eighteenth century. Grabbing Irons Greaver, so-called because he had six fingers on one hand."

"Pirates, eh?" The Major perched on the edge of his chair. "Now, that's a topic for you. Was he found with any booty?"

Since the cat was half-way out of the bag, Drayco replied, "One gold coin. Not exactly a treasure."

The Major stroked his beard. "Hardly surprising. Folks would have found it by now. Guess there wasn't a treasure map, either?"

"Sorry, but no."

"Well, now, I've never heard of any such maps being found on the Delmarva. Most of the pirates were up in Maryland. Or south near Jamestown and Norfolk. Like Blackbeard, you know, killed by a British naval officer. His head hung on a pole near the entrance to Hampton Creek."

Maida glared at her husband. "You do love those gory tales."

Drayco said, "No treasure with Blackbeard, either."

"But there's always the Charles Wilson treasure."

"Haven't heard of that one, Major."

"One of those legends that probably isn't true. An American sailor-turned-pirate by that name wrote a letter to his brother. Had directions to where he'd buried ten chests filled with gold bullion, silver, and gems. The Brits intercepted the letter, captured him, jailed him. Then hanged him in 1750."

"With directions that specific, surely it would settle the matter."

"You'd think. Allegedly buried near Chincoteague or Assateague. Never found. Lots of folks feel it's a hoax."

Drayco set his half-full glass on the table. Maida's rapid refills would have him falling down drunk in a few hours. "Marty and his friend Antonio often went beachcombing."

"With a metal detector?""

"Not according to Antonio."

The Major snorted. "Be impossible to find coins without it."

"Regardless, I'm not sold on the idea Grabbing Irons is connected with this case."

"Sure would be something, wouldn't it?"

Maida peered at him over her chartreuse glasses. "If not buried treasure, then why would someone want to kill Marty?"

Drayco replied, "Jealousy is a leading contender. Marty's group of friends had 'inter-attachments.'"

"Sex, you mean. But sex has a way of turning into something deeper. Add jealousy in, and there's trouble."

That was one thing Drayco loved about Maida. Her insights were spot-on. "At this point, it's hard to tell who had the most to gain by killing Marty."

Maida said, "If Deirdre Pinnick and Marty were serious, must have ticked off her parents. You don't think they'd go to such extremes?"

"It's not impossible. But I'm long on motives and short on evidence. For murder, that is, not suicide."

Maida poked her head in the oven and checked a timer. "Another sixty minutes. Hope you can wait that long."

Drayco's cellphone rang, and when he saw the caller, he answered. After getting a briefing from Sheriff Sailor, he hung up.

Maida put a hand on his shoulder. "You have that look on your face. It's got to be bad."

"I may have to wait longer than ninety minutes for your lovely meal yet again. Sorry I'm making this a habit. Can you put it aside for me later?"

"We could hold supper for you."

"Don't wait for me. I have no idea how long this will take."

Sailor's call had turned Drayco's stomach into a cement mixer, and he had a burning feeling in the back of his throat. He looked longingly around the kitchen, wanting to stay there. Not that it would matter—he doubted he'd be hungry for quite some time.

38

The majority of suicide cases Drayco worked on almost made a weird kind of sense. Usually, they involved drugs, psychosis, or people who didn't want to go to prison. Or who were already there.

Antonio Skye's, however, didn't have any of those markers. The sheriff's deputies had removed the body from the noose fashioned from polypropylene fishing rope and laid him on the floor before Drayco arrived.

Sheriff Sailor pointed to Antonio's hand. "Look what's he clutched there. It's why I called you in."

Drayco walked over, his feet making swishing noises from being wrapped in shoe covers, and bent over for a closer examination. It was a copy of the suicide song.

Despite having nitrile gloves on, Drayco put out his hand to smooth Antonio's hair and touch him gently on the cheek. Still warm, as if he'd laid down for a nap. "Who found him?"

"His mother. She hadn't heard from him in a while. So, she decided to bring him supper and found him then. Called us right away but is too distraught to talk. She also called her priest, and he's with her now. We'll see if she can chat tomorrow."

Drayco studied the paper. "This copy of the suicide song is different."

"How so?"

"No added verse, as with Marty."

"We'll fingerprint this one and match 'em up."

Drayco recalled Antonio's words to him about the song, that it was cursed. It certainly seemed to be so for poor Antonio, and maybe that was the true power of curses. Whether real or imagined, all that mattered was whether you believed.

Drayco looked past Deputy Giles, who was handling CI work solo. "Did you find his cellphone?"

Sailor pointed to a table. "Over there."

That was a second detail different from Marty's death. Spying a book lying next to the body, Drayco picked it up. He showed it to Sailor. "*The Akashic Records: Unlock Infinite Universal Purpose.*"

It was the same title the bookstore clerk sold earlier in the year. Drayco flipped through the pages, prompting Sailor to ask, "Find anything?"

"No margin scribblings." He handed the book to the sheriff. "He left no other note of any kind?"

"Just that blasted song."

Drayco stood there, surprised at how grateful he was to miss seeing Antonio hanging from his rope. But why? He'd witnessed death and its aftermath numerous times before. He shook his head. Yeah, who was he trying to kid? He knew exactly why, and he hadn't told Nelia the whole story.

That stormy June evening, Drayco trudged through a fierce downpour to see Alexander Vucasovich. Using his key, he went inside when Vuca didn't answer the doorbell. He made his way to the study where he found Vuca's body—draped over his beloved piano, blood dripping from the gunshot wound as it turned the white keys red.

Another of the violent images Drayco had crammed inside his mental lockbox to keep him sane. In its own way, Antonio's death felt every bit as personal. Twice Drayco missed the signs, and twice two men died.

A feminine voice heralded the arrival of Nelia Tyler, who'd donned her protective gear and joined Sailor and Drayco. She sighed when she saw Antonio. "I know it shouldn't be this way, but it's the young ones that are the hardest."

She added to Sailor, "Sorry I'm late. I was up in Baltimore staying with Tim this weekend."

"Giles can fill you in on what he's done so far."

She gave Drayco a quick wave before joining her colleague. He asked, "Sheriff, was Rosita able to give any details about Antonio's behavior recently?"

"Not much. You spoke with him, didn't you?"

"Two days ago, on the beach." Another reason Drayco's stomach was churning. Drayco considered his instincts to be decent, but this time, he'd not only missed—he'd maybe even dismissed—the signs.

After barking a command to Giles, Sailor said to Drayco. "Antonio owned the gun used to kill Marty Penry. You know what a psychologist would say—it contributed to Antonio's despair. And if he were the one who killed Marty? More so."

"We don't know that yet." But as Drayco studied the cramped space more intently, it took on the air of a Marty shrine. Photos of Marty graced the tables with one enlarged into a print hanging on a wall. All it needed were candles and incense.

The biggest surprise came from the drawings and paintings lying on a table next to pencils, pens, and watercolors. Drayco inspected them. A few were of Marty, but the rest depicted coastal scenes and a few abstracts. He was nearly as good as Virginia Harston and likely self-taught.

Sailor said, "All this Marty memorabilia gives weight to my guilt hypothesis."

Drayco picked up a frame with a faded photo of a man he didn't recognize with his arm around a boyish Antonio. "Is this Antonio's father?"

Sailor took a look. "Arrested before my era. They do share a resemblance."

"Rosita told me her co-workers at the plant whispered about Antonio and how he must have killed Marty. Like father, like son."

Sailor removed his hat to rub his forehead. "That's bullshit. Her co-workers should mind their own business. If there's one thing I can't stand, it's gossip."

"Can come in handy during an investigation."

"But I hate it in principle."

"I'd question your sanity if you didn't. Have you traced the source of the sertraline found in Marty's protein powder?"

"Working on it. No tracebacks to Marty yet. That clinic doctor at the plant turned out to be mostly clean. No malpractice reports, no censures, never met Marty. He *is* a little too free with opioids, something Giles is checking out. But the guy doesn't prescribe sertraline."

Drayco knelt next to the bookcase. Only a few books—a dictionary, school textbooks, a few graphic novels. He picked up a book on biology and flipped through the pages. A single white envelope floated out between two pages and onto the floor.

Addressed by hand, it read, "To Antonio." Pulling out the sheet of paper inside, he scanned the note, also handwritten, filled with writing on both sides.

Sailor strained to read the paper. "Secret message?"

"A love letter from Tess Gartin to Antonio." It was painful to read the raw, intimate outpouring from the then-teenaged girl's heart. Did she still feel the same?

Drayco stared at Antonio's body, newly photographed and being transferred to a gurney, then handed the note and envelope to Sailor. "Might not be relevant."

"You never know." Sailor added it to a small evidence stack.

Drayco opened a closet as he avoided getting in the way of Giles and Nelia. "Any guns or other weapons found?"

Sailor replied, "Nope."

Drayco pulled out the drawers of a chest along one wall. Each held different kinds of seashells—scallops, sand dollars, knobbed whelks, and a type of thin, brittle clamshell called angel wing.

He gathered a couple of the shells and asked Sailor, "Mind if I take a few of these when you're finishing dusting?"

Sailor gave him a "What the hell do you want that for" look but nodded his assent.

A small kitchenette drew Drayco's attention. And not just because Nelia was working in that area. He approached her. "Found any treasure, gold or otherwise?"

She closed a drawer. "Not yet."

Her eyes had dark circles, and her face was paler than usual. He asked, "Are you okay?"

She pursed her lips together in a hard line. "Lack of sleep."

It was more than sleep deprivation, but he wasn't going to pry, about that or Tim. She opened the door to a cabinet that served as a pantry, and one item immediately caught his attention. He pulled out a small unlabeled plastic container and held it up for Nelia to see as he unscrewed the top. The green powder inside was very familiar.

Drayco waved to Sailor, who ambled over to join them. "Whatcha got?"

Drayco held up the powder. "More to test."

Sailor's eyes narrowed as he grabbed the container. "If this is what I think it is, we could be looking at a much different ballgame."

When the crew rolled the gurney out the door, Barbara Pinnick's description of Antonio rang in Drayco's head—Deirdre's "ghost friend." Vuca's last words to Drayco also echoed back to him, one of his teacher's favorite Marcus Aurelius quotes, "Death isn't the greatest loss to fear, it's never beginning to live."

◈ ◈ ◈

Drayco almost didn't find his way in the moonlight. After some wrong turns and getting the Starfire's tires stuck in soft ground twice, he made it to his destination. He parked in the cutout by the side of the road and pulled out his flashlight. Once barefoot, he threaded a path through the seagrasses and sand dunes.

It wasn't too smart to be here at night where it would be hard to spot one of Antonio's Portuguese man-of-war blobs. But he didn't really care that much. He sat on a bank and turned off the flashlight, watching as the waves lapped against the shore. The light from the full moon reflected on the water in a shimmer of liquid gold. It was mesmerizing.

His thoughts kept returning to his last meeting with Antonio here on this beach. He'd missed something. He must have missed something.

The young man hadn't been talkative, but during Drayco's chat with him at the chicken plant, he was equally terse and brooding. What had Tess said? That "Antonio can be a drama queen. Named Best Actor at the school play and had me guessing what was real and what wasn't."

Maybe Drayco hadn't missed suicidal signs in Antonio. Maybe the young man was "acting" all along, and his façade hid a darker side, the sociopathic killer. Or he was covering for someone else, a partner-in-crime. Or maybe that damned song *was* really cursed.

A couple of crabs scuttled off to Drayco's right, diving into their burrows when he moved his feet. Chesapeake blue crabs only lived for about a year. Hardly enough time to even realize you were alive to begin with.

What would it feel like to *want* to die? Would Drayco even realize it if he did? And could music, the one thing that had kept him sane all these years, be a catalyst for that urge to end it all? He'd played the Suicide Sonata every night now. Had Antonio listened to the song one last time before he died?

As Drayco stared up the sky, a meteor, or "shooting star," passed overhead. Just like the one Antonio said he'd seen here once.

Drayco sat on the sand for the better part of an hour, listening to the whistling of the wind gusts and the spongy sienna-and-magenta pinwheels of the waves. Vuca, Drayco's mother, Marty, Antonio, so many others. Like waves on the shore, echoes in time.

Finally, he hauled himself up and trudged back toward the Starfire, flashlight in hand. Right as he cranked up the engine, his cellphone chimed the arrival of a new text. The number from the texter was unfamiliar, but the attachment wasn't. Another copy of the Suicide Sonata song. So much for Antonio being the sender unless he'd found a way to do it from beyond the grave.

39

Sunday, June 24

Drayco hadn't slept much. His dreams starred faceless figures in shadowed rooms, and he fell into a deep pit filled with water, nearly suffocating. Thanks to his insomnia, he was awake when Nelia called early with a tip that Rosita Skye would be at the sheriff's office at nine. Nelia probably shouldn't have told him, but he was grateful.

Sailor wasn't surprised to see him when he showed up—although the lawman gave a pointed look in Nelia's direction. "Since you're here, you may as well sit in on our chat."

Deputy Giles showed Rosita Skye to a small interview room. She gratefully accepted coffee from Nelia, who sat beside her at the metal table. Her priest was the one who drove her in, taking time out before a service, and hovered outside the room's window.

Sailor wasn't into sexist nonsense, but he'd asked Nelia to take the lead on questioning to ease Mrs. Skye's stress. Nelia started gently, "Mrs. Skye, we're grateful you could come this morning. We understand how hard this must be. We won't keep you too long."

Rosita folded her hands in her lap. Her red-rimmed eyes barely focused on Nelia as they blinked away a scrim of heartache and pain.

"When did you last speak with Antonio?"

"Two days. I think to myself, maybe he go off with a friend for a weekend trip or such. But I worry when I not hear from him. So I go to his apartment. And then I find him." Her voice trailed off, and she grabbed a tissue from her pocket to blow her nose.

"When the two of you last spoke, did he say anything unusual? Did he make any comments about hurting himself?"

Rosita shook her head vigorously. "He was like always."

Nelia pushed over a box of tissues to her. "He didn't seem distressed or upset in the past week or so?"

"Only the death of his friend. But that is over a month. I hoped he would be better by now."

Drayco kept quiet but was disturbed by her words. It would take Rosita much longer than a mere month to be "better," so why expect it from her son? Especially when her pressure on Antonio about his feelings for Marty may have contributed to his depression. But, then, did Drayco's own questioning of Antonio also play a role in his mental state?

Nelia pressed on. "Rosita, did you overhear anyone threaten your son at the plant?"

"No one would want to harm my Antonio. He was a good boy. He was good to his *mamacíta*."

"We only want the truth. If someone else was involved in Antonio's death, we want to bring that person to justice."

"I want that, too." Rosita grabbed another tissue to wipe her eyes.

"He had some green protein powder in his apartment. Do you have any idea where he got it or when he began using it?"

"What difference can it make now?"

"Marty used it, so we're curious."

"If Marty liked it, that is why. Antonio looked up to Marty. Wanted to do everything he did."

Drayco pulled out a chair to sit across from her, picked up a book on the table, and showed it to her. "Do you recognize this?"

She read the title. "Ah-kah-chick Records." Then she frowned. "That is what you asked me at my house."

Before Drayco could reply, her frown turned into a mix of anger and grief that cut Drayco to the core. "You told me not to worry, that it was harmless. If Antonio killed himself over this, it is not so harmless, is it? I told you it was evil, wicked."

He turned the book face down. The air in the room suddenly seemed thinner, colder. With the acute feeling of Sailor's laser-sharp stare aimed toward him, Drayco asked gently, "Did Antonio mention finding any valuables during his beachcombing trips? Coins or items more valuable than shells?"

Her scowl soon faded, and the grief took over. "He never mentioned such things. I did not pry. He should be his own man, I said. Unlike his father."

She paused for a moment. "I know what people say. That my Antonio killed Marty. Now they will say he killed himself, too much guilt. You do not believe it, do you?" She looked from Drayco to Nelia to Sailor, imploring each of them to agree.

Nelia was the one to reply, "Like Mr. Drayco said, we'll uncover the truth. You can rest assured."

Rosita's frail demeanor was crumbling by the second. Her eyes brimmed with fresh tears as she said, "What am I going to do? He was all I had left."

Nelia gave a questioning look at Sailor, who opened the door to allow the priest to escort her outside and home. After Rosita had left, Sailor said, "We didn't get much from that, but she's in shock. I spoke with Reverend Alvarez privately. He's a good man. Said he'd check in on her. Get her into a support group."

Nelia spoke up, "Too many parents not knowing their own kids around here."

Sailor replied, "*Maybe* she didn't know her son as well as she thought she did. Or she was in on it."

"Think that's possible?"

"In this business, you gotta consider all options. No matter how distasteful. Particularly if there's a treasure involved. Money can make good people do very bad things."

Drayco added, "She made it clear how upset she was with Marty because of Antonio's crush. It's not impossible she killed Marty to remove an 'evil' influence. If Antonio found out, maybe he couldn't live with the knowledge."

Nelia winced. "I'm not liking that scenario. Sorry."

Sailor sat on the edge of the table. "You get the fingerprint analysis done on the two copies of the suicide songs, Tyler?"

"I did a quickie comparison. The only prints on each were the victim's."

Sailor nodded. "No surprise. FYI, to touch all bases, I asked the M.E., Dr. Fireside, to add autoerotic asphyxiation to her list of things to check. Didn't see signs, myself."

Drayco had also noticed that and felt relief, surprisingly protective of Antonio and his reputation. He picked up the Akashic Records book and flipped through the table of contents, stopping on one page. "Soul vibration."

"What?"

"Something mentioned here. And the words Marty wrote in the margin of the song."

"That book tell us who killed him, then?"

"I researched the term. Near as I can tell, it's mostly used by people who claim they can read your 'soul vibration' for you. If you fork over some dough."

"Figures," The sheriff snorted. He folded his arms across his chest. "The two boys in Marty's group are dead, and the three girls are alive. Who knows? Maybe this is a feminist group that kills off men."

Nelia glared at him. "Really?"

"As I say, gotta consider all the possibilities." Sailor made a motion as if he was pulling her chain. "At any rate, their gang was quite the heartbreaker set. Lena loved Marty, who loved Deirdre, who doesn't love anybody but herself. Tess loved Antonio, who was in love with Marty. And there you go."

He turned to Drayco. "Got the lab test results of your coffee. Had the same antidepressant in the green powder, the liquid form. Not enough to kill. Would have made you feel sick if you'd drunk it all."

"Sheriff, if the protein powder in Antonio's apartment is the same that Marty used—"

"Still doesn't prove Marty Penry's suicide was murder. All those lawsuits over that class of drug causing suicides, remember?"

Drayco drummed his fingers on the metal table. "Which would make it the perfect weapon."

"A too-unpredictable one, as I've said." Sailor eased out of his chair as he added, "Oh, and thanks for tipping me off to that website with the Suicide Sonata piano music downloads. Got the site owner to give me names of people who'd downloaded it. Other than you, just one."

He handed over the piece of paper where he'd written the name. Drayco held it up to Nelia. "Tyler, you up for an interrogation? That is if your boss approves."

Sailor raised his hands in resignation. "I'm swamped. You kids go. Have fun. Report back ASAP, or your coach will turn into a pumpkin. A rotten one, at that."

40

Nelia stood with Drayco on the step of Cherie and Judson Kolman's house after ringing the doorbell. They allowed extra time for Cherie to navigate her way to the door with her crutches, and she cheerfully welcomed them inside. "If you want to see Judson, he's at the station. He likes being there on quiet Sundays. Gets more work done."

She pointed to a necklace lying on a table. It looked like the same necklace Kolman wore on the boat with a small key and a dolphin. "He won't be long when he realizes he's left that behind. It's his good luck charm. Doesn't go anywhere without it." She smiled. "Poseidon would be a better choice. I'll get him one for his birthday."

Nelia replied, "Actually, we wanted to speak with Lena Bing. We understand she's working for you this morning."

If Cherie was surprised by that, she didn't show it. "I love having her around. Such a hard worker. Pays attention to every detail."

Cherie called out for her aide, and Lena walked in from the back part of the house. "These lovely folks want to see you, dear."

Lena's gaze darted toward Cherie. "I told them I was here when they called earlier. Guess I should have asked you first."

"It's fine. Why don't you all take a seat in the den."

She led the way and soon had Nelia, Drayco, and Lena ensconced on ash-gray tufted armchairs. Dark wooden cabinets sporting narrow drawers lay against one entire wall. Drayco had a good idea of what was in those drawers, judging from the array of framed boxes on the walls filled with coins.

Cherie asked if she could get them drinks. Nelia looked at Drayco and replied, "Thanks, but we may not be here that long." Cherie left to give them privacy with the excuse she needed to attend to her bird feeders.

Lena looked at them expectantly. "You said you had something important to tell me?"

Nelia adjusted herself in her chair as if sitting on a row of tacks. Delivering bad news was never fun. To make it easier on her, Drayco took the lead this time. "There are two items we wanted to discuss. The first has to do with Antonio Skye. Sadly, he was found dead last evening."

Lena gasped. "What? Oh my god, where? And how?"

"In his apartment on his mother's property. We're not sure yet if it was suicide, but it looks that way at first blush."

"Oh, my god." Lena clutched her hands to her chest, then said in a whisper. "Suicide?"

Drayco added, "We found a copy of the suicide song clutched in his hand."

Tears started to trickle down her face. "This is all my fault."

Drayco said, "You were the one who downloaded the piano sheet music from the internet, weren't you?"

She wiped her eyes with her sleeve. "I printed it out as a joke."

"You have a computer at home?"

She shook her head. "Used the one at the library. At the time, I was still mad at Marty for dumping me for Deirdre. So I egged him on about that sonata." She sniffled and hiccupped, prompting Nelia to get up to pour her a glass of water from a pitcher on a nearby table.

Lena drank some and then continued, "Then I found a song version and sent it to him. I wanted him to suffer but not kill himself. It was just a prank, a lousy prank. Maybe that damn song really is cursed."

Drayco asked, "You never 'egged him on' about taking his life?"

"I would never do that. I loved him. Despite his whole Deirdre obsession."

Drayco studied her face and her body language, looking for telltale signs of lying. But her shock, at least, seemed real. "When I spoke with you before, you lied about this."

"I was scared, okay?"

"Did you go through Marty's apartment after he died looking for the sonata print music?"

She sighed. "And threw it away. I'm not very proud of it. Of any of it."

"Did you take Marty's cellphone?"

"What? No, not that. I didn't see it." Lena rocked back and forth. "This can't be happening. First Marty and now Antonio."

Drayco paused as her sniffling started up again. He waited for it to abate and then asked, "Antonio hadn't contacted you recently, had he? Indicating he was in trouble?"

"Nothing. Not depression, not worry, not that damn song." Lena stopped rocking to bend over and take some deep breaths. When she straightened up, her eyes had hardened. "I overheard Deirdre teasing Marty about that sonata, too. You should ask *her*."

Deirdre hadn't mentioned that to Drayco, but there were plenty of lies to go around. "We'll do that. I know this is an odd question, but does your aunt own a metal detector?"

"She did. Who knows where it is now?" Lena quickly changed the subject. "So you think Marty and Antonio were murdered?"

Nelia replied, "As I said, we don't know yet."

Cherie popped into the room, and when she saw Lena's teary face, she rushed over to sit beside her. "Child, whatever has happened?"

Nelia said, "One of her friends passed away last night. He was also a good friend of Marty Penry."

Cherie put an arm around Lena's shoulders. "Oh, Lena, dear, I am so, so sorry." She looked at Nelia and Drayco. "This was sudden?"

Drayco got up to stand near a mounted coin display. "The sheriff's office is looking into it, but that's all about we can tell you."

Knowing how the small-town gossip mill worked in town, he asked, "Have you heard about the skeleton found at the new condo site? Centuries-old, possibly a pirate."

"A friend told me, yes."

Drayco flipped open his cellphone photo gallery to the picture he'd taken of the coin. He showed Cherie the photo. "Does this look familiar?"

Her face lit up. "Why, that looks like a Queen Anne 1714 guinea. They're rare. One sold at auction in the UK for two thousand pounds."

"Come across any of these yourself? Or known anyone around who had one?"

"I'd give anything to get my hands on such a beauty. But couldn't afford it unless I sold other coins first."

Cherie pulled her covetous gaze away from the coin, and with a look at Lena's pale face, reached over to give the young woman a hug. "Is there any way you could ask Lena questions some other time? This has been such a shock."

Nelia stood up to join Drayco and replied, "Lena, if you think of anything important to pass along, please let us know."

Lena exchanged a quick glance with Cherie, who hastened to reply, "Of course, she will. Won't you, dear?"

As Drayco followed Nelia out the door, they ran into Judson Kolman, whose face blanched at the sight of them. "Is everything okay? Cherie?"

"Your wife is fine," Drayco assured him. "It's Lena Bing who's had bad news."

The other man's facial muscles relaxed. "Sorry to hear that. You gave me quite a scare, though." He wiped his forehead, newly bathed in beads of sweat.

Drayco stepped off the porch so he wouldn't tower over Kolman. "Marty Penry's friend, Antonio Skye, was found deceased last evening."

"Tess told me he visited her at the station. A few days ago, I believe. He was very upset, making her worry, and I guess with good reason."

"Antonio hadn't visited the station before then? Or after?"

"Not to my knowledge." Kolman's mouth dropped open. "Wait, are you saying this was another suicide?"

"We don't have all the facts."

"That poor young man. And poor Tess. I'll have to give her a call and make sure she's okay."

A chipmunk darted through the grass and scurried across Kolman's shoe. He jumped, but his laugh was hollow. "Guess that's my cue to get off 'his' property. If you'll excuse me, I'll go check on my wife and Lena."

When Drayco and Nelia were clear of the house and its occupants, Nelia said, "Lena ordering that sonata, pushing Marty over the suicide song, taking antidepressants. Doesn't look good. There's that infamous case of the girl arrested for encouraging her friend to commit suicide."

"And Cherie Kolman? You see how obsessed she is with coin collecting. If that skeleton's gold coin was part of a larger stash, she could be involved. Or they're in it together."

"I'm not seeing that frail woman being a criminal mastermind."

He massaged his temples. "Maybe she and her husband were partners in crime. But none of this seems right."

She studied him. "You sure you're feeling okay? Watching your drinks?"

"Just thinking about Antonio. He told me he couldn't get that song out of his head, had nightmares from it. That he wished he'd never heard it because it's cursed."

"Surely, you don't agree?"

He looked at a colorful scarlet ibis as it flew overhead in the direction of the Wildlife Refuge. Birds never committed suicide, did they? Their survival instinct was too strong. And they never sat around contemplating their lot in life.

Nelia repeated, a little louder, "You don't, right?"

He turned toward her. "What? Oh, I don't believe in curses, no. But I do believe in obsessions. And this is one I can't explain."

Before Nelia slid into the Starfire's passenger seat, she added, "Mom and Sebastien Penry will be at my apartment tonight. They hope to hear from you in person with updates. Can you make it?"

"Might disappoint them with lack of news."

"They know you're committed and working hard. That's all they ask."

Was it enough? Hard to say. But speculating himself into a loop of self-doubt wasn't going to help anybody. He cranked up the Starfire to drive Nelia back to the sheriff's office, apologizing for the lack of AC.

As he gave the house one last look, he was startled to see Cherie Kolman staring at him from a front window.

41

Like Marty Penry's place, Nelia's apartment was part of a house made into a duplex and equally humble. But unlike Marty's, her unit was on the top and didn't seem quite as post-apocalyptic. The architecture had a beach cottage feel with seafoam-green shake siding and mailboxes carved into dolphins.

She led Drayco up the outside stairs and through the front door that opened onto the kitchen. It was in decent shape other than the interior looking like it jumped out of the 1970s. The color scheme, on the other hand, could startle even a paint salesman.

"Pink walls?" He surveyed the chairs and sofa with matching pink flowers and plaid patterns. "That's so not what I expected."

"The place came furnished. And I haven't gotten the okay to paint, but as soon as I do, that Pepto pink is history." She added, "If it makes you feel any better, this place was the scene of a murder. One reason I got it cheap."

He grinned at her. "Only you would find a crime-scene apartment."

From the babbling of voices, he gathered that Sebastien and Olive were outside, and Nelia motioned for him to follow her to the back of the wraparound deck. The duo in question sat at a wooden picnic table with an umbrella deflecting the late afternoon sun.

He caught a citrus-y whiff of the citronella candle on the middle of the table, and potted marigolds stood in one corner. A mosquito problem. He should tell Nelia that citronella didn't work. Or maybe he'd buy her some of Judson Kolman's bug spray.

As Drayco took in the view, he saw why there were mosquitoes. He'd known the house lay close to the shore but hadn't expected to have glimpses of the water from here. As he looked toward the north, he spied something else surprising—the rising condo development in the distance. How many more views was that abomination going to ruin?

Nelia and Drayco sat opposite the other two on the table and, after a quick greeting, Nelia plunged right in. "I waited to tell you in person. Antonio Skye's mother found him dead last night."

Olive put a hand to her chest. "Dear lord, no. What happened?"

"On the surface, it appears to be suicide. There are some parallels to Marty's death."

Sebastien jumped in to ask, "What parallels?"

"He had a copy of the suicide song clutched in his hand. And we found more of the green powder with the antidepressant in his apartment."

Marty's father was stunned into silence, so Drayco prompted him, "When did you last see Antonio?"

"I don't know. A year, I think. He seemed quite normal."

"No mention of being bullied or anyone with a grudge?"

"Why would anyone do that? Antonio was a harmless soul." Sebastien looked smaller and older as he hunched over with his hands splayed out on the table. "Marty, now Antonio. Maybe I was wrong all along. Grasping at straws, a fool who can't let things go."

Olive placed a hand on his arm. "I got the impression Antonio worshiped the ground Marty walked on. Perhaps the suicide's a copycat affair."

After a few moments of silence, Sebastien straightened up. "No, I don't buy that, not then, not now. My son would never commit suicide. I know him. He made it through his mother's death and was stronger for it. He wanted her to be proud of him."

Drayco said, "Something's been added to the mix that might have a bearing on that."

"What do you mean?"

"Someone sent copies of the suicide song to my phone. And my coffee was spiked with the same antidepressant found in the green powder."

Sebastien asked, "But why?"

"The murderer wanting to throw me off is one possibility. The question is, why would they go to the trouble of trying to disguise murder as suicide and then bring attention to it?"

Nelia said, "Unless it's a sick game at your expense, Drayco."

"Or someone desperately wants me to believe this is murder instead."

Sebastien's eyes flashed as Drayco's words sank in. "We're back to that, are we? Accusing me of killing my own son?"

Olive jumped in before Drayco had a chance to reply. "I met Antonio once. The soulful type, one of those who become poets or artists. Such sensitive souls often have an undiagnosed mental illness. Look at all the poets who've committed suicide."

Drayco thought of the artwork he'd found in Antonio's apartment. She was right about the artist part.

Olive was still holding onto Sebastien's arm but aimed her words at Drayco, "Could he have sent those songs and spiked your drink? Isn't it possible he killed Marty? It was his gun. Case solved."

Drayco took note of Olive's facial expressions as she kept looking at Sebastien, intense and worried. More intense than one would expect from just a close friend. She was also very touchy-feely, giving him a quick rub on the back.

Drayco remembered first meeting Olive and the tightened skin around her mouth when he mentioned her husband's name. At the time, the notion Sebastien and Olive were having an affair briefly crossed his mind, but he'd dismissed it. If it were true, Olive's objectivity was compromised—and was the man genuinely interested in her or playing her for some reason?

Drayco replied to Olive slowly, "The scenario you describe is one possibility. But we can't close the case yet."

Nelia added, "I understand this is hard. The waiting, the questions, having to relive the unpleasant memories."

Olive reached under the table and grasped Sebastien's hand. Nelia didn't appear to notice.

Drayco asked, "Sebastien, did you own a metal detector by any chance? Or did Marty?"

Sebastien squinted at Drayco. "What makes you ask that?"

"An eighteenth-century skeleton dug up at the new condo development had a gold coin worth three grand. Marty often went beachcombing, and he told Lena Bing there was 'something big' coming soon. It's all conjecture, but what if he'd found a stash of coins?"

"He never said a word. But why hide it instead of telling someone? Or selling it right away?"

"Possibly, his accomplice wanted it all for himself. Or, if he had more than one partner and Antonio was in on it, the third accomplice killed both."

Sebastien's face turned even darker. "Heard rumors of the skeleton at my current job. Wouldn't put it past them to say I planted the thing over a grudge. The coin makes it look worse for me, right?"

Nelia tensed, and Drayco quickly added, "It's likely the skeleton was there for centuries. Too decomposed and fragile to be recently buried."

Sebastien said, "I knew going into the bid for that condo project I had a fifty-fifty chance. Hell, if I held grudges against every gig I've lost, there would be skeletons popping up all over the place."

Drayco smiled briefly at that. "Don't believe Grabbing Irons Greaver has any twins out there."

"Grabbing Irons Greaver?"

"The possible identity of our Mr. Bones. So named for having six fingers on one hand."

Sebastien pursed his lips. "Just when you think this whole insanity couldn't get any stranger."

Nelia spoke up, "That's probably enough murder talk for now," and her raised eyebrow signaled Drayco to agree.

"Nelia's right. I should let you folks enjoy this view in peace."

Olive stood up and smiled. "You must stay and join us for dinner, Scott."

"That's kind of you, but Maida has planned a special feast. I've stood her up too many times lately."

Nelia trailed him outside and down the stairs to his waiting Starfire. "I hate playing 'bad cop,' but it's even worse with people I care about."

"The odds are still long that Marty's father is involved. But not zero." He studied her face as he said, "Olive and Sebastien seem close."

Nelia nodded absently. "I'm glad she has such a good friend. Someone who shares her love of classical music."

No signs she knew or suspected anything deeper. It wasn't his place to bring it up unless it related back to the case. He'd avoided too many personal chats with Nelia lately—her mother, her husband, her divorce. And yeah, the big "and."

She patted the car. "Still in good shape. Darcie must enjoy riding around in it."

"She's enjoying her new beau's Mercedes instead. Or Rolls Royce. Or one of each."

"New beau?"

"Much older. Much richer."

Nelia chewed on her lip, making her best impression of a poker face. Was she sad? Happy? Indifferent? She asked, "How do you feel?"

"To be honest, I'm not sure."

She hesitated for a moment. "Perhaps there isn't any chance for true love for some people, do you think?"

"Depends on what you mean by 'true,' doesn't it?"

"If you find out, you can write a how-to book and make millions. Make that billions. A mega-bestseller."

"I'll get right on it. But not tomorrow. I have to make a quick trip into the District. I'll leave tonight to avoid traffic on the Bay Bridge."

"Detective business?"

He paused to let a gust of wind blow past, bringing a hint of a cooling sea spray along with it. "Detective and normal human business. I'll be back tomorrow night."

"Guess Cape Unity will have to cope for twenty-four hours. Poor, poor Cape Unity."

He took a bow and then said, "Just promise me you won't dig up any other skeletons, pirate or otherwise, while I'm gone."

42

After sleeping in the platform bed at his D.C. townhome, Drayco realized it wasn't nearly as comfortable as the four-poster at the Jepsons' B&B. Another reason he slept better over there. Perhaps not a fair test because he'd added a dozen mosquito and no-see-um bites from Nelia's deck to the scratches on his arms from Lena's motorcycle ride. Calamine lotion and aloe gel didn't make for the best aromatherapy.

Sheriff Sailor had paved the way for Drayco's mid-morning "port of call," although Drayco was dreading it. When he reached his destination, the block style concrete buildings with tiny window slits resembled the industrial chicken houses dotting the Eastern Shore. But these pens were created for people.

As state prisons went, it had run-of-the-mill lookout towers, miles of wire fencing, and security cameras everywhere. And lots of unsmiling guards.

Drayco handed over his ID, waited while they gave him a pat-down for contraband, and then walked through the metal detectors. Finally satisfied Drayco was a legitimate visitor and not a threat, a guard chaperoned him to a bank of small chairs in front of small windows. Each had a telephone handset, and a sign above read, "All visitor phones are subject to monitoring."

Moments later, the guards ushered in prisoner number NN7546, wearing an orange jumpsuit, to the other side of the window across from Drayco. He still resembled the man in the photo from Antonio's apartment, if a little older. Had Drayco met him on the street, he'd have thought the guy was an accountant or an insurance rep.

Conroy Skye stared at Drayco through the thick window glass, and Drayco picked up the phone, hoping the other man would do the same. Skye kept staring and blinking, not making a move. After several tense moments, he grabbed the phone on his side and said, "Who are you?"

"Scott Drayco. I'd like to ask you a couple of questions, a case I'm working on."

"You a cop?"

"Private consultant. But more importantly, I have news of your son."

Rosita Skye had wanted to notify her ex-husband and tell him of Antonio's death but couldn't bring herself to do it. When she'd learned Drayco planned a visit, she'd pleaded with him to pass along the news.

Conroy Skye said, "What about Tony? He in some trouble?"

"I'm afraid it's worse than that. He was found dead two nights ago."

Skye froze for a moment. "Two nights ago. I don't understand. How? Why?" Then his voice rose higher as he almost shouted, "Tell me why. Tell me now!"

After Skye's outburst, Drayco half-expected guards to come running. He waited for a moment. No guards. "It appears to be suicide."

Skye growled. "Appears? Appears? What the hell do you mean by that? How you can have a not-suicide?"

"His friend Marty Penry died a month ago, also allegedly a suicide. Penry's father hired me to prove it was murder."

"So you think my boy didn't kill hisself?"

"That's what I aim to find out. Are there any reasons someone might want to harm Antonio?"

Skye tightened his lips. "Nah, he was a great kid. I was always bragging on him to the other guys."

"There are questions about the gun used to kill Marty. I understand it belonged to you and your father before that. Antonio had it in his car where it was allegedly stolen."

"Allegedly? Appears? What game is this?" Skye growled, "Aw hell, I know what you're thinking. Like father, like son, right? That my son killed the other kid and then hisself because he felt bad. Or didn't want to end up like his old man."

"Or someone did steal the gun and tried to frame Antonio."

Skye considered that for a moment. "I been in here long enough to know all the tricks. It's possible. Look, maybe Tony was just a drunk like me, as I said, like father, like son."

"Did you ever see signs he was an alcoholic?"

"How the hell would I know that? Since I wasn't around him? Since I'm an animal in a cage?"

Drayco countered, "If it helps, no alcohol or drugs were found in his system." Sailor had the M.E. do a rush job and told Drayco the results only that morning. No recreational drugs, just aspirin and sertraline.

Skye closed his eyes and didn't talk for a moment. "I failed him. He needed me, needed somebody around to help him out, show him the way. But I let my drinking get the better of me, and here I rot. To think I outlived my son."

"When did you last see him?"

Skye's voice grew quieter and pinched, making Drayco strain to understand him. "Him and his mother used to visit more. Over the years, the visits trailed off. I saw Tony two Christmases ago. Or three. You lose track in here."

"Did he send you any letters or schedule a video visit? Mention any friends? Enemies? Threats?"

"Been a while since I got a letter. Longer since the last video. He had this one girl, Tess, I think he was friends with. But he mostly talked about Marty. Guess they was closer than I knew."

Drayco didn't enlighten him as to the real depth of Antonio's affection for Marty. "What were his feelings regarding Tess?"

"One of those love-hate relationships that reminds me of my wife. As in I loved her but she hated me. Or didn't approve. Couldn't live up to her high standards."

"Was it Tess judging Antonio or the other way around?"

Skye gave a half-shrug. "Got the impression she was bossy. Wanted things her way."

"Are you sure Antonio didn't have any enemies?"

"You shitting me? As I said, he was a great kid. Period. Other guys in here, they got kids who end up like them. Or worse. I never worried about Tony. Never."

"This is a long shot, but would the family of the man you killed be out for vengeance?"

"He was an older guy. Former drinking buddy. Ex-wife who hated him more than mine does me. No kids. And anybody and everybody else is dead of cirrhosis or car accidents or they OD'd."

Drayco figured he'd found out all he was going to. But there was one other thing he wanted to say. "Antonio had a framed photo in his apartment—of you with your arm around him from years ago. Thought you'd want to know."

Skye's jaw clenched, and his eyes narrowed, making him look much more like a violent inmate than the mild-mannered accountant he first appeared. "If you think my boy was murdered, Mr. Drayco, then you'd better find the guy real quick. Because if you don't, I'll find a way to get out of here. And I'll kill him myself."

❧ ❧ ❧

The jet noise at National wasn't as loud as the planes as Accomack, but that's what a thick wall and heavy glass panes could do for you. Drayco craned his neck but didn't see the gray-haired man he expected. A tap on his shoulder made him whirl around.

"Situational awareness on vacation, son?"

"I thought your flight was on the other end of the terminal."

"It is. Just keeping an eye out for you. And here you are."

Drayco squinted at his father's leather carry-on. "Still packing light?"

"Always. As I said on the phone, it's a quick trip. Since it's on the client's nickel, I *could* stay longer and see some sights. If I were that kind of investigator."

"Is this client the fellow from Accomack?"

"No, a new one. Hints of global money laundering, and you know how I feel about those types of shit-can cases."

"I remember. They always turned you into the Incredible Hulk."

"How's *your* case going?" Brock studied his son's face for a moment. "Tell you what. I've got time for a coffee. I'll bet they even have salt."

Drayco agreed, and they grabbed a quick brew from the kiosk and sat at a table nearby. Drayco added the salt, and his father made a face.

They sipped in silence for a moment before Brock asked, "So, your case. How much longer you think it'll take?"

"Wish I knew. There was a second death."

His father whistled. "Sorry, son. Definitely murder this time?"

"Alleged suicide. A friend of the first young man." Drayco rubbed his eyes. "They have to be connected somehow."

"Two suicides is not that surprising."

"A copycat. I realize that. It's just all wrong. Too curvilinear."

"Haven't heard you use that word regarding a case in a long time. The last one was that serial killer investigation at the Bureau. You're not thinking that here?"

"I'd give it forty-two to one. Although the way I've been feeling lately, I should probably refrain from betting on anything."

Brock blew on his coffee. "You usually don't seek out my advice on cases."

"Advice won't help with Antonio. It's far too late for that." Drayco took a sip from his own drink and realized he was getting a little sick of coffee.

Brock put down his cup and leaned forward. "Was this Antonio of yours obviously suicidal?"

"If so, I didn't pick up on it. Missed every single damn sign."

"Scott. . ."

Brock gripped Drayco's arm so tightly, it made him wince and ask, "What was that for?"

"You fell into a depression after Vuca's death. And didn't want to admit it then. Even refused to see my therapist friend, Franklin Kinder."

"Everybody gets the blues."

"This was different. You blamed yourself for Vuca's death. Still do, if I'm not mistaken."

Drayco shook his head. "See? You're pretty good at psychoanalysis. Always note my mistakes and have plenty of ideas about what I should and shouldn't do. I didn't need Kinder."

Brock sighed and studied the vaulted ceiling for a moment. "I've been in this business for forty years. Met a lot of law enforcement types in my day of all stripes and badges. But not a single one has your instincts."

Drayco's eyebrows almost flew off his head. "You've never said that before."

"I should have. My mistake. One among many where you're concerned."

How should he reply to something like that? Maybe it was true, but maybe they'd both made their share of mistakes in the relationship. Drayco met his father's stare. "Wish I felt that confident right now."

Brock leaned over and tapped him on the forehead. "You're overthinking it. Instincts, remember? I believe in you, and hopefully that counts for something."

Drayco contemplated his father's words for a moment and nodded. "Okay."

"Okay, then." Brock looked at the departure message board and added, "They're about to board my flight. Thanks for making the trip to see me. Although we've got to stop meeting like this."

"I can think of worse places for family reunions than airport terminals."

Brock stood up with a smile. "The guys in my basketball league are wondering where you've been."

"Hope I'll be back to nailing their asses soon."

"That's the spirit."

Drayco hopped up and reached his hand out to his father, who took it and pulled him in a hug. "Thanks, Dad."

"Any time, son."

43

Tuesday, June 26

Drayco couldn't stop rubbing his eyes as he drove into Cape Unity. He was more tired than he should be, not that yesterday's encounter with Conroy Skye was uplifting. And his brief visit with Brock had only left him craving more. Their relationship was still a work in progress, with emphasis on the "work" part.

What had his Monday in D.C. done for him? He'd paid bills, run errands, hooray. The only "fun," if you could call it that, was a brief trip to the National Archives to conduct research on pirate ships. A *Sea Strumpet*, to be exact, and the few names of crew members Reece had uncovered.

It was still early in the morning. He'd expected driving east in the off-hours would mean less traffic, but that hadn't gone according to plan—the Bay Bridge looked like a long car train. Sure, it was summer, but tourists mostly waited for the weekend to pack the bridge on their way to the beach.

When Drayco added chain-yawning to eye-rubbing, he knew he needed a liquid booster. But he hated to head to the Lazy Crab just to start guzzling caffeine. Deciding to give Grounds for Glory another try, he arrived right after they opened at eight.

What he didn't expect to find was a car parked in front with Tess Gartin and Emmerson Pinnick again, but they weren't so much arguing as talking in earnest. When Tess stepped out to head into the coffee shop, and Emmerson drove on, Drayco decided to corner Tess this time.

He moved behind her in line. "I hear their cinnamon lattes are popular."

She jumped when she heard his voice and turned to face him. "Oh, my god. You startled me."

"I saw you alone with Emmerson Pinnick. Twice, now. Want to tell me about it?"

With her rapid blinking and flared nostrils, he expected her to bolt, not talk. After a moment's hesitation, she whipped out her cellphone to call Judson Kolman. Drayco overheard her tell her boss she was going to be late to work but would bring his favorite coffee as penance.

Drayco grabbed his iced tea and led Tess outside to sit at the same drink-doctoring table as before. He waited until she'd blown on her hot drink and taken a tentative first sip before asking, "Are you and Emmerson having an affair?"

She exhaled deeply before replying. "Can't keep up the lies any longer. Long story short, the answer is yes."

"Were you 'with' him this morning?"

"We carve out time together whenever we can get a break. Sometimes early morning between when he leaves home and starts work. Or a long lunch hour. Or when he's supposedly working late. I know it's not honest on my part. But look who he's married to. Can you blame him?"

She had a point in some respects, but he had a twinge of sympathy for Barbara Pinnick. "Did either Marty or Antonio know of the affair?"

Tess opened her mouth to reply, then closed it and looked away. After another sip of coffee, she said, "I don't know."

"You've heard of Antonio's death?"

"Lena Bing called me. We're all in shock." Her hand holding the coffee shook, and she set the cup on the table, spilling a few drops.

"I know how much you cared for Antonio." He chose not to mention the love note he'd found.

"Thought I understood him pretty well. But not this."

"You said when he stopped by the station recently, his behavior scared you."

"And I told you I had no idea how much of that was acting."

She focused on a sparrow as it landed on a post beside the table looking for crumbs but disappointed, flew away. "I didn't go to see him that day. Or even give him a call. Never occurred to me think of suicide. Despite Marty."

"The cause of death isn't official."

Her eyes widened. "You think someone killed him and Marty? That we've got a serial killer running around?"

"I didn't say that."

"Serial killer, suicide. What the hell difference does it make? Antonio is still dead." She scratched the side of the cup, making polystyrene-foam flakes fall in a mini-snowstorm.

"Can you describe Antonio's behavior that day in more detail?"

"I've told you everything. Mostly."

"Mostly?"

"Antonio felt responsible for Marty's death. I guess I thought maybe. . ."

When her voice trailed off, he finished the thought for her. "He was the one who killed Marty?"

When she didn't reply, he added, "I spoke with him recently while he was beachcombing."

She sat up straighter. "Did he talk about Marty? Or mention anyone else?"

Another patron headed out onto the deck and started up a cellphone conversation so loud, Drayco had to lean in to avoid raising his voice. "Antonio was mostly looking for shells. But he appeared distracted."

Tess fell silent for a moment. "That's the impression I got, too. That he had something on his mind." She pushed the foam-snowstorm into little piles. "I should have gone to see him. Urged him to get counseling."

"He might not have agreed."

"Shit." She slumped deeper in her seat. "Everyone has frickin' traumas, ghosts, skeletons, heartache. But most people want to live."

To live, to love, to breathe, to learn. . .and maybe even to lie at times? "I had a chat with your boss the other day. He mentioned a heated argument between you and Marty."

"That was nothing."

"He said the two of you were ready to fight each other. That's not 'nothing.'"

"Judson loves to exaggerate. Marty and I worked it out. We were cool."

Drayco studied her clouded expression as he asked, "Must have been hard working with someone you blamed for your parents' deaths."

Her eyes flashed. "Who said I blamed him? Deirdre? Look, it was an accident. They could have been hit just as easily in Marty's car if he *had* picked them up. Besides, they're dead and Marty's dead. What does it matter now?"

"It matters if you wanted revenge."

She clutched the coffee cup so tightly, the liquid burst upward in a mini-geyser. She cried out in pain as a red patch formed on her wrist. Drayco fished out ice from his drink, wrapped it in a napkin and gave it to her to lay on the burn. It was the same hand as the one with the stingray barb days ago.

"Does that feel better?"

"Yes, thanks."

He gave her a moment to adjust the homemade ice pack, then asked, "You're not on social media much. Too busy?"

"Accusing me *and* checking up on me?"

"Checking up on everyone. It's my job."

"You won't find much 'cause I hate all that social crap. People only post happy news—photos of their families, parents, husbands, kids. Trips to some famous somewhere in the world. Their new frickin' house or car. Everyone's great, everyone's perfect."

Drayco gave her a brief smile. "People seeking validation?"

"Like kids to their Mommy—look at me, look at me! And I had plenty of bullies in high school. I don't need them online."

He took a sip of his now ice-less tea. But he was pleased to see Tess's hand wasn't hurting her much. "How long have you and Emmerson been having an affair?"

"Six months. Today's our anniversary." She pulled out a necklace from underneath her shirt. The glinting blue stone looked like a sapphire. "He gave me this last week."

"Sounds like it's getting serious."

She bit her lip. "I'm not sure we'll stay together or what. We do care about each other. Emmerson's been unhappy in his marriage for a long time. That whole social-climbing mania? It's not him that's into it. It's his wife. Makes a big deal out of it for her benefit. And to keep her from nagging."

"I can't imagine his firm would appreciate a soon-to-be partner having an affair."

"They all do it. What difference would it make?"

"Maybe more than you think."

Drayco glanced at the planters with the tall bamboo and thick fronds so very good at hiding things. "You're at the center of it all, aren't you? You're the nexus of everyone and everything around Marty. If I made a chart of all the ties to him and his family and friends, you'd be in the middle."

Tess stared at him. "I don't know what you're accusing me of."

"Not accusing, observing. By the way, do you still have your motorbike?"

"I sold it a year ago. Why?"

He started to answer when his cellphone rang. She hopped up, said she had to grab Kolman's coffee, and scurried into the building.

Drayco checked the phone number. Another unknown caller. He answered it, thinking it could finally be the person sending him the mystery texts. But it wasn't another copy of the suicide song, nor was it anyone at all who he was expecting.

44

The voice of Lydia Vucasovich Miles was strong despite her seventy-five years. "I've wanted to call you for some time, Scott."

"That's an odd coincidence. I was planning on calling you."

He heard the smile in her tone. "Really? That *is* a coincidence. As to why I haven't called sooner, well. . . Don't get me wrong, I'm happy now with Kent. But those memories of Alex remain raw sixteen years later."

"I understand."

"I've followed you in the news. Made quite a name for yourself during your career."

"I hope I've helped a few people."

"From what I gather, more than a few. But you said you were going to call me? Whatever for?"

He paused for a moment before replying. "Vuca's been on my mind lately."

"He will always be a part of you, Scott. As he is with me."

Drayco pictured the Chopin biography with Vuca's inscription lying on his nightstand at the Lazy Crab. "I never had any closure over his death, Lydia. Never figured out why he did what he did. And me being the last one to see him alive, I'd like to know. *Need* to know."

"That's one of the reasons I wanted to talk to you, Scott. But it would be better if we chatted in person. Do you still live in D.C.?"

"Ordinarily. I'm at the Eastern Shore on a case."

"When you get back to town, we can meet and reminisce over old times."

"I'd like that. Why don't I call you when I return."

After he hung up, he sat for a moment trying not to think too deeply about anything—just feeling the sea breeze through his hair, the condensation droplets from the coffee cup trickling down his fingers, the buzzing of a wasp as it bounced off his arm.

He counted the tiny, distant boats at the marina, and the strains of the Cousteau song *"Calypso"* started up in his head. Marty had loved going out on boats. He loved his job, had big plans and big dreams. Where had it gone so horribly wrong?

Drayco was still feeling "off." He looked at his tea, but his eye was on it the whole time.

After checking a text file on his phone with side effects of the SSRI drug in Marty's green powder, he ticked them off against his symptoms. Sleep disturbances, yes, but that wasn't unusual for him. Tired, check, headache, check. Weight loss—he *had* dropped a few pounds, but Maida always accused him of not eating and worked hard to fatten him up.

He was letting his imagination run away with him, not like him at all. No way he'd admit the Suicide Sonata was working on him, too, because it couldn't be. He was a rational, logical being, with a doctorate in criminology. The notion that a piece of music could be cursed was as scientific as the existence of a purple unicorn.

What, then? Maybe he should stop by the Opera House again. The distraction might help, but he cringed at facing that responsibility. The shaky finances were too grim.

Okay, back to the Lazy Crab. But Maida had another guest who was leaving this afternoon, and he didn't want to get in the way. He'd wait until dinner.

Darcie was out of the question. And Nelia? The oddly mixed signals from her made him think it wasn't a good idea at all. He could get more tea and people watch, but he wasn't in the mood for that, either. What was his problem?

He had a sudden urge to return to the clearing where Marty died. Decision made, he climbed into the Starfire and made his way to the site, stopping at the point where cars had a hard time going in—he'd hoof in the rest of the way. But first, he grabbed a pair of hiking boots he kept in his car. He'd learned his lesson after ruining a couple pairs of shoes tramping around in conditions like this.

No new flooding, but there were distinct signs someone else had visited the clearing recently. Fresh motorcycle tracks led in from the road and judging from the treads, all made by one bike. He checked the photo on his phone. These newer tracks matched the treads from the other mystery ruts he'd found on his first trip with Lena. Some of those lovers she'd mentioned? Or someone returning to see if they left any evidence behind?

The clearing was in a section of Cape Unity like so many others on the Eastern Shore. Emphatically flat. Isolated. Forgotten. Such a remote place would be a great site to find buried treasure or hide a body, like the old Victorian house Lena took him to.

He pictured what happened that fateful day. Marty rode in on his motorcycle, parked, pulled out Antonio's pistol, and allegedly shot himself. A couple of days later, he was found by the sheriff's deputies when Judson Kolman reported he hadn't shown up for work.

Simple enough. Suicide due to despondency over bad love affairs and job stress. But if he wasn't in love with Lena, why choose a suicide spot where he and Lena had visited? He could have done the deed anywhere—home, work, behind a grocery store.

If someone killed him, they had to have ridden in with him or around the same time. Lena was the obvious choice, yet she had no qualms about bringing Drayco to the crime scene.

Okay, so assuming whoever it was rode in with him, at some point they shot Marty and wiped the gun clean and then put it in his hand. And left the suicide song "note" in his pocket, then simply rode out.

Maybe this recent visitor *was* looking for those other skeletons. Or treasure, if it existed. Could that explain why Marty was here that day?

Sailor was right on one count. No evidence linked Marty to the pirate skeleton or the coin found with it whatsoever. Dead ends, dead ends, and more dead ends.

A rustling in the woods made him mindful of the attack from a rabid coyote in such a place a year ago. Should he get his Glock from the car? He listened and didn't hear a repeat, so he continued his search around the area.

Slivered rays of dappled sunlight peeking through trees flashed on a bright object among a pile of decaying leaves. He headed over and picked up a white fishing lure with a handkerchief from his pocket. A fishing lure? The clearing wasn't anywhere near any fish-filled creeks or ponds.

As Drayco examined the lure further, it was clean—no traces of dirt. Either the rains following Marty's death had rinsed it off, or someone left this at the same time as the new set of tracks. Did Antonio come here before his death as a last tribute? He stuffed the lure in his pocket.

Drayco paced outward from the clearing in a wheel-spokes pattern, underneath trees and over fallen branches and piles of leaves. If someone were here recently digging for treasure, surely they'd leave evidence behind. And no signs Sailor and his crew searched this far afield—virgin investigative territory.

Spying a hole in the ground, he headed for it and looked inside. When he saw bits of bark and dandelions, he bit back his disappointment. A groundhog burrow, most likely.

Something else caught his attention ahead of the hole, a patch of plants that didn't look native—plants with long skinny stems and large serrated fan leaves. Cannabis. Just as he made a note of the location to tell the sheriff, he spied something altogether different that made his pulse quicken. A tripwire.

Where there was a tripwire, there was a booby trap. Without moving a muscle, he looked around for the source of the wire, but it was too late. The ground shifted beneath his left foot and before he could react, his "groundhog burrow" collapsed into a gaping hole of dirt and rocks, taking Drayco along with it.

When the ground finally stopped moving, Drayco had fallen a good eight feet. He calmed his breathing to take a body check to see if anything felt broken. So far, so good. Now, how to get out?

He studied his hole in more detail, and that's when he saw something that made him break out in a cold sweat. His feet had landed on a shelf of sorts, keeping him from falling all the way into the hole. At the bottom lay a row of bear traps with steel jaws and some seriously wicked-looking teeth.

One false move and he'd slide right down into those traps. Bye-bye foot. Or leg. The excruciating pain from his mangled hand the day of the carjacking sixteen years ago came back in full force. He didn't want to go through that again. Ever.

He slowed his breathing further to keep adrenaline levels in check. What were his options? Sliding down and somehow managing to avoid the traps, a non-starter. And trying to ease his cellphone out of his pocket to call for help could trigger more dirt falls and pull him down toward a mangled leg. Option three was to go up somehow.

But first, he'd have to will his body to ignore the pain that was growing in his left side. Maybe nothing was broken, but he was well-acquainted with the feeling of bruised ribs.

Recalling the chimney climbing technique a friend taught him, he tentatively pressed one foot and one hand against opposite sides of the hole's walls. Slowly, he shimmied upward, bracing himself on exposed tree roots. On the first attempt, his right foot started to slide, but he stopped it in time.

A few inches, then a few more. What did that make—half a foot now? His pulse sped up when a clump of dirt avalanched into the hole, missing the traps. Every time he moved his left arm, the pain in his side set off a new wave of agony, but he let each wave pass and tried again. Inch by painful inch. After what felt like hours, he was near the top.

Seeing a nearby tree root, he grabbed hold of it and hoisted his body bit by bit back onto the forest floor. After allowing himself a moment to catch his breath, Drayco peered into his former prison. Bear traps, yes, but no skeletons and no treasure.

Not feeling like pushing his luck, he headed toward the central clearing, studying the ground for any other traps along the way. He hadn't forgotten about looking for signs of recent human digging, but that was a futile search. A few broken beer bottles, potato chips bags, and a used condom.

A screeching hawk appeared as if from nowhere. To Drayco's amazement, it swooped inches from him, grabbed a mouse from the ground in its talons, and fluttered away with its prize. Life here, then gone.

Suddenly bone-tired, he slid to the ground beneath an oak tree and sat on the cool bed of leaves and pine needles. He closed his eyes and pictured Marty in this spot. What would Marty have experienced as he lay here dying, alone. . .hearing what? Maybe the hawk, a woodpecker hammering away, the buzzing of flies.

If Drayco believed in the Akashic business, he'd pop into the Hall of Records and find out whatever he needed—the who, what, when, where, how, and most importantly for him, the why. If police could do that, there'd be no more crime because everything, everywhere would be revealed.

He stood up slowly, taking pains not to use his left side much, and dusted off his pants to head toward his car. He might not believe in those Records, but he did believe in the process of truth. Not a straight or an easy path, but it was the only one he knew how to follow.

45

Drayco handed the white fishing lure to the man behind a glass counter filled with an impressive array of lures and bait—a virtual psychedelic zoo. Mike Dickens, the owner of Limping Mike's Bait Shop, studied the lure carefully. "This is a jigging spoon. Used for deep-sea fish like bluefish, marlin, sea bass. I don't keep records of who buys what. But we sell a ton of those."

"I was hoping to find out if Marty Penry bought something like this. He worked at the Eastern Shore Lab of the Virginia Institute of Marine Science."

"Penry? That's the guy who killed himself, right? Saw his photo in the paper and recognized him from the shop. Didn't come here a lot but seemed like a nice kid. Too bad what happened."

Drayco called up a photo of Antonio on his phone and turned it toward Mike. "See this man here, too?"

Mike studied the picture. "Don't recall that one. He wanted or something?"

"He was a friend of Marty's and may have also taken his own life."

"Now that's a damn shame." Mike called out to someone in the back, "Greg, can you come out here a minute?"

A man several inches taller even than Drayco lumbered out. "Need something?"

Mike nodded at Drayco, who showed him the cellphone photo of Antonio, then asked, "Seen this guy in here?"

Greg shook his head. "He wanted for burglary?"

"Nothing like that. Thanks, Greg. Sorry to interrupt your box-opening joy."

Drayco thanked the two men and paid for more Manhattan Specials, complimenting the storekeeper for being the only one to sell them locally.

Mike replied, "I got addicted to these things when I lived in New York. We sell a few, but you're the only other addict down here I've met."

Drayco checked the time. Going on three-thirty. Safe to check back at the Crab. Once inside, he ducked into the kitchen briefly to wave at Maida and headed for his room to change out of his damp, muddy clothes.

He studied the left side of his chest in the mirror. No visible bruising. Taking a deep breath wasn't much fun, but he'd just get some ibuprofen and an ice pack from Maida later.

Deciding a shower was the best course of action in the short term, he hopped in and out in record time and then sat on the bed *au naturel*, letting the evaporation cool him off. Unlike the Starfire, the Crab's air conditioning worked, although it could use a tune-up.

An angel wing shell from Antonio's apartment lay on the nightstand next to the Chopin biography. So fragile-looking, that shell. But as with Antonio, that wasn't the whole story. Drayco had researched angel wing, or *Cyrtopleura costata*, live clams able to bore into wood, clay, and even rock. Antonio and the sea creature were a little of both—strong and fragile at the same time.

Glancing at another object on the nightstand, the necklace Drayco found in Marty's apartment, he grabbed it and held it up in the light. What did those symbols mean? His research had turned up squat—Native American codes, Sanskrit, Akashic Records, video games—he'd tried it all.

After pulling on clean clothes, he stuffed the necklace into a pants pocket. When he made his way to the kitchen, Maida was in a whirl of activity chopping fresh basil from the garden and checking on an Italian-smelling dish in the oven.

She turned her head to say, "I invited Nelia Tyler to join us. She's in the den."

Nelia was in the den all right, but she didn't look happy to be there. Was it because he was present or because she'd only agreed to come to spare Maida's feelings? But on closer inspection, he saw Nelia's eyes were watery and bloodshot.

He sat beside her. "What's wrong?"

She clenched her fists. "It's my parents. They're getting a divorce. Mom told me the news today, and we had the argument to end all arguments. I can't believe it, I just can't. Thirty-six years of marriage."

He searched for the right words. But there weren't any. "This must be tough on all of you."

She laughed briefly. "I'm supposed to be a cop who sees problems. Never saw this coming."

Drayco wasn't sure if or how to bring up the topic of Sebastien, but he didn't have to when Nelia continued, "Mom and Sebastien Penry have been having an emotional affair. She swears there was nothing physical."

He nodded but didn't say anything. Her eyes narrowed, and she said, "You knew this already, didn't you?"

"They didn't tell me. Something I observed."

She rubbed her forehead. "How blind I've been. You told me they seemed to be close. That was your way of warning me, wasn't it?"

"I didn't want to butt in unless it became relevant. Otherwise, it's none of my business."

Nelia flopped against the couch. "Had to go to Sheriff Sailor and tell him there's clearly a conflict of interest now. He agreed. I'm officially off Marty's case."

"He understands, as I do. We'll keep you apprised of developments."

She groaned. "How could Mom do this to me? She knows how hard I've worked. How it would look if this came out."

After a minute of silence except for the whirring fan noise in the room, she said, "My Dad's a former army guy."

"You mentioned that once."

"Left the service, formed a consulting business with military clients. He wasn't around much when I was a kid. But he always made those times he was home special."

"More like a grandfather, then? Spoiling you rotten."

"It was an unfair advantage over Mom. Dad got to come home and play the golden knight. Poor Mom had to be the day-to-day disciplinarian."

"Is he the reason you went into the Army Reserve?"

"Largely."

"I told Sarg that. As a former Ranger himself, he was even more impressed with you."

"That's a high compliment coming from him." Turning her attention to a small fraying patch on the couch, she said, "I always took my marriage vows seriously, inspired by my parents. What does this mean now? I mean, Tim? Two divorces so soon?"

She looked so miserable, he wanted to give her a hug. He settled for putting his hand on her shoulder and giving it a gentle squeeze. "You'll figure it out. I have faith in you."

He hated to pose his next question. "Did Marty know of the emotional affair?"

"I'm amazed I had the presence of mind to ask. Mom says he didn't, that they were careful. But who knows?"

Sensing she wanted to change the subject, he pulled out Marty's necklace. "I never showed this to you."

She took it from him and turned it over in her hand, examining it. "Figure out what the symbols mean?"

"No. But it looks hand-crafted. And that has given me an idea."

He got up, grabbed a handkerchief from a different pocket, and laid it on an end table. Then he put the necklace on top of the handkerchief and removed his shoe. Right as he started to strike the clay charm, Nelia grabbed his hand. "Is that wise?"

"I've got photos of it. Besides, from the shape, I have a sneaking suspicion I know what's inside."

She released his hand but made him wait as she grabbed her own camera from her purse to record the proceedings on video. Drayco hammered the shoe down on the charm. It took a few thwacks, but the clay finally broke off, exposing a shiny round object. "Look familiar?"

"Same vintage as the pirate's coin?"

He checked his photo from his phone and compared it. "Looks identical."

"It could be from a separate stash he found."

"Or, it might not have anything to do with his death. But otherwise, why hide the coin?"

She shook her head. "And why not just keep it in a safe deposit box or a home safe?"

"Hard to say at this point."

"Even if it led to murder, why go to the trouble to push him toward suicide? That method for murder wouldn't make my top one hundred."

Drayco made a note to avoid pissing off Nelia if she had a ready list of murder methods. "The killer may feel conflicted—needed Marty out of his way but didn't want to get his hands dirty. If it were made to look like a suicide, no one would question it. The perfect alibi."

She sighed. "I'd love to speculate with you further. This may fall under the category of me not working the case to avoid a conflict of interest."

"Free speech is protected, last I checked. We're two friends shooting the breeze. How about those Nationals, eh? Or do you prefer the Orioles?"

That elicited the first hint of a smile from her since he walked in.

He gathered up the shards from the necklace along with the coin into the handkerchief. "I'll deliver it to Sailor first thing tomorrow."

After returning to his room to place the remains of the necklace in a drawer, he took a moment to sit on the bed. His spirits had nosedived since he'd first headed into the den. Nelia's parents' divorce, her own marriage, bad enough. Along with the coin, he had a sinking feeling things had got much more complicated. And a hell of a lot messier.

46

Nelia could put on an award-winning act when she needed to. But at Maida's supper last night, it was apparent to Drayco she wasn't her usual self. Her grief did little to help his recent insomnia, and he awoke with the room spinning.

He'd promised to take Marty's gold coin to the sheriff first thing but had one stop to make beforehand. He parked in front of the Historical Society, and, once inside, Reece Wable immediately hammered Drayco for updates on Grabbing Irons Greaver.

Drayco had called Nelia earlier to see if she wanted to join them there, since she and Reece were friends, too. What was wrong with a simple chat on local history and culture, after all? She'd accepted, grateful for the distraction and, he suspected, for him finding a way to keep her in the investigation.

The trio compared the new coin with a photo of the coin from the construction site using Reece's magnifying screen. To Drayco's eyes, they looked like the same type and vintage. But only two of them? Marty's find would have been a one-in-a-million chance.

Nelia once again read Drayco's mind. "How did Marty come up with a coin matching one buried for centuries?"

Reece adjusted the screen and peered intently at the twin coins. "He found the original stash. The one Grabbing Irons hid before he was whacked."

Nelia shook her head. "Sheriff Sailor had us check around after the first coin. To see if anyone had seen signs of digging. Farm properties, gardens, remote places. Zilch."

Reece pointed toward the file room. "I've got oodles of news accounts. A boy who found a cache of Roman and Greek coins on the shore. Then there was the elderly lady up in Ocean City who found gold 1730s Spanish coins. Happens more often than you know."

Nelia asked, "But why encase a coin in clay to hide it? A form of insurance? Against what or whom?"

Reece grabbed a book and showed Drayco and Nelia photos and drawings of shipwrecks around the world. "Twenty thousand shipwrecks lie off the Mid-Atlantic. Eighteen hundred on the floor of the Chesapeake alone."

Drayco scanned the list and jabbed his finger on one entry. "Look at this one, the Swedish warship Makalös. Sank during a naval battle in 1564. Sent hundreds of sailors and a fortune in gold and silver coins to the bottom of the Baltic Sea."

"Why that one?"

"The extra stanza to the suicide song Marty Penry wrote. 'And peals of the church bells that reach out to Mars.' Makalös was also known as Mars."

Reece pointed at a world map hanging on the wall. "The Baltic's a bit far from here. Unless you're thinking there's a wormhole nearby. Under that construction site, maybe."

Nelia looked at the drawing of the ship. "Reece has a point."

Reece gaped at her. "About the wormhole?"

She grinned. "About a survivor from that Baltic wreck who made it all the way to the Eastern Shore." She shook her head. "Nope, wouldn't work. Virginia wasn't settled until 1604 in Jamestown."

Drayco countered, "Perhaps Marty meant Mars, the planet. An astronomical signpost pointing to where he stashed the treasure. I did find an astronomy textbook at his place. People have long used celestial bodies as markers. Like Stonehenge."

"On the Eastern Shore? Much as I'd love a Stonehenge ruin around here, seems dubious. But think of the exhibits. And the tourism. Boggles the mind." Reece headed to Andrew Jackson's cage to add more seed to the bird's feeder.

Nelia said, "Shore-henge? Honestly?"

Reece replied, "Maybe like that skeleton. Buried somewhere under a world of dirt."

Drayco ignored Reece's pun and read the full entry on the Mars shipwreck. Rumors said it was cursed after its cannons were made from melted church bells. When found by divers, historians declared it the best-preserved vessel of its kind—no curses or ghosts, but ordinary cannons, human remains, and a silver coin worth thirty-thousand Euros.

Just then, Andrew Jackson screeched, "In the hole!"

Reece said, "And there you have it. We only have to get Andrew J here to let us know which hole we need to dig up." He grabbed a stack of papers from a table. "Forgot to ask how our bet is going. Figured out the murderer of Grabbing Irons yet?"

"Have you?"

The historian grumbled, "Couldn't find a single link between the crew of the *Sea Strumpet* and our skeleton."

Drayco replied, "There is one possibility."

"You're kidding me. I checked every last one of them. Nada."

"George Graves."

"Didn't find anything on him."

"I'm not surprised you couldn't find anything on *him*."

Reece opened his mouth and then snapped it shut. "I don't follow."

"Grabbing Irons had a sister."

"I did find that. Georgina."

"Don't you feel that Georgina Greaver and George Graves are too close for coincidence?"

"Not necessarily." Reece chewed on his lip.

"When I was at the National Archives on Monday, I found out the Greaver kids were orphans and dirt poor, or so say the records. He became a pirate, she was married off to a moderately successful cooper. But Georgina's husband ran off with another woman and took everything they owned. She was poor, shamed, tainted goods in an era when women had few rights or status. What else to do but take on a male persona and enter the 'family business'?"

"A female pirate?"

"There were others. That book you showed me has examples. Anne Bonny, Mary Read, to name a couple."

"Okay, so she was on the same ship as her brother. But all mentions of the *Sea Strumpet* vanished around the same time Grabbing Irons did."

"And yet, Grabbing Irons made it to the Eastern Shore. Why not his sister?"

Reece snorted. "You're telling me Grabbing Irons' sister killed her own brother?"

"From the few accounts I read of her, she was fierce. And if you were abandoned by your brother as a girl and dumped by your husband, you wouldn't necessarily have a kind view toward men, would you?"

"The motive, my dear detective. Where's your motive?"

"A Miss Georgina Graves turned up in Canada a few years later. Her background was mysterious, but she was said to be a rich heiress running from a loveless marriage. Rich, as in she had a substantial stash of gold to her name."

"Hoo boy. Never would have guessed that in a million years."

"That's what they pay me for. Solving puzzles."

"Um, I don't think anyone's paying you for this."

"You mentioned a bet, as I recall." Drayco tilted his head.

Nelia had listened to the account with an amused expression, and she laughed. "Give it up, Reece. You can't win betting against this guy."

Reece huffed. "Very well. Although blood, meet turnip."

Drayco said, "I was thinking more of an exhibit here."

"On you? I'm already planning that."

Drayco wrinkled his nose. "Lord, no. And don't you dare. This would be on Marty and Antonio. Not so much their deaths, but celebrating their lives on the shore. Fishing, marine biology, and Antonio's artwork."

Reece nodded. "Sounds intriguing. We'll discuss."

The diversion of Grabbing Irons' murder didn't matter in the long run. Yet, that historical mystery quest was more fun to Drayco than any contemporary one—so much easier when you didn't have personal stakes. But ancient murder or modern, all victims deserved a voice, someone to say their deaths—or, rather, their lives—weren't forgotten.

47

"Where'd you get this?" Sailor grabbed his new reading glasses and examined the coin in the plastic bag.

After Drayco told him the story, Sailor replied, "I'll be damned. Sure looks like a duplicate to our skeleton's coin. I'll get my team on it. Maybe it'll keep the owner of the condo development off my back. Said he's filing a lawsuit over the first coin."

That made Drayco wince as it reminded him of the Chopin manuscript found at his Opera House—and the pending litigation. He should warn the condo owner that finders weren't always keepers.

Sailor held the bag up to the light. "Wonder if Marty was hiding it from his father? They were partners in a scheme. . .and this was insurance?"

"Hiding it from someone, anyway."

"Congrats on your find. You've been more successful than me. I finally got Marty's cellphone records—only friends and family. And oddly, no calls or texts the day he died. Except for a couple from Antonio."

Sailor cracked his knuckles. "Oh, and thanks for the tip about the marijuana plants and booby traps. Sent Giles and Monroe out there this morning, and they already made an arrest. Your dirt-diving stunt set off an alarm that lured our pot grower. Just in time for my men to nab him, too. Turns out, the guy has a rap sheet for dealing harder drugs."

"Glad it was me in that trap, not one of the young people who hang out nearby."

Sailor nodded his agreement, but when he got a call on his desk phone, his scowl showed it wasn't a congratulatory call from the lottery. He hung up and rubbed his shiny head. "Change of plans. After you told me what Lena Bing said about Deirdre and the sonata thing, I got Deirdre—and her attorney Daddy, naturally—to join us for a nice chat. They're in the conference room."

The two men joined father and daughter who sat at the table looking uncomfortable and annoyed. Sailor stayed standing while Drayco sat across from the Pinnick duo.

Emmerson Pinnick barked, "Yet another interrogation, sheriff? Is this necessary?"

Sailor put on his familiar poker face. "We're very grateful when our citizens cooperate fully in an ongoing investigation. Makes life easier for everyone."

Before the man could erupt more, Sailor addressed Deirdre, "You weren't entirely honest about that Suicide Sonata. Someone overheard you provoking Marty Penry, pushing him into listening to it. This after you told us you didn't remember how he got interested in the music."

She pushed her hair behind her ear and flashed Drayco a big smile and a wink as she replied to Sailor. "It's no bigs. Marty and I were friends, and I was having fun. It was all a game. I mean, it's not like I killed him."

"Of course she didn't, and you have no evidence to suggest otherwise!" The veins popped out on her father's neck into an angry, branching tree. "My daughter had nothing to do with Marty becoming obsessed with the sonata. Right, Deirdre? Not that she'd be surprised."

Once more, Sailor directed his question at Deidre, "Not surprised?"

The young woman glared at her father. "Antonio was in love with Marty. Obviously, he'd want to do whatever Marty did. Yes, they were both obsessed with the sonata. And both committed suicide. Duh."

She grumbled, "And I'll bet I know who that snitch was. Lena Bing. She'd try to frame me for anything."

The sheriff placed the gold coin found in Marty's necklace on the table. "Either one of you see this before?"

They looked at it and then each other and said in unison, "No."

"It belonged to Marty. Any idea how or where he found it?"

Deirdre blurted out. "That can't be his. He would have told me."

"Is that so?" Sailor's stare was as piercing as a laser beam when he wanted it to be, and this was one of those times.

She folded her arms across her chest. "We were close, that's all. And that coin looks important, expensive, and—"

Pinnick jumped in, "We've told you she doesn't know anything."

Deirdre spoke to her father through clenched teeth. "Dad, I'm twenty-five, not five. I can speak for myself."

"And I'm telling you as your attorney not to." Pinnick jumped up and grabbed his daughter's arm to haul her up with him. She wrested her arm out of his grasp, making her father glower at her. He bellowed, "Was there anything else you had to grill me about, Sheriff, or can we be free of this pointless charade?"

Sailor got up to open the door and motioned into the hallway. Deputy Daniel Wylie came into the room, and the sheriff said, "Escort Miss Pinnick here to the front lobby. I have a few questions for her father."

When Pinnick started to protest, Sailor held up a hand. "She'll be fine. There's even a coffee machine out there. I need to talk to you in private. Something personal."

Drayco walked with Deirdre and Deputy Wylie out the door and into the hallway. At first, Drayco thought Deirdre would ignore him, but she stopped in her tracks and whirled around. "I'm not going to marry him."

It took a moment for that to register in Drayco's brain. "You mean, your fiancé, Dale Messineo?"

"Do I have another one?"

"What do your parents think?"

"I haven't told them. Haven't even told Dale. You're the first. You should feel flattered."

Drayco didn't know what he was feeling, but it definitely wasn't flattered. "What will you do, then?"

"I don't know. Party, work as a stripper, go to school and get my biology degree. Maybe I'll look you up, Mr. FBI." She stood on tiptoe to kiss him on the cheek.

Deputy Wylie smirked at him and then turned to usher Deirdre down the hall.

When Drayco re-entered the interview room, Sailor said to him. "Why don't you tell Mr. Pinnick here what you told me."

"I understand you've been having an affair with Tess Gartin for the past six months."

The color drained from the other man's face, and he slumped into a chair. "This can't get out. Promise me."

Sailor shook his head. Yeah, fat chance of that. Drayco pressed further, "Was Marty Penry aware of this? Or Antonio Skye?"

Coming from an attorney who should have known better, Pinnick didn't fend off the questions. "I have no idea."

Drayco asked, "You're due to be a partner in your law firm, is that correct?"

"You know it is. You probably know everything about me by now. In case you don't, my favorite color is green."

"And this firm, which is known to be on the staid side, wouldn't take too kindly to a future partner having an affair?"

As the normal flush returned to Pinnick's face, he gripped the armrests of his chair. "What Tess and I do in our spare time is our business. It's not some tawdry affair, we care about each other. We're legal adults. And this has nothing to do with any of your cases."

Sailor chimed in, "We'll be the judge of that."

Pinnick grew a spine as he jumped up. "This conversation is finished, gentleman. I can show myself out."

Sailor held open the door. "Regardless, I'll come along to give you a proper send-off. A normal courtesy around here."

As they left, Drayco returned to Sailor's office and slumped into his favorite swivel chair, swinging from side to side as he waited. But when the motion set off the pain in his bruised ribs, he thought better of it.

Moments later, the lawman strode in after returning from his "escort service." Sailor glared at the mounted flounder on his wall. "That was a whole lot of wasted air."

"Not necessarily. Sometimes to find the right path, you have to pull out a few weeds."

The sheriff growled at him. "Start spouting clichés like that, and I'll arrest you for disturbing the peace."

Drayco stood up slowly, glad to see his dizziness from early that morning wasn't any worse. "Deirdre and Lena have little in common except for Marty—and stabbing each other in the back. Think I'll go have another chat with Lena."

"Don't know it'll accomplish anything. But what the hell, it's always the quiet ones, right?"

Drayco did a double-take. "Funny, that's exactly what Deirdre said."

48

After Drayco left the sheriff's office, he checked the address for Lena and navigated along a washboard dirt road through a lacy cloak of white-blossomed fringe trees. Remote, with few houses, it reminded him of the site where Marty died.

When he reached the end of the long, twisting path, he arrived at a trailer on concrete blocks abutting more of the Eastern Shore's tufted marshlands. Lena sat out front on a green and tan webbed chair, hunched over a pot on a portable barbecue grill.

She looked up as he exited his car—and immediately cried out in pain. He saw then she'd been peeling potatoes and had cut her hand with the knife.

She cursed as Drayco grabbed a first-aid kit from the Starfire. "Damn it, that hurts."

"Didn't mean to startle you." He wiped the cut and applied an antibiotic spray followed by a bandage. First Tess's burned hand the other day and now this with Lena, not to mention his ribs he'd doctored with a lidocaine patch. He was going to have to get an EMT certification if this kept up.

He studied his handiwork. "That better?"

She wiggled her hand in the air. "Yeah. Thanks for the bandage."

"It's too hot to be cooking outside today, isn't it?" He peered into the simmering pot that held a golden soup or stew with carrots and chunks of something white. Then he spied fish guts and bones on the ground.

She followed his gaze. "This looks hillbilly. But when I use the stove inside, it gets hot as hell. We've got a fan. But it doesn't help much."

He pointed to the carcasses. "Freshly caught fish?"

Lena waved toward the tidal pools and grasses. "When my aunt was healthy, she taught me how to fish in the marshes. Speckled trout, croaker, bluefish, black drum. Sometimes crab."

"You did mention your aunt was disabled."

"That's why I do all that extra work for Cherie Kolman. 'Cause I owe Aunt Peg so much. She raised me after my parents died."

Drayco admired Lena for her loyalty and work ethic, but at the same time, gold treasure would go a long way toward helping her situation. He pulled out his cellphone and showed Lena the photo of Marty's gold coin. "We found this among Marty's possessions. Have you seen it before?"

She examined the photo, and her jaw tightened. "Damn him. Are you telling me he had gold he was hiding? He knew how much I needed money, how hard I worked. How could he hold on to something like that and not want to share? Is there more?"

"We're not sure. Did Cherie say whether Marty brought her coins to appraise or sell?"

"Not a word." Her face turned red, but not from the heat. "It's not the only thing he didn't tell me."

Drayco took a guess. "Marty and Deirdre?"

Lena grabbed a spoon to stir the pot, the steam from the stew causing her face to sweat as she leaned over. "I found out from a friend—a real friend—Deirdre was still having sex with Marty after they broke up and me and him were dating again. At the same time she was engaged to her fiancé. And her father had that restraining order."

She stirred the pot with fury. Drayco stood by to try to deflect it away from her in case she flung it off the grill. She laughed bitterly. "It was all a lark to her. What a bitch. Or maybe she's just a sex addict."

After she had a moment to calm down, he asked, "Have you visited the suicide site recently?"

"Not since I took you there."

He pulled out the white fishing lure and showed it to her. "Do you use these?"

"Can't afford 'em. Worms are free. You should ask Tess since she's such an expert."

Drayco had that one on the list. "How would you describe Tess's true relationship with Marty?"

"They were rivals. And there was the accident. You heard about that?"

"You think she blamed Marty for her parents' deaths?"

"A little. But she's a scientist, right? Odds and all that crap. Accidents happen. Fate is fate. Everybody's got an expiration date, you know?"

"Is that from the Akashic Records?"

"Who can say? I mean, it says things like we don't have to be victims of fate. There are all kinds of realities where your soul lives. But can't see it's helped me much. Or it's the other-me in some other-universe that's living the good life."

"As you noted, Tess is a scientist. I can't imagine she swallowed the Akashic philosophy."

"Her philosophy was sex and more sex with drugs on the side. I'm just thrilled she wasn't interested in Marty."

"Does she get along with her colleagues and her boss?"

"She was pissed with Mr. Kolman for promoting Marty over her. But him and Marty were close. I got the feeling Kolman had a big influence on Marty. Kind of funny, right? Antonio worshiped Marty, and Marty worshiped Kolman. There's a religion for you."

Since she looked hot and tired, he asked "May I?" and she handed over control of the spoon while he stirred the stew.

He got a whiff of an aroma he couldn't identify. "Smells musky."

"That's wood sorrel. I know it sounds like the hillbilly thing again, but they grow wild around here. You can eat the leaves, flowers, and green seed pods. And they taste kinda like lemon."

Drayco pointed to a shovel leaning against the trailer. "You use that for digging roots?"

She looked at the shovel and replied, "Comes in handy. For lots of things."

Her stew smelled pretty good. "Have you considered going to college or a technical school? You could turn out to be an award-winning chef. Some get paid big bucks."

"Can't stop working. My aunt's disability check isn't enough."

"There are other options. A chef friend of mine didn't finish high school. He apprenticed with another chef, learned the craft, and struck out on his own. He's now making a six-figure salary."

"For real? But there aren't any chefs around here."

"More than you'd think. And you'd be paid for working while you're training."

"Sure would be nice to get out of the chicken plant." She took the spoon from him to taste the stew.

He smiled at her. "Let me ask around. See what I can find out."

"You'd do that for me?"

"I'm a lousy cook, ask anybody. We need more good chefs out there who can make food for lousy cooks like me."

She returned his smile and offered him a taste from the spoon. Damn, it tasted better than it smelled. "You did all that with trout and potatoes and wild sorrel?"

"And a pinch or two of this and that."

He would definitely be making a few calls on her behalf. One thing he hated in this world was wasted talent.

49

After speaking with Lena, Drayco drove around town working through things in his mind. But, it led to distracted driving. So, he called Maida with his ETA and headed for the one place he could puzzle through the turmoil in his brain in relative peace.

Drayco stood on the stage, looking out over the audience. That is, what *would* be the audience if the renovations on the Opera House were ever completed—an audience needed seats.

A quick visual survey revealed the workmen hadn't made much progress on the lighting and structural reinforcements. The money dribbling in from the grants he'd cobbled together resulted in work stoppages, as Troy Mehaffey had painfully reminded him.

But the piano, ah, the piano was there, hiding in its closet in the wings. He pushed it to stage center and gave it a once-over to make sure it hadn't suffered since he'd played it ten days ago. Was it only ten days? Felt much longer than that.

After a trip to the green room to soak his right arm in hot water, he headed to the Steinway and sat down for a few warm-up scales. Satisfied his right arm was more flexible, he launched into the G-minor Rachmaninoff prelude from Opus 23. He hoped his arm and his bruised ribs were up to it.

He made it through the *Alla marcia* section relatively unscathed and eased into the more lyrical chordal melody of the "B" section. The notes of the recapitulation of the march came fast and furious as his fingers pounded out the staccato sixteenth notes in both hands. The prelude was such a paradigm of Russian Romantic-era music. Melancholy, serenity, joy—all under four minutes.

Vuca had loved Rachmaninoff. All Russian piano music, for that matter. Drayco closed his eyes, transported to the time when he'd race through his schoolwork to sit at the piano and play with Vuca at his side.

When Drayco's father was busy or traveling, Vuca was always there, patiently encouraging, guiding, consoling. The same Vuca who'd told him he was going to be one of the world's premier soloists, a superstar. Had even entered him in the Van Cliburn competition the week before Drayco's "accident."

An image of Vuca draped across his piano, bleeding, and another of Antonio on the floor with purple ligature marks hit Drayco with a sudden jolt. An explosion of pent-up emotions surged through every fiber of his being. He banged his hands on the keyboard, the sound reverberating throughout the empty hall.

The stinging mustard and beet-colored tacks of that noise hit him full force, and he welcomed it. Welcomed the noise and the throbbing pain. For several minutes, he just sat there staring at the black and white keys as they mocked him.

He jumped up and paced around the stage for a few laps but eventually sat back down, rubbed his arm for a bit, and eased into the Schubert Impromptu No. 3 from Opus 90. Much more fitting. Hints of a deep sadness and acknowledgment of that sadness as part of being alive. Not a prayer or a plea, just an affirmation that dark and light belong to the same spectrum.

Any other time, he'd immerse himself in Bach to help focus his mind and go on a "reflection retreat" to take apart the case piece by piece—and then put it all back together in a picture that made sense. But this time, he was pretty sure he had most of the picture. It was the *sense* that was missing.

Buoyed by the fact his arm hadn't cramped after his hand banging or the Rachmaninoff and Schubert, he began playing the Suicide Sonata in its original version. The music was so reminiscent of Bela Bartók—perhaps the folk-inspired Romanian Folk Dances or the *Marche funebre*.

He was still feeling a little lightheaded, but he plowed through anyway. That dizziness was popping up more and more, even before the incident with the drug grower's trap. He only recalled feeling it after first playing the Suicide Sonata at the Lazy Crab—but no it wasn't that, it couldn't be that. To prove his point, he hammered away at the second section more forcefully than usual. Dizziness be damned.

As the last notes died away, someone started clapping. He squinted in the glare of the stage lights and saw Olive Tyler walking up to the edge.

She said, "I didn't recognize that piece. What is it?"

When he told her, she replied, "So that's the infamous Suicide Sonata. It's unusual, for sure."

"Perhaps it's the fact this piece is in the key of hysteria."

"Key of hysteria?"

"Hysteria as in rumors, superstitions, fears, and the copycat effect."

"Lucky they didn't have the internet way back when. Could have made that song's effects much worse."

She walked up the stage stairs with an air of apology around her. "Maida said you'd checked in with her and told her you were here. I've wanted to see the place ever since Nelia described it."

He swung his legs around on the bench. "As you can see, it's in a state."

"But it has character. Newer halls can't match it. Too clinical and perfect."

"This faded rose is far from perfect."

She walked up the stairs to join him on stage. "I listened to your recordings. You were marvelous then, and you're still masterful. Despite the accident years ago and not doing this for a living."

"I try to practice most days. And I miss it when I can't."

"Nelia also told me of your uncle's scholarship he set up in your name. And your upcoming recital in Maryland."

He corrected her. "Possible recital. We're working out the details."

"Are you going to perform at the Opera House, too?"

"I'd hate to jinx the place."

She laughed. "Oh, hardly. You and I should play duets. Wouldn't have to be a violin sonata. How about the Duo Concertante by Stravinsky? If audiences here would like modern music?"

He ran his finger silently along the piano keys. "I'd love that. If this place is ever finished."

"Financial problems?"

"In spades. I was counting on funds that might not happen now."

Olive looked thoughtful for a moment. "You must mean the Chopin manuscript. Nelia mentioned that, too. I suppose there are lawyers involved?"

"Always."

She grabbed a chair in the wings and brought it over to sit across from him. "I'm staying with Nelia for a few days."

"I'm sure Nelia welcomes your company. If you can stand all that pink."

That made her smile. "Funny how that was Nelia's favorite color as a girl. For all of a year. Then it was purple everything."

"Thankfully, not deputy brown."

Olive shifted around in her seat. "I must confess to ulterior motives for coming here. I wanted to talk to you directly. Alone."

"Regarding the case?"

"And Sebastien and Nelia. And to chat with you."

He held an arm indicating the empty building. "We have all the privacy you could want."

She rubbed her hand along the armrest of the chair. "My relationship with Sebastien has hurt Nelia emotionally. And hurt her on this case, even with her boss—"

"I disagree with you there. Sheriff Sailor respects Nelia highly."

"Hope you're right. Despite how this all looks, nothing has changed for me. Marty couldn't have killed himself."

"I agree with you on that point. I don't believe it was suicide, either."

Her eyes widened. "I hadn't heard you come right out and say that so bluntly before."

"Wasn't as sure before."

"What's changed?"

"My interpretation of the facts. And an understanding that relationships aren't always what they appear to be."

"If you don't believe the suicide angle, you have to believe someone killed him. But who? And what about Antonio? And what does that song have to do with it?"

Drayco smiled grimly. "The song was just a tool, albeit a brilliant one, thanks to its checkered history."

He closed the piano's fallboard. "As for Marty and Antonio, that will have to wait for another time until I'm certain."

"I'll try to be patient, but it's hard."

"Perhaps you can help me with something. Has Sebastien spilled any details of Marty's work and his colleagues, like Tess? Or was he jealous of Marty's relationship with Kolman?"

"Sebastien understood. Marty's idol was always Jacques Cousteau, and here was the real-life version. Or, the closest thing. Marty was dying to dive in a submersible like the one used on the Titanic wreck."

"Kolman told me the station couldn't afford a manned version. But the robotic ones are cheaper, faster, and go down deeper."

"Guess it's the difference between having a lander on Mars and having people there."

He nodded. "Touché. Like astronauts, marine biologists are quite dedicated. Tess Gartin works long hours, Marty did, Kolman often works weekends. Can take a toll on family—Kolman's wife Cherie has a disability, and his travel leaves her alone frequently."

She pursed her lips. "You're drawing a comparison between them and my husband and me?"

"Nelia did mention the travel issue contributed to your divorce."

"It was so much more. I pray Nelia can understand that one day. Couples get together when they're young and idealistic. Granted, an army man like J.B. wasn't naïve, but he hadn't been in a real relationship before I came along."

"Then one day years later, you realize the two of you have nothing in common?"

"And the person you married and thought you knew is a stranger. Life can be like that."

Olive leaned toward him, her eyes locking with his. "You and Nelia have become close through your cases. I'm pleased she has such a good friend, someone she admires and trusts. And cares about."

Was Olive now drawing her own comparison? They always say you can't fool a mother. She reached over to pat his hand. "I'll tell you what I've always told her. True love finds a way even if it has to take detours here and there."

50

Thursday, June 28

The next morning, Drayco ignored his pounding headache and drove to the marine biology station under leaden skies. He'd overslept after the tonic Maida gave him to help with his insomnia.

Navigating his way through the station, he saw that gear had been moved around. Items that Tess said Marty purchased weren't in evidence. Sold already? Or stored elsewhere?

When he popped out the rear door, he didn't see Kolman, but Tess was busy with the algae pots. She glanced up at him with an air of exasperation. "I should be on a first-name basis since you've become my shadow."

"Scott, if you wish."

"No, that doesn't feel right. I'll stick with Dr. Drayco."

"Sorry to interrupt what you're doing, but I have two questions. Make that two items." He pulled out the white fishing lure. "Do you recognize this?"

"A bunch of people use those. We've got some here. But we catch fish to keep and study, not kill and eat."

He replaced the lure in his pocket to show her the photo on his phone of Marty's gold coin. She stared at it. "Where was this found?"

"Where was what found?" Judson Kolman strolled around the corner of the building, overhearing Tess.

Drayco turned the cellphone toward Kolman, who peered at the image while Drayco answered, "Marty had this. He'd encased it in a clay necklace we found at his apartment."

Tess narrowed her eyes. "What the hell was he thinking?"

Kolman looked equally shocked, and Drayco asked him, "Marty never said anything about this?"

"I had no idea. Is that the same necklace you showed me at the Lazy Crab?"

"It is." Drayco slipped the cellphone in his pocket. "He never hinted at coins or gold?"

Kolman rescued a long-handled net that had fallen on the pier. "I'm more into the living treasures of the sea. Thought he was, too."

Tess piped up, "That coin would be hard to sell, wouldn't it?"

"Unless you're a shady dealer." Kolman chuckled. "Dealing with government types is bad enough. That's another category of shark right there."

"Speaking of sharks," Drayco pointed at a large, gray finned creature in the waters a few meters beyond the marina.

Kolman grabbed a pair of binoculars on a table and surveyed the animal. "A bull shark. They're aggressive, preferring shallow coastal waters. It's why they're more likely to attack humans. But that's not Nessie."

"Nessie?"

"We've tagged a few juveniles to track them. Must be a new neighbor."

Drayco was glad to be on dry land at that moment. "I know this is an odd question, but do you keep any metal detectors here?"

Kolman lowered the binoculars. "Don't have much use for them. Maybe I should. But with my luck, I'd just find useless cans or wire. It can be dangerous, too—think I recall a woman finding a loaded gun buried in her back yard, along with old military ordnance."

Drayco countered, "It's unfortunate Antonio's gun was left in plain sight to be stolen."

The other man's eyes widened. "Doesn't the sheriff think Antonio killed Marty and staged the theft?"

"Where did you hear that?"

Kolman looked at Tess, who ducked her head over the algae pots. Neither answered Drayco's question, so he changed tacks. "I noticed some of your new gear last time, but I don't see it now. Was hoping you could give me a tour since I'm a scuba diver myself."

Tess snorted. "Marty and his crazy idea of becoming the next Cousteau."

"He was driven, all right. But in retrospect, I can't blame him." Kolman dipped his hand into a small cooler filled with bottled water and grabbed two, offering one to Drayco.

Drayco asked, "Then all that lovely gear—"

"Will be sold. I've put it away in a separate locker for now. Marty meant well, he truly did."

"Are those the 'questionable purchases' you mentioned on my first visit?"

With a frown, Kolman replied, "As I said, he was learning. I hardly see how it helps now to defame the poor boy's judgment."

"No defamation intended."

Kolman shared another look with Tess. "If the sheriff doesn't believe Antonio killed Marty, then it must be suicide, after all. Not to be rude, but why are you here? Don't see how we can fill in any more gaps regarding his motives."

"You've helped more than you realize." Drayco looked at the water to where he'd spied the shark, but it had disappeared. Too bad the motives of human sharks were murkier than those of the *Elasmobranchii* variety. It was time he consulted one of the human kind.

❧ ❧ ❧

Drayco spent a few hours on the phone with a few less-than-reputable contacts he used. It took a while to get to the right person with the right information, but he finally struck investigative gold. The results had Drayco driving up US 13, off onto a state road, and then along a densely forested path that seemed to head to the ends of the Earth.

His GPS couldn't be wrong, could it? But after another bumpy five minutes, the Starfire arrived at a break in the trees. He saw what must be his target, the old abandoned Dolphin Island amusement park on the banks of the not terribly friendly sounding Duck Guts Creek. He didn't see any duck guts, but the acrid odor of sulfur and putrescine told him some corpse, hopefully animal, was decaying nearby.

He got out of the car, taking in the rotting pier with the faux lighthouse threatening to fall off. The exterior of the sole remaining building had a sign with faded and smeared red, yellow, and blue primary colors that read *Barrel of Fun*. The location of this tiny unincorporated area went by the name of Painterville. A bit of irony in that.

He looked around for the man he was meeting, a shady figure known to handle gold when the owner didn't want to have the sale tracked. No signs of Eddie Skenderi, and Drayco's car was the only one around.

But when he walked around the rear, he saw a motorboat moored at a rickety but still-standing pier post. A nice, quick getaway. No wonder the guy arranged a meeting here instead of his normal haunts up in Baltimore.

Returning to the front, Drayco scanned the building for an opening, stepping over the remains of a miniature train track and a lone rusting car with tandem seats. He walked through the one door he could see and paused to let his eyes get dark-adapted.

It took a few seconds to spy a figure standing in front of the old distorted funhouse mirrors. But if it was Skenderi, he wasn't alone. Drayco soon noticed a duo of goons Skenderi had brought along.

"Eddie Skenderi?" Drayco's question echoed through the building.

The man in the middle of the trio said, "You Drayco?" Skenderi resembled a walrus with his domed bald head and thick gray mustache split into two sides curling toward his chin.

Drayco replied, "Arlin Barlow said to tell you the lilac is lovely this time of year."

Skenderi studied Drayco, paying particular attention to his pockets. "Looked you up. Big-city private detective. Pretty gutsy to come way out here in the boondocks alone. Unarmed." He rocked back on his heels. "Barlow said this had to do with gold coins."

"I'm working a case involving coins from the eighteenth century. Gold, British, Queen Anne era. Worth three grand by themselves. And I imagine a cache of them would fetch a tidy sum."

"You think I know something about that? Me, a regular businessman who likes to help people out with trades? Why I'm just a human eBay."

All the distorted mirrors were making Drayco lightheaded. "I'm not interested in anything other than solving a murder."

"Murder?" Skenderi stiffened and eyeballed the other men. "Look, I don't wanna be tied up with no murder."

"Good, then we're on the same page. You help me out, as a regular businessman with your 'expertise,' and I'll walk away. With any luck, you'll never see me again."

"How do I know you ain't wired?"

"You can pat me down if you want. And we don't have to say any names aloud if you'd prefer. I'll show you a photo. I'm going to reach into my pocket for my wallet—"

"No, you're not. Zaine, go get the wallet."

Drayco angled his head toward one side. "Left front pants pocket."

"You left-handed?" Skenderi's thin lips formed a crooked smile. "Me, too."

Zaine handed Drayco the wallet, and Drayco pulled out a photo he'd printed out, unfolded it, and held it up. "Look familiar to you?"

Skenderi nodded but didn't speak.

"Is this your client? Assuming you have such a client. The one who hypothetically approached you wanting to sell antique gold coins like the ones I described?"

Another nod, then, "How do I know you won't come after me on all this?"

Drayco folded the photo and returned it to his wallet. "No gold changed hands, right? It was only a potential deal?" With any luck, he was making the right call on this.

The other man held out his hands with a smile.

"There you go. You've committed no crime. As for your other 'business practices,' I have no knowledge of those. Far as I know, you sell cotton candy on the side. Goes with the whole Fun House scene."

Skenderi grunted out a sound like a walrus barking. Drayco imagined it was meant to be a laugh. Drayco took out some hundreds from his wallet and handed them over to Skenderi. Skenderi had earned that laugh and then some.

51

Drayco woke up once again with a headache, this time accompanied by a strange sense of dread. Nightmares? He couldn't recall any. Save for one with Eddie Skenderi shooting at the Fun House mirrors, the shards morphing into pieces of bone.

His meeting yesterday with Skenderi was enlightening, but it left out a few crucial details. The burning question was how to plan his attack. Hopefully, the meeting he'd lined up with Sheriff Sailor after noon would help sort things out.

But first, he had to face his visitor who'd shown up at the Lazy Crab unannounced. He took Darcie to the den and sat with her on a love seat, probably not the best decision. She fiddled with the object on her hand—her left hand—that he'd noticed when she first entered. Not that it was possible to miss the Gibraltar-sized diamond.

He pointed at it. "People don't usually buy those for themselves. Not to put on that particular finger."

Her words came out in a rush. "Harry and I are going to divide our time between Cypress Manor and McLean. It's closer to his headquarters in the D.C. area. And you'll come, won't you?"

"I take it this means you are engaged?"

She nodded.

"And you want me to come visit you?" He didn't want more talk about three-ways and being some gigolo on the side.

"To the wedding, silly."

"I appreciate the invitation, but I think it's best I didn't attend."

"But I want to see you. I don't want to give you up."

"Darcie—"

She babbled on, "I have to marry him. I need the money, or I'll lose everything. Randolph's finances were worse than I knew, and there are now liens on the property, and there are the divorce attorney fees, and insurance and—"

"And I can't keep you in the lifestyle to which you've become accustomed?"

"I'm not that shallow." She was the most miserable-looking engaged woman he'd ever seen, and he felt truly sorry for her.

"I know. I understand."

"You do?"

He put his hand on her shoulder. "I once asked you 'what do you want from life'? Do you remember what you said?"

"That no one had asked me that before. And that I wanted freedom."

"Freedom to be who you are, not somebody else's idea of who you should be. And not spending your life as a portrait people hang on their walls but don't expect to be a living, breathing person."

"You have a good memory."

He smiled gently. "Have you finally found out who you want to be? Will this give you the freedom you desire?"

"I think so, but I'm so confused. Tell me what to do."

Her sad expression was more than he could bear. "Just one word for you—prenup."

A small smile spread across her face. As they hopped up off the sofa, she wrapped her arms around him and gave him a passionate kiss. She said, "You can't get rid of me this easily. Rest assured you'll be hearing from me."

He walked her to the door and closed it behind her, shaking his head the whole way. Those were the exact words Deirdre had said to him. But there wasn't time to dwell on his strange love life. Before meeting Sheriff Sailor in an hour, he had to see someone about a box and what he hoped was a very special key.

ej ej ej

The confab with Sailor went as well as Drayco had expected. He had to give the sheriff credit—Sailor was *almost* always open to Drayco's crazy ideas and odd requests, even when it meant devoting extra manpower. After his meeting with Sailor, leaving behind Drayco's newly obtained key and a slightly exasperated lawman, Drayco drove to Marty's apartment.

The rain was so heavy, the roads were turning into ponds. At one particularly low spot, the wheels of his car started slipping to the side as the Starfire hydroplaned. Just when he thought he'd have to hop out and push it out of the muck like Judson Kolman had with his boat, the Starfire found firmer ground and surged onto the road.

Pulling in the parking lot of Marty's duplex, he waited for a tiny break in the deluge and made it to the door, grateful for the small overhang. As he stepped inside the apartment, he didn't need a slight crease in the carpet behind a file cabinet to tell him someone else was here recently. That someone was less careful this time about masking his efforts—books, papers, and drawers littered the floor, and boxes of food were open on the countertops.

He stood still and listened. No banging or rustling from the bathroom or bedroom. He crept around the piles on the floor and stopped short of the bathroom. Then he barged in and ripped away the shower curtain, but the room was empty. With the creaking wood floor making it impossible for him to be stealthy, he took the plunge and forged ahead into the bedroom, checking behind the door first.

But the bedroom was as unoccupied as the rest of the apartment. And as messy if not more so. The papers from the closet seen on Drayco's first visit littered every surface. The bed was pulled away from the wall with the mattress askew and sheets and bedspread on the floor. Hindsight was always twenty-twenty, but he wished he'd suggested Sebastien Penry put a camera in the place until the man got around to cleaning it out.

Drayco sat on the bed, looking around. Had the intruder or intruders found what they were seeking in such a hurry? And why hadn't he anticipated this? Even worse, the intruder's whirlwind destruction served to obliterate some of the last intact traces of Marty's presence here.

He stared at the wall where Marty hung the three framed photos of Cousteau's *Calypso*. Then he saw it—the spacing of the three photos formed a triangle. With two on top and one on the bottom, you could even say it was a downward-pointing triangle. Just like the ones etched on Marty's clay necklace and written on his copy of the suicide song.

Drayco got up and removed the bottom frame from the wall. He flipped it over and released the slick metal clasps to pull out the cardboard backing, separating it from the photo. Between the cardboard and photo, Marty had wedged a thin piece of paper, folded over once.

The paper was unmistakably a map, complete with GPS coordinates. As evidence on its own, it was pretty flimsy, but with everything else taken as a whole, the map could be an invaluable clue. It was a gamble on Marty's part, but if he'd intended the hidden coin and map to be a form of insurance, it hadn't worked.

Still, as Drayco sat on the bed surrounded by the last traces of a murdered young man, it was like Marty was reaching out to him from the Great Beyond. Or the Hall of the Akashic Records. Reaching out in a way Vuca and Antonio hadn't or didn't know how to do, perhaps.

The whole thing made Drayco angry. Angry at the senseless loss of life, angry at how he seemed powerless to stop it, angry that once again, at least in Marty's case, it all came down to greed.

Drayco slipped the map inside the frame and secured it, taking the entire frame and one of Marty's fleece shirts with him toward the front of the apartment. When he neared the door, he spied something he hadn't when he'd arrived—the telltale sign of a small clump of mud on the left.

Drayco hadn't set foot there yet. Meaning, the intruder was there mere moments before Drayco's arrival. Maybe lurking outside even now, escaping notice in the rain and gloom. Even more irritated now, he wrapped the frame in the shirt to keep it dry and ducked out into the elements.

He studied the parking lot and nearby roads. His Starfire was all alone. But if his intruder saw Drayco and felt the noose tightening, flight could be the next logical step.

A chime from his cellphone told him he had a new text. No suicide song, only a simple message, *Have info for you. Condo construction site. At six-thirty. Come alone, or I'll leave.*

Drayco tried calling Sheriff Sailor, but it went straight to voicemail. What to do? Sailor had better not strike out on his end because there was a good chance they were running out of time. He swiped over to his cellphone address book and quickly dialed Nelia Tyler.

ও ও ও

Sheriff Sailor held the door open for his deputy, Wesley Giles, as they headed into the bank. The manager understood when Sailor informed her of the need for the visit. She'd waited patiently for them and unlocked the door to let them in after-hours at six. After Sailor's meeting with Drayco hours earlier, he'd pushed through an emergency search warrant he now handed over to the bank manager to appraise.

The manager, Gigi Smith, walked them to the large safe room and asked, "Are you going to have to use a drill or a punch?"

Sailor pulled out a key. "This is from the owner we were able to get our hands on." That is to say, Drayco had managed to get *his* hands on it.

She studied the key. "The box number tag is missing. Do you have the number?"

Sailor grimaced. "Unfortunately not. We'll have to try them one by one."

She replied, "Do you mind if I watch? It's not that I don't trust you. I want to be sure it's all handled to the letter. For our board and customers."

Sailor and Giles dutifully started on the first box as Sailor looked at the rows of boxes with a grim smile. The sooner they got through them, the better. After two dozen tries and not a single "hit," Giles inserted his key into a box, and it fit perfectly.

It was surprisingly heavy as they brought it out to the table in the center of the room. Sailor quipped, "Drayco had better be right, or I'll never hear the end of it from Judge Jackson."

Sailor held his breath as they opened the box. When Giles flipped open the top to reveal the contents, Sailor's held breath flew out in a mini-tornado. "Will you look at that? And we didn't have to dig up a single skeleton to find this buried treasure. Guess we have our motive. And evidence."

His deputy asked, "What was that other thing Drayco asked you to check out yesterday? About fishing gear?"

"More than rods and reels. Expensive gear. As in, who bought it. Funny how a phone call from law enforcement can make companies gladly turn over their records."

Giles smiled, "Guess you'll have to call Drayco and eat crow. Where is he? Why isn't he here?"

"He said he had something to check into." And that made Sailor uneasy. He trusted Drayco's judgment but worried he was striking out lone-wolf style as he often did. Nah, he wouldn't do anything hasty and without a backup plan. Not this time.

52

Drayco parked in a spot where he hoped his informant couldn't see him or his secret "cargo." He slipped the hidden Glock from the Starfire into his pocket and prowled around the condo construction site. Thankfully, the rain had stopped. It was half-past six, and the workers had all gone, no doubt in a hurry on a Friday evening.

An alert from Drayco's phone revealed a new text message, *Come to third floor via stairs at north end.*

Drayco found the stairs and dutifully headed to the third level. He looked past the columns on the partially finished floor, skirting the perimeter, but didn't see anyone at first. Until he came face to face with Judson Kolman.

Drayco asked, "What's this important info that couldn't be discussed at the station?"

"Not so much information as closure."

"Closure for Sebastien Penry?"

"For you. You wanted to know why Marty died, didn't you?"

"And you've decided to tell me?"

"I doubt you're going to like it."

Drayco stepped toward him, but Kolman pulled out a gun. "My brother's a policeman. Taught me a few tricks."

Drayco said, "Did you steal another firearm?"

"Guns are easy to find. But you're referring to Marty. Overheard him talking about Antonio's gun, how he left it in his car."

Drayco was far too close to the edge of the open building. A sudden move could prove fatal. "All this for the marine biology center?"

"You can't possibly understand. Doing important work no one appreciates. Barely scraping by, begging for grants. I want to build our center into one recognized worldwide. With money left over to treat my wife to the retirement she deserves."

"If you're in jail, that won't happen, will it? Doesn't seem you thought this out clearly."

Kolman's eye twitched. "I'm not going to jail. Cherie needs me too much, especially after losing our boy, our Jack. Can't leave her alone with no money, no help, no future. It would kill her."

Drayco gauged his surroundings—distances to the wall, possible escape routes. "You knew Marty was troubled. And obsessed with the Suicide Sonata. You took advantage and spiked his drink with an antidepressant known for suicidal side effects. Rather shaky for a murder plan."

"I had a Plan B. But Plan A worked nicely."

"Did you shoot Marty?"

The twitching around Kolman's eye went into overdrive. "He was supposed to do it. I gave him the gun. But he wavered, changed his mind at the last minute."

"'Assisted' suicide, then?"

"It was his hand on the trigger."

"Yet you were the one holding the gun."

"Technically not murder, wouldn't you say?"

Drayco bristled at that but forced himself to focus. "Why did you pick that spot, in the clearing?"

"Marty took me there once. Told him I was interested in remote spots for a photography hobby. I keep a motorcycle garaged in a rental unit. We rode in together."

"And you returned the other day?"

"Had to make sure I didn't leave any evidence behind, with you poking around. How did you know?"

Drayco made the mistake of looking over the side of the building. He was still dizzy, and it made his head throb. "You never believed in the Suicide Sonata."

"Not at all. Or that Akashic nonsense. But Marty did. I played up that whole curse and paranormal business."

"Was Antonio part of the plan, too?"

Kolman gave a brief shake of his head. "I had nothing to do with that."

"Oh, but you did. He'd borrowed some of Marty's protein powder with your sertraline in it. Antonio was more depressed than Marty. And more susceptible."

"Never intended for that to happen. Only Marty."

"Because of the gold coins you found on the shipwreck?"

Kolman laughed. "You really are good, Dr. Drayco. We were out searching for a tagged shark when our sonar spotted something big. After using our ROV, we saw what it was. Got lucky, too. It's down a mere two hundred feet. We found coins embedded in the old wood and the sand and sent in the ROV with a grabber."

"Why not sell the coins in public?"

"The Shipwreck Act. Our wreck is within U.S. Territorial Waters. Federal and state governments override a finder's rights to the wreck."

"But Marty went along with your scheme to keep the gold discovery quiet."

Kolman's gun hand wavered. He might know how to shoot a gun, but he wasn't used to holding one. "I told him the money would buy a manned submersible. His dreams of being the next Cousteau would be a step closer."

"Why silence him if he was going along with your secret?"

"Couldn't trust him. He was becoming unstable. As you told me yourself, he'd blabbed to a friend that 'something big was coming.'"

Drayco shook his head. "Marty idolized you."

"Everyone has their breaking point. I knew Marty would crack."

"Did Tess find out?"

"Her nose is too buried in tanks to notice. But I feared Marty would tell her the whole scheme. Eventually."

As Kolman stood framed in the fading twilight, his sneering figure resembled a bull shark ready to charge. Drayco needed to buy more time. "You spiked my drink. And sent me the copies of that suicide song on burner phones. Why do it after going to all the trouble to make Marty's death look like a suicide?"

"At first, it was to make it look like you were going nuts, too. When it became a murder investigation, I hoped to deflect attention away from me."

Kolman crept closer to Drayco. "Take three steps back."

When Drayco hesitated, Kolman insisted, "Do it now, or I shoot."

Drayco took the steps, teetering on the edge of the open-structure building. He saw all the way to the ground below, three stories down. "If you're expecting me to jump, think again. And if you shoot me, it won't look like a suicide."

"But it's your weapon they'll find beside your body. With a copy of the suicide song."

"That's not my gun."

"It will be. I see the outlines of one in your pocket. You are going to take it out very, very slowly and lay it on the floor."

Drayco was a quick draw, but even a non-expert like Kolman could nail Drayco before he got his gun out. Especially with his painful bruised ribs slowing his reaction time. He complied.

"Kick it over here."

Drayco gave it a slight kick. Kolman slowly bent down, staring all the while at Drayco as he hoisted Drayco's Glock from the floor and exchanged it for the gun he'd been holding.

"You're missing one important thing, Kolman."

"What's that?"

"Suicides don't wear a hidden microphone."

Kolman laughed. "You're stalling for time. It won't work."

Drayco said a little louder, "The cavalry may have something to say about that."

Kolman raised his gun arm and pointed it at Drayco. "I'm sorry. I have to do this."

A female voice yelled out from behind him, "Drop the gun, Kolman."

The man stiffened, his face contorted into a mask of uncertainty. Drayco's secret "cargo," Nelia Tyler, strode closer to Kolman, her gun drawn and pointed at his back. "Drop it. Now."

Drayco looked over the edge of the building where Sheriff Sailor and Deputy Giles had arrived and were racing up the stairs. Drayco turned back to Kolman just as the man gave a quick glance at Nelia out of the corner of his eye.

Drayco took advantage of the split-second distraction. He lunged at the other man and grabbed the gun from his hand. Kolman's bravado quickly crumbled, and he fell on his knees, weeping. Nelia made short work of cuffing him.

As soon as Sailor and Giles entered the floor, Sailor surveyed the situation. "Looks like we missed the party. Everything okay here?"

Drayco replied, "It's all on tape for your listening pleasure. How did the safe deposit box turn out?"

"Evidence. And lots of it. You should have told us earlier about this plan of ours."

"I tried. Got the mystery text while you were at the bank and suspected it was Kolman. But I couldn't reach you on your cell. I picked up Nelia and her wire on the way here, and she called dispatch."

Giles hauled the handcuffed Kolman off the floor with the man still blubbering. Drayco wanted to feel sorry for the guy, but Marty and Antonio had deserved help, not chemical fuel for their depression. Drayco was sickened by the image of Marty wavering, not wanting to go through with the suicide, only to have Kolman "help" him do it.

Drayco gave Nelia a brief smile of thanks. Before she turned to follow Giles and Kolman down the stairs, she asked, "You okay? You look pale, and you're sweating more than usual."

"I'm fine."

Sailor sidled up to him and said, "She's right. You don't look all that great. Giles and Tyler can book Kolman. I'll follow you to the Lazy Crab."

Drayco grabbed the copy of the suicide song that had fallen from Kolman's pocket, the one supposed to be found with Drayco's body. The words jumped out at him, *I live in the shadows, and alone I shall be;*

Gone are the days that were bright and carefree; The flowers are fading, the light becomes dusk; Ashes turn to ashes and dust turns to dust.

53

Olive, Sebastien, Nelia, and Drayco gathered around the picnic table at Nelia's apartment watching the weekend boat traffic in the bright afternoon sun. Almost two days had passed since Kolman's arrest, which is one reason Drayco felt better. The other was the fact he'd discovered Maida had unintentionally poisoned him with her pretzel dip and sleep tonic that both included saffron.

She was horrified when she found out he was allergic, but he assured her it wasn't a common allergy. There was no way she could have known. But it did explain his recent nausea, headaches, and dizziness. Maybe even his funky mood.

Sebastien didn't notice the boats and the view, staring instead into his glass of wine. "Wish I knew why Marty agreed to the gold conspiracy. I worry it wasn't only to finance his Cousteau dreams. That he did it to help with my financial problems."

Olive put a hand on his shoulder. "I doubt that, dear. But if he did, it shows how much he loved you. He was an adult and capable of making his own decisions. Sometimes our children don't always make the best ones." She gave Nelia a little side-eye before turning to Drayco. "How did you figure out it was Kolman?"

"It wasn't any one thing but many. Opportunity. The coins. Marty's hidden map."

Drayco had opted for a soda instead of wine. He would have preferred the wine. He took a sip and continued, "The final straw was the fact Kolman kept saying Marty bought all that expensive gear. The type most often used for finding shipwrecks. But I couldn't find records of it in the purchase orders on Marty's computer. Sheriff Sailor helped track the real purchaser, Kolman."

Nelia chimed in, "And the gold coins stashed in the bank sealed the deal. Cherie was kind to give you the spare safe deposit key, Drayco."

Olive asked, "Cherie didn't know what it was for?"

Drayco shook his head. "Knew he always wore it on his 'good luck charm' necklace. And that he had a duplicate key in a home wall safe. When I first saw the key, I assumed it was for a safe deposit box. But the question of why he'd carry it with him all the time only made sense later." He smiled at Nelia. "It was something Nelia said that made me think of it—she wondered why any treasure hunter wouldn't have just tucked their find away in a safe somewhere."

Olive asked, "Cherie never asked her husband what it was for?"

"Trusted him completely."

Olive sighed. "That poor woman. Had no idea about any of this."

Drayco replied, "She's distraught, as you might imagine. Lena Bing is checking up on her. And surprisingly, Tess Gartin has offered to stay with her."

Nelia spoke up. "Had my money on Tess all along."

"She was an early candidate for me, too." Drayco had a hard time finishing the soda. Regular soda tasted like pure sugar after being addicted to his carbonated espresso. "It was all fueled by Lena's suicide song pranks and Deirdre's Akashic Record project. But it turned deadly in the hands of Kolman."

Sebastien was still holding Olive's hand. Now that their relationship was out in the open, they were more affectionate to each other in front of others. But Nelia looked away whenever it happened.

Sebastien asked, "Was that skeleton and Kolman's shipwreck gold-related?"

"Only time, historians, and archaeologists will tell."

Sebastien rubbed his eyes. "He had that coin all along. I never knew."

"Buried treasure was always a possibility. I just thought it was on land, something requiring a metal detector."

After they paused to let a squawking crow fly overhead, Cherie asked, "How did poor Antonio Skye fit into this?"

"We'll never know if the sertraline pushed him over the edge, or he would have been suicidal without it. Or if a misinterpretation of the Akashic Records had anything to do with it. At any rate, my early suspicions that his death was murder were way off."

Drayco surveyed the sky, hoping to see where the crow had flown. Lucky bird. The one life-or-death issue it had was its next meal.

Nelia said, "Drayco," in a sharp tone of voice that got his attention. "You weren't to blame. And if anyone gives you some pat BS answer about easy solutions to mental illness, they're full of it."

Drayco nodded, but only so he wouldn't have to discuss it further. Antonio, in his isolated, alienated state, had needed someone to help him, and Drayco could easily have become that someone. Powder or no powder.

Cherie asked, "Will Kolman get life?"

"Depends on various mitigating factors. And the abilities of his attorney. Emmerson Pinnick has agreed to defend him."

Sebastien scowled at that. "He would, wouldn't he? Trying to stick it to me until the end."

Drayco pulled out his wallet and withdrew a folded piece of paper that he handed to the other man. "You may enjoy taking a look at this."

"What is it?"

"Found it on Marty's computer. It's a schematic he dreamed up. A project to clean up the giant trash debris islands in the oceans."

Sebastien stared at the paper as Drayco handed it over.

Drayco added, "After I showed it to Tess, she contacted her colleagues and found one interested in developing a prototype. If it works, it could help solve disasters like the Great Pacific Garbage Patch. Tess and the partner said Marty will get full credit."

Sebastien studied the printout as a slow smile crept across his face. "I don't know what to say, other than his work will be remembered. That he made a difference. It's all he really wanted."

Drayco smiled back. "Least I could do." He checked his watch. "I hate to leave, but it could be a three-hour drive to D.C. on a Sunday."

Sebastien released Olive's hand to shake Drayco's. "Can't thank you enough. For believing in me and in Marty."

Nelia walked Drayco to the front of her apartment and the stairs that led to his car. "Have to go so soon?"

"Got a potential new client I'm meeting tomorrow morning."

"You'll be returning to Cape Unity to check on the Opera House?"

"Yep. We're not through with each other yet."

It came out as innuendo by accident. She didn't notice or didn't want to acknowledge it, saying, "We may bump into each other, then. If not, I'll see you through Benny Baskin's office in the fall when I return to law school."

So, they were back to the cool, professional, at-arm's-length relationship. He suspected she'd given up on her previous talk of divorcing Tim in light of her parents' situation. She hadn't mentioned it to Drayco, another obvious clue.

As if to seal the deal, her cellphone rang, and she looked at the number. "It's Tim. I have to—"

"Take it, I know."

She walked toward the deck until she was out of sight. Right as he was heading down the stairs, Olive popped out the front door to the apartment and walked over to him. "There's one thing I wanted to ask you but keep forgetting. Make that two things. Why didn't you play piano pieces for the left hand after your accident?"

She wasn't the first to mention it, and he gave her the same answer. "Not very satisfying, is it? And the repertoire is limited."

"Have you tried the exercises by that teacher, Dorothy Taubman? She worked with Leon Fleisher, who had to play with one hand for years."

"I dabbled with those techniques. But I got frustrated. And I had to make a living."

"You should revisit them. They could help with that hand cramping you have. I'm going to hold you to that duet at the Opera House."

He smiled but inwardly cringed. It was much too late for his arm and his piano career. "You said two things?"

"That last verse of the suicide song. Why did Marty write it?"

"Perhaps part of Marty sensed what was coming and his subconscious left behind a clue. Guess that's another thing that will remain a mystery. Another unknowable."

Olive gave him a quick hug. "I do plan on seeing you again, one way or another." Then she whispered in his ear. "Don't give up." And with that, she waved and headed into the house.

Don't give up on what? The piano? Nelia? The Opera House? Life? He didn't want to dig deeper into any of that mess, not now. And he certainly didn't want to hang around while Nelia talked to the abusive Tim on the phone. He bounded down the stairs two at a time toward his faithful companion, his Starfire. That was one girl he could always count on.

৶ ৶ ৶

For once, the Bay Bridge traffic hadn't been all that bad. Drayco headed straight for his townhome where he was expecting an unusual guest.

He hurried to the door when the knock came and opened it for Lydia Vucasovich, who still had a stately and unbowed walk as she came inside. He spotted a waiting car outside with its engine running. "You can't stay a while?"

"I'm afraid not. I've love to reminisce and catch up on your career. But my driver has a doctor's appointment later. You and I will have to get together some other time for a longer meet-up."

She smiled, handing him a book. "I was cleaning my husband's things out of the attic and found a copy of that book he wrote about Chopin with an envelope inside. Addressed to you."

Drayco took the book and opened the front cover where the envelope with Vuca's distinctive feathery handwriting had penned his name. It was sealed. He asked, "Do you to see what's in it?"

"That was a private note meant for you. Besides, it's ancient history. Nothing can change the past. I've made peace and moved on." She gave him a quick peck on the check. "You should, too."

After she'd left, he sat staring at the envelope. Part of him didn't want to read it. Would it confirm his injury was to blame for Vuca's suicide? The teacher who'd put so much faith in Drayco—was he driven over the edge?

But no, that felt too narcissistic. Like Sebastien and his concerns that Marty's death was due to his father's financial problems, it didn't matter now.

Drayco put on a CD of Bach's English Piano Suite No. 5 in E Minor, grabbed a Manhattan Special, and sat on his favorite red chair. Then he slit open the letter and started reading.

Dear Scotty,

If you are reading this, I must be dead. Sounds harsh, I know, but there it is. I shared with you one of my favorite quotes, "Death isn't the greatest loss to fear, it's never beginning to live." You probably wondered what I meant by that. It's pretty simple, really. You have within you a great strength, something rare, something remarkable. It doesn't come from the piano, it's far better. No accident, no loss, no disappointment will ever change that. You must never give up, for giving up would deny the world your considerable talents and deny yourself a universe of wonder.

I don't have many regrets of my own. It would have been nice to have more time with you and Lydia and my music. But, the other day I got the news every musician dreads. My doctor told me I have carcinoma of the bony ear canal in both ears. He also told me I should have bought a lottery ticket, such a case is so rare. But even with surgery and radiation, I would likely lose my hearing. Beethoven was a greater soul than I, for I cannot bear to live without the ability to hear music. I haven't told anyone other than you in this letter. I think you'll understand.

Some would say this is the coward's way out. I like to think that out there in the Great Beyond, whatever it is, music will be everywhere, and I will be immersed within it forever. And cheering you on wherever your life's course may take you. You have always, and will always continue, to make me proud.

With love, Vuca

Drayco laid the letter on the end table beside him and picked up an object next to it. He fingered one of Antonio's shells, a shark's eye, marveling at the intricate beauty of nature's design. What was it the Akashic Records beliefs stated? That the universe is one giant organism where all art, science, and inventions come from. Maybe Vuca was right. And even now he was immersed within a rapturous symphony of the cosmos.

And Marty and Antonio? He'd leave that one for the theologians and philosophers. But in a dream he had last night, the duo were off fishing in a boat that had the name *Calypso* on the stern.

CPSIA information can be obtained
at www.ICGtesting.com
Printed in the USA
FSHW022214161119
64179FS